BACK HA...

Not much is going right for amateur jockey Alan
Mor... ly
need... ck
part... ne
busi... es
£100... ed
race... ll
that... on
that

Thin... ax
Ashw... is
affai... is
gaml... is
fathe... of
anot... ut
surel... th
abou

Two... ut
over... ne
cosy... ne
noos... al
emp

BACK HANDER

John Francome

WINDSOR
PARAGON

First published 2004
by
Headline Book Publishing
This Large Print edition published 2005
by
BBC Audiobooks Ltd by arrangement with
Headline Book Publishing Ltd

ISBN 1 4056 1058 1 (Windsor Hardcover)
ISBN 1 4056 2047 1 (Paragon Softcover)

British Library Cataloguing in Publication Data available

Printed and bound in Great Britain by
Antony Rowe Ltd., Chippenham, Wiltshire

Thanks to Captain David Williams RN,
Gail Paten and Gary Nutting
(www.harrythehorse.net)

Prologue

As Max left the flat, the temptation to slam the door so hard it shattered the wall was almost irresistible. If there'd been a cat on the stairs he would have kicked its head off. There are good days and bad days, he told himself, and then there are days like this. Total crap.

He punched the light switch on the thinly carpeted stairwell and went down fast, eager to leave the evening behind. He'd lost again; he should have known better than to go gambling on a day when his luck was plainly out. He'd woken to the news he'd been jocked off a stone-cold certainty at the weekend, then he'd lost a race on the run-in at Newbury when his horse's bridle had snapped, and he'd arrived home to a phone message that he'd been dumped by his twice-weekly secret shag. At least, that's what he thought Crystal's message had amounted to, she'd sounded so hysterical he couldn't make out much. Well, good riddance to her.

The light timed out just as he reached the front door. Jesus Christ, what kind of cheapskates ran this building? He'd half a mind not to come back again—he could find classier games even on a Tuesday night. Except that would mean settling his debts with Paul, the ex-jockey who hosted the card school. At present, Max's liability was in paper form only and if he baled out he'd have to stump up the cash. Laying his hands on six grand plus would not be easy—it was three months' allowance, for God's sake. Of course, he could try and get it

1

off his father but he didn't want to go that route again. As Dad had said last time, the point of the allowance was so he didn't have to keep asking for a handout.

But Paul wasn't giving him grief, he was cool about the money Max owed him. And why wouldn't he be? Paul might be a devious little wide boy operating out of a tatty gaff in Kilburn but he knew all about the *Sunday Times* Rich List and exactly where Max's father came in the Top Hundred. Number sixty-three, as it happened, just behind a mail-order fashion king and ahead of a mobile-phone millionaire. Lewis Ashwood: property and leisure. Estimated net worth £481 million. No wonder Paul wasn't all that bothered about Max owing him a few quid.

Outside, the autumn night was warm and starless. The thick clouds that had dulled the afternoon at Newbury had rolled in from the west and Max, with a horseman's appreciation of the weather, calculated it would rain soon. He rounded the corner into the high street, relieved to see his Lexus parked where he'd left it, on a yellow line in front of a boarded-up off-licence and an Asian dry-cleaners. Frankly, this area of inner-city north London was such a dump it was a miracle it was still there.

He pointed the remote-control and the car's sidelights blinked and the lock clicked open in recognition of his signal. He couldn't wait to get home.

'Hey, wait up.'

A big shambling figure was lumbering after him, Tortoise Jacobs, the oldest of the punters and former racecourse reprobates who made up Paul's card school. Max had seen quite enough of Tortoise for the night. As usual, he'd pocketed almost all of Max's gambling money. What's more, Max knew what was coming next.

'Give us a lift, mate, will you?'

'No.' The only lift Max felt like giving him was under his jaw with his fist. He'd once made the mistake of allowing Tortoise into his car and it had stunk of his unwashed tobacco-smoked presence for days afterwards.

'I'm not going your way,' he added.

The big man had his hand on the passenger-side door.

'Just to the tube station. It won't take you a minute.'

'Get a taxi.'

'I've got one right here,' and Tortoise opened the car door with a giggle, an irritating sound that Max had heard a lot during the last four hours. Most things about Basil Jacobs irritated Max—the length of time it took him to make his play (hence his nickname), the way crisp crumbs clung to his dirty grey beard, and the fact that the jammy sod rarely lost.

Max wedged himself between Jacobs and the vehicle. 'You're not getting in my car, fat man.'

The grin faded from Tortoise's face. 'Daddy didn't teach you any manners, did he?'

'Get lost.'

'Just like he didn't teach you how to lose. You really shouldn't play poker, Max. I can read the cards in your face every time you pick them up.'

Tortoise's bulk was pressing him against the Lexus and his whisky breath soured the air. Max tried to push him away.

3

'Get off me, you useless tub of lard.'

Jacobs didn't budge. 'If I'm so useless, ask yourself why I'm walking away with your money in my pocket. I do it every week. You know what, Max, I'm thrilled every time I see you at the table. You're like a blank cheque in my name. Goodie, I say to myself, that's the gas bill paid and the phone bill—and maybe I'll have filet mignon tomorrow. Little Maxie's paying.'

Max didn't think. He just hit him, putting as much weight into it as he could. It was like sinking his fist into a pillow. Tortoise grunted with pain as the breath gusted from his mouth and Max shoved the big man away from the car, the key fob spilling from his grasp as he did so.

Jacobs doubled over, winded. He was obviously completely unfit. Max scanned the surface of the road, looking for the key. There it was, in the gutter, just a few inches from the drain. That was the day's one stroke of luck; if the key had gone down the drain, Tortoise would have got more than a thump in the bread basket. Max bent to retrieve it.

As he did so, he was grabbed from behind and hurled across the pavement. He looked up to see Tortoise running at him, arms swinging. It was out of character—Max couldn't believe the old lard bucket could move that fast—and took him by surprise. The first blow cuffed him on the ear but he dodged the second and ducked inside the big man's reach to whack him in the gut once more. This time the punch did not have such a dramatic effect. Instead Tortoise wrapped his arms round Max, enfolding him in a nauseating bear hug. It was like being embraced by some old wino.

4

'Teach you some manners,' Tortoise muttered.

Max said nothing, just jabbed with his elbows and tried to twist free. The pair of them stumbled in a grotesque dance down a pedestrian alleyway between the post office and a supermarket car park.

Max found himself wedged between a wall and some kind of obstruction against his thigh.

'Say you're sorry,' hissed Tortoise and began to squeeze.

Max hacked at the big man's ankles and, suddenly, the obstruction collapsed and the pair of them crashed to the ground. In the dim light Max registered a red and white painted barrier and a stack of new paving stones piled against the wall.

Tortoise was on top of him, one big mitt now fastened round Max's throat, his dead weight pinning Max to the ground like a huge smelly sandbag. All he could move was his right arm.

'You may think you're the bee's knees,' said Tortoise, 'but you're just a stupid boy, and I don't give a monkey's who your daddy is.'

Max's hand closed round something hard and jagged, a kind of stone, and he thrust his arm up from the ground like a shot-putter. He didn't have much of an angle to work with but the stone was a good weight. It made a funny clonk as it smacked against the side of Tortoise's head.

The big man gave a little grunt but still held Max fast.

'Let go of me!'

He swung his arm again and made a solid connection. Something wet dripped down.

Max struck again and the grip on his throat relaxed. With a sigh like the wind escaping a pair of

5

bellows, Tortoise rolled sideways amongst the paving stones and bags of cement.

Now it was Max's turn. He had an unhampered swing this time. Smack!

Take that, you fat bastard.

And this.

It felt good, but he made himself stop.

His breath rasped in his ears and his heart was banging against his ribs.

Tortoise said nothing.

Not so full of it now, are you, fat man?

Max climbed shakily to his feet. A sudden acid rush of bile doubled him over and vomit spilled from his throat. He had to get away before the old fool came round.

The street was still deserted and his car awaited. He felt in his pocket for the key and remembered that it was lying somewhere on the road.

He couldn't see it! But it had been there—right next to the drain!

For a few seconds, he panicked. Tortoise would be back on his feet any moment now.

There it was! Under a piece of newspaper that had blown along the gutter.

Max's hand shook as he reached for the key and the fob seemed to squirm out of his grasp. His fingers were wet.

He held them up to his face. They were inky, stained with something.

He looked across at the piece of stone he'd used to get free from Tortoise. He'd dropped it by the car: a chunk of broken paving slab that glistened wetly in the pale street light.

Oh Lord, what had he done?

Whatever, he wasn't going back down that

alleyway to have a look.

He wiped his hand on the newspaper and then used it to wrap the paving stone. On his way back to his flat in Holland Park, he stopped by a skip full of builder's rubble and chucked it in. He knew he was being silly but why take risks?

By the time he'd reached home the rain had come, drenching him thoroughly in the short walk to his front door. He welcomed it.

<u>Part One</u>

Chapter One

Alan Morrell woke in the darkness and reached for the bedside light. A lance of pain stilled his movement. Damn—he'd forgotten about the collarbone. As injuries went, it wasn't too bad, a sight better than the two broken legs he'd had in the past eighteen months. All the same, it wasn't much fun first thing in the morning. As a jump jockey you never got any sympathy with a broken collarbone. It was regarded as little more than a minor inconvenience. If you took any more than ten days off you were considered a sissy. The truth, however, was that getting your head off the pillow for the first few days after the break was incredibly painful.

He listened out for sounds of movement elsewhere in the old cottage. The luminous display on the alarm clock read 6:03 and he knew his companions would be stirring. When you worked at a training yard your day started early.

He heard footsteps coming up the stairs. The bedroom door opened, silhouetting the familiar curly head of Noel Dougherty, his friend, landlord and—for a few more weeks—his housemate. Soon Noel would be returning to Ireland to work at his father's yard. Alan and Lee, the other member of the household, would be sorry to see him go.

'Give me a hand, will you?' said Alan.

Noel stepped into the room and flicked on the light, grinning hugely.

'Are you not mended yet? I thought you jockeys healed overnight. You should be up making

11

breakfast for us workers.'

Alan scowled at him but it wasn't possible to look fierce lying flat on your back with a six-foot tough guy looming over you. But Noel's touch was gentle as he eased Alan into a sitting position.

'Thanks, mate,' he said. 'I'll be OK now.'

'I'll fetch you some tea once Lee's finished brewing up. That might take a while, the state he's in.'

'Nervous, is he?'

'You could say that.'

Alan's broken bone, sustained after a fall at Taunton three days ago, had done more than put him on the sidelines, it had caused repercussions for his two friends. Lee, a keen amateur rider, had been offered Alan's ride today at Haydock on a horse who was well thought of at the Lambourn yard of Tim Davy, where Alan and Noel both worked. Lee had jumped at the opportunity but he was not the most confident of jockeys.

'He'll be fine,' Alan said. 'He's got the easy job compared to me.'

In return for taking his ride, Alan had agreed to fulfil Lee's role for the day and the prospect was much more daunting: he had to bid for a horse at Tattersalls' horses-in-training sales that afternoon.

Noel wasn't entirely sympathetic. 'For God's sake, if you want to be a bloodstock agent you've got to know how to bid for a horse.'

That was true enough—and there were loads of other things involved as well. Being a bloodstock agent was a bit like being an estate agent, only you were dealing with horses not houses.

The idea to set up Blades Bloodstock had come from Lee. He was a bit of a bookworm on the quiet and an expert on form and breeding; he'd also been doing business studies in his spare time and was the brains behind the whole venture. His first idea was that the three of them should operate as a team but Noel had ducked out, being committed to a return to Ireland. Alan, however, had been swept along on the tide of Lee's enthusiasm and, for their first purchase, they'd earmarked a Flat horse in Tim Davy's yard. Having the inside track on a horse was a big advantage when it came to buying one. Just to be certain an animal was sound was a plus. But Alan had particular knowledge of Grain of Sand: he'd schooled the horse over some baby hurdles recently on the way home from the gallops and Grain of Sand had turned out to be a natural.

He rushed home to tell Lee, who had worked some magic with his contacts and soon announced that he'd got a buyer lined up. Then Alan had fallen off at Taunton and suddenly Lee was heading to Haydock and it was up to Alan to secure the horse. If Lee was nervous, he was petrified.

Noel seemed to know exactly what was running through Alan's mind.

'Cheer up, man. It'll be a piece of cake.'

'Yeah, sure.' Alan tried to sound positive.

'Anyway, I'll be there to hold your hand.' Noel had volunteered to drive him to the sales in Newmarket. 'Honestly, the pair of you would be lost without me.'

'Oh bog off,' said Alan. He wasn't going to admit that what the Irishman said was true.

He struggled into his clothes and went to look for Lee.

'Good luck, mate,' Alan said. 'He'll hack up.'

Lee gave him one of his sceptical looks. His thin face looked particularly pale and drawn this morning and his earring no longer seemed a jaunty adornment but a mistake. Then his usually perky grin reasserted itself. 'You just worry about yourself. I did mention the bidding was in guineas, didn't I?'

'You did.'

'And a guinea is worth how much?'

'We have been through this a dozen times, Lee, and I understand about the bidding. What concerns me most is that this bloke Ian Redmond is prepared to let us spend a hundred grand of his money.'

'He gave me his word. I told him if he got the horse for that he'd have a bargain.'

'The word of a stockbroker. Shouldn't there be something in writing?'

Lee laughed. 'A lot of business is done on the nod. It's the way of the world, my friend.'

'And you're the expert?'

'More expert than you. And, excuse me, haven't we been through this a dozen times too?'

Alan nodded. They had indeed.

Lee put his hand on Alan's good arm. 'Anyway, just suppose it went pear-shaped with Redmond, am I not the best horse salesman you know? I can drum up half a dozen guys in the City who'd kill for a chance at a horse like Grain of Sand.'

Alan cheered up. It was true Lee had produced their buyer like a rabbit out of a hat and he didn't doubt his friend could do it again. All Alan had to do was successfully bid for the horse and he had every confidence Lee's nous and enthusiasm would see them home with a profit on their first deal.

14

Their fee for brokering the sale was five per cent of the selling price, which they would split between them.

If Lee could take half his positive attitude into his ride at Haydock, tonight the pair of them would be celebrating a double triumph.

*   *   *

Max found himself a half-decent mug from the dirty pile in the sink and spooned in coffee granules. The cleaner came today, thank God, so he could close the door on the squalor in the flat and return later to find the place smartened up and squeaky clean. It had been a good idea of Dad's to have the woman come in a couple of times a week. Pity it wasn't possible to clean up the rest of his life so easily.

As he sipped his coffee he tried to get his head round the night before. He'd slept the sleep of the innocent, deep and dreamless, and it still blanketed his thoughts, making it difficult to focus. Too much vodka hadn't helped. Maybe he'd go back on the wagon for a bit. The booze always shortened the fuse on his temper.

He was clear about one thing though, he'd shown that sack of lard Tortoise that he wouldn't stand for being shoved around. Who did the fat man think he was, demanding a lift and making fun of Max's card skills? He was simply on a bad run— it happened to all poker players. Especially one who played a high-risk take-no-prisoners style like he did.

He'd definitely taught the fat man a lesson— he'd be feeling a little sore this morning. Served the smelly git right, making him lose his rag like that. Max hadn't been so wound up since that incident at Bangor when he'd laid into a stable lad with his whip after being touched off at the end of a three-mile chase—the little fool should have kept his sarky remarks to himself. The whole affair had turned out a complete pain in the neck and he'd lost a lot of rides.

All the same, in the circumstances Tortoise should think himself lucky he hadn't been hit a couple of times more.

There'd been blood and sick all over him when he got home. Max remembered washing it off his hands last night and sponging the stain on his jacket. Lucky he'd not been wearing his new suede one—you'd never get a bloodstain out of that.

He'd better have a thorough check through what he'd been wearing—get it all in the wash and down to the cleaners. And check out the car, too. Drop it in to the valet service and ask for their Gold Star top-to-toe clean.

Just in case.

*   *   *

Alan was still buzzing as he entered the crowded refreshment room at Tattersalls' horses-in-training sale at Newmarket. He was known as a good man in a crisis, able to keep a cool head when others were getting hot under the collar; it had always been one of his chief attributes as a jockey. In the crush of an oversubscribed novice hurdle or when it came to holding a horse up for a late challenge, Alan could be relied on to get the job done. So it was a shock to find himself getting nervous in these civilised surroundings.

'Tea?' suggested Noel.

'I'd rather have a brandy.'

Alan wondered if he'd ever get used to spending so much money. Ninety-five thousand guineas was a powerful amount to say goodbye to on the nod of a head, even if it wasn't his money.

Noel dived purposefully into the crush in front of the bar and Alan hung back, all too aware he had to protect his left arm which hung awkwardly in a sling under his jacket. Noel reappeared with unlikely speed and put a glass in Alan's good hand. He took a large gulp and savoured the fiery progress of the liquid down his throat. He only drank spirits on special occasions and this was certainly one of those. It would probably go straight to his head but that was OK, the tough part of the afternoon was over. He felt his mouth stretch into a grin.

'I got him, didn't I?'

'Only just, mate.' Noel had spotted a couple of seats and quickly manoeuvred Alan into position ahead of a couple of suited business types. 'Once the bidding went over ninety I thought you were going to freeze.'

The truth was, he *had* frozen. He'd never bid at an auction before and he'd found the atmosphere of the bidding ring intimidating. Everyone else seemed so familiar with the drama of the process: the well-oiled efficiency of the auctioneer, the nerveless concentration of the bidders and the flickering of the electronic board, as bids in five currencies escalated like the score of some giant video game. He'd felt as if he were at the performance of a play—except that he knew he had lines of his own to speak. That's what had gripped him with fear.

At first, it had been OK. It was a relief to see Grain of Sand led into the ring. The sight of that familiar white-muzzled head was like recognising an old friend in a crowd. Others recognised him too, Alan could tell from the whispering and shuffling that greeted the horse's appearance. Grain of Sand had been a pretty useful performer on the Flat but the question was, did he have a career ahead of him over the sticks? Alan knew that the chances were good but, in truth, the only place to find out if the horse had the bottle for the job was on the racecourse.

The bidding had opened at fifty thousand guineas. He'd waved his catalogue at the middle-aged lady in the aisle whom Noel had identified as one of the auctioneer's spotters. There were a handful of people interested at that price but, as the bidding went over seventy-five, it was down to just two of them: Alan and a man in a camel-haired coat. It had taken Alan a moment or two to locate him.

The man seemed completely at ease, obviously accustomed to the business of blowing substantial sums of money on unpredictable animals. Alan tried not to look at him but couldn't help it. After each bid of his own, conveyed by a nervous flap of the catalogue, he'd turn anxiously towards his rival sitting in the front row. The man would pause just long enough to let Alan think he'd seen him off, then incline his head in a patrician nod and inch ahead again.

When the bidding reached ninety-four, the auctioneer turned expectantly in Alan's direction.

Alan did not move. His mind was racing, trying to compute whether he could bid further. What had Lee said? A guinea amounted to £1-05. Or was it £1-10? He had an upper limit of £100,000—if he bid on, would that take him through his ceiling? Lee would kill him if he got this wrong.

Noel had jabbed him in the ribs, hissing, 'Go on!' And he had, thrusting his arm out just as the auctioneer was about to bring down the hammer against him.

Alan stared anxiously at his opponent. He'd worked it out now: 95,000 guineas amounted to £99,750. It had to be his last bid.

You could have heard a pin drop in the small amphitheatre as all eyes settled on the man in the camel coat. He sat impassively, just as he had done throughout, and then, with heart-stopping deliberation, shook his head. Alan had won. It was then he'd started to shake, suddenly aware of the sweat beading in his armpits. He'd signed for his purchase in a daze as Noel had nipped off to arrange for Grain of Sand to travel back to Tim Davy's yard in Lambourn and then they'd made for the bar.

'Well done, Mr Morrell.' Alan looked up to see the man who had run him to his limit extend his hand. 'I only carried on bidding when I recognised you. I reckoned you must know the horse from Davy's yard and therefore he must be pretty promising.'

'Oh, he is,' said Alan just before their new acquaintance disappeared into the crowd. He'd introduced himself but Alan, the brandy already taking effect, had failed to catch the name.

'Pleasant sort of fellow,' said Noel. 'He probably

just cost you twenty grand.'

Alan reflected on Noel's words. Let that be our first lesson: get someone else to bid for you when it's obvious you have inside information. But what did that matter? He was spending money on behalf of someone else, this contact of Lee's. Alan glanced at his watch and indicated to Noel the large-screen television in the corner. It was time to see if Lee could do his side of the business on Olympia.

*　　　*　　　*

Lee sat next to another amateur in the changing room. He loved the atmosphere and the banter between the riders, with amateurs and professionals mingling together, regardless of whether they'd ridden one winner or a thousand. The only difference was that the jockeys at the top of the tree got the best seats, handy for the showers, the tea room, the exit—and, of course, the trial scales.

Lee didn't get many chances to ride a decent horse, especially one as good as Olympia. As an amateur rider, he'd only managed nine winners in five years and these days it was getting hard to wangle any rides at all. He'd taken up riding too late in life to be really good. He looked and felt stiff in the saddle but his enthusiasm and effort had never been in doubt. And when Tim Davy had offered him the chance to pilot Olympia, he'd jumped at it. Who knows, he might even take his winners into double figures.

He'd ridden at Haydock a couple of times. It was a fabulous galloping track where the fields were

usually small but always competitive and where—
there was no getting round it—you had to be on a
quality horse or an exceptional jumper. The fences
there were more upright than any others in the
country and you slept a lot better the night before
if you were on a horse as agile as Olympia.

He was confident that the race would mark a
change in his fortunes. Olympia was an animal with
real talent, one he'd been riding out on a regular
basis. If he couldn't get this horse home first then
he'd know for certain that he was destined never to
win on this track. Well, he could live with that.
Better men than him had drawn a blank at
Haydock.

But this was no time to think of failure. The
owners, a couple of footballers, were waiting for
him in the parade ring. Luckily it wasn't necessary
to come up with a load of flannel for their benefit.
They were here for a fun day out when the
pressure, for once, was not on their shoulders. The
three of them traded pleasantries for a couple of
minutes before they wished him good luck.

As Lee turned to Tim Davy for some last-minute
instructions, a steward appeared in front of them.

'Mr Davy, I've just had a phone call from
Portman Square'—the headquarters of the Jockey
Club, no wonder the steward was positively puffed
up with importance. 'This horse of yours is drifting
in the betting. Is there any reason to think he won't
be running at his best?'

Lee stared at the man blankly, at a loss.

Tim was equally taken aback but spoke for both
of them. 'As far as I know he's in great shape.
We've come to win. Who's been laying him?'

'No one in particular and it might be nothing but

we thought you should know.'

'Take no notice,' muttered Tim as he legged Lee up into the saddle.

'What was that all about?'

Tim shrugged. 'Don't worry about it—just concentrate on the race. Your father's here, by the way.'

His dad was here? They'd spoken just last night but the old man had said nothing about driving over to Haydock.

Tim was grinning. 'He said not to tell you in case it put you off, but I reckon that's bollocks. You're going to ride a blinder in any case, aren't you?'

'Sure.'

'You'd better. Your dad says he's put a pony on the nose.'

Jesus—his father never bet.

No pressure then.

*　　*　　*

Alan suppressed the jolt of jealousy that gripped him as on the television he watched the horses lining up for the start. Lee deserved the ride on Olympia and it wasn't fair to begrudge it. Besides, if he'd been fit to race himself then he wouldn't have had the satisfaction of securing Grain of Sand, no matter how ineptly he'd gone about it. He sincerely hoped that Lee would make a better job of piloting Olympia—though not so good that Tim would prefer him to Alan next time out. It was a selfish business being a jockey and Lee's seven-pound allowance would always be useful off an easy ride with plenty of weight.

The camera dwelt for a moment on Olympia as

the TV commentator announced that his price had lengthened once more; he was now two whole points bigger than at the start of the day.

'He's a powerful-looking beast,' said Noel. 'What's he like to ride?'

'Your granny could ride him.'

As the race began and the field set off away from the stands, Olympia had a perfect position on the inside, about four lengths off the leader. Lee did what Alan had told him and cut off the dog-leg to steer a direct line from the first to the fourth fence. You could only do that on a horse that was big and strong enough to ease other horses off their line. The ground looked soft and Lee had Olympia in a good rhythm. It was like clockwork. As Noel and Alan watched, they could count off the strides before each fence like a metronome: one, two three—ping! One, two, three—ping! With each fence they could see Lee's confidence growing. He began crouching lower in the saddle.

'This is the best I've seen him ride,' said Alan.

For a circuit Lee just let Olympia make ground at each fence and then took a pull, keeping him nicely on the bridle. But as they rounded the bend away from the stands, the horse's head began to get lower and his stride shortened.

Alan thought straight away that maybe the horse had broken a blood vessel.

*   *   *

At the next fence the horse made his first mistake—nothing serious but, instead of standing off, he got in close and was clumsy. He gave the fence a belt with his front end. Lee, who had been sitting further up his neck than he'd ever been before, suddenly found himself thrown right back on the buckle end of the reins with legs locked out in front of him as if he were the anchor man in a tug of war.

Lee's confidence seemed to vanish in an instant. He tried urging the horse on but it didn't have much effect. It was as if Olympia had run out of petrol. Olympia wasn't a shirker, he never needed shaking up on a racecourse and it seemed unfair to bully him. If he wasn't performing, it wouldn't be because he didn't want to.

Lee felt sick about the whole thing. Here he was, in a good quality race on a rated horse with the whole world watching—well, a packed grandstand and a television audience, not to mention his dad— and Olympia was having an off day. And he knew who'd get the blame. People would be bound to think that Alan would have rung a tune out of the horse and that Lee had cocked up.

He pushed the thought to the back of his mind. He just had to do the best he could and avoid ignominy if he could. He decided to jump a couple more fences and, if nothing happened, he'd pull up.

They scrambled over the next fence but landed safely. A knot of three horses lay just a few lengths ahead and Lee gave his mount a slap on the shoulder, urging him to hunt them down. But the horse felt dead.

That's enough, thought Lee and went to pull out from the next fence when a tailender came past and unintentionally kept him on line for the final ditch. Olympia had lost all momentum. Lee couldn't find a stride. Suddenly he was flying through the air on his own, instinctively curling into

24

a ball to lessen the impact of slamming into the turf. Bang goes Dad's pony, he thought in the instant before he hit the ground.

*   *   *

There were groans of dismay from the crowd around Alan in the bar as Olympia somersaulted the fence and landed on top of his rider. These were horse people and they knew at once that this was no ordinary fall.

'That's a bad one,' said a voice and others murmured agreement. The TV coverage followed the progress of the race but Alan hardly noticed.

'He bloody buried him,' murmured Noel.

Alan said nothing, but scanned the screen above him, looking for clues to Lee's welfare. A long shot across the course to the scene of the accident showed an ambulance and other vehicles in attendance.

'There are screens up around Olympia,' said the TV commentator. 'Let's hope he's just winded. That looked pretty nasty.'

'What about Lee?' muttered Alan beneath his breath. He could make out two knots of people; one by the green canvas screens that surrounded the horse, the other grouped around a shape on the ground.

The television picture switched to a replay of the incident, with Olympia on the charge approaching the open ditch.

'You can see his front foot going over the guard rail ahead of the ditch,' said the other commentator, a well-known former jockey. He sounded as sick as Alan felt. 'He tries to push off

25

but the ground's not there and he flips over. There's nothing the rider can do.'

'Except pray the horse doesn't land on top of you,' added his colleague as the screen showed the event in slow motion.

Alan turned away; it was too sickening to watch. He walked to the door past a cheerful crowd of drinkers and other sale-goers unaware of events at Haydock. Outside, away from the noise of their chatter, he groped in his pocket for his mobile and speed-dialled Tim Davy. Unsurprisingly, he was switched to a message centre; Tim would have his hands full right now.

Jesus, he hoped Lee was all right. The fall had probably looked worse than it was. Sometimes the most spectacular spills were the most innocuous. Anyhow, Lee was like a cork, always bobbing back up.

Ten minutes later, his mobile rang. Tim Davy's voice was brisk.

'The ambulance is taking him to hospital right now, Alan.'

'Is he serious?'

'Nobody knows, it's too early to say.'

*   *   *

There were roadworks on the M6. Alan admired the way Noel dealt with the frustrations of driving; the drive from East Anglia's flatlands up the A14 across the Midlands to this last flog up the motorway had taken over three hours, as dim day turned into a rain-filled evening. They'd not stopped for any kind of refreshment, in fact they'd hardly eaten all day, not that either of them cared.

When Noel had heard what was happening to Lee, he'd simply said, 'Let's go.'

Doing his collarbone had had some bloody awful consequences, Alan reflected. Would Olympia have cocked up that fence if he'd been on board?

He was a better, more experienced rider than Lee. He'd ridden Olympia before and won on him too. He couldn't imagine the horse making the kind of mistake he'd made this afternoon. His whole performance had been out of character. Alan couldn't fathom it.

'Nearly there,' Noel said. They were off the motorway now, negotiating rain-slick urban streets. Noel appeared to know exactly where he was going and Alan didn't question it. It was like being in a dream.

'Wait till you tell him about Grain of Sand,' Noel murmured. 'That'll cheer him up.'

It would too. Alan found himself smiling. There was no need to get too down about things.

They pulled into the hospital car park and found a space. It was a relief to get out of the car and breathe the damp evening air.

Ahead of them, outside the glass doors of the hospital reception, a burly bare-headed figure stood in the rain, silhouetted by the pale orange light. As he mounted the steps to the entrance, Alan recognised Lee's father, Geoff.

'Mr Finney,' he called.

The man turned towards him, his face a blank, but he gripped Alan's hand hard and held on to it. In the other, he held a cigarette burnt down to an unnoticed stub.

'How is he?' Alan asked.

Geoff opened his mouth but no words came out.

27

He swallowed and tried again. 'They operated on him but they couldn't stop the bleeding.'

Alan saw Geoff's cheeks were wet and not with rain.

'Lee's dead, son.'

As the three of them stood in shock and silence, Alan's thoughts went from Lee to Grain of Sand and the unknown client who was supposed to be buying him. With his partner dead, Alan's exposure had suddenly doubled to a hundred thousand pounds.

He guiltily banished the thought from his mind. How could he be so selfish at a time like this?

Chapter Two

Tom Dougherty squinted down the row of hurdles into the morning sunlight. Beyond the long paddock where it dropped suddenly to the beach— a cause of alarm to visiting riders on a misty morning gallop—the light sparkled on the Atlantic waves, making it even more difficult to pick out the distant horse and rider. Not that Tom needed to look—he saw this horse day and night, in the flesh and in his dreams. Tom Dougherty, farmer and horse trainer of County Kerry in the far west of Ireland, lived and breathed for his champion hurdler Black Mountain.

It had been a stormy relationship between man and horse; no other animal had ever given Tom so much trouble—and no other had given so much in return. He supposed it was like bringing up a rebellious child who suddenly made good, which was not, thank God, part of his own experience. His three children had not dished out anything like as much grief as this one stroppy horse. But he didn't own Black Mountain; the man standing by his side did, and Tom was profoundly grateful to him.

Lewis Ashwood was kitted out in what looked like a brand-new waxed jacket and he was holding a pair of high-specification binoculars to his suntanned face. Taken in conjunction with his well-groomed head of hair and finely manicured hands, some might have taken the tan to be a beauty-parlour affectation—after all, what businessman in the public eye wouldn't want to present his most glamorous face to the world? But Tom knew for a fact that Lewis had acquired it lying on a beach in Mauritius. Lying, what's more, next to Tom's daughter Roisin. Tom would never have thought he'd get used to the idea of Roisin being romanced by a man approaching his own age, but who couldn't warm to a fellow like Lewis?

He reminded himself that he'd liked Lewis even before he'd stepped in and bought Black Mountain, ending the speculation that the horse might be moved to another trainer. That would have been a blow.

Lewis lowered the binoculars; they were unnecessary now as the horse and rider ahead grew larger in their sight. At this angle, it was almost as if the pair were galloping straight at them out of the rising sun. The jingling of tack and the thump of hooves rang louder, mingling with the huffing breaths that seemed to come from deep within the barrel chest of the thundering horse.

Black Mountain was the colour of night, a

29

silhouette cut from coal-dark cloth as he charged at them. Though the air was warm and a balmy autumn sun was on his back, Tom had seen the horse like this in all weathers. No wind or rain or sleet or snow ever slowed him down or dented the fury that thrust him forward.

The horse was closing on them now, devouring the ground in a stride that seemed to reverberate beneath their feet. As he took the last hurdle in the line, just a couple of yards from where they stood, the wind of his passing was like the wake of an express train.

'Fantastic,' cried Lewis, thumping Tom's back in delight. 'Just fantastic.'

Tom said nothing. He wasn't a fellow for unnecessary words.

In response to his rider, Black Mountain had slowed at the end of the straight and now allowed himself to be swung round in their direction. His jockey, Tom's youngest son, Connor, clapped the horse's shoulder in appreciation, a grin splitting his face. Con had been asked to show the horse off for his new owner and he knew he'd done just that.

'Well done, lad,' Lewis said and somehow, before Tom could intervene, a couple of banknotes were transferred into Con's hand.

'Shall I take him down again?' the boy asked but Tom shook his head and told him to take the horse back to the farm.

When he was out of earshot, he said to Lewis, 'You shouldn't tip him like that. You'll spoil him.'

'He'll start asking for wages, you mean.'

'He does all right.' The lad was still at school, after all. And much as Tom appreciated Con's dedication to the horses, he'd rather the boy put

30

some of the same effort into his homework.

*   *   *

Lewis would happily have given the entire contents of his wallet to the lad after what he'd just seen. That horse was a wonder. Such speed and strength. Such bloody brute strength. Black Mountain was a marvel and, if he had anything to do with it, the next winner of the Champion Hurdle at the Cheltenham Festival, the best and most prestigious hurdle race in the racing calendar. For the past ten years Lewis had had at least one entry, fine animals all of them—two had gone off as favourites—but they'd always come up short. Black Mountain could not conceivably ever come up short. He looked as if he'd rather die.

But Lewis had a few hurdles of his own to jump before he could be sure of getting the horse to the starting line. It was well known the animal was temperamental and he'd never raced outside Ireland. Tom Dougherty was the key.

'So, Tom, don't you think it's about time you gave Black Mountain a tilt at some English prize money?'

He knew Tom would appreciate the 'you'—as if he alone would make the decision where the horse would ride in the future, much as he had when Michael O'Brien owned him. But things were different now that old Michael had pocketed Lewis's shilling. Tom would know that Lewis hadn't paid well over half a million pounds just so the horse could continue to clean up in Ireland.

'Cheltenham, you mean?' Tom said.

'Exactly. He's not the best horse until he's

31

proved it on the biggest stage.'

'He's not much of a traveller, you know.'

Lewis laughed. 'Come on, Shannon airport's only a few miles up the road. Short flight, Bob's your uncle.'

Tom lifted his cloth cap from his head and wiped his brow. 'You must be joking. It's been the devil's own job to get him in a horsebox, you'd never get him on a plane.'

'Seriously?' Lewis was incredulous.

'When I changed my old lorry, it took two days before he'd put a foot on the ramp and four before we could coax him inside. You can't make this horse do anything he doesn't want to do. The only way we could get him to England is on the ferry.'

Lewis calculated the length of the road journey to the east coast and the sea journey on top of that. It seemed a long way round but he simply nodded. 'Whatever you think's best. I'd like a trial run.'

'Oh yes?'

'It's not a good idea just to take him over for the Festival, is it? First time away from home and all that craziness to put up with. He won't do himself justice. There's time for him to pop across for a less frenzied rehearsal.'

Tom appeared to consider the matter, though it would surely have occurred to such a wily old bird already.

'Or am I being too pushy?' Lewis had a conciliatory hand on Tom's elbow. 'Your daughter tells me I'm always trying to take over but when it comes to Black Mountain I defer to you entirely. You're the expert and you know your horse.'

Lewis thought it was nicely done—the mention of Roisin combined with the offer to take a back seat. But he'd never taken a back seat in his life and he wasn't going to start now.

He could picture himself all over the papers next March, holding aloft the Champion Hurdle trophy: the culmination of a personal quest.

*   *   *

Roisin Dougherty checked her appearance before she stepped onto the gaming floor: hair tied off her face, lipstick discreet, dress demure, name tag in place. She looked like a bank teller or a schoolteacher or a restaurant manager and, she supposed, her job had a little in common with all these: she was a casino croupier.

She relieved her colleague Alvin at the roulette table and he shot her a look of mock surprise in recognition of her recent absence; this was her first day back at work after her holiday. She didn't have to return, Lewis had made it clear he'd pay for her to be a lady of leisure or else find her a job with more sociable hours but she'd resisted the idea. Much as she adored Lewis, he couldn't be allowed to take her over completely.

Besides, she liked her job. It was better than serving time in an office—which was where she had worked nine to five when she had first lived in London two years ago. The glamour of life lived outside the conventional still appealed to her, perhaps because this indoor world of no clocks was such a contrast to her upbringing on a farm in County Kerry. Also, she was good at it. Her brain and her fingers were deft; dealing cards, sorting chips, reckoning up wins and losses all came naturally to her.

But maybe the chief appeal of this work was that she carried it out in secret. None of her family or friends from back home knew what she did, except her brother Noel and he would never tell. She knew how lucky she was with her elder brother. How she wished he wasn't going back to Ireland, but that was another story.

There were the usual crew of punters at the table: some tourists, some blow-ins and others who looked as if they never saw the light of day, which was probably the case. A couple she recognised and she acknowledged them with a polite dip of the head and quick eye contact. One of them, an American regular, said, 'Hey, Irish, I missed you—where you been?' But she just cast him a smile as she spun the wheel. She never talked to the customers, the management didn't approve.

She'd lucked into the job through Danielle, a girlfriend of Noel's who worked in what she referred to as 'the gaming industry'. Roisin had looked shocked until Danielle had explained that it wasn't the same as being on the game and Roisin had felt like a complete hick from the sticks. But as Danielle had explained what she actually did, the advantages had been obvious to Roisin. There was the money, for a start—it was far better paid than office temping. The hours also appealed to her; working evenings and nights meant that she could drive out to the Lambourn yard where Noel was working to ride out and catch up on her sleep in the afternoon. The car, of course, would be paid for out of her new wages. So she applied for training as a croupier and it had worked out much as she had hoped.

But she hadn't dared tell her parents. Dad would

34

probably be amused but her mother, she knew, would not understand. Mum was a keen church-goer and did not approve when Dad had a few pounds on a runner at the races. Though she might not ask Roisin to give up her job, she would be deeply unhappy about it and berate herself for bringing up her daughter so badly. Roisin could do without inflicting such pointless breast-beating.

Roisin relished being independent, having a life that was all her own. She wasn't going to give it up just yet.

A man of about her own age took a seat at the table next to a middle-aged player in an expensive suit. The lad looked familiar and she studied him peripherally. He reminded her of Noel's friend Alan—only, now that she looked at him more closely, nowhere near as handsome. She'd been rather taken with Alan when she'd first met him—at a charity ball soon after she'd come over from Ireland. There was a brooding intensity about him that made him look like one of those soulful heroes out of a French movie. As the evening had progressed he'd revealed a dry line in humour and, when he smiled, his whole face lit up. Later, he'd whirled her round the dance floor with some skill. She'd been rather disappointed to discover that he already had a girlfriend.

But that was ages ago, well before Lewis entered her life like some overwhelming force of nature. Lewis was handsome too—in a different way, of course—and could handle her on the dance floor and much more besides. His aura of self-assurance was such that she couldn't imagine ever being with anyone else ever again.

There was another reason the new punter was

familiar—he was a jockey and she'd seen him interviewed on the television recently. He'd been full of confidence then but here in the casino he looked quite out of his depth. He was fiddling with a small pile of chips—£5s, she noticed—and chewing on his bottom lip. When she asked the table to place bets he wagered one chip on black.

The ball landed on black 17 and Roisin quickly settled up, raking in the losing chips and paying off the winners. As she pushed two £5 chips in the jockey's direction she noticed his meagre little pile had grown. Grown, what's more, with counters of a much higher denomination. Suddenly he was sitting with around £2,000 at his disposal.

Roisin's swift and certain movements did not falter. But, as the next play began, she probed the mystery.

It had to be the man next to the jockey in the made-to-measure suit. His face was round and smooth, his features doughy and undistinguished. She had no idea who he was and had not seen him here before—though that didn't mean a great deal; he could be a regular she'd never come across. Whoever he was, he was lucky at the table—she'd been paying him on almost every spin—and he'd just paid a man off under everybody's nose.

Well, it wasn't her business, just one of those little side shows that kept life in the pit interesting.

The jockey scrambled to his feet, clutching his chips, and without glancing at his benefactor headed for the cashier in the corner of the room.

Roisin wondered what her mother would have made of that. She'd be bound to make a fuss about the immorality of working in a casino but was that any worse than making a living out of horseracing, where jockeys were regularly paid off?

She kept the smile off her face as she spun the wheel.

*   *   *

'May I speak to Mr Ogilvie, please?'

It was the second potentially embarrassing phone conversation Alan had initiated in the past couple of days and he hoped it wasn't going to end as badly as the first.

'Speaking,' said an instantly recognisable voice at the other end of the line. So Noel's information had been correct: Cyril Ogilvie of Ogilvie Tompson, Antiquarian Bookseller, was the underbidder for Grain of Sand.

'We met the other day at the horses-in-training sale. Alan Morrell. I don't know if you remember but we were both bidding for the same horse.'

'Of course I remember. How can I help you, Mr Morrell?'

This was the awkward bit.

'I was wondering whether you were still interested in Grain of Sand. There's been a change of plan at my end and I'm looking for a buyer for him. Naturally, I'd be prepared to let you have him for the underbid.'

'I'm very sorry but I can't help.' The man was apologetic but explained that he'd bought another horse later on in the sale.

Damn.

'Tell me,' Ogilvie continued, 'what's made you change your mind?'

'I haven't changed my mind about Grain of Sand. But I was buying him for someone else and

37

he's had second thoughts.'

That was a polite way of encapsulating the first embarrassing conversation, when Alan had called Lee's buyer, Ian Redmond.

In the days immediately following Lee's death, the ownership of Grain of Sand hadn't seemed important. There had been too much shock and emotion in the Lambourn air, both at Tim Davy's yard and at the cottage, where Alan and Noel sat up late into the night hashing and rehashing the whole horrible business. But after the funeral had come and gone—a hysterical, bitter-sweet affair attended by hundreds—Alan woke up to the unpalatable fact that Lee's buyer for Grain of Sand had not got in touch with him to confirm the deal was still on.

Redmond had been blunt.

'I cancelled the deal that morning when I read in the paper that Lee was riding at Haydock,' he said. 'I reckoned if he couldn't be bothered to spend my money himself then he wasn't looking after my interests.'

'Lee didn't say anything to me.'

'Sorry, mate, not my problem.'

'What did Lee say when you told him?'

'I sent him a text, actually. I couldn't get through on the phone.'

'He was riding—he'd have had the phone turned off.'

'So? As far as I'm concerned, I pulled out of the deal. It's a shame what happened to Lee but what can I say? I don't want the horse. End of story.'

Hence Alan's call to Cyril Ogilvie. Tattersalls gave credit depending on who you were and how much business you did with them during the year.

The majority of trainers bought horses on spec and then paid the debt off when they sold the horse. In Alan's case, as a new customer, he had thirty days—less than that now—to find almost one hundred thousand pounds. He didn't know what he was going to do.

'I was very sorry to hear about your colleague up at Haydock,' said Cyril Ogilvie. 'Racing can break your heart at times.'

In all sorts of ways, thought Alan as he replaced the phone.

*   *   *

Lewis Ashwood gazed down from his office on the thirty-third floor of his Docklands tower at the dirty grey river snaking its way to the sea. He was proud of the view and always keen to show it off, though on some days—murky autumn ones with skies of lead, like today, with wind whipping raindrops against the great glass windows—it could seem a trifle bleak. Right now, however, it looked downright beautiful to Lewis. After the phone call that had just ended, everything looked beautiful.

'Jackie!' he called and his PA appeared on cue, as she always did. A woman just a few years younger than himself, she was smartly turned out in a paisley-patterned blouse and neat pencil skirt. She looked tired, but that wasn't surprising as she'd been holding the fort for the past week while he—he had to admit it—had been bunking off. But sometimes it paid to bunk off, to stop fiddling neurotically with problems that would resolve themselves in their own time. As had just happened.

He smiled at Jackie. 'We've got Elmwood Glade. Jerry says planning permission is going through.'

Jackie's face lit up. It had been a long battle to secure the right to develop the hundred-acre site and she had witnessed every skirmish with East Downham council. In fact, she'd carried the fight herself on many occasions, not least in escorting council leader Jerry Rubak to every current West End musical and turning down his advances at the end of the evening without offending him. Lewis knew all this and more and he appreciated it.

'Go and buy yourself a nice outfit,' he said. 'And take Mike to dinner somewhere smart and show it off.' It was the least her husband deserved, boring fart though he was. 'Be extravagant.'

For a second, her grey eyes narrowed, as if she were looking for the catch—she knew him too well. But she evidently decided there was no ulterior motive and said, 'Thank you, Mr Ashwood.' He'd long given up the attempt to make her use his Christian name.

'And get something for Roisin, too, will you? You're good at it. That pink blouse went down very well last month.'

She gave him one of her inscrutable looks. 'I'll do my best.'

Of course she would—she always did.

As she left the room he picked up the phone but his fingers hovered over the keypad. He wanted to call Roisin but at two thirty in the afternoon it was quite possible she was sleeping after her stint at the casino. He was never quite sure what she got up to during the day and more than once he'd woken her up. More to the point, he didn't want to ring just for the sake of it. They'd seen a lot of each other recently and he was aware he was in danger of crowding her.

Since the death of his first wife more than ten years ago, he'd enjoyed the company of many women. In his experience, he knew there was a time to get in close and smother with affection and, similarly, a time to back off. Most of his lady friends, of course, were overwhelmed by his money and status and were only too keen to be smothered—for life, preferably. As a rule when he sensed as much, that's when he backed off.

Roisin, he was convinced, was different. She was younger than his other women for a start, half his age, and at first he'd found that off-putting. But she didn't behave like an irresponsible twenty-something; she had her life sorted out, spending time on things that mattered to her, like horses, her brother, even that damn job at the casino.

At first, he'd been intrigued. He'd met her at Whitbread Gold Cup day at Sandown in another owner's box and had simply thought she was remarkably fetching, in a flashing-eyed Irish colleen fashion. But when he'd been introduced as the owner of a runner in the big race she'd started quizzing him about the horse in a manner that revealed she was more than just another pretty face. It turned out that she'd already backed his runner so they both looked on downcast as the animal made a hash of the second-last with the race at its mercy. He'd taken her with him to the stables to check that all was well with the horse and, next thing he knew, offered to take her to dinner.

'I work at nights,' she'd said.

'Lunch then.'

'I'm usually catching up on my sleep. But . . .' she'd treated him to the full blaze of eyes as black as pitch and a smile full of sly laughter, 'I don't mind missing sleep for some people.' He'd been surprised to find himself as thrilled as a teenager. He also realised she wasn't just pretty, she was a beauty. And though he might end up making a fool of himself, he wanted her in his life. The months that had gone by since had not changed his mind.

But it was her mind that mattered at the moment. He had the impression she wasn't entirely thrilled by him buying Black Mountain and travelling to Ireland to talk horse business with her father. She was a girl who valued her independence and he respected her for that. He wouldn't crowd her at the moment.

The same applied to his son. He'd left Max a message to say he was back in the country but the boy hadn't returned the call. That wasn't necessarily a bad thing. Max's calls often brought news he could do without: a whinge about poor horses, a complaint about a trainer, a request for money. Sometimes no news was good news.

His fingers tapped out the number of one of his co-conspirators in the matter of Elmwood Glade. It was time to forget about personal issues and spread the good news that he'd finally got East Downham council where he wanted them—in his pocket.

*　　　*　　　*

'Where were you, you lousy bastard?'

'Hello, Crystal,' said Max. 'How delightful to see you.'

This was debatable. It was certainly a surprise to

42

find her standing on his doorstep, her green eyes blazing and her sulky mouth spitting fury.

'Don't think you can get away with treating me like dirt. You stood me up this morning and I want to know why.'

To be honest, not that he could afford to be in these circumstances, Max had forgotten all about Crystal and their mid-morning date at a Swindon hotel. He'd had more urgent matters on his mind. However, he summoned up a defence—a good one too, in his opinion.

'But you cancelled me, don't you remember? You left a message saying we should cool it.' He looked over her shoulder at the maroon Space Wagon parked outside on a yellow line. 'You don't want to leave your car there.'

'Why not? I'm not staying, if that's what you're thinking,' she spat, shouldering past him into the hallway in a cloud of perfumed contradiction. As she bustled ahead through the open door of his flat, Max admired her rear in the spray-on high-fashion jeans he'd bought her for her birthday. He grinned as he followed her inside.

'You've got a woman in here, haven't you?' she demanded.

'No.'

She was standing in his sitting room, staring round suspiciously. The room was a mess. Clothes, food cartons and newspapers were everywhere—newspapers in particular. Since his fight with Basil, Max had been scouring the papers, including all the local rags, for news of—well, he didn't like to think what precisely. So far, he'd found nothing.

Crystal picked up today's *Kilburn Times* and hurled it petulantly across the room. It separated

43

into several sheets and fluttered down to join the chaos on the carpet.

'I don't believe you,' she said, sounding less sure of herself, and made for the bedroom.

Crystal knew the layout of the place. They'd wangled a couple of afternoons together and, once, an all-nighter when her husband had stayed over at Ayr. Now she flounced from room to room, poking into drawers and wastepaper baskets and making a thorough search of the bathroom, hunting for evidence of a female presence. He watched her with some amusement—it was the best entertainment he'd had in days.

Finally, she turned to him in triumph, a tortoiseshell hairclip in her hand. 'Whose is this?' she demanded.

The fury was back in her face and the way her swollen bottom lip thrust forward was rather appealing.

'Well, whose is it?'

'It's yours, sweetheart. You left it here last time.'

She looked at it suspiciously, turning it over in her hand. 'I've got one like it.'

'And that's it, you daft woman. I was hanging on to it as a souvenir but you can have it back, if you like.'

'Oh.'

He judged that it was safe to step closer. 'When you left that message you sounded so upset, I thought it was all over.'

'Cliff was acting all suspicious. I was in a bit of a panic.'

'You said I shouldn't get in touch with you. Naturally, I thought that meant everything was off. Is it?'

44

She paused, readjusting to the situation. How seriously did she take herself? he wondered. Or was it all just an act? Not that he cared.

'Cliff seems OK now,' she murmured.

'Great.'

He made no move to touch her but they were standing very close. She tilted her head up, the anger replaced by a lazy sensual look he knew well. She would never make the first move but the invitation was there.

He loved moments like this, the anticipation was intoxicating. In a moment he'd peel her out of those jeans and put her naked on the bed.

It was a damn sight better way to pass the time than wonder if he'd killed a man.

*   *   *

Noel considered himself a happy-go-lucky sort of fellow; he didn't stew over things, he tried to fix them. But it was easier to be happy when things weren't going arse over tit. Unfortunately, since he'd made the decision that the time was right for him to go back to Ireland to help his father, life had been one big banana skin.

Lee's death had been the start of the slide. It was difficult to face the world with a smile on your face when one of your best mates had been killed like that.

But it didn't end there. Thanks to the accident, Alan now found himself with a hundred-grand horse on his hands and no buyer. Lee could have sorted the situation, Noel had no doubt, but Alan wasn't a wheeler and dealer in the same league. His strengths were with the horses. Together, he and

Lee would have made a great team. Too late for that now.

Noel picked up the phone. He wasn't much of a horse dealer himself but he'd had an idea that might just help.

'Hi, Noel.' His sister sounded pleased to hear from him, but then she always did these days, since she'd come to London and become the new Roisin. It was hard to believe what a temperamental pain in the jacksie she'd been as a kid back home. He guessed it had something to do with growing up and—give the man credit—Lewis Ashwood. He imagined Lewis appreciated some maturity in the behaviour of his female companions.

'I'm after a favour,' Noel said. No point in beating around the bush. And he told her about Alan and Grain of Sand. She was sympathetic, as he'd expected; she'd once had a soft spot for Alan.

'But how can I help?' she said when he'd finished. 'I don't have a spare hundred thousand pounds.'

'Lewis does though.'

There was a short pause. 'Noel,' she said finally, 'just because Lewis bought Black Mountain doesn't mean he can run around getting everyone out of trouble.'

'I'm not suggesting that. This horse is going to be a tiptop hurdler, take it from me.'

She laughed. 'Come off it, you're just trying to help your mate out. I know you too well. You can't solve everyone's problems, Noel.'

'You could at least ask Lewis, couldn't you? He owns a whole string of horses, so what's another?'

'Well, I would like to help Alan.'

So he'd persuaded her. She was a good kid.

46

*　　　*　　　*

The thought of returning to Paul's place the week after the dust-up with Tortoise filled Max with dread. The news and local papers had carried no mention of an injured man on the streets of Kilburn last Tuesday night, so the chances were that Basil Jacobs was in roaring good health and had forgotten all about their disagreement. After all, he'd been drinking a fair amount. Maybe he'd woken up in the alley none the wiser.

Get real. That couldn't be possible. There'd been something about those last couple of cracks he'd landed, a kind of yielding, splintering sensation as the stone in his fist had gone in, jabbing through the man's skull like a teaspoon smacking into an eggshell. He could still feel it in his arm. It gave him the effing creeps.

If he'd hurt Basil and the old sod turned up at Paul's looking for revenge, that would be bad news. But he could smooth it over, surely? Some grovelling apologies, an exchange of money. It would be embarrassing with all the other guys looking on, but the situation should be salvageable if he took it on the chin like a man. It would be a sight worse if Basil showed and he didn't. Tortoise could badmouth him all evening and his absence would condemn him.

But—and there was no getting away from the worst-case scenario—suppose Basil didn't show *because he couldn't*? Like, he was in a coma or his brain was scrambled and the hunt was on to find who'd thumped him? What would it look like if Max then missed the Tuesday night game for the first time in six months? Apart from Paul, he was the most regular player.

It would look bloody suspicious if he wasn't there.

So Max drove to Kilburn. He parked in a different road, a good five minutes' walk away, and with a sinking heart and a guilty conscience climbed the stairs to Paul's flat.

'Cor, look what the cat dragged in.'

'It's Millionaire Maxie.'

This familiar chorus instantly lifted Max's spirits. Please God let nothing have changed since last week. He handed Paul a plastic carrier full of Doritos and canned beer—a contribution he frequently forgot to make—and looked round the small room, which was already blue with cigarette fog.

Three regulars sat round the dining table, together with a man Max did not recognise. There was no sign of Basil.

Paul did the honours. 'Max, this is Victor,' and Max exchanged a firm handshake with a pleasant-looking middle-aged bloke wearing neatly pressed slacks, which was not exactly the dress code for this particular card school.

Max had heard of Victor. Paul was prone to the odd story about his underworld friends and the name Victor always featured. This Victor, according to Paul, was 'the dog's bollocks', a great gambler and a great guy but you would not—repeat not—want to dick him around. Not if you wanted to stay in one piece, that is. Victor was a hard man.

To be honest, Max was a little disappointed. Victor looked like the kind of fellow who washed the car at weekends and went on caravanning holidays.

It was obvious Max's arrival had interrupted a tense hand, for the game resumed the moment the introduction was over. Max took a seat and waited, pretending interest in the show of cards.

Where's Tortoise? he wanted to ask. But not yet. He mustn't appear anxious.

Maybe Tortoise was late, as he himself had been. Not that he'd ever known Tortoise to be late.

Maybe Tortoise was having difficulty negotiating the stairs with his head in a bandage.

Max played conservatively, which was not his usual style, and folded holding triple 7s when the bidding got hot fighting over a big pot. Victor won in the showdown with a full house and Max congratulated himself on playing it cool. He even won the next pot himself with two pair, king high. Though it wasn't worth a lot, £50 or so, it made him feel better. Things were going OK after all. Just like a normal evening at the card table.

'I hope you're coming to the funeral,' said Double Top as Max collected his chips.

'What?' He wasn't sure he'd heard correctly.

'Basil's funeral. Friday, Golders Green Crematorium.'

'Tortoise Basil?' His voice came out high and flutey, like a squeaky schoolkid. He'd wondered, if it came to it, how he would pretend to be shocked. The truth was there was no need to pretend.

'Christ, Max, don't you know?' Paul looked accusingly at Jimmy Park. 'I thought you were going to ring round.'

Jimmy shrugged. 'He wasn't in when I called. It's not exactly something you can leave a message about.'

'You could have rung back, couldn't you?'

'Oh, for God's sake!' Max shouted. Paul and Jimmy were always bickering over something but tonight he wasn't in the mood to put up with it. 'Just tell me what happened.'

Paul pulled a face—sorr-ee—and stopped shuffling the cards.

'Basil got mugged on his way home last week. Some bastard smashed his head in and he wasn't found till six o'clock the next morning. They carted him off to the Royal Free and he died over the weekend.'

'Oh Jesus, that's terrible.' The others nodded. 'Do they know who did it?' That was the important question.

'They haven't got anyone for it,' said Fat Seth.

'I bet they don't get anyone neither. The cops are bloody hopeless.' That was Jimmy.

'I dunno.' Paul's foxy face lit up with a grin. 'I had a smashing little DC round here, asking if I'd seen anything. Freckles like fairy footsteps all over her cute little nose.'

'You should have given her my number,' said Double Top. 'She can take down my particulars any time.'

Seth managed a tired snigger but Paul said swiftly, 'As a matter of fact, I didn't think any of you would fancy me handing out information. I told her I had a quiet night in last Tuesday, all on my own. I mean, it's not as if we can help poor old Tortoise now, is it?'

Victor spoke for the first time, in a voice of quiet authority. 'Quite right, Paul.' And began to deal the cards.

Max's heart was pounding as he played the next

50

few hands.

So he really had killed him.

And the police had been round. But Paul had kept their names out of it.

It was looking OK. Considering.

'Your shout, Max,' said Seth. They were waiting for him to bet.

'Raise you fifty,' he said, his reckless spirit suddenly liberated.

By the end of the evening he was over two grand down to Victor and he didn't have that much on him.

Victor just smiled. 'Don't worry about it, son,' he said. 'We'll work something out next time.'

Now there was a sensible man.

Max drove home in a daze.

It was official. He was a murderer. He couldn't believe it.

Chapter Three

Alan patted Grain of Sand enthusiastically as he skipped over the last in the row of practise hurdles.

'You've really got the hang of this jumping lark, haven't you, old son?' he murmured into the horse's ear. Grain of Sand bobbed his head as if he understood and took the compliment as his due.

There were compensations, Alan decided, in being the owner of a racehorse like Grain of Sand. Though the horse might be about to plunge him into bankruptcy, he was still an inspiring animal. He couldn't figure out a man like Redmond, Lee's prospective buyer. If he'd been convinced Grain of

Sand was worth having one day, why change his mind? The horse was still the streamlined thoroughbred he'd always been. The thought occurred that Redmond probably had no interest in Grain of Sand as an individual animal with a career ahead of him and the prospect of becoming a champion. He probably thought of him as an item indistinguishable from many others, a commodity simply to be traded. Redmond was a stockbroker, after all.

The fellow would think differently, Alan knew, if he could see the world from Grain of Sand's back. Now that his collarbone was strong enough, Alan had been up at Tim Davy's yard to ride the horse out as often as possible, depending on his other riding commitments. As ever, there were never quite enough of them, certainly not sufficient to sustain a living as a rider—which was one of the reasons he had gone into the horse-buying business with Lee. Alan knew he had talent as a jockey; he'd learned from his father who'd been among the best of his generation. But his father had been a few other things as well, such as a liar, a crook and a self-destructive gambler—not necessarily in that order—which had blighted his career. Alan had been fortunate that his father's reputation hadn't interfered with his own career—trainers could forgive most things if they saw someone with talent. It was injuries that had held Alan back.

He booted Grain of Sand into motion once more. They'd have one more run over the line of schooling hurdles and call it a day.

They took the first two jumps conservatively and then Grain of Sand began to pull, as if he were impatient with the sedate pace. He was, after all, an animal who'd won races at Goodwood and Newmarket on the Flat: he was built for speed. Let's see what you can do then, thought Alan, and gave the horse his head.

Grain of Sand quickened in an instant and flew the next hurdle as if he were already leading the field at Cheltenham. Oh yes! He was a thrilling prospect all right.

Maybe Alan was too slow in putting the brakes on—or maybe, like the horse, he was simply carried away by the glimpse of what he could do—but the last hurdle was one too many. The horse cleared it easily enough but, as he landed, Alan felt him stumble and suddenly he was like a car running over cobblestones. It's a stomach-churning feeling when a good horse goes lame on you. Especially when you own it yourself.

It took a moment or two to pull the animal up so that Alan could get off and check to see what he'd done. He looked down to see a two-inch deep cut just below the fetlock on the off fore. It was a typical over-reach, his rear foot striking the front leg—a common injury amongst novice hurdlers. Alan had tried to protect against it by putting 'boots'—like rear-facing shin guards—on Sandy's front legs but the cut was just below the boot. It was the last the horse would see of the practise hurdles for a few weeks.

Fuck it, he thought to himself as he led the animal back to the yard on foot. He wouldn't be selling this horse to anyone for a while. Still, at least Sandy hadn't done a tendon. That would have kept him off the course for a year and knocked eighty per cent off his value.

All the same, Alan had just damaged the biggest

investment of his life—one he hadn't even paid for yet.

*   *   *

The phone was ringing as Max opened the front door.

Crystal in freak-out mode again. If ever there was a case for padlocking a woman's jaw, she was it. He thought at first she was simply moaning because she'd picked up a parking ticket outside his flat. Well, there was a surprise—he'd told the silly tart she was bound to get one. But it turned out to be another 'Cliff's-on-to-me' drama, on account of the ticket which, naturally, itemised the time and place of her offence. Since she'd told her husband she was spending the day with her sister in Chichester, he wasn't happy. It looked like Mrs Miles was going to have to keep her nose clean for a bit.

Too bad. The things about Crystal that he'd miss could be counted on one hand.

The phone rang again and he waited till the answer-machine cut in, just in case it was Cliff or Crystal. When he heard Paul's nasal drone he picked it up.

'Got good news and good news,' Paul began. 'The first is that you don't owe me money any more.'

'How come?'

'Victor cleaned me out at backgammon after you'd gone last night. So, rather than you owe me and I owe Victor, I've passed your markers over to him. See?'

Max did see, just about. He now owed some

54

smooth character he didn't know the best part of ten grand.

'So what's the other good news?' he grunted.

'Victor wants you to go down to his club for the evening—so he can get to know you better.'

That was good news? Max wasn't sure that getting to know some gangster was to his advantage but he obviously had no choice.

The phone went off again almost immediately after that. This time it was his agent, Pete, and Max grabbed the receiver gratefully. He could do with some rides.

But Pete wasn't calling to offer him work—rather the opposite.

'Cliff Miles has just cancelled you for Bangor on Friday.'

'Why?'

'I don't know what you've been up to,' Pete continued, 'but he was spitting blood. He says if you show your face at the yard again he'll set the dogs on you.'

Obviously Crystal's other half had checked out the address on her parking ticket and put two and two together.

'Cliff's a bit of a hothead,' Pete added. 'I expect he'll calm down in a day or so and I can straighten things out.'

Max didn't say so but there wasn't much chance of that.

*   *   *

Alan was reluctant to leave Grain of Sand, even though the wound on his foot had been dressed and the horse was contentedly nibbling at his feed.

'Cheer up.' Tim Davy was looking at him from the door. 'The vet says it's not that bad.'

Alan shrugged. It was true the injury wasn't serious but, in the circumstances, any time the horse had to spend convalescing gave him a problem. But he didn't want to get into his financial problems with the trainer—they'd been through that recently. Tim had been sympathetic and told Alan not to worry about the stabling fees for the moment, which was generous of him, though Alan swore to himself he'd settle up somehow.

'How's Olympia?' he asked.

'Fine.' Tim confirmed that there had been no repercussions to the horse after the accident at Haydock. Once Olympia had regained his breath, he'd simply got up and walked away—unlike poor Lee.

'Did you ever get to the bottom of why he ran such an odd race?'

Tim shook his head. Olympia's uncharacteristic behaviour had been much discussed. 'The Jockey Club took a blood sample of him on the day and fast-tracked it through. That showed nothing unusual, no trace of dope. The next day we scoped his lungs and he was fine. Our vet gave him a blood test and that was fine too. He wasn't anaemic, there was no sign of a virus and he seems perfectly normal. Full of himself, in fact.'

Alan could vouch for that, for he'd caught sight of the horse up on the gallops and he'd looked in good fettle. Like much associated with horses, it was a mystery.

Before he left the yard, he sought out Kevin, the travelling head lad, who'd made the journey up to

Haydock with the horse the night before the race. Kevin had seen more of Olympia prior to the accident than anyone else.

He ran him to ground in the small tack room that was Kevin's private territory.

'Got a moment?' Alan asked.

Kevin grunted; it could have been a yes. He was a tall man in his thirties, beanpole thin. The story was that he'd been apprenticed as a jockey but a late growth spurt had put paid to that. At the moment, his gangling frame was huddled over the sink as he sponged mud from dirty racing bridles.

'It's about Olympia,' Alan began. 'Did you notice anything different about him before the race up at Haydock?'

'No,' Kevin said in the tone of one who'd been asked that same question many times before. Alan knew that the Jockey Club had also been down to the yard to interview the stable staff.

'What about on the journey up?'

Kevin didn't look up. 'No.'

'Is he a difficult traveller?'

Kevin shook his head.

This was awkward but Alan couldn't just let it lie. 'I only saw the race on television but he looked as if he was just knackered. That's not like him, is it? Was it the ground, do you think? Or was he just taking the piss out of Lee?'

Kevin chucked his sponge into the sink and turned to glare at Alan. 'Look, mate, I don't know. Go and ask the bloody horse, why don't you? I've got work to do.' And he jabbed his thumb at a pile of dirty tack waiting to be cleaned.

Alan bit back the retort that sprang to mind and retreated. 'What's got into him?' he muttered to

57

Frankie, one of the stable girls who was sweeping up in the yard outside.

'He's taking it badly. He feels responsible for what happened.'

'That's ridiculous.'

She gave him an exasperated look. 'It's how he feels. He could do without people getting on his back.'

Alan brooded over this exchange as he drove home. On reflection, Lee had been pretty pally with Kevin—Kevin had been the first to tip him off about Grain of Sand. Any inference that Kevin might have spotted something not right about Olympia and refrained from mentioning it was bound to rub him up the wrong way. So, charging in with a load of questions had not been the most sensitive thing he could have done. Next time he saw Kevin, he'd apologise.

* * *

Alan wasn't exactly brooding but it wasn't easy to banish certain matters from his mind. Until this morning, he'd known his principal task was to find a buyer for Grain of Sand; much as he appreciated the animal, he couldn't afford to keep him. But now, following the horse's mishap over the practise hurdles, he had no hope of selling him. He didn't know what he was going to do.

The doorbell interrupted his train of thought and he opened it to Roisin Dougherty. He'd not seen her since Lee's funeral though he knew from Noel that she'd been up to the yard to ride out.

He led her into the kitchen and put the kettle on. Her presence made him uneasy but all distractions were welcome at the moment. The one that got away—that's how he thought of her.

Her unfathomable black eyes came to rest on his. 'How are you doing, Alan?'

'I'm OK,' he said and turned to making tea. He was irritated with himself but he really ought to be able to handle being around her.

When they'd first met he'd just started going out with Jane, the latest in a string of fun-but-never-going-anywhere relationships. Noel had got him to squire his kid sister from Ireland for the evening. She'd made quite an impression on him with her low lilting voice and her blue-black raven hair flowing like a river down her back. It was rare, he thought at the time, to be in the presence of someone so naturally beautiful. In retrospect, he wished he'd told her so at the time, for the Jane affair had turned into a cheerful friendship soon after. By that time, naturally, the Irish beauty had a boyfriend—though 'boyfriend' didn't quite cover this particular admirer. Lewis Ashwood was rich and flashy and at least twenty years Roisin's senior. He also owned companies and racehorses and wielded the kind of power that a penniless rider like Alan could never hope to match. It made him sick.

Ashwood's son, Max, was another reason to dislike Roisin's current lover. He wasn't the most popular face in the jockeys' changing room and Alan avoided him whenever he was around—which wasn't, to be fair, as often as his talent might suggest. But Max had an ugly temper—he'd lay into a horse after it was beaten—and he fell out with trainers on a regular basis. Wild rabbits don't have tame parents and Alan wondered what Lewis

59

was really like.

Roisin had gone down in his estimation. Though he couldn't help being captivated by those flashing eyes, he now noticed the designer labels in her clothes, the expensive new riding outfit she wore on the gallops, the way she swanned around during the day when the rest of the world was trying to earn a crust. But, of course, she was exempt from doing that. She was just an ornament, he decided, an exotic luxury that a man like him couldn't afford, lovely though she was.

He plonked a chipped mug of tea in front of her and proffered a packet of digestives. To his surprise, she took one and dunked it. Slumming it for his benefit, no doubt.

He took a biscuit and copied her. Raising it to his lips, the biscuit broke in half and splashed into his mug.

She giggled in childish delight and he joined in, he couldn't help it.

'Noel says you've got to find a buyer for your horse,' she said after a moment.

That brought him back to earth. He gave her a quick précis of the situation, finishing with that morning's fiasco with the hurdles.

She listened closely, as if she knew just what he was talking about. He reminded himself that she was a trainer's daughter; she did indeed know what he was talking about.

'Didn't you have boots on him?' she asked.

'Of course. But the cut's below the binding. It was just bad luck.'

'It's not serious though, is it? He's not going to be off work for more than a few weeks, surely?'

He nodded. 'All the same, I won't be able to sell

him like this.'

'I might know someone.'

He didn't quite take in what she'd said at first. Her bottom lip was a fascinating mulberry pink which he found distracting.

'Someone who'd buy Grain of Sand even though he's not fit?'

'He might if I vouch for the horse. He trusts me.'

Then the penny dropped. She was talking about Lewis Ashwood. The same Lewis Ashwood who had just bought Black Mountain, the Irish hurdler, so he could stay at her father's yard. Alan had read a piece about it in a tabloid racing column, headed 'No greater love'; it had been illustrated with a photo of a sombre-faced Roisin and a grinning Ashwood, done up in a dinner jacket.

He laughed without humour and said, 'Does your sugar daddy buy you everything you fancy?'

Roisin's face froze in shock, as if he'd slapped her. Then the fascinating mulberry pink spread to her cheeks.

She sprang to her feet.

He began to apologise but she was already rushing down the hall. At the front door she turned. 'Maybe you should get someone to buy you some manners.'

She left without another word.

If only, Alan thought as the slam of the front door echoed in his ears, he'd kept his big mouth shut.

* * *

Tom Dougherty had never wanted to run a large training operation. He was a farmer first and foremost, like his father and grandfather; the horses were just a hobby. At least, that's the way he'd always looked at it. So how had he ended up in this situation?

'You're going to have to ring some of these folks back, you know,' said Pauline the moment he stepped into the office. She waved a scrap of paper at him on which he could see a scribbled list of names. 'I've not got through half those letters because the phone's not stopped. It's a tiring business making excuses.'

He scanned the list as she continued to scold him. There were pluses and minuses to using your wife as a secretary but these days the minuses were weighing heavily in the scale. He'd take on a local girl if he could find one he could rely on to stay. The smart ones all upped sticks and left, like Roisin.

The names on the paper were all journalists, they'd been dogging him for days once the rumour had started about Black Mountain running at Cheltenham. How they'd got wind of it he didn't know—he'd not let anything slip. He dropped the paper back on the desk. 'I'm not rushing to talk to that lot,' he muttered.

'Please yourself.' She was on her feet heading for the door. 'You'd better call Lewis, though. His office have been on twice.'

So why wasn't Lewis's name on the list? he was about to ask but thought better of it. He knew the reason well enough: Pauline wanted to tell him herself. She just liked saying his name. Lewis Ashwood could do no wrong in her book ever since he'd had a frank discussion with her about Roisin. In twenty minutes he'd reversed her poor opinion, turning himself from a lecherous cradle-snatcher into a golden-hearted pillar of society with her daughter's best interests at heart. From the way she now spoke about him, Tom suspected Lewis had admitted to a basic religious faith, which would have scored heavily in his favour. The man ought to be a politician.

At any rate, Tom thought as Pauline left him to it, this was one call that couldn't be postponed. He'd been agonising over Black Mountain's racing schedule for long enough.

His call was put through to Lewis without delay.

'I think we should go for the Bula Hurdle next month.'

The Bula was a well-known prep race for Champion Hurdle contenders, which had the advantage of also being run at Cheltenham. It was an obvious target for Black Mountain, and they'd discussed it several times, but Lewis reacted as if Tom's decision was a blinding revelation.

'Brilliant choice, Tom—couldn't be better.'

Tom said nothing.

'Are you sure,' Lewis added, 'you don't want me to fly him over?'

'I am. We'll give the ferry a try.'

'Whatever you say. He's going to take it all in his stride, just you see.'

Tom wished he could share the Englishman's optimism. But Lewis didn't know Black Mountain like he did. He just saw the fearless powerhouse of muscle and sinew who pounded all opponents into submission on the racecourse. He didn't know the horse's history.

Tom didn't know it all himself, but he knew enough. The horse had been bred by an old farmer,

Michael O'Brien, and left to run wild in a field till he was three. According to Michael, his dam was a useful chaser and he had inherited her big frame, so there were hopes for a racing career. Being past the age of breaking in horses himself, Michael had sent Black Mountain to a local trainer where he turned out to be a slow learner, resistant to instruction, which infuriated the lad charged with breaking him in.

One morning, while on a long rein, the horse had hesitated when faced with a large puddle and, refusing to walk through it, earned a beating. Black Mountain kicked out in retaliation and broke the lad's thigh. From that moment on, he was classed as untrustworthy.

When the boy returned to work, he took his revenge, tying the horse up after everyone else had gone and laying into him with the stiff bristles of a yard broom. He did this regularly over the next few weeks, until his anger had gone. At least, that's what Michael told Tom—he claimed to have heard it from the lad's brother.

As a result, Black Mountain withdrew into himself, sulking and eating poorly. Entered for a couple of bumpers—Flat races for potential jumpers—he fared badly, obviously hating every moment. Over hurdles he was worse, jumping poorly and refusing to learn. Finally, he was returned to his owner and pronounced hopeless.

Michael turned him out into a field for the summer and sent him to the sales, where Tom first laid eyes on him. There had been no bidders for the horse, despite his powerful build. 'He's got an evil look in his eye,' said a groom as Tom looked him over. 'Broke a lad's leg last year, you know.'

Tom took the warning with a pinch of salt, as he did most opinions heard at the sales. Old Michael had been a friend of his father's and it was hard to conceive of him breeding an evil horse. A wild and ill-disciplined one maybe, but he'd never yet come across a horse that wouldn't respond to fair handling—and he did like the look of the black one's build.

The upshot was that he made Michael an offer. He'd take Black Mountain home and train him in return for his keep, provided his horse-mad son Connor could ride him. Even if he didn't prove suitable for Con, Tom was sure he could turn the animal into a hunter.

Old Michael showed only nominal reluctance and, after an hour and a half trying to get the horse on to his lorry, Tom understood why. He nearly gave up then. It was funny to think now, but he was a whisker away from abandoning the best horse of his life as the pair of them stood locked in silent conflict at the foot of the ramp leading up to the horsebox.

But he did finally go in, suddenly dropping his head and walking inside as if he'd decided to waste no more time. When Tom got him home he took him down to the beach and encouraged him to get his feet wet in the surf; he appeared to enjoy the sensation. On the way up to the farm he allowed the horse a long pick of grass, before coaxing him into the stables. After supper, ignoring Pauline's disapproving glare, Tom told his youngest son to put away his schoolbooks and come into the yard. The boy stared open-mouthed at the great black beast while Tom told him the story of his past, as related to him by old Michael.

At last the lad said, 'He doesn't look evil to me, Dad.'

'Nor me, son. But I don't want you going in with him yet. We've got to get to know him first.'

Tom spent a long time with Black Mountain, observing his moods and his fussy eating habits. For all his powerful build, he put little into his work and moped around his stall.

'Perhaps we ought to find a companion for him,' Tom suggested. He'd known it work with some animals.

'What about Patch?' offered Connor, volunteering his pony.

The pair of them had watched with some anxiety as Black Mountain was let loose into Patch's field. At first the horse ignored the pony but by lunchtime Connor reported that the two animals appeared to have hit it off. Tom observed for himself the way they stuck close together. That night, Black Mountain ate all his supper for the first time.

Lewis had no idea of the effort that had gone into turning Black Mountain into a manageable beast, let alone a racehorse. Tom knew it was due to his own dedication—and Connor's too; at a bigger yard, no one would have taken the trouble.

Since Black Mountain had been in Tom's care the horse had won twelve times out of fourteen starts—a phenomenal record. His victories included the Bank of Ireland Hurdle at Naas and the AIG Champion Hurdle at Leopardstown, the top race for Irish hurdlers, which he had claimed for the past two years.

But Lewis Ashwood was unlikely to be interested in the past. He'd be too busy calculating

Black Mountain's chances in the Bula Hurdle.

Tom stared out of the small office window at the distant ridge of mountains. In his opinion, winning the Bula Hurdle was less of a problem than getting the horse to the racecourse in the first place.

*   *   *

Conditions were officially described as 'soft' at Towcester but, by the time of the fourth race, 'heavy' would have been a more accurate description in Alan's opinion. Soft, steady rain had been falling since midday, turning the clay soil into a gluey bog. It had taken him five minutes to pick the mud out of his ears after the last, in which his mount had made no attempt to jump the penultimate hurdle and had dumped him halfway up the steep run-in.

All the same, he was feeling more cheerful than he had for days, as if the clouds that had covered his sky since Lee's death were thinning at last. The primary reason was the call he'd received that morning from Geoff Finney, Lee's father. Geoff had rung him regularly since the accident, usually late at night and not the best time for a jockey who was planning to be up at six the next morning. But Alan had not complained; he didn't sleep much these days anyway.

So he was surprised to get a call from Geoff at breakfast time this morning, just before he left for the racecourse.

'Don't worry, son, I'm not going to hold you up,' Geoff began. As a rule, their conversations were one-sided, with Geoff reminiscing about his son and Alan listening. 'This is just about the business.'

Business? Alan was floored.

'I've been talking to the solicitor about Lee's affairs and you ought to know that we're still in. Grace and I want Blades to carry on.'

Blades Bloodstock was the name Lee had picked for their joint enterprise, based on his love of Sheffield United. Geoff was a lifelong Blades supporter too, but that was hardly a sensible reason for him to step into Alan's doomed venture.

'Hang on, Geoff, that makes no sense. There's no business to speak of. Lee and I had hardly got going.'

'There's you, isn't there? Lee thought the world of you. He told me you had a champion eye for a horse.'

That was good to hear, though hardly relevant.

'And there's that Grain of Sand,' Geoff continued. 'Lee told me he was going to be special.'

'He might be someday but I've got to find a buyer for him quick. The whole thing is a fiasco, Geoff. You don't want to get involved.'

There was a short pause before the other man spoke again. His words were delivered with intent.

'Listen to me, young man. The life insurance company are due to pay twenty thousand pounds on Lee's death. His mother and I have talked long and hard about what to do with it and we think it should go into this horse that Lee was so keen on. That's what he would have wanted and so that's what we're going to do, with no arguing from you, right?'

Alan had felt like laughing. Not because it solved his money problems—it didn't—but because he heard Lee in his father's tones; it was the voice he used when the fooling stopped and he wanted to

68

be taken seriously.

'Is that clear?' said the voice.

'Absolutely,' Alan had replied. 'Thanks, Geoff.'

'No need to bloody thank me, we're in this to make money, aren't we, lad?'

Alan wasn't so sure about that, he'd just settle for getting out of trouble, but all the same the promise of twenty grand towards the outstanding debt on Grain of Sand cheered him no end. And, he thought as he pulled on clean silks for the next race, Geoff's call was a bit of a boot up the backside. He didn't have to find just one buyer with a hundred grand to spend; he could put together a syndicate of owners, all chipping in smaller amounts. It wouldn't be easy but it was worth a try.

Outside, the rain was falling harder. To be in with a chance of winning the next race—a three-mile one-furlong handicap chase over eighteen fences—it was essential to be on a mudlark with bottomless stamina. Fortunately, in Nightswimmer Alan was on just the right kind of animal for the job, a big-built gelding who was something of a course specialist. Alan had won on him before at Towcester and also at Wincanton and Exeter, other tracks where his tendency to jump to the right was an advantage. By virtue of a couple of ordinary performances on left-handed routes and harder ground back in September, the handicapper had been kind.

'You know what to do on this fellow, don't you?' said Ian Rafter, the trainer, as Alan settled onto the horse's broad back. 'Don't let them get away from you and make his strength tell from the bottom of the hill.'

Alan smiled at the girl who was leading

Nightswimmer round. Jane was the girl he'd been going out with when he'd first met Roisin. She was now working at Rafter's yard. 'Piece of cake, Al.' He gave her the thumbs-up in return. When he'd talked to her in the weighing room she'd been bursting with optimism about Nightswimmer—she clearly doted on him.

Some riders were less than thrilled by Towcester racecourse. The steep hill going down away from the stands got horses travelling with their weight on their front ends and the slightest error when landing over a fence meant that they easily lost balance and knuckled over. But Alan relished the track, in particular the long uphill run to the finish that put stamina at a premium. It was made for Nightswimmer, in his estimation.

If any race could be said to go to plan, this one did just that, for the first two and a half miles. The big horse cruised round effortlessly, tracking the front runners, and then, going down the hill for the last time, kicked up a gear and moved to the front. This was the point where Alan expected his horse's experience and superior strength to tell. He was already anticipating Nightswimmer's relentless stride up the stiffest finishing slope in British racing.

But it didn't turn out like that. Instead the horse began to labour, as if he was running out of steam. As they took the gentle bend into the long challenging home straight Alan asked the horse to dig deep, as he had done for him in the past. Try as he might, however, Nightswimmer could find nothing and the other runners began to pour past him. They finished eighth out of a field of ten.

It was an uncomfortable group who stood

in the unsaddling enclosure. Beneath Ian Rafter's habitual perkiness Alan could read disappointment; the owner, a TV company bigwig, wore the long face of a man who has seen his stake money go west; and Jane looked on the verge of tears. They all stared at him, expecting an explanation for this unexpected reverse.

Alan did the best he could. 'Sorry, folks. He tried his hardest but there was nothing in the tank at the end.'

'I thought he was meant to be in great shape,' said the owner with bitter emphasis. He was obviously quoting Ian's words back to him.

The trainer shrugged. 'I thought he was. But the important thing is that we live to fight another day.' He slapped the owner on the back. 'The battle may be lost but the war is not yet over. He'll be back to his best next time, you'll see.'

Alan grinned at Jane, amused at Ian's trainer-speak, but she was too miserable to raise a smile. He caught up with her as she led the horse back to the stables.

'Cheer up,' he said.

'I don't understand it. He *was* in great shape. He's been in the best form of his life at home.'

Alan said nothing. It was clear she was inconsolable.

Chapter Four

Max didn't know what to expect as he drove over the river to south London. He was dressed casually but smartly—a jacket and no tie—hoping he'd

71

blend in and not stick out in unknown surroundings. He wasn't looking forward to the evening ahead but Paul had made it clear that his attendance was not optional. Victor had commanded his presence and, from what he had gathered about his new acquaintance, Max guessed it would be foolish not to obey.

The Poison Ivy Club was more discreet than Max had anticipated. It occupied a large detached building on the corner of a residential street and, beyond a small gold plate on the gatepost, did not advertise itself. The door was opened the instant Max rang the bell and he was greeted by a middle-aged man in a dinner jacket. 'Of course, sir. Please follow me,' he said when Max gave his name and hesitantly asked for Victor.

He was led up a wide carpeted staircase hung with oils of seascapes, past rooms humming with conversation and the snick of cutlery; through a doorway he glimpsed a row of snooker tables and smelled cigar smoke. For a moment, following the uniformed figure ahead, he fancied he was stepping into an Edwardian country house party. Dodgy though Victor may be, he was a smooth operator. Max was impressed. He was no stranger to nightclubs but they tended to be noisier, flashier affairs where the birds fell out of their party frocks as the booze went down. He wondered what kind of women you might pull in a classy joint like this.

Max followed the butler, as he now thought of him, into a small book-lined room with a desk in one corner and an open fire. A jacket was draped over the back of the chair behind the desk but the room was empty. Soft piano jazz played in the background.

'Mr Bishop will be with you shortly,' said the butler indicating an armchair by the fire. Max sat and the man left.

Max wasn't sure what to make of it so far. He was expecting some tough talking on the matter of his debts and had been relying on his gift of the gab, and a few judicious mentions of his father, to provide a little wiggle room. Of course, if there were heavies with knuckledusters lurking in the wings then he'd have to go straight to Lewis and grovel.

But, from the look of things, Victor wasn't going to go the tough guy route—not yet at any rate. This was an old-fashioned gentleman's set-up. Max might be able to string matters out long enough to scrape up the money from other quarters. A few good punts could be a start.

*   *   *

Cherry Hamilton observed the newcomer closely on the CCTV as he entered the club and was shown upstairs to Victor's private sitting room. He was her project for the evening and she'd not been too thrilled at the prospect when Victor told her.

'I've got a new pal of mine coming over this evening and I'd like you to take him in hand.'

'Who is he?' she'd demanded and not got much of an answer.

'A jockey and his dad's a bit of an operator.'

So was it the son or the father Victor was interested in? Cherry didn't know yet but she'd find out soon enough. Victor didn't tell her everything but, by virtue of their once-special relationship, she had a good chance of finding out. So far she knew this Max had been brought to Victor's attention by Paul, one of his gambling contacts. Victor always had his eyes open for potential marks.

In the meantime she'd been rather dreading the evening ahead. She'd met plenty of jockeys in Victor's company and most from the Flat had no conversation outside of horses—and the jumps lads just wanted to get inside her pants.

Then she'd picked up some gossip in the bar which had added some piquancy to her assignment and she studied the TV pictures closely. Broad-shouldered, floppy fair hair and a strong jaw—quite the rugged action-man type. Maybe this wasn't going to be as grim as she had thought.

*   *   *

'Would you like a drink, Mr Ashwood?'

Max hadn't noticed her come in—or maybe she'd been here all the time and, preoccupied, he'd not seen her in the shadow by the window. A pretty remarkable state of affairs given how honey-blonde gorgeous she was: a heart-shaped face and wide-spaced eyes, and lots of leg on view beneath the little black dress—a classic combination in his book.

'Whisky, please,' he said, getting to his feet and noticing that he wasn't much taller than her. There really was an awful lot of leg. 'And water,' he added—he had to keep a clear head.

'Vic will be through in a moment,' she said, handing him a heavy cut-glass tumbler. 'Cheers.'

So she was drinking, too. Not one of the staff then.

She looked at him with an expression he couldn't

fathom, unless it was a smirk. 'So you're the naughty boy.' The smirk broadened to reveal a row of small glistening white teeth. 'She's got better taste than I thought.'

What? Her act would have angered him if he hadn't been confused by her physical presence. He found her irritatingly sexy.

'Who do you mean?' he said. 'Who's got better taste?'

'Crystal Miles.'

He was instantly suspicious. 'Are you a friend of Crystal's?'

'I've never met her. But we get all the racing gossip in here.'

Just what he needed. People discussing him behind his back.

'What's it to you then?' he snapped.

'Nothing.' She took a sly sip of her drink. 'Not yet anyway.'

Before he could take it further, a door opened behind the desk and Victor stepped into the room. He was in shirtsleeves—no tie, thank goodness—and he greeted Max like an old friend.

'Great to see you, mate.' Mate? 'Thanks for coming down.'

Did I have a choice? Max wondered, but he returned Victor's two-handed shake with a smile. There was something about the man's bluff, open-hearted manner that he couldn't help liking. The fact that he owed him ten grand was also a powerful reason to be polite.

'So, tell me about Robber Baron,' said Victor, motioning Max back into his chair and sinking into a small sofa on the other side of the fire. 'I thought it was a bloody scandal when you got jocked off next time out.'

So Victor wanted to talk horses. That was fine by Max. The blonde woman had slipped out of the main door.

'I wasn't really jocked off,' he said. 'His regular rider was banned so I was only filling in.'

All the same, he'd felt he should have kept the ride on Robber Baron. His win at Newbury in the spring had been as good as any professional could have achieved. The trouble was, he didn't get enough rides. His father had eighteen horses in training and he rode most of those. He was always in demand for races confined to amateurs but he wanted more.

'Bloody scandal,' Victor repeated. 'And I say that as a punter who dropped a packet because of you. Believe me, you weren't Mr Popular round here that night.'

'Oh.' Max wasn't sure how to react. 'I was just doing my job.'

'Of course you were, sunshine.' Victor beamed and laugh lines disturbed the smooth surface of his round, genial face. All his features were nondescript, apart from eyes that were yellow, like a cat's. 'You're a top class jock on your day, in my opinion. What I want to know is, why don't you get better rides? Some of the nags you sit on would be late delivering the milk.'

Max shrugged but Victor wasn't expecting him to provide an answer.

'I'll tell you why, son. It's because you're trouble.' He produced a half-smoked cigar from somewhere and flicked a lighter. 'You get in with some owner or trainer and then you screw up. You don't know when to keep your trap shut, or your

76

hands in your pockets.'

Max realised he was being given a lecture by some ponce he barely knew. A ponce to whom he owed money, however. He managed a thin smile.

'Or else,' Victor was now dragging heartily on his cigar stub, 'you don't know when to keep your pants zipped.'

Max steeled himself for another crack about Crystal Miles but Victor just blew smoke at the ceiling. 'I always think it's a shame to see talent go to waste.'

They sat in silence for a moment, disturbed by the sound of hearty male laughter from below.

Victor pointed with his cigar. 'Some of Ian Rafter's lads are in tonight. Does he ever give you any work?'

'No.' Max knew Rafter well enough to nod hello but that was about it. His agent had sounded him out on a couple of occasions but had been met with a blank wall.

'I've got a couple of horses with him. I'll put in a word for you, if you like.'

'OK. Thanks, Victor.' He mustered sceptical enthusiasm. If Rafter had blown Pete off he couldn't imagine that Victor would get very far.

'Excellent,' Victor said with satisfaction, as if some tricky negotiation had finally come to a conclusion. 'Now let's go downstairs.'

Max stood up and followed his host. He was puzzled—what was all that about? More to the point, there'd been no mention of his debt.

'Victor,' he said as they stood at the top of the stairs, 'about the money—if you could just give me a week or so—' He stopped, his clumsy speech halted by Victor's heavy hand on his shoulder.

'We're both gambling men, Max. I know you'll honour your obligations. Just take your time.'

The relief hit him like a gust of wind and he began to burble his thanks.

Victor's big yellow eyes twinkled as he pushed him towards the stairs and the sound of men making merry. 'Come and meet the boys.'

*   *   *

Max woke to a world of pain. He was in his own bed, he knew that much, but he had no recollection of getting into it. Or of how he'd got home. Only of being at Victor's club, having a laugh with a group of racing lads. It had got a bit riotous. They were celebrating a win of some kind, throwing money at the bar and packing the booze away.

But they didn't have to make a riding weight. He'd stuck to tonic water. So why did he feel so bad?

'So you're awake.'

The voice was soft and feminine. In the gloom of the bedroom, lit only by wintry light leaking round the blinds, he made out a shape sitting by the side of the bed. There was a glint of blonde hair, thick and curling, a white flash of teeth. The girl from Victor's club.

'What?' he managed. It came out as a croak, his throat was so dry.

'Here, sit up.'

She leaned over him, hooked her hands under his armpits and levered him into a sitting position. He found himself supported by a bank of pillows. It hadn't even hurt that much.

'Drink this and take these.'

78

He did as he was told. The tea was hot and sugary, which he detested but right now it tasted like nectar. God knows what the pills were; he didn't care provided they relaxed the vice that gripped his skull.

'Who?' he said.

'We met last night at Victor's club, though you might not remember. You were having a whale of a time.'

But I was drinking tonic!

'You passed out so Vic asked if I'd take you home. We found your address in your wallet and your car outside, so I drove you back. I put you to bed. I hope you don't mind.'

What could he say to that?

'Thanks . . .' He realised he'd forgotten her name.

'Cherry.'

'Thanks, Cherry.' He shut his eyes and opened them again. She was still there. He could make out her face more clearly now—the smooth brow, the clear-eyed stare, the intriguing slope of her nose. 'Have you ever been a nurse?'

She shook her head and the blonde locks swayed. He was beginning to feel a fraction more civilised. Maybe this angel would care to minister to him for the rest of the day, until he felt better. She was wearing a sludge-green cable-knit sweater he recognised as his own. Perhaps, later on, she'd tug it over her tousled head and slip between the sheets with him. Those spectacular legs wrapped round his would soon put him back in the land of the living.

'You have two messages. One from a trainer wanting to know why you didn't turn up this

79

morning. The other's from your father's office. He's expecting you at twelve forty-five.'

He stared at her blankly.

'For lunch,' she added.

Damn! It came back to him now. He'd arranged to see the old man in case he needed to sweet-talk some money out of him after the evening with Victor. But he didn't need to do that now.

'What time is it?' Perhaps he could cancel.

'Ten to eleven.'

Too late to cancel, at least not without causing offence. Dad had cleared a window in his diary to accommodate him.

'Hadn't you better get a move on?' she said. 'I'll fix you a cup of coffee while you're getting dressed if that would help.'

It would indeed. The way he felt, he needed all the help he could get.

*　　　*　　　*

Alan studied Grain of Sand morosely as the horse delved into his manger. Because the horse was confined to his stable with no exercise for a week, his rations were restricted.

Grain of Sand looked up when Alan spoke to him, favouring him with a long-lashed stare and throaty wicker of acknowledgement. Then he plunged his head back into the bin. At least the animal was in good spirits.

'How's it going?' said a voice at Alan's elbow. Tim Davy had emerged from his office.

'He seems happy enough.'

'I didn't mean him, I meant you. Still looking for a buyer?'

Alan turned to him. 'Yes. I'm trying to put together a syndicate but the horse carrying an injury doesn't help.'

Tim studied Grain of Sand. 'It shouldn't make all that much difference.'

A thought occurred to Alan. 'You don't know anyone who might like to come in, do you? I mean, it's not as if he's going to be out of action forever.'

Tim grinned. 'As a matter of fact, I might be interested in a share myself.'

'Seriously?'

'Definitely. I never thought he'd have the balls to jump hurdles but the way he schooled the other morning before his injury he was as good as I've seen.'

'Lee's dad says he'll invest twenty grand in him—would you match it?'

Tim considered for a moment, then nodded his head. 'OK.'

Fantastic. Alan felt a surge of excitement. *Forty thousand pledged—I'll make a go of this yet.*

Instantly, he had misgivings.

'Tim, don't come in just to help me out.'

The trainer looked at him in amazement. 'Don't be stupid. This is business.'

That was fine by Alan; it was just as it should be.

*   *   *

Cherry stood in the centre of the shop, debating whether to try the jacket on again. The money Victor had given her for taking care of the Ashwood fellow was burning a hole in her pocket and her eyes kept returning to the powder-blue suede jacket on the rack in the far corner.

81

There were more mundane uses for £400, like replacing that old washing machine in her kitchen but, what the hell, she'd earned it.

She could have left Max to sleep it off and got a taxi home last night, but a little voice had told her to be careful. He'd managed the stairs up to his front door but had collapsed in the hall. Thank God, he had a flat on the ground floor. It had been hell getting his clothes off and rolling him into bed.

'What is this stuff?' she'd asked Victor as he'd handed her the pill to put in Max's drink.

'Mexican valium,' he'd said. 'It's what you don't want some bloke giving to you.'

A date-rape drug, then. Vic had assured her Max would be fine after a good night's sleep but she didn't like the idea of just abandoning him. Suppose he threw up? Drowned in his own sick like some zonked-out rock star. As she was the one who had dosed him up and brought him home, she'd be first in the frame.

So she'd watched over him for a while, checking his pulse and temperature, making sure his airway was clear. Having decided to stay the night, she was in no hurry to get down to business.

Finally, when she was sure he was sleeping peacefully, she'd begun her search of the flat. Vic had given her a good idea what to look for.

'Any business papers, sweetheart. Anything to do with his dad.'

There hadn't been much. Victor had assured her Max lived on his own but all the same she'd first checked for another presence in the flat. It was immediately obvious he had no on-site girlfriend. Apart from a shoebox containing some flimsy knickers and a bra—a collection of trophies, no doubt—there were no female clothes.

Naturally there was plenty of bachelor mess in evidence and the guy seemed addicted to newspapers. She ignored all that and turned to the computer on the table in the living room. It wasn't password-protected so she'd been able to read his emails, which were uninformative: round-robin funnies from like-minded cronies, undeleted spam and the odd memo from his agent. The internet sites he visited were more interesting: horseracing pages, on-line casinos and porn. She flicked through some of the latter and gained an impression of a regular hetero jack-the-lad. There were no nasty surprises. Max liked looking at pictures of good-looking women and she guessed she couldn't complain about that.

It was obvious he didn't spend much time on the computer, apart from surfing the internet and playing PC games—she found a stack next to the machine. There were a few letters, boring stuff about buying the flat and insuring his car, but nothing that counted as 'business'. The table drawer contained a mess of papers: bills paid and unpaid, joke postcards from friends, a ten-page letter of recrimination from some ex, but nothing from Lewis Ashwood.

All she found of the father was in an album of photographs charting Max's boyhood. In some early shots of Max as a toddler on an unspecified beach, a handsome man and a thin blonde woman took it in turns to pose with him. A year or so later, there were photos of the three of them in a leafy garden. After that, the woman disappeared, replaced by schoolfriends and horses and, regularly, Dad. The best shots were halfway through the album. Max and his father sailing a dinghy, then standing on the deck of a large yacht—a Maxi, she recognised it—the wind in their hair, laughter on their lips. Cherry put the album back in its place, conscious she'd not found much to keep Victor happy.

Not that he'd seemed bothered when she'd reported in at midday. She'd turned up a few phone numbers, including that of Lewis Ashwood's office, but that was it.

'No problem, sweetheart,' he'd said, pulling a bundle of notes from his pocket. 'I know I can rely on you to keep your trap shut.'

Of course he could. She knew who buttered her bread and the money in her purse proved it. Victor could be very generous if you caught him in the right mood.

'You *are* going to get that, aren't you?' A woman's face was peering over her shoulder in the mirror. 'I tried it on but it's not my colour. It looks fabulous on you, though.'

The jacket did look good, there was no denying. It was tailored just so above her hips and the pastel blue made her hair seem richer and blonder.

Cherry turned to the woman by her side, making a snap judgement—great figure, face like a bag of nails and, she was right, the blue would be no good with her muddy brown bob and washed-out complexion.

'Yes, I think I will buy it,' Cherry said.

'Go for it. I'm glad someone's found what they want.'

Cherry smiled politely, putting an end to the conversation, and walked to the sales counter at the back of the shop. As she paid for the jacket she

84

was aware of the woman still standing by the mirror, observing the transaction at the till. She didn't look a likely customer for an upmarket New Bond Street fashion store. Cherry would lay money she was strictly M&S.

The assistant handed over her purchase and Cherry made for the door.

The woman fell into step beside her. 'Do you fancy a coffee?'

'No.' The word came out louder than Cherry had intended but this woman was giving her the creeps. Perhaps she was a dyke out on the pull. 'I'm in a bit of a rush,' she added to soften the rejection, and reached for the door handle.

The woman stretched round her and held the door closed. Her bag-of-nails face was up close and Cherry could see camouflage make-up on a pimple on her chin.

'I suggest you come for a coffee now, Cherry,' she murmured. 'Or you'll never get a chance to wear that jacket.'

*   *   *

The high-speed lift to his father's office did not aid Max's recovery but as he stepped out onto the penthouse floor his stomach settled, then grumbled restlessly. What he needed was solid food inside him. Maybe this lunch with Dad was good timing after all; they always went somewhere decent.

Jackie greeted him in the corridor like a surrogate mum, which she was after a fashion, and ushered him towards his father's door. As she did so, she whispered, 'He's just had a call from Clifford Miles.'

Oh Lord. He could do without that.

Lewis did not look up from his desk as Max entered nor did he offer him a seat. Max slumped onto the black leather sofa anyway and drawled, 'Hiya,' in a tone guaranteed to set the old man's teeth on edge. When he knew he was about to feel the rough edge of his father's tongue, he behaved as if he were a fourteen-year-old again. He couldn't help it.

Lewis raised his head and glared. 'Why on earth were you playing around with Crystal Miles?'

A few reasons sprang to mind but Max kept his mouth shut.

His father sighed heavily. 'Your mother would be ashamed of you.'

This was a familiar beginning and Max had the usual retort to hand.

'I don't see why—she lived with you long enough. Let's face it, we both like married women, don't we?'

Lewis continued as if he hadn't heard. 'You're such a selfish little fool. It's only your pleasure that matters, isn't it? You don't think of the consequences for anybody else.'

'Come off it, Dad. Cliff Miles is a turd. You don't want to feel sorry for him.'

Lewis paused, as if controlling himself. 'Listen, Cliff's a good man and you've made him so angry he's told me to take both my horses out of his yard.'

Oh. He hadn't foreseen that. No wonder Dad was peed off; he'd had horses with Cliff Miles for years.

'He's an idiot,' Max blustered. 'What's it got to do with you and him?'

Lewis shook his head. 'Have you no idea how he

86

might be feeling? After the way you've behaved he wants you out of his life completely. And he doesn't want to be doing business with the father of the man who's been bedding his wife.'

'Oh, for God's sake, she's hardly a vestal virgin.'

'I'm sure she's not but he was honest with me and I must respect his feelings. I can't tell you how much I resent this. It's expensive and inconvenient, not to mention bloody embarrassing.'

Max suppressed a yawn—just. 'Well, I'm sorry, Dad. Now can we go to lunch?' He got to his feet.

'Sit down. I haven't finished.'

Oh please. He slumped back onto the sofa.

'This has all come about, Max, because you don't have a decent woman in your life. As far as I can tell, you hang around with a bunch of loose-knickered tarts.'

'Like Crystal? I hope you didn't say that to her old man.'

'Don't be facetious. I'm trying to make a serious point which it would be worth your while listening to. It's about time you found a woman of your own age, who is unattached and, preferably, who is able to teach you some decent moral standards.'

Max laughed. 'You're not giving me a marriage lecture, are you? Find Betsy Boring and settle down and have a family and all that old bollocks?'

'What's so funny about that? Your mother and I may not have had a perfect marriage but we built a home and a family. We stuck together. If she were still alive we still would be.'

Max got up and walked to the window, staring without seeing at the muddy curve of the Thames down below. He kept his back to Lewis as he said, 'If Mum were still alive she'd have waltzed you

87

through the divorce courts twice over. You could never keep your hands off the young birds.' He turned to face his father. 'In fact, you're still at it, aren't you?'

Lewis was on his feet, his mouth set in a thin line and his jaw jutting—the way he always looked before he smacked the young Max round the head. Max was relieved that a desk and a sofa stood between them.

'Your mother's dead and I can see who I want,' his father said.

Max smiled. He was feeling a hundred per cent better all of a sudden. Turning the tables on the old man was an effective cure for a hangover.

'How old is the lovely Roisin? Twenty-two? Twenty-three? Younger than me. Less than half your age. I swear the older you get, the younger you like 'em.'

Lewis stood rooted to the spot, shaking with silent fury—or impotence. For once, Max felt he had the upper hand. He was determined to make the most of it.

'With your track record, Dad, you've got some nerve lecturing me on my choice of women. I admit Crystal was a bit of an error, she's quite a bit older than me. Hey, what about a swap? You take Crystal and I'll have sweet Molly Malone.'

The moment he said it, Max realised he'd gone too far. Something in Lewis's face changed—his jaw sagged and his eyes flicked down to the papers on his desk. He sat heavily and reached for the phone. 'Jackie, call the restaurant and cancel the table. My son is leaving.'

'It was just a joke, Dad. I didn't mean anything by it.'

Lewis lifted his head. 'Just go away, Max. And grow up.'

As he travelled down in the lift, Max worried that he'd blown more than lunch.

*   *   *

Cherry was in shock. A drink of some description—had she agreed to tea?—was in front of her, untouched and cooling rapidly. Next to her, shutting off her exit, was the woman from the clothes shop—Janice—and across the table her partner, a square-headed fellow with greasy hair called Ray. They weren't police but as good as: Customs and Excise filth. This was a nightmare.

The Ray bloke had appeared on her other side the moment they'd stepped out of the shop and they'd steered her down a couple of side streets and into the back of a half-empty café. She could have made a run for it but there wouldn't have been much point. The first thing Ray had said was that they'd been watching her for a fortnight; she wouldn't have got away for long.

Her hands trembled as she leafed through the three pages of stapled-together A4 they'd placed on the table in front of her.

'Read this, then we'll talk,' Ray had said—he seemed to be in charge. 'Take your time.'

Though the words swam in front of her, she forced herself to concentrate. She'd been in worse spots than this, she told herself, and she'd survived by keeping her head. She suppressed her urge to dash the tea in Janice's beaky face and tried to make sense of the document.

It was a poor photocopy of a fax and some things

were illegible, others blacked out, but the significance of the papers was all too plain. This was a statement given to the US Customs Service by one James Morton, currently serving nine years in Florida for the illegal importation of drugs.

Cherry knew Jimmy Morton well. They'd been lovers briefly—you had to do something to pass the time while stuck in Poole harbour waiting for your ship to come in. She'd first met him while crewing on a charter in Greece and they'd hit it off because of their south coast background.

Now Jimmy, her old pal, was staring at four walls in a US jail and had obviously decided that it would help his cause to confess past sins. Maybe he had an appeal pending or was wiggling out of new charges. Whatever the reason, he was grassing up some old mates. Like her.

She'd been on a job with Jimmy four years ago. Using a local boat, they'd rendezvoused in the Channel with one of Victor's yachts sailing in from the Caribbean. They'd off-loaded a quantity of drugs—according to this statement approximately 500 kilos of cocaine—and brought it into Poole. The technique was known in the trade as coopering. They'd done this twice and all had gone without a hitch; being local, their boat had raised no suspicions. She'd earned a combined total of £65,000, most of which she'd sunk into the lease of her tiny house in Fulham. It had been the most profitable work she'd ever done in her life, made all the sweeter because she'd walked off scot-free. At least, she thought she had. Now it didn't seem so sweet at all.

Janice was smiling, transforming herself into the friendly soul who had struck up a conversation in the clothes shop. 'Thought you'd got away with it, didn't you?' she said. The two-faced bitch.

The man jabbed a blunt finger at the statement in front of Cherry. 'Mr Morton is willing to testify against you in any proceedings we may decide to bring.'

'He hasn't got much else to do,' added Janice.

'Of course, we wouldn't just rely on his testimony but I don't think we'd have trouble building a convincing case against you once we got going. As I'm sure you are aware, smuggling that quantity of drugs carries a severe penalty.' He looked at Janice. 'What did those two characters from Manchester get recently? Ten years, wasn't it?'

'Twelve each.' She turned to Cherry. 'They hid ten kilos of coke in the sills of a Vauxhall Vectra and brought it in at Dover. You shifted rather more than that, didn't you?'

Cherry tried to blot out Janice's ugly estuary-English tones and concentrated on the spot on her chin. She hoped it would grow and grow until the woman's horrible head was one great septic pustule.

Another part of her brain spoke to her in Victor's voice. She was Vic's girl, one way or another, and he'd be disappointed in her if she screwed up. 'Ask yourself why they haven't arrested you,' said the voice. 'Why haven't they stuck you in an interview room in some smelly nick while they record what you say? Think, sweetheart.'

'What exactly do you want?' she said, her voice as chilly as she could make it, finally lifting the cup to her lips. The tea was lukewarm by now, but she drank it all the same.

The two of them exchanged a glance. Maybe they'd expected her to make a scene—to cry and plead, or just explode in a torrent of abuse. They must get the lot in their shitty line of work.

She'd show them she wasn't that stupid.

'We want to help you, Cherry,' said Janice.

'Just so long as you realise the gravity of your situation,' said Ray.

She realised all right, but what would she have to do to get out of it? Whatever it was, she'd go along with it. She'd been inside briefly, when she was still almost a kid. It had been no picnic and she shuddered to think how Holloway would compare to Bellwood Young Offenders Institution.

'What have I got to do?' she said, still cool. She placed the cup back on the saucer with a steady hand. She was conquering her nerves.

Ray leaned forward. 'You're very friendly with Victor Bishop.'

Suddenly it all became clear. It wasn't her they wanted, it was Vic. Of course it was; compared to Vic she was nothing.

'Someone in your position could provide us with a regular flow of information on his business affairs,' continued Ray.

'No!' she spat. It was an instinctive reaction. 'He'll kill me.'

'Not if he doesn't find out,' said Janice.

'But I don't know what he's up to. I'm not involved.'

'How would you describe your work then?'

That was a good question. Basically, she was Victor's creature and had been since she'd met him crewing on a charter yacht on St Lucia. She'd disappeared into his cabin for an entire week and when she emerged she discovered she'd been romancing a genuine gangster. Most girls would have run a mile. Where she came from, with a boyfriend who'd put her on the game at sixteen, it had been a scramble up the greasy pole to survive. And Victor Bishop, in her opinion, lived right at the top. Even more remarkably, now they were no longer lovers, she'd remained at the top of the pole right next to him, under his wing. Protected—until now.

'I work behind the bar,' she said.

'Is that all?'

'Sometimes I fill in when they're short in the restaurant.'

'Don't fart around with us. We've been watching that club for two months.' He leaned closer to her across the table top. 'You're no effing waitress, Cherry. Mr Bishop doesn't take a dump without you there to wipe his arse.'

Janice gave a snort of laughter at this witticism, then picked Jimmy Morton's statement off the table. 'If you help us,' she said, 'this goes away.' And she stuffed the paper into her handbag.

Ray ignored his partner and stared at Cherry. She felt a shiver of revulsion for his cheap suit and gluey hair and pale pee-coloured eyes.

'So,' he said, 'what's it going to be? Have we got a deal or not?'

Cherry didn't speak—she couldn't. They were asking for the ultimate betrayal and she couldn't give in just like that.

'I need time,' she said at last.

He continued to glare at her, his stare unblinking, as if he were trying to decide whether she was worth bothering with any longer. Cherry told herself it was an act, a whole lot must be hanging on her cooperation. Eventually he leaned back in his seat and nodded at Janice.

'You've got twenty-four hours,' the woman said, scribbling a number on a paper napkin and pushing it across the table. 'Call me any time.'

Cherry grabbed the napkin and pushed past her. She had to get into the street before she was sick. She almost ran towards the door.

'Hey, Cherry, wait a minute.' Janice was behind her, holding something in her hand. 'Don't forget your jacket. It really did look good on you, you know.'

Cherry yanked the bag from the woman's hand and bolted through the door.

Chapter Five

In his first season, when he'd ended up leading conditional jockey, Alan had won the Victor Chandler chase at Ascot. It had been the highlight of a wonderful season and he anticipated it would be just one of many more to come at the Grade One course. But for one reason or another—mostly his bad run of injuries—he'd never again got close to winning another race there, not even a small one. When you are riding well, you are in demand every day of the week and, as an apprentice, you have the added advantage of an allowance to reduce a horse's weight. Unfortunately for Alan, he rode out his final three-pound claim two days before he broke his leg for the second time. When he returned to the fray four months later he had

94

struggled to pick up the pieces.

Today was just another scrub round on an ordinary horse of Tim Davy's called Itsmyparty. The truth was he wouldn't find it easy to win at Ludlow, never mind Ascot, but the owner wanted a day out to entertain his mates from London. Today, however, Lady Luck decided that it was time for Alan to visit the winner's enclosure again. The ground was an absolute bog and his horse handled it while the others didn't.

With none of his rivals even close, Alan had the luxury of dropping his hands and easing off the gas as he steered Itsmyparty past the post. What made it all the sweeter was that the race was the most valuable of the afternoon—and shown on TV too. Alan was determined to savour the moment.

Even Tim Davy, who was famous for not allowing the rough or the smooth to disturb his laid-back manner, couldn't help grinning from ear to ear. Alan was pleased for him too; Itsmyparty had been off for four months with a bruised heel and it had been a training feat to produce him in such form. Not to mention the fact that Tim was being so stalwart in the matter of Grain of Sand.

Not everyone shared their glee, however. It was plain from the angry shouts behind him that a few spectators were unhappy.

'What's all that about?' he asked Tim.

'Just someone having a moan about the favourite.'

Gremlin had been every pundit's tip for the race.

'Why, what happened to him?'

'Fourth or fifth. Twenty-odd lengths behind our fellow anyway.'

How satisfying, Alan thought as he changed out

of his riding clothes. If only there were more afternoons like this.

On impulse, just before he started the drive home, he picked up his mobile. He didn't often call his father. He'd learned the hard way that the best method of avoiding criticism was to avoid talking to the critic. Today, however, he had done something worth shouting about.

The phone was answered with a familiar grunt. He knew his father would be parked in the kitchen of his Holloway flat, drinking tea and chain-smoking, and following the racing on the portable TV in the corner by the microwave. Ralph Morrell, disgraced former jockey and trainer, had been warned off every racecourse in the land but they hadn't managed to ban him from watching television. Or having a bet.

'I hope you were on my horse, Dad.'

'Hello, son,' said a gravelly voice. 'Congratulations.'

Good Lord, he sounded as if he meant it. This *was* a red-letter day.

'You gave him a good ride,' the voice continued. 'Except you won too far. I've told you that often enough.'

And a few other things besides. There was no denying that Ralph Morrell knew how a National Hunt horse should be handled. He'd ridden 756 winners in eight seasons before a fractured skull sent his career in a different direction. He'd been successful as a trainer too—for a while.

Alan's sister, Dawn, remembered the glory years when their father was a jump-jockey hero and a winning trainer. Being younger, Alan didn't have such positive memories to savour. He recalled the frostiness between Mum and Dad and the sounds of their rows drifting up the stairs at night when he was supposed to be asleep. Most of all he remembered the police arriving at their house at six thirty in the morning and the headlines in the papers and the whispering behind his back at school.

The house and the yard had gone soon after the trial and he'd ended up with his mum in a rented semi in Swindon. She'd divorced Dad while he was serving his time and married a prison officer, of all people. Dawn had bolted from home as soon as she could but Alan had had to serve an uncomfortable, horse-free three years before he was old enough. And when he'd set off to become a jockey himself he found that his father's notoriety closed more doors than it opened. But at least he had taught him how to ride.

'I once won the SGB Chase at Ascot,' Ralph said. 'That's the last race Arkle ever won, you know. Bloody bottomless it was the year I won it. Just like today, from the look of it. I had to carry the horse for the last furlong—at least, that's what it felt like.'

'Yes, Dad.' Why had he ever thought he could impress his father? The old war stories were always too vivid.

'I'll tell you another thing, you were bloody lucky.'

Lucky? How did he figure that?

'I should think that Gremlin was got at.'

'Come off it. What makes you say that?'

'Because he could hardly put one foot in front of the other by the time he finished.'

'Or maybe he's just not very good.'

97

'As you wish.'

A thought occurred to Alan. 'I don't suppose you had money on Gremlin, did you?'

His father grudgingly admitted that he had. 'When he drifted out to 4/1 he was value.'

Alan grinned. So Ralph was now thinking like every other punter he knew. There could be any reason for one of his selections running badly but never that his judgement was wrong.

All the same, he put the phone down in less cheerful spirits than he'd picked it up. Talking to his father always had that effect.

*   *   *

Cherry called in sick, she couldn't face the club tonight. In the hope of avoiding a conversation with Victor, she told the restaurant manager she was off to bed. Five minutes later, the phone rang.

'Are you all right, sweetheart?' The familiar voice sounded genuinely concerned and Cherry felt a stab of guilt. *Why? I haven't even decided to grass him up yet.*

'Sorry, Vic. I've got a thumping headache.'

'Sure you don't want me to come round and give you my special cure?' He chuckled lasciviously.

What was it about men? It had been a year since he'd shown an interest in her like that. A year since he'd given her his special neck massage which didn't end at the neck. Why would he open up that possibility tonight of all nights?

She killed it off swiftly. 'The way I feel, I'd die if anyone touched me. I think I'm going to throw up.'

'You take care of yourself then. Get some sleep.'

'That's what I need. I didn't get much last night.'

She was glad she'd got that in, the reminder that she'd been taking care of his business all night.

After he'd got off the line, she sat in her small front room watching the evening turn to night, too weary even to draw the curtains.

Suppose she left the country? She could go to her mother, see how life was treating Mum in Australia with her new husband. Not that Cherry fancied spending much time with the middle-aged lovebirds; she'd not taken to lazy Les, the Aussie town-planner who was now her stepfather. On the other hand, it would play all right with Victor. He'd understand her wanting to catch up with her mother. He'd probably find her some work in the Sydney clubs if she asked him; he had plenty of contacts.

But going to Australia wouldn't exactly put her out of reach of the UK authorities. She might win some time but they'd catch up with her and she'd be extradited.

It would be better to change her identity and bum around on the yachtie circuit. She'd crewed on charters on the Med and in the West Indies and there were many other parts of the world, out of the way places, where itinerant boat workers could escape the notice of the police. South Pacific islands, for example, or Sri Lanka. Or the Mergui Archipelago of Burma; eight hundred islands dotted like jewels in ten thousand square miles of lonely and beautiful ocean—according to an old sailor she'd met on her last trip to Victor's place in St Vincent. Those two horrible Customs officers would never find her there.

But it needed planning and she had no time, unless she told Ray and Nail Face that she'd do the dirty on Vic and then ran for it when she'd got herself sorted out. She'd have to go to Vic for help though. He'd find someone to fix her a new identity. If she didn't tell him and he got wind of it, he'd be suspicious. Or maybe she should come clean with Vic, tell him about Jimmy fingering her and the Customs offering a deal if she spied for them. Then Vic could help her get away.

But—there were too many buts—suppose he asked her to play along with them? He might get her to offer duff information while he covered his tracks.

And then, when it all went pear-shaped at their end, she'd be left blowing in the wind. No thanks.

Cherry tried to put the whole horrible mess out of her mind and think about something else. She was too shell-shocked to cope—this way she really would get a headache.

But it was futile. She kept returning to one underlying thought that nagged like a toothache. Suppose Victor's days were numbered. He'd had a good run—God knows how much charlie he'd smuggled into the UK over the last five years. But a shipment had gone down, in every sense, six months ago when *Ice Maiden*, one of his yachts, had been caught in a storm in the Bristol Channel and ended up in fragments on the north Devon coast. Two hundred kilos of cocaine had been picked out of the wreckage—less than half the amount on board, in fact, but more than enough to trigger the arrest of the surviving crew members.

According to Victor, only the yacht's skipper knew anything of value and he'd been lost at sea, his body washing up on Lundy a week after the disaster. Victor had been delighted at this stroke of luck and accepted the loss of *Ice Maiden* and its cargo as a necessary write-off. As far as he was concerned, it was business as usual. Cherry wasn't so convinced by his optimism. Suppose the skipper of *Ice Maiden* had opened his mouth to one of the crew? They hadn't appeared in court yet and God knows what they'd been saying.

Adding the *Ice Maiden* fiasco to today's news about Jimmy Morton was ominous. The police and the Customs weren't the quickest but when they finally got their act together they weren't to be deflected. The more Cherry thought about it, the more convinced she became that Victor's operation was doomed. Knowing him, he'd probably skip out of the country just before the trap closed and set up shop somewhere else. Could she rely on him taking her with him?

The phone jolted her out of her unpleasant reverie. She considered letting it ring but she needed the distraction.

'Hello,' she murmured tonelessly, just in case it was Vic checking up on her.

'Hi, Cherry, it's Max.'

She had to think for a moment before she placed him. The blond jockey she'd driven home last night. Why was he calling? Didn't he realise she was off-duty?

'How did you get my number?' she said.

'I got it off Victor. He said you wouldn't mind if I called.'

Had Vic really said that? She supposed he might have done.

'I just wanted to say thanks for looking after me last night,' Max was saying.

'That's OK.'

'Suppose I take you to dinner to make up for it?'

The suggestion took her by surprise. She wasn't functioning as she normally did. Her first impulse was to put him off but then her Vic reflex kicked in. 'That would be nice but I work most evenings.'

'You're not working tonight.'

'Yes, but—' she reached for one of the usual glib excuses but was too slow.

'Cherry, I'll be honest. I've had a dreadful day and I'm desperately hungry and I don't want to eat on my own. We'll go wherever you like.'

It was not the most romantic offer she'd ever had but she said yes. Anything to get out of here before she cut her throat.

*　　　*　　　*

Alan brooded on the conversation with his father for the rest of the journey home. He should never have called him. Ralph's comment that Itsmyparty had only succeeded because Gremlin must have been nobbled had taken the gloss off his Ascot victory—an entirely predictable outcome.

Grow up, Alan told himself. You're not a little boy any more. You don't need Daddy's approval.

This wasn't entirely true. Evidently, he did still need a pat on the back from the old man. He just couldn't remember when he'd last had one.

It wasn't till he reached home that he began to think about the wider implications of his father's comment. Suppose, just for once, that Ralph hadn't said it simply to put Alan down.

Maybe it was true. After all, who better to spot a nobbled horse than a man who'd made a living out of nobbling them? In the field of manipulating a

102

horse race to get the right result, it could be said that his father was an expert.

Alan never thought about race-fixing in any specific sense. He knew it went on—given his father's history, he could hardly believe otherwise—in fact he'd been asked to give a horse a quiet run on more than one occasion. But he'd never been asked to stop one. He assumed that it was rare and, like the bad accident that was a statistical possibility, it was always going to happen to someone else. To think that he might have been the beneficiary of a horse being got at was a sickener.

It was more than that.

He emptied a can of tomato soup into a saucepan and heated it up, mulling the matter over as he stirred. Once he began to consider what his father had said, his thoughts turned to Olympia at Haydock.

Ouch! The soup was bubbling furiously, spitting drops of scalding orange liquid across his fingers as he stood distracted by his thoughts. He turned out the light under the pan and held his burned hand under a cold tap. With his other hand he reached for his mobile.

Gary Beal, the jockey who'd been on board Gremlin at Ascot, was a mate. Alan speed-dialled his number.

He got quickly to the point. 'What happened to Gremlin this afternoon?'

Gary barked a small bitter laugh. 'Nothing. Apart from him chucking in the towel after he'd gone two miles.'

'Is that what happened?'

'Yeah. He was fine going down but as soon as we

went round Swinley Bottom and faced up to that hill again he just said no thank you, the lairy sod.'

'Couldn't or wouldn't go?'

'I'm not sure, to be honest. It was like he was knackered. Why are you asking me anyway? You won, mate, isn't that enough?'

No, it wasn't enough. Not the way Alan was thinking now. He explained about Olympia and the horse he had ridden at Towcester.

Gary's theory was that it had been very wet recently. 'It catches some horses out. You know as well as anyone that the going is the biggest single factor in a horse's performance.'

Alan thanked him and put the phone down.

He poured the still warm soup into a mug and sipped without tasting, his brain working overtime.

*   *   *

Max couldn't keep it to himself any longer. 'I think someone spiked my drink last night.'

Cherry stared at him as if she didn't believe him.

'I'm not just saying it to look better,' he went on, 'but apart from that whisky you gave me I was on tonic, remember?'

'I remember,' she said.

Well, so she should, she'd been keeping an eye on their table. She'd even brought him over a drink.

'I've never been out like that before. I've been completely bladdered many times but not so I couldn't put myself to bed. I'd have been lost without you.'

She shook her head, her shaggy blonde locks rippling across the shoulders of that fantastic blue suede jacket. She looked even more gorgeous to his sober eyes than when he'd been woozy last night— the opposite of the usual state of affairs.

They were in the back booth of a Chinese restaurant he'd never been in before. He'd planned a ritzy French meal but when he'd picked her up she'd obviously had second thoughts about accepting his invitation. She'd said she wasn't going anywhere fancy as she couldn't face dressing up and so they'd blown in here.

He had no complaints. She wore that jacket, a simple white top and a pair of faded denim jeans without rhinestones, tassels or appliquéd slogans of any kind—Crystal Miles would not be seen dead in them. If Cherry looked this good without making an effort, Max hoped he'd get a chance to see her when she had.

'But who would have spiked your drink?' she said.

'Those stable lads I was chatting to—one of them, I expect. Or maybe all of them were in on it. You didn't notice anything, did you?'

She'd been in and out, floating around like some manageress—which is what Max assumed she was. She might have seen something.

She shook her head. 'Why would they do that?'

'For a laugh. Stable lads do all sorts of mad stuff when they're on the piss.'

She popped a piece of duck pancake into her mouth and took a sip of China tea. She'd said she wasn't hungry but she seemed to have an appetite after all.

'I'm sorry,' she said.

'What for? It's got nothing to do with you.'

She shrugged and reached across the table to

take his hand. 'Is that why you've had such a bad day?'

That was nice, her touching him. Like the way she'd soothed his forehead this morning. It wasn't just because he fancied her. He had the feeling he could talk to her.

'I had a row with my father,' he said.

'At lunch?' she said.

'We never got as far as lunch.'

'Oh?'

The invitation to talk about it was there but he wasn't going down that road. Whingeing about Dad was no way to impress a woman. He twined his fingers round hers and said, 'If you could go anywhere on the planet right now, where would you go?'

Her hazel eyes widened in surprise. 'Why do you ask that?'

'Answer the question.'

'OK.' Her grip tightened on his. 'I'd like to sail around the world.'

'On the QE2 or something?'

'No!' She dug her nails in playfully. 'On a proper sailing boat.'

That was a surprise. When you meet a girl in a nightclub you don't associate her with a healthy outdoors ambition like sailing round the world— though, looking at her, she was lean and athletic. She wouldn't be out of place on board a yacht.

'Sounds good,' he said. 'Can I come?'

She grinned. 'You might be a liability.'

'My dad kept a boat at Chichester when I was a kid. We used to cruise the Channel Islands in the holidays but I haven't been sailing for years.'

'Why not?'

106

Because Mum was the sailor in the family. After she died he hadn't wanted to go on the boat and he knew Dad felt the same—the boat had been sold and Dad had gone back to horses. And, of course, he'd got into horses too.

But now, sitting here holding Cherry's hand, he could see the appeal of sailing round the world with her at his side. It would be one in the eye for the old man—he could just picture his father's face when he announced he was off for a few years. He could leave his debts behind too. Above all, he could escape from Basil the Tortoise and the horrors of that night in Kilburn. Take that bulky, sweaty, whisky-breathed vision out to sea and drown it forever.

Cherry was sitting patiently across the table, bathing him in the pale light of her gaze, waiting for his reply. Maybe she's my salvation, he thought as he began to speak.

*   *   *

Alan tried Noel's number but he'd turned his phone off—which wasn't surprising. He was on a golfing trip to Spain and, round about now, would probably be finishing off his tapas and heading off for a late dinner; dinner, in Alan's short experience, was always late in Spain.

He should have been with Noel. They'd booked the trip back in the summer, together with a couple of other lads, a school friend of Noel's and a vet who played off scratch and had promised Alan a couple of sorely needed lessons.

But that was a lifetime ago. After Lee's funeral Alan had approached Noel and suggested they find someone else to take his place.

'Why?' said the Irishman. 'A holiday right now might do you a bit of good.'

'I know but to be honest I can't afford it.'

Noel had laughed. 'You owe a hundred grand—saving a few hundred isn't going to make much of a dent in that.'

But Alan had insisted. The thought of going on holiday when he owed that sort of money was beyond him. Anyway, they'd soon turn up someone else keen to take his place.

'Are you quite sure about this?' Noel had said. 'If it's really just the money, let me pay and you can owe me.'

'Thanks, mate, but I owe enough already.'

Noel, he saw, had been tempted to argue the point but had thought better of it.

The Irishman was a good friend and Alan missed him right now. He didn't have anyone else with whom to chew over the business of Gremlin and Nightswimmer.

He pulled himself together and headed for bed. Why not get an early night? In any case, he'd have to get used to Noel's absence. After the bugger got back he was finally packing his bags for Ireland. Alan wasn't looking forward to living here on his own.

Once Noel had gone, Roisin would be keeping an eye on the place for her brother. Alan wasn't looking forward to that either. He wasn't even certain he'd be able to afford the rent.

*　　　*　　　*

Cherry cautiously eased herself onto her side,

ungluing the skin of her hip from the naked figure in the centre of the bed; she didn't want to wake him. As for herself, there was no chance of sleep.

Spending a second night in Max Ashwood's flat hadn't been on her agenda. But whatever that agenda might have been, it had been left in pieces by the arrival of Janice and Ray in her life. They'd pulled the rug from beneath her and she was looking for any kind of foothold to steady herself.

She couldn't face a lonely night at home, sleepless and brooding, as the minutes of her deadline ticked away. Also, who was to say someone wasn't watching her place? They'd told her they'd been keeping an eye on her. The thought gave her the creeps.

So she'd accepted the invitation for a nightcap back at Max's flat. Truth to tell she'd probably been angling for it. Once she'd allowed herself to be talked into an evening out, she'd slipped back into her angel-of-mercy role, holding his hand and making goo-goo eyes at him. And encouraging him to spill a few secrets. It made her feel less guilty about Vic.

He had the hots for her, that went without saying, so she knew she'd have to box clever if she wanted to keep him at arm's length. But she might not want to. Victor had dumped far worse men in her lap.

That, at any rate, had been her attitude at the start of the evening. Then he'd thrown that question at her about where she'd most like to go if she could, as if he knew what was on her mind. She wanted to escape, of course, and he'd unexpectedly given her the chance to imagine it might be possible.

The round-the-world idea had just popped out of her mouth. She'd been thinking about crewing on a charter but this was better. It could take years and, done properly, neither the Customs nor Vic would catch up with her. She could just drop out of the whole silly mess she'd made of her life and start again.

Max seemed all too keen to indulge her fantasy. In the restaurant, then back at his flat killing off a bottle of brandy, they'd talked boats—the kind a round-the-world voyager might need. Max had fired up his computer and they'd surfed the Web, lingering over photographs of yachts for sale. He'd been thrilled by a two-masted steel schooner, almost a small ship, with an enormous saloon and three cabins but she'd shouted him down; at sixty-five feet it was a hell of a proposition for a two-person crew. She'd preferred a high-performance cruising yacht, smaller, with a single mast, which was capable of covering 200 nautical miles in twenty-four hours in the right conditions—a cosier and more manageable proposition for two people.

'OK, you win,' he'd said. 'We'll get yours. It's only three hundred and sixty thousand pounds.' And he'd laughed with a bitter edge.

She'd looked closer at the spec on screen. 'It was custom-made for the present owners by some America's Cup design team.'

'That would explain it.'

'Why don't you ask your dad to buy it for you?' she suggested.

He laughed again. 'Oh sure.' Then the smile faded from his lips and he gripped her wrist. It hurt but she did not flinch. 'You *are* joking, aren't you?'

'Just thinking out loud. He'd only have to cash in

a horse or two, wouldn't he?'

His face was up close, steel flashing in his blue eyes, lust for the moment obscured by fury. 'I make my own way in life, understand? My father doesn't pay for me.'

So he had a temper. He didn't frighten her, however; she was used to playing with true hard nuts. It made him more interesting.

'Are you aware you're leaving your fingerprints on my skin?' she said.

The anger disappeared in a flash and he released her. She held out her arm to show him the red bracelet left by his grip.

He didn't actually say sorry—she'd bet it wasn't a regular in his vocabulary—but he bent his head to kiss the bruised skin. She allowed the caress and its progression up the tender flesh inside her forearm. So this was the pass she'd been anticipating ever since they'd returned to his flat. She put her other hand on the back of his neck and scraped him with a fingernail, a minor revenge.

As the seduction—if that's what it was—took its course, she reflected on his words. So Max paid his own way, did he? This flat, for example, on the ground floor with two bedrooms, an enormous sitting room and a garden, less than a minute from Holland Park—what would that be worth? Well over half a million, that was certain, maybe a lot more. He'd said he owned it but who had bought it for him in the first place? The same went for the Lexus outside. She knew he had a jump jockey's licence but he was an amateur. He'd be riding for nothing so that wasn't what was keeping him in this kind of style.

Daddy, on the other hand, was rolling in it. Vic

had tipped her off about him. Max had not been slow to refer to his father's apartments in New York and Monte Carlo. Then there were the racehorses that had apparently replaced sailing in his affections. Really, it was a scandal he didn't have a spare yacht bobbing at anchor somewhere, just waiting for her to sail away into the sunset.

Now, in the small hours, with the horrid reality of daytime looming, she put aside the fantasy of the night before. She'd run if she had to, but first she had to keep immediate disaster at bay. The more she considered her position, the more it seemed that the boozy debauch she'd indulged in with Max might have been a good move.

Whatever happened next, her time with Victor was running out. She needed a new protector. On his own, Max was hardly that but he wasn't on his own, was he? Despite the current breakdown in relations, Lewis Ashwood was behind his only son. And Lewis Ashwood had money and political connections—real power in anybody's book. If she could hitch herself to Max's star then maybe she would gain the protection she needed.

The man beside her suddenly jerked in his sleep, as if a bolt of electricity had shot through his body. He moaned something incoherent in a low, hoarse voice.

Cherry turned towards him, circling his chest with her arms and pressing her cheek to his. She saw his eyes open in the half light, staring at her in panic. He was shaking.

'Shh, darling,' she murmured, 'it's all right.' Then she added, 'I'm here,' and he stopped trembling. How satisfying.

She'd stick close to Max from now on. The

beauty of it was that she would only be doing what Victor wanted.

*　　　*　　　*

The trouble with early nights was the early mornings, especially when sleep was fitful. Alan's suspicions about horse-fixing wouldn't leave him alone. He went downstairs and replayed the video of the afternoon's racing.

The TV coverage concentrated on the front-runners at Ascot and in particular on the winner, which was him on Itsmyparty. But Alan wasn't much interested in that. The focus of his attention was the poor performance of Gremlin, finishing well down the field. Given Gary Beal's comments it was clear now that the horse was dead on his feet. He was running on auto-pilot in the last furlong and could barely manage a trot as he stumbled past the finishing post.

Was it just the ground? Could soft going really make that much difference? Alan got the form book out and went back through every one of Gremlin's races. It was true he'd never won on heavy ground but he'd run plenty of sound races in those conditions. He'd never once finished out the back. Horses could always run badly for no apparent reason and maybe that was it, but Alan doubted it.

He turned to the other video he'd dug out, one that, until now, he'd had no intention of ever watching again. He'd played it twice before he'd gone to bed. At first he had been sickened and shocked and, on the second viewing, he'd begun to feel the flickering flame of anger. Now, watching

Lee's fatal ride on Olympia for the third time, the anger was blazing.

He was convinced that whatever had happened to Gremlin at Ascot and to Nightswimmer at Towcester had also befallen Olympia. In which case, he thought as he watched the exhausted horse bury his friend in the Merseyside turf, whoever had done it was guilty of more than fixing a horse race—they were guilty of murder.

Chapter Six

'*Et voila!*'

Roisin kept her amusement to herself as Lewis manoeuvred a tray piled with breakfast things through the door of her bedroom. He liked to play the French waiter when he stayed overnight at her flat and he took his efforts seriously.

'Bravo,' she said as he plonked the tray on her bedside table, managing to slop coffee into only one of the saucers. A pile of muddy-looking scrambled eggs covered a plate and the aroma of burned toast filled the room.

'You're laughing at me,' he accused her.

She shook her head vigorously, not trusting herself to speak. She thought it was sweet the way he tried to prove himself domestically, even though it was obvious he'd never lifted a finger in the kitchen in his life—just like her dad. Not that she minded, she'd always been a daddy's girl. Maybe that's why she had a boyfriend who was twenty-odd years older than she was.

Still, there were things Lewis did for her that

had nothing to do with their age difference. She noted that he was already dressed.

'You're not coming back to bed?'

'I wish but I'm trying to squeeze a lot in today.'

She understood. He was making space in his schedule so he could take her to Kempton the following afternoon. She was looking forward to it.

He sat next to her on the bed and picked at the eggs.

'What's the matter?' she said. Something was up and it wasn't just a spoiled breakfast. They'd not talked much when she got home from the casino in the early hours and found him already in bed.

He put the plate down. 'I had a bit of a ding-dong with Max yesterday. He's not in my good books at the moment.'

He rarely was, in Roisin's observation, and she listened without surprise to Lewis's account of his son's latest transgressions.

'I read him the Riot Act, of course,' said Lewis, 'but it never seems to do much good.'

He fell silent but Roisin could imagine the rest of the unspoken conversation. 'If only his mother was still alive' would come first, followed by 'How do you think I should handle him?'

Every time they'd had this conversation it made her uncomfortable, which was why he was keeping his mouth shut. How the hell did she know how to handle Max? He was older than she was. She found him charming, as a rule, always arrogant and, she knew, deeply suspicious of her role in his father's life. To be fair, she couldn't blame him, she'd feel much the same in his shoes. And she didn't have a clue how Lewis should treat him. The whole topic only illustrated to her how unsuited she and Lewis were in some areas. She wasn't cut out to be a surrogate mother to a spoiled rich kid who treated her like an insignificant younger sister.

Time to change the subject.

'I've got a bone to pick with you,' she said, aware even as she spoke that this wasn't the best moment to choose. But when would be? She'd been putting it off for too long. 'About Black Mountain,' she added.

Lewis faced her with what she thought of as his sphinx look—closed, unreadable—one she imagined his subordinates saw frequently in business meetings. 'We're going for the Bula Hurdle at Cheltenham. I've finally persuaded your father.'

If he was trying to put her off it wouldn't work.

'Why did you never discuss it with me before you bought him?'

'I'm sorry?'

'Black Mountain—you only bought him to help Dad out, didn't you? I think you should have talked about it with me first.'

'I thought it would be a nice surprise for you,' he said. 'Would you rather I hadn't bought him and he'd been moved to some other yard?'

No, she hadn't meant that. It was hard to articulate exactly what was troubling her without sounding ungrateful. She couldn't precisely think it through herself except that it was to do with the balance of their relationship. It wasn't the age difference that worried her, so much as his wealth and power. How could she be equal with a man as rich as Lewis? It had hit home on their trip to Mauritius. He'd told her she wouldn't need money while they were away and she'd taken it at face

116

value, enjoying the feeling of being pampered. But when she'd gone into a shop on her own to buy postcards and realised she couldn't, it had unsettled her. 'You should have asked me,' he'd said later but that wasn't the point. She didn't want to ask him for money. She valued her independence, it was hard-won and relatively newfound and it would disappear in an instant if she stayed around Lewis.

Also, and maybe it was this that rankled more than anything else, she worried about what others thought. Some, like her girlfriend Danielle, would call her a lucky cow and wonder what she was complaining about. Others, like Alan, would take her for a woman on the make, without substance, looking for an easy path through life. That irked. Though she might have misjudged Alan—he'd hardly been pleasant to her at their last meeting— she loathed the thought of him making snide remarks about her.

Which brought her back to the horse. It was bad enough Lewis taking over her life—it was inevitable, she supposed—but her father was another matter.

'Don't think I'm not grateful Dad's still training Black Mountain,' she said, 'but if you're trying to buy your way into my family, it won't work.'

Lewis gave her his sphinx look once more. 'It was a business arrangement, Roisin. It's got nothing to do with you and me.'

'Come off it, Lewis. You're trying to take me over.'

He shook his head. 'Honestly, you've got the wrong end of the stick. I bought Black Mountain so my son can have a decent shot at the Champion

Hurdle.'

Oh. She hadn't thought of that.

He grinned ruefully. 'Not that he bloody well deserves it.'

*　　*　　*

'Morning, doll.'

Victor made Cherry jump, coming up behind her as she stuffed envelopes in the Poison Ivy office. It was a menial job she could have delegated but she wanted to do something mindless—it was all she was capable of at the moment.

Vic slipped his arm round her shoulders and gave her a playful hug. She forced herself not to stiffen. Relax. Act normally. Don't make him suspicious.

'Feeling any better?'

'Much better, thanks.'

'A bad one, was it? That headache.' He was grinning at her. 'So bad you couldn't bear to be touched, as I remember. At least, not by me.'

The implication was clear—he knew about her night with Max. She hoped that was all he knew about.

The grin had turned into a smirk. 'Tell me, has young Max got the tender touch?'

She knew better than to ask how he had found out.

'It's what you wanted, isn't it?' she said. 'Max was your idea, not mine.'

'True enough. I'm glad you two have hit it off.' He said it with a straight face, as if he meant it, but she knew him better than that. 'So you won't mind coming to watch him at Kempton Park tomorrow.

118

He's riding for Ian Rafter.'

'Really? He didn't tell me.'

'He didn't know about it. Ian's just had a word with his agent and it's all fixed. Max is very grateful.'

So Max had been on the phone to Vic. Was that how Vic knew she'd spent the night with him?

'Just what is it you want from Max?' she asked.

'Nothing too painful, sweetheart. Mind you, his dad's got a runner at Kempton tomorrow and I quite fancy an intro.'

Given the state of affairs between Max and his father, pain might not be out of the question, but Cherry kept the thought to herself. If Victor thought father and son were at loggerheads he might lose interest in Max and she didn't want that.

'I thought it might be better coming from you,' Vic added. 'I don't want to look pushy, if you know what I mean.'

Cherry had a fair idea. He wanted Max to introduce him to Lewis but he didn't want to ask. 'Leave it to me,' she said with a confidence she did not feel. The sooner the Ashwoods patched it up the better for all concerned.

'Thanks, my love.' He bent forward and kissed the top of her head. 'I can always rely on you to sort out the tricky stuff.'

She watched him go with relief and wondered how he would have reacted if he'd known about her conversation with Janice this morning. She'd made it on a cheap pay-as-you-go phone she'd bought for the purpose. If she was embarking on a relationship with Customs and Excise agents it was essential to keep all communication with them separate from the rest of her life.

She hadn't expected any kind of warmth from Janice and she didn't get it.

'So you've seen sense, have you?' the woman said. She'd sounded almost disappointed.

Janice had decreed another meeting that afternoon and named a Starbucks about a quarter of a mile from the club. Cherry had objected.

'Look, I can't afford to be seen with you.'

'Why not? I'm your old mate from Bournemouth. We went to school together.'

Nail Face certainly reminded her of some of the girls she'd known at school, although the real resemblance was to some of the nasty bitches she'd met in prison—the ones with uniforms on.

Cherry didn't like any of this, but what could she do?

*   *   *

'Fancy another?'

Alan still had half his lager in his glass but he could see that Clive Jones had a thirst.

'Just an orange juice,' he said, which was better than saying no but nowhere near as satisfactory as joining his companion in a pint. 'Got to watch the weight,' he added unnecessarily as Clive made for the bar through the lunchtime crowd.

On second thoughts, Clive probably didn't give a monkey's whether Alan joined him in a drink or not. The ex-copper was a solid, confident figure who gave the impression of ploughing his own furrow in life.

Except, that is, in the matter of Alan himself. Nine months ago, when he'd thought his second broken leg might keep him out of the saddle for good, Alan had applied to Clive for a job, working beneath him in the security department of the Jockey Club. It would have suited him, or so he thought, as his employers would have been tolerant of his need to get in the saddle when he could. He had the impression the interview had gone well and afterwards, as they had a drink in this very pub, Clive had only just stopped short of saying the job was his.

So Alan had been surprised to get a phone call the following week telling him that someone else had been appointed. Clive had sounded more than just apologetic but Alan had resisted the temptation to ask for an explanation. He thought he knew the answer, and it had been confirmed by the first thing Clive had said to him as they sat down.

'I wanted you on the team, chum, but the powers that be weren't happy. You've got a black mark against you.'

'My father, you mean.'

Clive had nodded his big balding head and swallowed half his beef sandwich in a gulp. 'I didn't agree with it but they told me to belt up and look elsewhere. There was eff-all I could do about it.'

One of these days, Alan thought as he watched Clive return with a pint glass in his fist, he'd meet a member of the racing establishment who had a soft spot for his dad but God knows when that would be.

'So what's up?' said Clive, finally giving Alan the opening he'd come looking for. At the conclusion of their conversation nine months back, the big man had invited him to keep in touch. After watching the race recordings over and over, Alan had decided to take him up on the invitation.

He started with the non-performance of Gremlin, then turned to the poor runs of Nightswimmer and Olympia. He didn't mention the part his father had played in placing suspicion in his mind.

Clive kept silent as he heard him out. When Alan had finished, he said, 'What exactly are you asking me?'

'Whether it's possible these horses could have been drugged.'

The big head moved slowly from side to side. 'Unlikely, at least as far as Olympia and Nightswimmer are concerned. I don't know that we've seen the results of blood tests on Gremlin yet.'

'So you have been looking at those particular horses?'

'Oh yes.'

'But couldn't they have been doped with something that you can't detect yet? They always say the dopers are a jump ahead of the testers, don't they?'

Clive smiled. 'If the evidence isn't there we can't say a horse has been drugged.'

'But suppose it's something new. Like that drug they just discovered athletes are taking. I mean,' Alan added as he caught a look of scepticism on Clive's face, 'a new drug for horses, of course.'

Clive sluiced beer round his mouth. 'I know what you're saying, Alan. The answer, of course, is that anything's possible. But on the evidence we have, those horses weren't doped.'

'Oh.' Alan was instantly deflated.

'It's a shame we can't ask them, isn't it? Maybe

the nags were having an off day and just didn't feel like running round to keep us happy.' Clive seemed amused at the prospect. 'I often think it's a pity horses aren't like cars. Then you could just worry about the mechanics and not temperament.'

Alan raised a smile though he wasn't sure he agreed with him. You couldn't discount temperament where his car was concerned.

'Doesn't mean to say you're wrong,' Clive continued. 'There's a lot of odd results at the moment. The runners you're talking about aren't the only ones who look a bit iffy. The exchanges are on to us all the time.'

Alan realised he was talking about the internet betting exchanges.

'You mean they pick it up from the way money is wagered?'

'They watch what prices are being offered and let us know if something looks strange—usually before the race is run. Gremlin, as I remember, started the day at six to four and drifted to four to one. Considering he was the best-rated horse in the race and two and a half miles is his distance, that looked a bit dodgy. You wouldn't lay him at those odds unless you had a pretty good idea he couldn't win.'

Alan digested the information. The arrival of internet betting had changed the basic concept of trying to beat the bookmaker by finding the winner. Now, on the exchanges, anybody could play at bookmaker and 'lay' a horse.

Put simply, nowadays you could bet on a horse to lose.

'What about Nightswimmer and Olympia?' he asked.

'I can't remember the precise odds but it was a similar situation, a fancied runner being offered at a silly price. Unless, of course, you were confident that the horse wasn't going to perform.'

Alan stared moodily at the stained wooden table. 'Somebody must be fixing them somehow, then cleaning up on the internet.' He lifted his head and stared at Clive. 'What are you lot doing about it?'

Clive held his gaze. 'We're doing plenty. The internet people are on our side and we're hand in hand with the police but it's not easy. We need hard evidence of race-fixing.'

'What have you got so far?'

'I can't tell you that, Alan.'

But Alan was pretty sure he knew. They'd got nothing. At this precise moment, whoever was responsible for Lee's death was getting away with murder.

*   *   *

These meetings with Janice were certainly putting Cherry off cappuccino. She stared mulishly into the pale tasteless froth while the other woman harangued her. Janice had made it plain that Cherry was being left at liberty on sufferance and that if she, Janice, felt she was being pissed around, circumstances would change.

'I want regular contact from you, all right? Where you've been, where you're going and the same for Victor. Also for his right-hand men like the Spot brothers.'

Brian and Chris Spot were loyal team players. Brian was an accountant, Victor his only known client; Chris handled the distribution of drugs. Cherry didn't know exactly how far back they went with Vic but it was way before her time. They'd made life difficult for her when they'd realised she'd become more than one of Vic's bits of skirt. If they thought she was stepping out of line, they'd tear her to pieces and love every moment. If she was going to grass on Victor, she'd make sure she put those two snakes in the pit with him.

'Are you listening to me, Cherry?'

Janice was giving her the prison-warden look. She had two basic ways of treating Cherry: it was either 'I'm your pal' or 'I'm your jailer'. Cherry wasn't sure which one she disliked most.

She took her time before replying. 'You were saying I needed permission to take a piss, right?' She shouldn't react but it was a reflex. Learned as a teenager in Bellwood probably.

Janice narrowed her eyes and made what looked like a deliberate effort to suppress the response that sprang to mind. 'Look, Cherry,' she said in a softer tone—switching to best-friend mode—'I know this is difficult for you. It's going to take time for you to adjust to this situation and I appreciate that. But you're a smart woman. Too smart to spend the best years of your life rotting in Holloway.'

And that was the bottom line. She faced certain jail or—well, who knew? But it might be escape to a new life. Round the world on a yacht with Max. Right now she'd grab that with both hands—and ditch Vic to do it.

'If I cooperate,' she said, 'I want a guarantee that I won't face charges.'

Janice leaned closer. 'I can't get you anything in

writing. I can't protect you from things we don't know about or crimes you may commit in the future. But you can take my word that if you play ball with us you won't be prosecuted on those two drug shipments.'

Cherry stared into the woman's slate-grey eyes. It was the best deal she was going to get.

'Vic's going to the races tomorrow, to Kempton. He wants me to go with him.'

'OK. Why?'

'I don't know. At least,' she knew she had to get used to making things sound good, 'I won't know till I get there. There might be something in it for you, I suppose. Depends if you lot are interested in horses.'

'I'm interested in anything to do with Mr Bishop.'

'Vic's a big gambler and he only likes winning. It might be one of those days when he's got a touch on.'

'A touch?'

'A betting coup. When he fixes the race and bets accordingly.'

'Does Victor launder money this way?'

'Sure. He can't lose. Fix the race, bet with dirty money and get a load of clean cash back. It's good business.'

Janice looked pleased. Cherry felt a stab of guilt but suppressed it. What, after all, had she revealed? If they hadn't worked out how these things were done then they were thicker than she took them for. The important thing was that they thought they were getting something.

Cherry smiled sweetly. 'May I go now? Someone will be wondering where I am.'

126

Janice looked at her watch, a crappy digital—couldn't the woman afford anything decent? Judging by her clothes, she must get paid peanuts. Why the hell do a job like hers?

'Yeah, OK, but call me tomorrow. Fill me in on this trip of yours.'

Cherry got to her feet and Janice stood with her. To Cherry's amazement, the other woman kissed her on the cheek, muttering, 'Pretend you like me. We're old friends saying goodbye, remember?'

Cherry managed a feeble smile and made for the door. She'd come up with an answer to her own question—Janice must do her job because it mattered to her. Because she was a zealous crusader against crime.

The thought scared the hell out of Cherry. She couldn't get out of there fast enough.

*　　　*　　　*

Alan rode out two lots for Tim Davy, then went to find the trainer in his office. With rides thin on the ground at the moment, the money he earned from riding out was helping to keep him afloat. On the way home from the gallops he'd learned that Kevin, Tim's travelling head lad, had gone home to Ireland. He felt slightly guilty that he hadn't apologised to him for being so insensitive over Lee's death.

He found the trainer in his office, dealing with some paperwork.

Tim looked up. 'How's it going with Grain of Sand? Found any more takers?'

The truth was that Alan hadn't yet unearthed any prospective buyers for the horse. He'd been through his address book—he'd even tried Clive at lunchtime ('Put money into a horse?' he'd said. 'Do I look crazy?')—but without result.

Tim absorbed the news and gave it thought.

'Have you tried the underbidder at the sale?'

'Cyril Ogilvie? He was my first port of call after Lee's buyer dropped out. He said he'd bought another horse instead.'

'But have you gone back to him? You only want to sell him a bit of Sandy now.'

That was a good point. Ogilvie might not have the cash to buy the whole horse but perhaps he'd be prepared to invest in a piece of him.

'I hadn't thought of that.'

Tim plucked some papers from the printer out-tray and began to scribble his signature across them. Alan was aware he ought to go.

'I hear Kevin has left,' he said.

Tim stopped writing. 'He just walked out.'

'But why?'

'Search me.' The trainer no longer looked calm and efficient. 'It's bloody inconvenient, that's all I know.'

'What did he say?'

'Nothing. He just rang in and said he was going back to Ireland. I offered him more money but he wasn't interested. I sent his stable pass and a reference round to his place in Swindon. He worked here for three years and did a great job. One of my top men.'

'Have you been in touch with him since?'

'I've tried. There's no answer on his phone. Honestly, you think you know people but you don't.'

'Do you reckon this has anything to do with

Lee's accident on Olympia?'

Tim looked up at the ceiling, as if taking a moment to collect his thoughts, then back at Alan. 'It's everything to do with it. Kevin took it really hard. I told him these things happen in this game and it's no one's fault.'

'But they happen on poor horses who are badly trained. Not on a horse rated over a hundred from a top yard like this.'

Tim's chin sunk onto his chest. 'I know. It's a cruel sport sometimes.'

Alan was tempted to say that, in this instance, it hadn't been sport at all. But how could he prove it?

*   *   *

Max knew he ought to pack his cards in. They were playing seven-card stud with 2s and 5s wild, which was pretty silly but it was the last hand of the night and there was £500 or more in the pot. He was sitting on a king-high full house. If he could win he'd at least finish the night a few quid ahead.

The trouble was, considering the open cards on the table, he didn't much fancy his chances. But what the hell.

He leaned forward and pulled two of the £50 chips out of the pile.

'Hello,' said Double Top, 'the drag queen's at it again.'

Dragging—borrowing from the pot—was frowned on but everyone did it at some time or another.

Seth shrugged and Jimmy didn't care either. 'You can owe me, Maxie,' he said as he laid his hand down.

He'd got five clubs: 6,7, jack, all natural, and two wild cards—just a squeak away from a running flush. But it was OK, a simple flush didn't beat a full house.

Seth couldn't keep the satisfaction off his face as he showed. Full house, queen high. Bloody hell, thought Max, I've short-headed him.

The others took it well.

'Law of averages, I guess,' said Jimmy. 'You usually chuck everything at the last hand.'

He did too, Max thought, as he collected his winnings. It was about time his bold style paid off. 'Classic bull poker play,' he announced. 'Learn from the master.'

Only Double Top didn't seem amused. 'I can't say that you deserve it. You didn't turn out for old Tortoise's funeral, did you? Bloody poor show.'

Max had an excuse at hand—he'd thought this through before he arrived.

'I couldn't, could I? I was riding at Newbury.'

'Not at ten in the morning, you weren't,' said Double Top. 'Your first race wasn't till one forty, you had plenty of time to pay your respects to Basil.' From the tone of his voice he'd been brooding on the matter. Obviously he'd thought it through as well.

'Yeah, but I was booked to school a horse that morning. For a trainer I've not ridden for, so I couldn't exactly get out of it.' Max glared at the others, daring them to contradict him. 'Ian Rafter. I'm on a couple of his at Kempton tomorrow.'

Double Top looked mollified so Max guessed he'd been convincing. He changed his tone to add, 'I'm really sorry I missed it. Were there many people there?'

'Loads. Sixty or seventy, I reckon,' said Double Top.

Seventy! Max was amazed. How could seventy people have turned out for that smelly old git?

'Yeah,' said Jimmy. 'All his pals from the Wheatsheaf in Finchley and some pub in Soho, apparently.'

'Half the staff from William Hill and Coral's, too,' said Double Top. 'A betting shop manager said they were there to celebrate. He was joking, of course.'

Paul lit up a Panatella. 'Would have been more if the Blackpool Bonanza hadn't been on. Bloody poor timing, old Bas having his funeral on a tournament day.'

'He wouldn't have wanted us to miss it though,' said Jimmy.

Max was puzzled. 'But I thought you were at the funeral.'

'I couldn't go, could I? Me and Paul and Seth were in Blackpool.'

'We were there in spirit though,' said Seth.

'Jesus.' Max was indignant. 'You're trying to make me feel bad about not making it and you lot are off playing poker.'

Seth nodded gravely. 'Tortoise would have understood.'

'My little DC turned up, though.' Paul looked to Double Top for confirmation. 'Nice of her, wasn't it?'

'The police always show up at funerals of murder victims,' said Jimmy. 'That's how they find the murderer.'

'You mean to say the murderer always goes to the funeral as well?' said Seth.

131

'Absolutely, if you believe all those shows on TV.'

'Oh yeah?' The fat man laughed. 'If I'd bashed Basil's head in, the funeral's the last place I'd show my face. I'd make sure I had a bloody good excuse.'

'So what's this detective like then?' said Max loudly, jumping in to kill off this line of banter. It was too damn close to the truth. 'Is she as hot as Paul makes out?'

Double Top pulled a face. 'She's OK.'

'OK?' Paul was affronted. 'She's ten times better looking than any woman I've ever seen you with.'

To Max's relief, the others all chipped in as the conversation took the turn he had intended, away from murder and on to other well-trodden paths.

At least this time he left without owing money. Really, there was no reason why he should ever go back.

Chapter Seven

Max was in a good mood even before he won the second race at Kempton. Since he'd decided to jack in Paul's card school and avoid the weekly return to the scene of his fight with Basil the Tortoise, it was as if a ton weight had been lifted from his back.

Other factors helped, of course. As in the hazel-eyed blonde who had turned up at his flat with breakfast and fed it to him in bed, almost making him late for the meeting. What's more, she'd accompanied him to the course and made him promise he'd ride a winner for her—which he'd just done. Cherry brought sunshine into his life.

Compared to her, Crystal Miles was a pale old slapper, unworthy of a second glance.

To think he'd only known Cherry a few days—how amazing was that? And he had Victor to thank for introducing him to her. He wouldn't forget that. He was in the man's debt in more ways than one.

Here, for instance, was a beaming Ian Rafter, thumping Max on the back as he helped him unsaddle in the winner's enclosure. Until a couple of days ago, he'd never got a sniff of a ride on one of his horses. That was down to Victor too.

'I wasn't sure you could handle him,' said Ian, 'but it just shows what I know. Well done.'

Max accepted the praise modestly and allowed the owner, an elegant woman in her sixties, to give him a perfumed hug. In truth the victory had come fairly easily, once Max had realised that Brown Sugar, the animal beneath him, had enough confidence for the pair of them. He'd concentrated on preventing the horse hitting the front for the first circuit of the track and then given him his head. Brown Sugar had surged into the lead and pinged the three fences in the straight as if jumping for fun—and to be fair he probably was. He was a grand animal, the best Max had sat on for months, and he made a point of saying so to the perfumed lady. Ian had mentioned that she owned two other horses in his yard so it couldn't hurt.

The other aspect of proceedings, the icing on the cake, as it were, was the knowledge that his father had been watching. Max had noted that one of Lewis's horses was a late entry for the two-mile novice hurdle, a discovery that had irritated him. He'd not been offered the ride which, he reckoned, was probably punishment for their recent disagreement. As a rule, he rode all of his father's animals except for the really big races. He'd not ridden on any of Lewis's Champion Hurdle contenders and that really pissed him off. It was as if, when it came to the crunch, his dad had no faith in him. 'One day' his father always said when he complained about it. Max had a feeling that that day would never come. It was impossible to satisfy a father like Lewis Ashwood.

So it was pleasing to score a victory knowing that his father would be looking down from his box surrounded, as he always was on these occasions, by his business cronies. Their row still rankled. They'd not talked since and Max was damned if he was going to make the first move.

'Max!'

A woman's voice hailed him as he stepped outside the weighing room. He had plenty of time before his other ride of the afternoon and he was hoping to catch sight of Cherry.

Instead he found Roisin approaching, a coat thrown over her shoulders, the wind whipping strands of her blue-black hair across her face. Her cheeks were flushed with the chill but her smile was broad as she took his arm to give him a sisterly peck.

'Congratulations!' she said. 'You gave him a grand ride.'

Max was tempted to tell her it had been the other way round but where was the mileage in that?

'Where's Dad?' he said, looking over her shoulder for the familiar figure.

'He's tied up playing the host, but he was thrilled about Brown Sugar. He asked me to give you a message.'

'Oh yes?'

'He says will you come up to the box later.'

So the first move had come from him—most satisfying. Max pretended to think about her request.

'I'm riding in the novice chase. I'll see if I can manage it after that.'

'Great.'

She turned to leave and then stopped, maybe catching the scepticism on his face. She spoke again.

'I don't know what went on between the two of you the other day but he was very upset. He wants to put it in the past, I know that much.'

'Sure.' He nodded his head. 'Me too.'

He watched her slender figure as she walked away through the crowd towards the stand. His father had good taste in women, he'd say that for him.

*   *   *

Cherry waited for the dark-haired girl to leave before she stepped into Max's field of vision. His face lit up at the sight of her. How gratifying—and how reassuring. She needed everything in her favour for the next few minutes.

First, though, she was curious. 'Who's that girl?'

Max seized her in his arms. 'I won. Like I promised. What do you think of that?'

'Fantastic.' She hugged him back. 'So who is she?'

He chuckled. 'Not jealous, are you? That's my father's girlfriend, so you've no need to worry.'

Cherry had done some basic research on Lewis Ashfield on the club computer and discovered references to his current girlfriend, together with a couple of uploaded press photographs. So she'd had a fair idea that the dark girl was Roisin Dougherty. However, it was good to have her suspicions confirmed. People always seemed different in the flesh.

Max was looking pleased with himself which, she guessed, he had a right to be. He was telling her he'd been invited up to his father's box and asking her to go along with him. She agreed, just to keep him happy, though she wasn't sure it was a good idea. For the moment, though, there were other matters to discuss.

She took him by the arm and steered him away from the crowd outside the weighing room. Time to get down to business. Vic had given her the responsibility of sorting out 'the tricky stuff'. She was confident she had read Max right but you could never tell how a man was going to react until you put him on the spot.

'Victor was very impressed with your riding,' she said.

'A piece of cake.'

'Well, now you've got your winner, he'd like you to ease off.'

He looked at her, puzzled. 'Ease off what?'

She took the racecard from her jacket pocket and opened it to the fifth race—the three-mile novice chase. She pointed at the third runner on the list, Spanish Eyes, the horse Max was booked to ride. 'What's his prospects?'

'I've not ridden him but he looks the business. According to the paper, he's got a real chance.'

136

'Don't try too hard, will you, Max?'

He glared at her, suddenly understanding. The blue of his irises seemed to darken at the rim. 'You're telling me to stop it?'

She held his gaze. This was the crunch. 'Yes.'

His mouth was set in a thin tight line and he appeared to be fighting the impulse to shout, or turn on his heel. Or backhand her across the face.

Instead he said softly, but with intent, 'I've never chucked a race in my life.'

'Look, Max.' She risked a hand on his arm. She could feel the sinews tense through the thin silk but he didn't pull away. 'How much money do you owe Victor?'

He didn't reply, just looked at her sullenly.

'This is an easy way to start wiping the slate clean, isn't it? The chances are you're not going to win anyway. All you've got to do is make sure you don't. That must be easy for a jockey like you.'

'How would you know? I bet you've never sat on a horse in your life.'

She laughed. 'No, but I've sailed in competition. I let a guy beat me once in a Laser race and nobody was any the wiser. I sailed fractionally too close to the wind, put in a couple of short tacks—everyone thought I was trying my hardest but I wasn't. Don't tell me that with your skill you can't make it look good.'

He was chewing it over now. His jaw had relaxed and that crazy look had gone from his eyes.

'Why did you let the guy win?' he said suddenly.

'Because I was mad about him and I knew he couldn't stand being beaten by a girl.'

'This is hardly the same.'

She slipped her other arm round his waist and

137

put her lips to his ear. 'Isn't it? I'm mad about you too.'

He pulled away but only far enough so he could look at her, as if weighing her sincerity.

'Victor's a good man when he's on your side,' she added. *And a dangerous bastard when he's not.*

But she didn't need to say that surely. She'd said enough.

*   *   *

Alan found the address in an area of Swindon he'd never visited before. He parked by a row of mean terraced houses and approached the shabbiest. The smell of fresh paint hit him in the face as the door opened in answer to his knock. A very pregnant girl, who looked barely old enough to be in that condition, confronted him, brush in hand.

'I'm looking for Kevin O'Shea,' he explained.

'Sorry,' she said. 'He don't live here any more. We've just moved in.'

That much was evident, from the uncurtained windows and the boxes piled behind her on the bare floor of the hall.

'Do you know where he's gone?'

She shrugged. 'Never met him. He left the place in a shocking state though. We're just trying to get it straight.' She gestured with her loaded paintbrush. 'Barley white,' she added. 'The landlord gave us tons of it and said he'd let us off the first month's rent if we did the place up. Nice of him, ain't it?'

Alan could tell she was a bit of a motormouth.

'Who's that, Kylie?' came a male voice from up the stairs.

138

'Some guy looking for Kevin,' she called back.

'He ain't here no more. Tell him to sling his hook.'

Kylie made an apologetic face. 'That's my husband. He don't mean nothing.'

The husband appeared, overalls, spotty face and also armed with a paintbrush. The pair of them looked like they ought to be still in school.

Obviously they weren't going to be of much help. 'I'm sorry to bother you,' Alan said, backing away.

The boy stepped forward. 'You a mate of this Kevin bloke?'

Alan considered his answer. 'I've been working with him at a stables in Lambourn.'

'Oh right.' The lad broke into a grin. 'He left a box of his stuff. Would you give it to him?'

'The landlord said we was to chuck it but it don't seem right,' added the girl.

Five minutes later, having loaded a cardboard box into the boot and turned down the offer of tea, Alan drove off.

*　　　*　　　*

Max had an hour before the chase, plenty of time to brood on what Cherry had said. He couldn't get it straight. She'd asked him to throw a race. And she'd said she was mad about him. The two things overlapped in his mind.

Though Max was as pragmatic as the next rider, he'd never deliberately lost a race. Sometimes it had been made clear to him by the trainer that a horse wasn't expected to win. At other times, he'd made a mistake which had prevented him winning. But he'd always followed instructions and the

139

mistakes he'd made had been so-called honest ones. Not to win when he could—that was a different matter.

He acknowledged to himself that he wasn't the most honourable man in the world; if he could have cheated at the card table and got away with it, then he wouldn't have thought twice. This was different. It was one area of his life where he still had the opportunity to go for glory. He was a good enough jockey. Good enough to turn professional if he could just get on the right horses.

If anyone else had suggested he lose on purpose he would have allowed his temper full rein. But it had been Cherry who'd made the proposition, wrapped up in a declaration of—what? *I'm mad about you*. Was that a declaration of love? Or lust? Or a sweetener to get him to do what Victor wanted. He only knew the moment she said it that he was mad about her too.

Victor Bishop was a cunning bugger, no doubt about it.

After weighing out, Max quizzed Ian Rafter's travelling head lad about Spanish Eyes. After all, he might be agonising over nothing. Although the horse was heavily tipped in the press, it could well be that his connections weren't nearly so confident, which often turned out to be the case. If Max stopped Spanish Eyes when the horse wasn't fancied, the result of the race was much less likely to attract unfavourable comment. And Victor would be satisfied.

Unfortunately, the lad was enthusiastic. Over this track, on this going, against this field, they thought the horse was going to win.

It irritated Max to listen to him talk the horse

140

up. Was this just the party line he was feeding him or did he genuinely believe it? Whatever, it didn't help him. He wanted a reason why the horse was going to lose. And, listening to the lad, he didn't hear one. He was going to have to come up with something off his own bat.

Max was aware of his heart thumping as he lined up amongst the other runners for the three-mile chase. He'd always been a danger junkie. When he was younger he'd tried his hand at off-road biking and hang-gliding; bungee-jumping had also been a thrill. His father had called him stupid—but pissing the old man off had been part of the buzz. And his old man would be very, very pissed off if he knew what Max was up to right now.

He'd been among the first to leave the parade ring, trying to get a feel of the unfamiliar horse under him as they cantered down to the start. Spanish Eyes seemed a nimble, well-balanced type but he took a strong hold. That could help with what Max had in mind. He circled around, waiting for the other runners to join him.

Reaching down with his right hand, he pretended to adjust his stirrup leather. Loosening the strap, he made just enough play to slide the pin of the buckle out of its hole. I must be a nutter, he thought to himself as the starter called them into line. But it was too late to change his mind.

The field went off at a fair clip and Max kept Spanish Eyes right in the middle of a bunch. The less that spectators or TV cameras could see, the better. They raced towards the first fence as if it wasn't there. Spanish Eyes took off but as they landed Max felt his right stirrup go and his right side gave way as if he'd walked over a mantrap.

He'd been prepared for it but all the same it was a shock. His jerk in the saddle and the struggle to stay on board was not play-acting. By the time he regained his balance Spanish Eyes was running away.

Max kicked his left foot clear of its stirrup to straighten himself up and gripped the horse's flanks with his thighs, his feet dangling uselessly. It was a strange but familiar feeling, reminding him of the summer he'd spent as a twelve-year-old learning to ride bareback. He'd thought he was a real daredevil then, racing his pony across the meadow behind the house without a saddle. But this was the real thing.

*   *   *

Roisin saw straight away what had happened. She was watching the race from the balcony of Lewis's box.

'What's the matter with Max?' said Jerry Rubak, a barrel-shaped man in a business suit clutching a glass of champagne. 'He's wobbling around a bit, isn't he?'

Lewis was watching through his binoculars. 'I can't really tell.'

'He's lost his irons,' Roisin said. 'Maybe the leather broke.'

'Will he be OK?'

'He'll have to pull him up. He can't race without irons,' she said.

They watched silently as the pack of runners came down the back leg of the triangular course and turned into the home straight for the first time.

'It doesn't seem to be holding him up any,'

said Jerry.

As Spanish Eyes took the fence almost directly below them he was about a dozen lengths in the lead.

*   *   *

It was only the fear of hitting the ground at thirty miles an hour that kept Max astride the horse. The muscles on the insides of his legs burned from gripping so tightly. They were now half a furlong in front of the field and going further away.

I've got to pull him up, Max thought as they completed the first circuit. But for the moment he couldn't; he'd have to let Spanish Eyes have his head and stop him when he finally began to slow down. That was provided he could stay on his back, of course. They took the first open ditch for the second time and rounded the bend into the back straight with Spanish Eyes still jumping like a stag and setting his own pace. They were well in the lead.

Suppose he doesn't stop?

Max thought about pulling him onto the hurdle track but he didn't want anyone to accuse him later of not trying. He'd have to sit tight for a bit longer.

Suppose he bloody well goes on and wins the race?

Max hadn't bargained for that.

*   *   *

As she watched the race unfold on the screen in the bar, Cherry was surprised to find that her overriding emotion was concern that Max would get hurt. She didn't know much about horse-

143

riding—Max had been right about that—but it was plain from the commentary that accompanied the television pictures that he was in trouble.

'Bloody hell,' murmured Victor by her side. 'He doesn't do things by halves, does he?'

She didn't reply. She just felt sick.

'I tell you what,' Victor added, 'the boy can ride. Most of those jocks would have bit the dust by now if they'd lost their irons.'

'Aren't you worried?' she said. 'I mean, the way he's going he might win.'

Victor laughed. 'No chance. Look, they're coming back at him now. Spanish Eyes has shot his bolt.'

With relief, she saw that what he said was true.

*   *   *

Turning into the home straight, Max felt the strength drain from his horse and as they approached the first obstacle on the run-in he glimpsed the leading pursuer coming alongside. He almost willed Spanish Eyes to keep his nose in front as they scrambled over the fence but Ice-Skater, the chasing horse, gained a good half-length in the air and was ahead as they hit the ground.

It had been fun while it lasted, he thought. And, after all, he wasn't meant to win the race.

With Spanish Eyes flagging, now he could pull him up. Mission accomplished.

On the other hand, why pull him up so close to home?

He urged the horse on with hands and knees, his whip long discarded. Incredibly Spanish Eyes

144

rallied and popped the penultimate fence in tidy fashion. He hit the last but managed to stay on his feet as another horse came by. Max expected a pack of others to overtake him but, remarkably, none did.

He finished a gallant third to Ice-Skater, with the crowd in the stand on their feet. It was a better reception than he'd received earlier when he'd come home first.

*　　　*　　　*

Max found Cherry waiting for him outside the weighing room.

'You're mental,' she said.

'It was an accident.' He grinned. It was what he'd been saying for the last twenty minutes to the horse's connections. They seemed to accept it. It was not unknown for buckle pins to pull out of their holes under pressure. 'Anyhow, I could do with a drink so let's go.'

'I think I'd better not go up to your father's box.'

He was taken aback, he'd thought it was agreed. 'OK, somewhere else then.'

'Listen.' She took his arm. 'It's not that I don't want to meet your father—I'd love to. But I'm not sure that saying hello amongst a group of boozy businessmen is the right moment—if you see what I mean.'

He wasn't sure that he did. Was it that she didn't want to appear just another piece of racetrack totty? He could understand that.

She gave him no time to argue. 'I've a better idea. Take Victor up with you. He'd enjoy meeting your father and he's good with a crowd.'

145

Over Cherry's shoulder Max saw Victor approaching, looking the model of propriety in a well-cut dark-blue suit. Well, why not?

'A fantastic ride, my boy.' Victor was pumping his hand. 'Even more impressive than your winner, I'd say.'

Max couldn't disagree.

'I'm just off to my father's box,' he said. 'Would you like to come and meet him?'

As Victor beamed, accepting the invitation, Max glanced at Cherry. She looked relieved; keeping Victor sweet was obviously important for her too.

*   *   *

Roisin recognised the man who came into the box at Max's side. She'd seen that unremarkable doughy face before, though it took her a moment to place it: the casino punter who'd been sitting next to the jockey she'd noticed on TV. The man who'd slipped the jockey a stack of betting chips. She wasn't surprised, though a little dismayed, to see him with Max.

The last race had just been run and some of Lewis's guests had already said their goodbyes. Half a dozen remained, some still sitting at the dining table amongst the ruins of the afternoon's abundant hospitality, the others on the balcony surveying the fast-emptying racecourse. Despite the bustling presence of a couple of waitresses who were clearing coffee cups, brandy glasses were still being topped up.

Roisin felt a little tipsy herself, having decided the only way she could put up with the patronising company—were they really all local councillors?—

146

was to get stuck into the champagne. And her win in the fifth race had naturally justified a nip of cognac.

She scrutinised Max's friend closely as they were introduced. Did he recognise her? If so, he showed no sign of it, enclosing her fingers in a warm, dry handshake. Though the face was nondescript the eyes, she noticed, were a disturbingly pale yellow with tiny pupils—like pinholes into a void, she thought boozily. Maybe he had recognised her after all.

Lewis was making a fuss about Max's adventure on Spanish Eyes, telling him he should have pulled up as soon as the stirrup strap gave way. Though Max told him to cool it, that it hadn't been a problem, he couldn't fail to notice his father's concern. Maybe it was a good thing it had happened, Roisin thought; the drama of events had superseded the embarrassment of their last meeting.

'You did me a favour, Max,' she said. 'I was on Ice-Skater. I reckon you'd have beaten him if you'd had a set of irons.'

'There's no doubt about that,' said the friend. He turned to Roisin. 'I was on Ice-Skater, too. Stroke of luck, eh?' And he laughed, though not with his eyes. Just for a second the pinholes bored into her.

God, she must be drunk.

The man was now talking earnestly to Lewis. 'Seriously, your son is a very fine horseman. Not many jockeys could have stayed on a horse without stirrups in a three-mile chase and finished in the frame. You must be very proud of him.'

She watched Lewis closely. This amounted to a

test.

'Oh, I am proud,' said Lewis, 'very proud indeed. Well done, Max. That was an impressive display.'

They were all smiling now; even the stranger—Victor—had a twinkle in his eye that had to be genuine. She felt a stab of gratitude. She'd done him a disservice, after all.

She placed her brandy glass on the table half finished. She'd had enough to drink, no doubt about that.

*   *   *

Cherry took the wheel of the Lexus on the way back. Max had reappeared whiffing of alcohol so it was a no-brainer of a decision. After all, it wasn't the first time.

Frankly, it was a relief to get away from Victor. Since the heavy hand of Customs and Excise had landed on her shoulder, a cloud hung over the relationship with her mentor. She just hoped to God he hadn't noticed it.

It wasn't exactly a long drive back to west London but the traffic was bad. After the first twenty minutes, when Max had been buzzing from the day's events and keen to rehash his races, she'd persuaded him to put on the radio. She soon tuned out the pop music and adverts so she could think.

Victor wasn't expecting her at the club, so that was all right. Max obviously did expect her to spend the night with him and that was all right too—up to a point. She had to have some time alone to call Janice. It was tempting to forget all about the horrible cow but she couldn't allow things to get off on the wrong foot. This business might have to go

148

long term and it would be pointless to fall out over the matter of a phone call.

So what was she going to tell the bitch?

She'd think of something.

* * *

Roisin could see one advantage to being hung-over: it brought out the best in Lewis. He'd driven her to his St John's Wood house, dosed her with painkillers and tucked her up in bed. A couple of hours later, as she was slowly surfacing, he produced a soup and chicken salad supper which revived her with each mouthful.

'This is a sight better than one of your breakfasts,' she said as she broke off a length of baguette.

'Thanks to my housekeeper. She leaves an evening meal that even I can't spoil.'

She squeezed his hand and smiled. She appreciated it all the same.

When she'd finished, he moved the tray and sat on the bed beside her, circling her with his arms. With her head on the warmth of his broad chest, she was tempted to drift off once more. Then a thought surfaced, preventing her progress into sleep.

'Who was that man with Max?' she murmured.

'Victor someone. Seems a pleasant fellow but I've never seen him before.'

'I have.'

'Really? You know him?'

'No. I just remember him from the casino. He sat at my roulette table once.'

Lewis began to stroke her hair, smoothing it off

her face.

'That makes sense,' he said. 'He's obviously a bit of a gambler.'

'I think he might be a bit more than that, Lewis.'

'What do you mean?' His fingers stopped their soothing.

'I saw him pass betting chips to another punter, a jockey.'

'You mean he gave the fellow some chips to play with?'

She sat up. 'It wasn't that. The jockey sat down next to Victor but they didn't say hello or anything. The next thing, the jockey's sitting in front of a pile of chips and they must have come from Victor. I didn't see the handover but he started with about thirty pounds and suddenly he had about two thousand.'

'Then what happened?'

'The jockey cashed in. He didn't even pretend to play.'

'And?'

'That's it. I'd forgotten all about it until I saw Victor this afternoon.'

'With Max.'

The words hung there. Lewis's face was grim and, for a moment, Roisin regretted telling him. But she had to, it was only right—though her timing could have been better.

'It probably means nothing,' she said. 'Max should be careful, that's all.'

He sighed, his face softening. 'I wish.'

'This isn't going to spoil our evening, is it?'

He put his arms back round her, in a more purposeful fashion this time. 'There's no chance of that,' he said and kissed her in a way that showed he meant it.

*   *   *

Cherry finally summoned the courage to phone Janice. She made the call on her mobile from the garden of Max's flat.

'Nothing much happened at Kempton,' she said. 'We watched the racing, mixed and mingled. That was it.'

'Who did Sinbad associate with?'

Sinbad? For a second Cherry was lost, then she remembered that Janice had given Victor a code name: Sinbad, as in Sinbad the Sailor. All things considered, it was quite imaginative. Cherry had wondered if it was Janice's idea. Probably not.

'Sinbad,' Cherry said, her voice dripping with irony that would be wasted, 'associated with half the bookmakers on the rail and just about everyone in the owners' and trainers' bar.'

'Was he laundering money, as you suggested?'

'No. Brian organises all that and he wasn't there.'

'Organises it how?'

'He uses a team. He tells two guys what to bet, they tell two more and so on—it's like a pyramid. They synchronise their watches and place the money simultaneously, before the bookies can adjust their odds. They can easily sting them for forty or fifty grand.'

There was a pause. Janice was probably writing it down.

'Can I go now?' Had she said enough to get herself off the hook for tonight?

151

Another pause. 'OK, Scorpio. Call me soon.'

Scorpio was her own code name—Cherry had forgotten.

She put the phone down with a trembling hand. She'd find this funny if she wasn't so terrified.

Chapter Eight

Mist still hung in the mid-morning air as Alan led Grain of Sand down the empty lane behind Tim's yard. The horse was making a good recovery from his injury but, to Alan, it still seemed like slow progress. In a few days' time, Sandy would be able to resume normal exercise but for the moment he was just being led out with a bridle on. Alan observed that there was a wonderful confidence about him. It didn't matter if a pheasant flew out of the hedge or a tractor rumbled up behind, the horse took it all in his stride.

After they'd gone a few hundred yards, Alan hopped up onto the horse's back. Even at this dawdling pace he could feel the power beneath him. As they meandered along, he allowed the horse to pick at the grass in the hedgerow. Soon, Grain of Sand would be allowed off the tarmacked surface but, for the moment, it was important that his wound was kept clean and the fields were wet and muddy. Alan kept him out for the best part of an hour.

When they returned to the yard Alan noticed a splendid old Bentley parked next to his scruffy Toyota. He presumed it belonged to a visiting owner. He wasn't far wrong.

Tim stepped out of the office the moment the pair of them appeared. Beside him was the familiar figure of Cyril Ogilvie.

Alan jumped off the horse's back, his confusion plain to read.

'I don't know why you're so surprised to see me,' said Ogilvie, shaking the hand Alan offered. 'You've been badgering my secretary all week.'

'I didn't think I was having much effect. I just wanted you to know I was putting together a joint ownership for Grain of Sand. In case you were still interested in him.'

Ogilvie grinned. 'As you see, I might be.' He stepped past Alan, his eyes on the horse. 'Where's the over-reach?' he said.

Alan slipped off Sandy's back and lifted his off fore. 'Two more days and he'll be ready to canter, won't he?' he said looking at Tim, who nodded.

Alan found himself enthusing about Sandy's history on the Flat and his hopes for him as a hurdler. It made no visible impression on Ogilvie, whose genial old buffer air had disappeared the moment he turned his attention to the horse. He asked Alan to walk him gently round the yard.

'I love beautiful things,' Ogilvie said eventually. 'Years ago, I was clearing a library for some old aristo who'd fallen on hard times—at least he thought he had. Had to sell his books to finance a new roof for his castle. Ugly old pile. In his place I'd have kept the books. Anyway, I put my hand behind a shelf and pulled down a fourteenth-century psalter. Every page was exquisitely illuminated, hand-painted by some long dead master. I must have been the first person to look at it for centuries. Incredible, the most lovely object

153

I've ever seen outside a museum—which is where it ended up, of course. I was tempted to keep my trap shut and take it home with me.'

Ogilvie paused, then added, 'When all's said and done, though, I'd rather own a beautiful horse.'

Alan didn't know quite what to make of this digression. He'd not considered Sandy in these terms.

'He's a handsome fellow, all right,' he ventured. Out of the corner of his eye he saw Tim suppressing a smile.

Ogilvie turned to Alan. 'I suppose you could say I've got a sentimental attachment to him. He won me a few bob on the Flat.'

So was he in or out? Alan had the impression the old boy had made his mind up ages ago and was stringing him along for fun.

'I assume,' said Ogilvie, 'that you intend to be part of this syndicate yourself?'

'Yes,' he blurted. What else could he say? He must be able to borrow the money somehow.

'Excellent.' The bookseller pumped his hand. 'Count me in then.'

As the Bentley purred down the drive, Alan scrutinised Tim.

'This is down to you, isn't it? You knew I was having trouble getting hold of him.'

Tim shrugged. 'I've known Cyril for years. He used to send horses to my uncle.'

Which explained why Ogilvie hadn't asked about the cost of his share—Tim must have told him.

'Thanks, mate,' he called after Tim as the trainer stumped back to his office. He was quickly learning that when it came to selling horses, you could never have enough contacts.

Geoff, Tim and now Cyril Ogilvie had all promised money for Sandy. Now all he had to do was find another £40,000.

*   *   *

'I've got a Mr Bishop on the line,' said Jackie. 'Again.'

Lewis pulled a face. He'd been hoping Bishop would take the hint but he was a persistent type, obviously.

'I can get rid of him,' Jackie continued, 'but I've a feeling he'll be back unless I can give him a good reason why you won't talk to him.'

'Put him through then.' Lewis knew he'd have to hear him out eventually.

The conversation was predictable. Bishop mentioned Max straight off, thanked Lewis for his hospitality at Kempton and offered lunch in return in order to discuss a business proposition.

Lewis said no as firmly as he could to the lunch but suggested a ten-minute meeting in his office at the end of the day. After what Roisin had told him about his new acquaintance he'd already decided to give him a wide berth. But Max had been singing his praises, saying his Kempton rides were down to Victor. For his son's sake, he had to go through the motions.

*   *   *

Cherry rang Janice from the scrap of common a few streets from her house. She was paranoid about being overheard. She'd been with Victor that afternoon when he'd taken a call she knew would

155

be of interest to Customs and Excise.

'If you lot have been following one of Chris Spot's men then you've been rumbled. A guy called Conrad. Someone's been tailing him in a Rover.'

Only silence came from Janice's end.

'It doesn't make life any easier for me if Vic—'

'Sinbad.'

'If Sinbad thinks you're sniffing around.'

Another silence. Then Janice spoke.

'The extent of our operation is not your business.'

'OK. I just thought you'd like to know Conrad's been told to keep away from the farm in Sussex because of you.'

'What farm?' Janice sounded interested.

Cherry told her. The last time she'd been to Cookfield Farm had been in the company of Jimmy Morton. They'd driven up from Poole in Jimmy's old Escort with the boot stuffed full of coke. Reggie Jenkins, the farmer, had helped them offload it into the cellar of the main house, and then insisted they stay for tea, served in the gloomy front parlour. Jimmy, who'd had the munchies after smoking a spliff in the car, had demolished all the sandwiches and half a chocolate sponge, leaving Cherry to make awkward small talk to Mrs Jenkins. It had been a bit odd—not exactly how you'd imagine a big drug deal going down.

She thought about Mrs Jenkins now, a thin harassed woman with fly-away grey hair, as she gave Janice the farm's address. Did she have any idea what her husband and her two sons were up to on the side? She'd have a cock-eyed view of farming economics otherwise. Her eldest son was driving a Porsche in those days and his brother had been out in Spain overseeing the building work on the family's villa.

Cherry was only too aware that this phone call was liable to bring the Jenkinses' gravy train shuddering to a halt. Even if Mrs Jenkins was a complete innocent, she'd be left to pick up the pieces while the rest of her close family spent a few years inside and their assets were seized.

Too bad. Cherry couldn't afford to turn sentimental about an old biddy who'd served her a cup of tea five years ago. Time to get real.

'The farmer's name is Reggie Jenkins. Apparently Chris Spot was at school with him. On the farm there's his wife and two sons and they work the business between them.'

'Anything else?' said Janice when Cherry had finished.

'No.' That was enough for now, there was no point in coughing up everything all at once. Besides, what else she knew about the farm was largely unsubstantiated. Like the rumours of what happened in that cellar. When she'd been down there with Jimmy it had just been an empty space with whitewashed walls, one of which was flecked with brown stains. It could have been blood—she'd not lingered long enough to examine it at the time.

'Thanks,' said Janice grudgingly. 'That's useful.'

Useful? It was 22 carat and they both knew it.

*   *   *

To Alan's knowledge, none of his acquaintances lent money to their fathers. As far as he could tell, the process worked in the opposite direction and he had several pals who'd benefited from a handily

157

timed dollop of parental largesse. So why did he feel guilty about asking his dad to repay the four grand he'd loaned him last year?

When the request had been made, he'd been embarrassed on Ralph's behalf—which was more than his dad had been. He'd wanted it, he said, to buy a car which was essential to take advantage of a job opportunity. Naturally, when pressed, the specifics of the job remained hazy though the specifics of the money did not. 'I need cash, son. That won't be a problem, will it?' As it happened, it hadn't been. Thanks to a windfall bonus from a satisfied owner and hard graft, Alan had a bit of money in the bank. He'd handed it over on the condition that Ralph wouldn't bother his mother and sister for any more. And he'd had no expectation of ever seeing it again.

He'd thought long and hard about asking for it back. It didn't take him far towards his £20,000 share of Grain of Sand but it was a start. And it was his money after all.

Ralph sounded cheery when he answered the phone—that was something—and Alan launched nervously into his preamble. His father cut him off.

'If this is about business, son, you'd better come to my office.'

Office? For a moment Alan's heart leaped. Maybe his father did have a job after all.

'Where's that, Dad?'

When Ralph told him, Alan almost burst out laughing. Not that it was funny. Fancy him thinking his old man had gone legit.

*　　　*　　　*

158

Lewis hadn't taken all that much notice of Victor Bishop when he'd turned up in his hospitality suite at Kempton racecourse. Now he took in the well-cut grey suit and highly polished handmade shoes, the firm handshake and broad smile, the unreadable eyes and the studied neutrality of the speaking voice. He pegged Bishop as a boy from a council estate who'd made his way on graft and native intelligence; a self-made businessman operating in the motor trade or estate agency, who had racing connections. Whatever, he wasn't much concern to Lewis except that Max seemed to like him and Lewis was keen to mend fences. Despite his reputation as a ruthless operator, Lewis could not play the hard man with his own son for long. Infuriating though he was, and disappointing in so many ways, Max was his only child—and he was Max's only parent. Losing your mother at the age of thirteen excused many things, in Lewis's judgement.

So if Max considered this relationship with Victor Bishop to be of value to him, if it gave him an introduction to a new set of trainers and owners, then Lewis was happy to play along. He offered Victor a seat but no refreshment. This was an interview for politeness' sake and it wasn't going to take long. Ten minutes, tops.

It turned out to be rather longer than that and when Jackie rang him on cue he didn't take the offered escape route. Victor was a charmer and obviously well-informed about the racing world. Lewis found himself listening to a string of stories about trainers and yard staff that were funny, indiscreet and, quite possibly, useful.

'Do you own horses yourself?' he asked.

159

'Not exactly,' said his visitor. 'But I know a lot of people who do.'

Lewis couldn't quite get a handle on him. What did 'not exactly' owning horses mean?

He himself had owned horses for more than a dozen years but when it came to their training and maintenance he was in the dark. He'd never been able to tell if the mystery men he employed to house and run his animals really knew what they were doing. There were always plausible reasons why his horses performed the way they did on a particular day but these reasons were always delivered in hindsight.

'So, what's your line of work?' said Lewis eventually.

'You mean why am I sitting here bending your ear?' Victor grinned affably. 'I'm interested in Elmwood Glade. I've been following developments in the press.'

That made sense; the plans for a nine-hole golf course and sports centre had attracted a degree of national publicity.

'It sounds great,' Victor continued. 'You've got planning for a hotel with a casino, haven't you?'

Lewis agreed that he had and his visitor opened his briefcase to produce a selection of glossy leaflets for casino hotels, all situated in sunnier, more exotic climes—Caribbean islands, southern Africa, the Far East.

'When it's built, I assume you're going to need someone to run the business,' Victor said with a smile. He indicated the brochures. 'I've got a bit of experience in that line.'

'I'm sorry, Mr Bishop, but I've already granted the option to someone else.' It was no less than the truth.

Victor's smile did not waver. 'I guarantee he won't get as much out of it as I would.'

Lewis had no doubt about that but the avaricious gleam in Victor's eyes had just confirmed all the suspicions that Roisin had put in his head. This was not a man he wanted to do any kind of business with.

He brought the meeting to an end with a speed that bordered on rudeness.

*   *   *

Cherry made Max sit on her bed while she changed. She couldn't remember when there'd last been a male presence in her Fulham cottage and it felt strange. Her little house was the one place she felt safe and here was this new man in the heart of her sanctuary. She should have made him wait in the living room but she didn't want him snooping around in there on his own. It was best he was here where she could keep an eye on him—just as he was keeping an eye on her, the weight of his glance heavy on her bare limbs as she rummaged in her underwear drawer. She couldn't say it was disagreeable.

Her fingers closed on the new packet of tights and then rejected them in favour of something flimsier. Life was perilous at the moment, she might as well have a bit of fun while she could.

'Wow,' he said as she eased the stocking up her leg and clipped it to the suspender belt. She fastened the other one and stood casually for a moment, pretending to examine a nail. She knew she looked good. He placed a hand on the bare

161

flesh of her thigh, just above the stocking top.

'Off,' she said and smacked it away. He captured her hand in his and pulled her on top of him onto the bed.

'I thought we were running late,' she said.

That stopped him. Dinner with his father was obviously as important to him as it was to her—for different reasons, of course.

There'd been a change of plan. They'd been in bed at his flat—two rides at Ludlow had done nothing to dampen his ardour—when the phone had rung and he'd only answered reluctantly. Then his tone had altered and Cherry had guessed at once it was his father—Max was being summoned to dinner that evening. She was surprised to hear him say, 'Only if I can bring someone along.'

There'd been a pause, followed by, 'No, she's not.'

'Not what?' she asked when he put the phone down.

'Not one of my cheap nightclub sluts.'

'Are those the kind of girls you take to dinner with your father?'

'I can't remember when I last took any girl to meet my father.'

So that made tonight important for both of them. She'd insisted on a quick dash to her house to effect a makeover.

'What do you think?' she said, as she turned from the mirror and faced him. 'Will I pass?'

He appraised her carefully, no longer with lustful eyes but with calculation. They'd discussed her look in the car on the drive over.

'It's a bit serious,' he said at length. 'You look like a schoolteacher.'

162

She bristled. 'Schoolteachers can afford a suit from Valentino?'

'A solicitor then. Or some kind of city trader.'

That was better. She turned back to the mirror. Victor had fronted up for the suit for a meeting with some European business types in Paris a year ago. He'd been getting them to invest in one of his importation schemes and she'd been cast in the role of company accountant. The outfit—blueberry crepe, the jacket nipped in at the waist, the pencil skirt barely an inch above her knee—had worked its magic that night. Some smooth Italian had been very taken with the cut of her jib. But she'd retired to Victor's suite at the George V at the end of the evening and the pair had celebrated at length— after she'd carefully packed the suit away. It was the last time she'd made love to Victor. Definitely the last time.

Now she posed for Max. She'd put her hair up and kept the make-up to a minimum. Nevertheless, something extra was needed. She scrabbled to the bottom of her jewellery box and found her old silver chain and crucifix. When had she last worn this? Years ago.

Max was behind her already fastening the little catch on the nape of her neck. The small silver cross nestled into the modest V-neck of her plain cotton shirt.

'Perfect,' he murmured into her ear. 'He's going to love you.'

She sincerely hoped he was right.

*   *   *

One second thoughts, Alan reflected as he swirled

163

the ice in the dregs of his Scotch, there were worse places for a man to do business than the bar of the Golden Thread casino. It was plush and comfortable, with just the far-off rattle of roulette wheels and the click of gambling chips by way of background interference—which beat piped music any day. The only thing it lacked was another party to do business with. Where was his father? The svelte waitress in a scarlet cocktail dress had offered him one refill already. Though tempted, he'd declined. He anticipated some tricky negotiation ahead.

Just as he was about to duck the waitress for a second time, Ralph Morrell appeared from the direction of the gaming room and sauntered across the maroon carpet towards him. He wore a navy velvet jacket over a collar and tie and looked, for once, sleek and prosperous. Maybe Alan's luck was in. By the law of averages, his father had to hit a winning streak every so often.

Alan switched to mineral water, his father had a small beer; a good sign, meaning his dad was planning to keep his wits about him too. Ralph grinned encouragingly and Alan plunged straight in.

'Do you remember that money I lent you last year? I could really do with it back.'

Ralph didn't turn a hair. 'Five grand, wasn't it?'

'Four, Dad.'

His father shrugged. 'Whatever. Call it five, son—I owe you a bit of interest.'

'Just the four will do, thanks.' Alan was suspicious. This was a bit too good to be true.

Ralph tilted his head to one side, a characteristic pose, as he studied Alan's reaction. 'You're wondering what the catch is, aren't you?'

'To be honest, Dad, yes.'

Ralph laughed. A belly laugh that stripped away the years and took Alan back to the good times when he was little and his father was a hero and the family were together. He quickly shut off that line of thought.

Ralph finished his drink in one hungry swallow and got to his feet. 'Come on, then,' he said. 'Let's get you your money.'

'Now? You've got it here?'

His father gripped him by the elbow, his deep-set dark eyes gleaming. 'I haven't got it, son. The casino has. All we've got to do is take it off them.'

Alan's heart sank. It was just as he feared.

*   *   *

For the purposes of the evening, Cherry had cast herself in the role of hardworking businesswoman. The marketing manager for a software company, to be precise; a sphere, Max assured her, that his father had little knowledge of. She had precious little knowledge of it either but what did that matter?

Max had entered the restaurant first while she ducked into the late-closing bookshop across the street. She spent five minutes flicking through literary novels she had no intention of reading and then made her entrance. Father and son were at a table in the rear. They rose to greet her.

'I'm so sorry I'm late,' she said, gripping Lewis's hand and meeting his curious gaze. 'The phone went just as I was leaving the office.'

'I know the feeling,' Lewis replied and they both

165

laughed. So they were conspirators already—excellent.

The place was one of Lewis's favourites, Max had said—an old-fashioned chophouse with leathery waiters and a lot of gilt and mirrors. The menu was strictly for the red-blooded brigade which was not entirely to her taste. But she ordered sirloin steak cooked rare and earned a nod of approval from her host.

That was the easy part.

'I hope I haven't spoiled your plans for the evening,' Lewis said to her, 'but until a couple of hours ago I wasn't aware of your existence.' His smile was warm but his eyes were wary.

'No, this is great,' she said. 'I'm thrilled to meet Max's famous father.'

Was that too gushing? She didn't want to come over as an arse-licker.

'Not as thrilled as I am,' he said drily. 'You're the first female Max has deigned to introduce me to since he was seventeen.'

There was an uneasy silence as the wine waiter poured. When he'd retreated, Lewis raised his glass. 'To a rare creature—a woman my son is happy to be seen with in public.'

Max laughed. 'You're embarrassing Cherry, Dad.'

Lewis's face softened but he kept his eyes on her. 'I wouldn't want to do that.'

Cherry sipped her wine nervously. Better go easy, she thought.

'So, how did you two meet?'

It was a question they'd anticipated. She fielded it as agreed.

'At the opera—I was taking a client to *La Bohème*.'

166

Lewis's eyes flicked suspiciously towards his son. 'I didn't know you liked opera.'

'I didn't think I did, Dad. But one of Ian Rafter's owners invited me along and I ended up next to Cherry.'

'It was so romantic,' she gushed. 'I was in tears at the end and Max lent me a handkerchief.'

Lewis turned back to her. Max had assured her his father hadn't a clue about opera and wouldn't quiz them about the performance—which was just as well. 'Well,' he said, 'I can tell you've been a civilising influence on my son already. Good for you.'

Max placed his hand over Cherry's on the tablecloth. 'Cherry's just what I need, Dad, wouldn't you say?'

Lewis chuckled, scrutinising her hard. 'Absolutely.'

Cherry managed a demure bob of the head. She caught sight of the waiter making for their table with a tray. The first course was on its way—thank God for that.

*　　　*　　　*

Alan felt out of place. Ralph had led him down a corridor and up in a lift to a separate, smaller room containing card and roulette tables. On the way, there had been conversations with dinner-jacketed casino staff and, on more than one occasion, he had seen his father produce a banknote which had disappeared in a twinkling. On the second occasion Ralph had murmured, 'You can't tip the dealers but the rest of them expect it.'

At the door they had been held up by a further

167

conflab which required Alan to produce his driver's licence. Since he'd already been through the rigmarole of becoming a member he wondered why this was necessary but kept his mouth shut. 'This is the no-limit room,' Ralph explained. 'Because you're with me, they'll let you watch, but you can't play.' Ralph sounded apologetic but that suited Alan just fine.

So now he stood behind Ralph who had taken a seat at the roulette table with easy familiarity. Around them the clientele were conspicuously better dressed than in the room downstairs. So this was the big boys' game. To his surprise, his father did not look out of place.

Ralph settled into his chair and placed his mobile by his elbow. Nonchalantly he placed one or two chips on the table and lost them. He repeated the process and lost again. This did not discourage him. 'I'm just getting the feel of the table,' he murmured over his shoulder.

Alan's spirits sank. If it hadn't been pathetic it would be funny. Roulette was simply a game of chance, he knew that much. Why on earth didn't his father stick to horses? For all racing's fickle nature at least you could make a judgement on form, looks, going and a dozen other things. Here it was just blind luck and his father had long ceased to be blessed by that.

The wheel stopped spinning and the little white ball found a home amongst one of the thirty-eight compartments. The croupier plonked a marker on the winning number and cleared away the losing bets, then began to pay out. Remarkably, Ralph's small pile of chips was left standing, to be matched by a larger pile which he claimed. He turned to

Alan and said, 'Won't be long now.'

What won't be? Alan wanted to ask. Won't be long before I've got your money? Or won't be long before some flunkey, his pocket full of tips, is kicking me out into the street?

The wheel turned again and, to Alan's amazement, another pile of chips was pushed in Ralph's direction.

Maybe his father wasn't such a mug after all.

*   *   *

Cherry was feeling more relaxed. The wine was going down and Lewis had mellowed with its drinking. The origins of her acquaintance with Max appeared to have been swallowed without question and the conversation had inevitably moved to horses, which had given her a breather.

'Cherry's more of a boat girl than a horse girl, aren't you, darling?'

'Yes,' she'd said with enthusiasm, noting the interest in Lewis's eyes as she launched into tales of sailing in Poole.

Naturally, he took the bait and told her about his days as a yacht owner.

'Do you still have a boat?' she asked.

'No. I got rid of it after Ruth died. She was the real sailor in the family, not me.'

'Ruth was my mum,' Max explained unnecessarily. Cherry had already researched the information.

Lewis was staring at her moodily. 'As a matter of fact,' he said, 'in her younger days she looked a bit like you.'

Really? Now that was something she didn't

know.

*   *   *

Alan watched his father's steady accumulation of betting chips as if mesmerised. He couldn't discern any pattern in his distribution of the little discs on the table, except that when Ralph lost he reverted to low-odds wagers, black or red, odd or even—and he always seemed to guess correctly. And a guess was what it was, surely. Either Lady Luck was smiling or she wasn't. Luck was a big factor in Alan's own sport but here, around the hushed rectangle and the spinning wheel, it was everything.

Ralph turned his head and indicated the pile of chips by his elbow. 'There we are, son.'

'That's four grand?'

'Shall I cash up?'

His father's eyes were on him and he read a challenge there. In the wars between his mother and his father, naturally he'd always been on his mum's side. His father's profligacy, greed and, in the end, dishonesty, had broken the family apart. Even at a young age Alan had taken the moral high ground and disapproved. He'd never for a moment understood what drove his father on to take risks he couldn't afford. But at this moment, he had an inkling.

Four grand, to be honest, wasn't that good to him. Right now, in this high-roller atmosphere, it looked particularly feeble. It wasn't enough.

'Can you play for more?'

'More?' His father looked amused.

'I really need twenty.' Twenty would be his share of Sandy. It would put him on a par with Tim and

Lee's dad and Cyril Ogilvie. They'd find another partner for the final share and between them they'd own a top-class hurdling prospect.

Ralph stared at him. 'Are you serious?'

'Sure.' And he was. He'd seen the way Ralph had been playing. Tonight was his father's night—he was on a roll. Of course, that roll could finish right now—but maybe it would stretch to one more spin of the wheel. 'Put it all on, Dad. Now. Whatever feels right to you.'

Ralph nodded, waited until the croupier had spun the wheel and the ball was rolling, then quickly pushed the stack of chips onto the table. 'We're on six numbers,' he murmured. 'It's a fifteen per cent chance but it pays off at five to one.'

Alan couldn't believe he was doing this.

*　　　*　　　*

At the end of the meal Lewis ordered champagne but told the waiter not to open the bottle for a moment.

Max looked surprised. 'What's this in aid of?'

'I'm running Black Mountain at Cheltenham.'

Max nodded. 'I always assumed you would.'

'We'll give him a run-out in the Bula next week, so he gets the feel of the place. Then go for the Champion Hurdle at the Festival.'

'I'd save the champagne till he wins, Dad.'

Lewis took no notice but angled his head towards Cherry. 'I've been trying to win the Champion Hurdle for ten years. I've had some decent horses but they've never been quite good enough. This one's different.'

Max rolled his eyes. 'I've heard that before.'

171

'Max is just jaundiced because he's never ridden for me in the Champion Hurdle.'

Cherry looked at Max. She could tell from the tensing of his jaw that this was a sore point.

'Now I've just bought the best horse I've ever seen,' continued Lewis.

'Black Mountain,' she ventured.

'A heart of fire and runs like the wind. He's going to be my first Cheltenham winner. I can feel it in my bones.' Lewis turned to his son. 'And I want you to ride him, Max.'

Cherry could see Max digesting the information. She could tell he was holding his emotion in.

'Are you sure, Dad? I thought you were going to let Billy Flynn keep the ride.'

'That was when you were behaving like a prat. Now I want you to ride him.' Lewis held out his hand and Max clasped it. 'You'll have to get over to Ireland this week and get to know him. He's a bloody-minded beast.'

'Sure. No problem.'

Lewis included Cherry in his smile. 'Now, how about some champagne?'

*　　　*　　　*

'How on earth did you do that, Dad?'

Sitting in the bar once more, with a casino cheque for £20,000 nestling in his back pocket, Alan was in a daze. This was unreal.

Ralph winked at him. 'Roulette's always been my game.'

Was that true? He seemed to remember, from acrimonious conversations overheard in the past, that the opposite used to be the case. All the same,

172

he wasn't going to debate the point now.

'Look, Dad, some of this money is yours.' He had the feeling he'd said this before too. One spin of the roulette wheel had scrambled his brains.

Ralph shook his head. 'No thanks, son. Your stake, your call—it's all yours. Why do you want it anyway?'

In normal circumstances that would be a funny question. Why did anybody ever want money? But Alan knew what Ralph meant. Why did he need twenty grand? He'd not told his father about Grain of Sand. He did so now, clearing his head in the process.

Ralph heard him out, sipping slowly at a celebratory Scotch. When Alan had finished, he offered no comment, just put down his glass and announced he had to go.

As they made for the exit, Alan glanced in at the main gaming room, feeling for a moment a flash of superiority. Courtesy of his father, he'd played with the big spenders—and won. This small-beer gambling was not for him.

As he gazed across the room he saw something that wiped the smile from his face. There, dealing blackjack on the far side of the pit, was a slender dark-haired girl who looked remarkably familiar. She turned to face the player on the nearside of the table and Alan studied her face. Unless his wits had completely deserted him, the girl was Roisin Dougherty.

Chapter Nine

As he clasped his father in a bear hug outside the restaurant, Max felt a warm glow of pure happiness. For all the material advantages of being a rich man's son, it was rare for his father to bestow a gift without strings, especially one like this. Dad was going to put him up on Black Mountain. They were having a tilt at the Champion Hurdle. A top ride in a top race—at bloody last.

His father's car was waiting at the kerb, the engine idling. When Lewis turned to say goodbye to Cherry, Max watched as she kissed his cheek and allowed herself to be clasped briefly in his arms. The old man had warmed to her, no doubt about that. It had been a masterstroke to bring her along.

'Did I do all right then?' Cherry demanded the moment they were in the Lexus, safely out of Lewis's sight.

'I'll say. He fell for that whole trendy female exec thing and he lapped up all your strokes. You were a star, my darling. An absolute star. Not to mention the most beautiful woman in the room.'

'What are you after?'

'Who says I'm after anything?'

'I can tell.'

She was right. Even tipsy, she was on to him. That was another thing he liked about her—she wasn't thick like Crystal.

They'd arrived outside his flat. He turned off the engine and swivelled to face her in the half light. He hadn't been bullshitting—she was beautiful. He told her so again.

She put her hand to his face.

'What is it, Max?'

'I've got to go to Ireland.'

'To ride the wonder horse. I know.'

'Why don't you come with me?'

She hadn't been expecting this, he could tell. Her eyes widened in surprise.

'What do you think? You can get round Victor, can't you? A little holiday for you and me. You deserve it.'

She laughed, a sexy throaty chuckle. 'And you don't?'

That was a question he wasn't going to answer.

* * *

Not for the first time in recent days, Noel Dougherty reminded himself that he had just started a new job. He should not make waves—not yet at any rate. But returning to Ireland to work for his father was not a conventional situation. For a start, this was more than just a job, it was his future. His father couldn't go on for ever—which was how Tom had put it while persuading his eldest to return—and he wanted Noel in place so that, eventually, the whole business could be handed over from father to son. Furthermore, Tom had argued, Noel's experience in England would help them capitalise on the tiny yard's recent successes on the racecourse.

All of which was very fine in theory, but in practice Noel knew his father was hardly likely to turn his attentions to the farm and leave the horses to him. Not when Black Mountain was one of the horses in question.

It was Black Mountain, as usual, that was the point at issue between them.

'Why can't Billy Flynn carry on riding him?' said Noel. 'He's done a good enough job so far.'

They were sitting in the office—now neat and unfamiliar since Noel had spent three days putting it in order—debating the edict from Lewis Ashwood that his son, Max, would be riding Black Mountain in future.

Billy Flynn had piloted Black Mountain in all his recent races; the pair were unbeaten.

'He who pays the piper,' said Tom.

Noel shook his head in resignation. With the change of ownership they could get who they liked to ride Black Mountain.

In which case, why choose Max Ashwood?

Silly question.

All the same, he had to make his point.

'Look, Dad, I've seen Max ride plenty of times. He's OK but that's all. Black Mountain deserves the best.'

Tom replied in his slow, infuriating way, 'I think he's not too bad now.'

Noel disagreed. 'And he's whip-happy too.'

Tom nodded. 'Look at it this way. The lad's coming over to get acquainted with the horse. And if he's a complete disaster we'll just have to tell his father.'

And that would be one duty Noel would be happy not to undertake.

*   *   *

Cherry told Victor she and Max had been to dinner with Lewis. He was interested, as she knew he would be. It was important to keep on Victor's right side.

'Sounds like you had more luck with Ashwood than I did.'

She couldn't resist. 'Don't tell me you made him an offer he could refuse?'

'Very funny. I've got a little plan,' he said by way of explanation. 'Good for Lewis and good for me. He just can't see it at the moment.'

She knew what that meant: Victor would be having another tilt at Lewis. She knew of old that he was nothing if not persistent.

She returned to the issue which had put Lewis's name on her lips in the first place.

'You don't mind if I go to Ireland for a few days, do you?'

He looked away, then ran a big hand over his rubbery features. He was considering something, she could tell. Surely it wouldn't matter that much if she disappeared for a bit? Or maybe he'd changed his mind about Max in the light of his rebuff from Lewis and didn't want her associating with him. She hoped not.

'Let's go for a walk,' he said.

She picked up her coat and followed him out of the door of the club. The wind cut into them as they walked down the street—winter was at hand— but Vic, in an open-necked shirt and jacket, didn't appear to notice.

She wondered what he was going to say. This walk-around-the-block ploy was reserved for conversations he particularly didn't want overheard. The club was regularly swept for listening devices but Vic was ever vigilant. He was also a believer in simple solutions. She'd often had sensitive conversations with him in the middle of a crowded high street where eavesdroppers and directional microphones had little chance of picking anything up.

They joined the mob outside the supermarket waiting to cross the road. His hand was on her arm, gripping her just tight enough to let her know that this was the point of their excursion.

Suppose he said, I know you've been talking to the filth?

Jesus. The grip on her arm suddenly felt like a shackle.

'I've got a job for you,' he murmured in her ear, 'when you go to Ireland.'

Relief flooded through her. He wasn't suspicious of her—and she could go away with Max.

'A fellow in Dublin owes me a bit of money and he hasn't got it.'

This was hardly a novel situation but not one she was usually involved in rectifying. Putting the frighteners on non-payers was man's work in her book—in Victor's too.

'You should see your face,' he said to her as he steered her inside a large and smoky Victorian pub. 'I'm not asking you to go round there with a baseball bat.'

He bought her a gin which she drowned in tonic—after last night she wasn't feeling up to much.

'This Irish friend of mine,' Victor continued once they were seated in a far corner, 'is offering me something instead of the money. Something up your street.'

'The suspense is killing me, Vic.'

He took a sip of his pint. 'It's a boat moored on the south coast, in Cork somewhere. You can give

178

it the once-over while you're in the Emerald Isle.'

She digested the information.

'You just want me to look her over?' she said.

'I value your opinion in matters nautical.' He winked at her. 'Tell me whether you think she's up to the trip.'

The trip. Cherry knew what he meant by that. She'd made the trip once, from St Vincent to the Channel, loaded to the gunnels with high-grade cocaine. Her pals at Customs and Excise didn't know about that particular voyage.

'Sure,' she said. It occurred to her that this development might be useful in any negotiation with Janice. 'It would be a pleasure.'

*   *   *

Alan was late arriving at Tim's yard thanks to a detour to his bank in Swindon. He didn't believe in good luck unless you made it yourself. He believed in graft and toil and working at things till you'd earned that luck. Even after he'd paid the casino cheque into the bloodstock account, he was in a state of disbelief.

As he crossed the yard to Sandy's stall, he was hailed by Tim.

'You should have been here a couple of hours ago. You've missed her.'

'Missed who?'

'Mrs Ballard. She was expecting you to show her Grain of Sand and I couldn't get hold of you.'

Alan realised he'd forgotten to turn his phone on. He apologised. 'But I don't know any Mrs Ballard,' he added. 'And I didn't arrange to meet anyone. What was she like?'

179

Tim grinned. 'Blonde, well-dressed—not understated, if you know what I mean. Drove up in a new Alpha Romeo just as I was organising third lot. I'd have asked her to leave but she said you were going to show her Grain of Sand.'

Alan was mystified.

'Anyhow, we sorted it out. I led Sandy round the yard for her and she made a big fuss of him. She hasn't got much of a clue about horses but,' Tim's grin had got wider and now split his face in two as he handed Alan a slip of paper, 'she knows how to write a cheque.'

Alan glanced down. It was made out to Blades Bloodstock for £20,000 and signed 'B. Ballard' in a schoolgirlish scrawl. It looked genuine enough, but surely it couldn't be.

'Are you taking the piss?'

The smile froze. 'Believe me, mate, I'm not joking. Look, she wrote me one too, for training fees. I told her I'd sort that out later but she insisted.' And he showed Alan a separate cheque, made out to him for £3,000.

Alan was lost. He still didn't believe in luck but after recent events his conviction was cracking.

'Did she say how she knew me?'

'As a matter of fact, she said she's your father's girlfriend.'

*   *   *

Cherry rang Janice the moment she got the opportunity.

'You're leaving the country?' Janice didn't sound thrilled about it.

'Is there a problem?'

180

'Just as long as you don't get any ideas about forgetting to come back.'

Cherry had imagined they might be unhappy about her ducking out of their jurisdiction. 'It's only for a few days.'

'OK,' said Janice. 'But if you don't return, our deal's off. We'll get an international warrant and put you on our most-wanted list. You won't be able to show your face in the civilised world again.'

The bitch.

If only she'd got her act together, Cherry thought, she'd go anyway. Put Plan B into action and disappear into the world of sailing boats and fly-by-night crews. But, right now, Plan A might well work out. Plan A was Max. She wasn't falling for him or anything. She could walk away from him without a backward glance if she had to. But right now seemed too early.

For the moment, she'd just have to string the woman along.

* * *

Lewis put down the phone after his evening conversation with Tom Dougherty and fetched his briefcase. Days at the races and restaurant dinners were all very well but they ate into his time and he had a stack of papers to go through, including a new set of plans from the firm of architects contracted for Elmwood Glade. He thought of that suspicious operator, Victor Bishop, trying to muscle his way into the deal. Bloody cheek. Lewis chuckled to himself. He'd seen Bishop off smartly enough.

Before he turned to his paperwork he poured

181

himself a drink—a small malt whisky. Better make it the only one after last night's indulgence.

Lewis had carried a glow of satisfaction with him all day. The evening before had turned out much better than he'd expected. For once Max had behaved like an adult and he'd been genuinely thrilled to be offered the ride on Black Mountain, accepting with the kind of warmth that was guaranteed to gladden a father's heart.

It couldn't be denied that much of the credit had to go to the girl Max had brought along. Reading the Riot Act about Crystal Miles had certainly borne swift fruit. If his son could rustle up a woman like Cherry—a smart, self-motivated career girl— why on earth did he bother with the others? Though he might not have dined with Max's previous girlfriends, Lewis had run across them on occasions, at race meetings and in bars. Bars was where they belonged, in his judgement—serving behind them.

So, naturally, he'd been suspicious of this new girl at first; she seemed too good to be true. But by the time he'd spent half an hour in her company he could see her appeal—and that she hadn't just been brought along to keep him sweet. Max was in lust with her, that was obvious. And why not? Beneath that crisp businesswoman exterior Cherry was damned attractive. He'd spotted Max's hand on her thigh by the end of the meal, his finger playing over the bulge of something beneath the cloth of her skirt. The sight had hit Lewis with a little thud of excitement: the little minx was wearing suspenders and stockings. It might be a cliché but it was still a sexy one. No wonder his son was smitten.

182

It was hard to concentrate on the report in front of him. The minutiae of projects always bored him. Lewis was a big-picture man. Conceiving a grand plan and moving heaven and earth to get it off the ground—that was his skill. Others could nitpick over the details later. Delegation, that was the art of a man in his position.

But personal matters were not so easy to delegate. He hadn't been able to delegate being a husband and he'd damned nearly cocked-up his marriage to Ruth. If she'd not contracted breast cancer she'd have gone ahead with the divorce. Funny that. In a weird way cancer had saved the marriage. For the last eighteen months of her life he'd really made an effort. 'The things I do to get your attention,' she'd said to him after her second, futile operation. And they'd both laughed. It was better than the alternative.

He pushed the whisky glass away from him. He was getting maudlin and he knew why. That girl last night, the challenging jut of her chin even as she agreed with you—that was pure Ruth. He hadn't meant to comment on the resemblance but he'd not been able to help himself. Max had looked puzzled but maybe he'd not been aware. Subconsciously though, it had to be part of her appeal for him—Max had worshipped his mother.

The appearance of Cherry was unsettling. In a way he couldn't define, it put pressure on his own relationship with Roisin. He'd taken Max's remarks about her age to heart in the days after their quarrel, and concluded that the age difference was superficial. Young as she was in comparison to him, Roisin was a special woman. He was in love with her—insofar as a man of his age and experience

183

could be. Not head-over-heels puppy worship, but alive to her strengths and weaknesses, aware that she was what he wanted in the long run. There was a substance to Roisin, as there had been in Ruth, that would endure to her last breath and that owed nothing to youth and beauty.

Seeing his son with a suitable woman made his own situation even more obvious. He wanted Roisin at the centre of his life. He wanted the kind of commitment from her that meant she was here with him now and not dealing cards in the permanent night of some gambling den. He wanted to marry her but he knew that the M word had to be introduced with caution. She was a young woman enjoying her first independent life and to take that away would be fatal to his cause.

In the long run, he couldn't deny he wanted to cage the bird but first he had to let her sing.

Tonight, though, in the aftermath of meeting his son's lover, he longed for his own woman, here and now, in his own house—in his own bed. If he could have done so without ruining all his hopes, he'd have driven down to the casino and dragged her out, never to return.

He pushed his papers aside and rose to his feet, impatient with this train of thought. Only one thing would clear his mind and soothe his spirit. He turned on the television and pushed a video cassette into the machine. Tom Dougherty had sent the tape of Black Mountain over from Ireland and he watched it every night, sometimes more than once. The sight of the great horse in scarlet and green crushing the opposition in the AIG Champion Hurdle at Leopardstown was balm to Lewis's spirits. And the next time he ran, it would be in Lewis's colours. It drove every other thought from his head.

*　　　*　　　*

The thought of Roisin dealing cards in the casino had been niggling at the back of Alan's mind. What on earth was she doing there? Noel had never said she worked at all, there'd been references to past jobs in an office but nothing current and certainly nothing like this. From her frequent daytime visits to Lambourn and, of course, the rich boyfriend factor, he'd simply assumed she was not one of life's wage slaves. It seemed he was wrong.

Now he had the perfect excuse to return to the casino. He phoned his father to arrange to meet him there that evening. They agreed to have dinner in the casino restaurant when Ralph promised to come clean about Mrs Ballard.

As a boy, he'd never thought of his father as a ladies' man and infidelity was not a charge his mother had ever laid at Ralph's door. But since his parents' divorce he'd realised his father didn't live like a monk. Sometimes, when visiting his dad's flat, he'd be aware of a woman's coat in the hall, a display of flowers, a hint of scent in the air. Once he'd surprised his father in a hotel bar cosying up to a woman younger than he was himself. Good luck to the old man, he'd thought.

But Mrs Ballard was obviously no slip of a girl. Was she the source of his father's current prosperity? He was itching to find out.

Alan arrived at the Golden Thread early and made for the downstairs gaming room. After all, why shouldn't he play a little? He was a member

185

here, wasn't he?

At first he couldn't see Roisin and he wandered round the tables, just watching other players but not lingering too long in any one place. Suddenly he saw a slim dark figure approach a blackjack dealer and tap him on the shoulder. It must be her turn to take over the table.

Alan still held back. She hadn't spotted him, he was sure; she was concentrating on the game she was running, He enjoyed watching her precise, nimble movements, her fingers flipping cards and sorting chips with magical dexterity. She wore a simple black dress, with her raven's-wing hair pulled back off her face. The light caught on her high cheekbones and on the bridge of her long, straight nose. She looked formidable and in charge. And beautiful.

A player vacated a seat and Alan took it. He placed five £20 notes flat on the table. Roisin acknowledged his arrival with a nod of the head but that could just have been a reflex. As she passed him his chips he looked her full in the face, searching for some emotion beneath that mask of professional politeness—surprise, dismay, even pleasure. There was nothing.

He'd only played blackjack once before but he'd played pontoon as a kid. How hard could it be?

The idea of the game was to get as close to 21 as possible without going bust. More to the point, it was to get better than the dealer. In effect, Alan was playing one on one with Roisin. He liked the idea of that.

On his first hand she dealt him 4 and 9, making 13, and her up card was 7. He said, 'Card, please,' remembering at the last moment it wasn't done to

186

say 'Twist' as he'd done in those childhood games against his sister. He received a jack, making his total 23—bust. Her second card was 10, so she played 17, losing to the players on either side of him but taking his chip.

After five minutes, half his money had gone. It was unfortunate that the minimum stake on this table was £10. He was blundering along. He knew there were strategies of play which would improve his chances—if only he could remember what they were.

At last he was dealt good cards: 5 and 6, making 11. Sure enough, his next card was a court card, valued 10, giving him 21. Roisin drew a king to her 9, beating everyone but Alan.

He was down to £40 now but feeling more confident. It was about time he got the better of Roisin. This is personal, he told himself, staring at her impassive face. As yet, she'd not acknowledged that she knew him by even the flicker of an eyelid.

This time he had a pair of 3s. That was OK, he knew what to do. At his turn, he placed another chip next to his first bet and she split the pair so that he was now playing with two hands. On the first, she dealt him an 8 making his total 11—excellent.

He placed another chip on the table and she dealt him a card. Another 8. Good—19 gave him a reasonable chance.

She dealt to his other 3—a 7 this time. This was more like it. He wagered his last chip. She dealt him a 10, bringing the hand to 20. He kept his face as stony as hers but inside his chest his heart was thumping.

It made no sense. Last night he'd won £20,000.

Now he was as thrilled—more so, maybe—by the prospect of winning £40.

Roisin's card was 6—not promising. She dealt her second, a jack of spades, Black Jack himself. According to the rules, the dealer could not stick at 16. Her chances of busting were now high.

She dealt herself another card—a 5. Now her hand was worth 21.

Alan had lost.

He looked hard into her face as she cleared the table. This time he imagined he read a glint of triumph in her mysterious black eyes.

'Goodnight, sir,' she said as he stood up. He'd been playing for just over ten minutes.

Alan calmed down in the casino bar. He felt as if he had been personally taken to the cleaners by Roisin. He didn't care about the hundred pounds he'd lost but he cared about being humiliated by a woman who didn't even have the grace to acknowledge their—their what, exactly? It wasn't friendship, not since his stupidity the last time they had spoken. But she was the sister of his best mate and, in Noel's absence, she was also his landlord. Whatever the casino rules, she could at least have said hello, couldn't she?

He didn't have far to go to find the restaurant, a large busy room where dinner service was already at its peak. He spotted his father's mop of thick pepper-and-salt hair in an alcove by the window. Opposite him was a small woman with a lot of blonde hair.

'So you tracked us down,' said Ralph. 'This is Linda.'

'Delighted to meet you.' Her small bejewelled hand was offered in a satirical kind of handshake.

Up close, Alan could see she was his father's age, if not older. Her big features were softened by an artful arrangement of fair locks more suitable for a younger woman. The face was familiar though he couldn't place it.

Where had they met before?

'Mrs Ballard,' he said. 'I gather you've met Grain of Sand.'

She inclined her head in acknowledgement. 'He's adorable,' she said.

'I can't tell you how grateful I am you've bought a share in him.'

She laughed, a raucous sound from such a small body. 'There'd better be more than gratitude in it,' she said. 'Ralph says this horse is going to make me a lot of money.'

'I hope so, Mrs Ballard.'

More ear-splitting laughter. 'You haven't got a clue who I am, have you, darling?'

'Should I?' He turned to his father.

'Linda's on TV a lot, son.'

Alan never watched soap operas or read more than the back pages of the tabloids but the penny finally dropped. 'You're Linda Parsons,' said Alan.

'That's right, dear.'

His father, of all people, was bedding one of the biggest names in show business.

Chapter Ten

Chewing a lifeless cud of gum, Connor Dougherty stared fixedly from the hilltop down to the long meadow below where a horse and rider cantered back and forth. It hurt to watch but he couldn't look away.

'Hey, Con.' His big brother Noel squatted next to him on the log that served as a seat. 'I thought I'd find you up here.'

'Yeah.' So bleak was his mood, Connor had made up his mind to resist human contact. He'd stay here on the hill till night fell, avoiding all company. But Noel was different.

'So how's the new fellow doing then?'

Noel's voice was neutral but Connor wasn't fooled. He could tell Noel didn't think much of Max Ashwood either.

'Blackie doesn't like him.'

Noel let the comment lie and watched as horse and rider kicked into a gallop, jarring the earth as they powered away into the distance towards a square-shaped rectangle of brown—their father, Tom, in his shabby old raincoat.

'They seem to be getting on all right.'

Connor spat his chewing gum into the grass by way of an answer.

'You're not going all jealous on us, are you?' Noel said.

'What? Me jealous of him?' Connor knew his voice sounded reedy and shrill. 'What's to be jealous of with an eejit like him?'

'Well,' Noel considered the question, as if Connor seriously expected an answer. 'There's the car for a start.'

Max had turned up at the yard in a sleek silver machine that looked like it had zoomed straight out of a TV advert. Connor had been pleased to note the mud splatters down one wing—you'd knock the bejasus out of a car like that round here.

'And the arm candy,' Noel continued.

A blonde girl had extricated herself from the passenger seat. She wasn't from round here either; she wore a blue suede jacket and jeans so tight they could have been sprayed on. Connor had noted her uncertain smile as she took in the battered old stables and the whiff of slurry from the cow yard.

'And,' Noel continued, 'the fact that he's turned up to ride your horse.'

That was the clincher. 'Doesn't bother me.'

'Get away with you, of course it does. You don't like anyone else riding Black Mountain, do you?'

'It's just him.' Connor couldn't admit to the accuracy of his brother's remark. 'Blackie's just going along with it for now but he doesn't like him. You watch. He'll have him off if he gets a chance.'

'You wish.'

Connor switched tack. 'Anyway, you don't rate him yourself. You had ructions with the old man about it.'

Noel laughed. 'Listening at the door, were you? We had no ructions. I just said that as Black Mountain was the best, we should get the best to ride him. Max Ashwood's a decent rider but I wouldn't call him the best.'

Connor turned to face him and grinned. 'So we agree then?'

Noel just returned the smile.

It was great to have him back home. Connor had prepared himself to be disappointed by the return of his brother. Maybe Noel would come the big I-am after his time in England and push his little brother back down the pecking order. But he hadn't. Having him at home, sticking up for him with Ma and giving him good jobs in the yard, it

191

was better even than he had hoped. One day soon Noel would be running the business and Connor would leave school and work alongside him. Noel would let him ride and together they'd win big races. He knew it.

Noel nudged Connor's arm and nodded towards the horse below. 'He's jumping him.'

Connor shifted his attention and watched keenly as Max steered Black Mountain into the row of four practise hurdles laid out across the lush damp meadow. It was a familiar stretch, one that he'd ridden countless times on this same horse's back. Black Mountain could jump these in his sleep.

The jockey had quickly found the horse's rhythm. With a stab of disappointment Connor saw Black Mountain instantly lengthen his stride and flick over the hurdles as if they didn't exist.

They soared over the last and the rider went to pull up.

'Now we'll see if he can ride or not.'

Max leaned forward to pat the horse's shoulder and turned him back towards Tom. As he did so, Black Mountain whipped round the other way.

'Yes!' cried Connor. He knew it. Blackie wanted this interloper off his back.

But Max did not go tumbling to the floor in ignominy. Somehow he stayed glued to the horse's back, fighting the bucking beast beneath him.

'Did you see that?' said Connor. 'I told you he hated him.'

The horse was now still and Max was stroking his neck, speaking into his ear. After a few seconds, the pair set off again, in harmony now, back alongside the row of hurdles. Connor and Noel watched in silence as they took the jumps again, even more sweetly than before.

'I was right, wasn't I?' said Connor.

Noel put his arm round Connor's shoulder. 'You were. More than I was, anyway.'

'What do you mean?'

'Max Ashwood's a damn sight better rider than I thought. I reckon he might do after all.'

Connor didn't like the sound of that. But if it was what Noel thought, he supposed it must be so.

*   *   *

'When were you going to tell me about her, Dad?' Alan tried to inject reproach into his tone but, given the circumstances, it was difficult.

Ralph took a sip from the mug of tea Alan had just handed him. 'About Linda?'

'Who else?'

'You've got to realise, it's a bit awkward. I know you talk to your mother. I don't like to involve you in our differences.'

'She doesn't care about your girlfriends. She'd be happy for you.'

Ralph raised his eyebrows and drank some more.

'So you weren't going to tell me at all?' Alan wasn't sure why he was pressing the point. Guilt probably. As far as emotional support went, he'd left his father to sink or swim in recent years. It looked like he could swim all right.

'Me seeing Linda's a bit of a state secret. Officially, I'm her driver. That's how it started anyway, when she lost her licence.'

Alan thought of the shiny old BMW sitting outside. So his dad hadn't been lying when he'd borrowed the money for a car to take up a job opportunity.

'She drove herself up to Tim's place the other day,' he said.

'She was only banned for a year. Fortunately,' Ralph added, with a frankly lascivious grin, 'she found me another position.'

Alan began to chuckle and when his father joined in, it felt too good to stop. He didn't know when they'd last enjoyed such a laugh.

When they'd finally recovered, he asked Ralph the question that had been at the back of his mind for weeks.

'Dad, in your opinion, what's the best way to stop a horse from winning?'

*　　　*　　　*

A wet wind was gusting as Cherry stood on the quay; it rattled the standing rigging of the boats bobbing at their moorings in the swell. She'd borrowed Max's Barbour jacket, along with his car, for the trip but it didn't keep out all of the winter chill. By contrast, the young man at her side wore just a short-sleeved T-shirt over his strapping torso and seemed unaffected by the weather. Perhaps his tan kept him warm.

'That's her,' he said, indicating the *Cecilia*, a big solid yacht at the end of the row.

She rode high in the water, the sleek line of her hull immediately appealing to Cherry's eye. 'Lovely,' she said.

'She is that.' Her companion turned to her, his teeth glistening white in his bronzed face. Cherry had not been sure who to expect when she'd asked for Ciaran Fitzmaurice at the marina office but this vision of boy-band loveliness was definitely a surprise.

He helped her on board with some gallantry though his hands lingered unnecessarily on her waist beneath the Barbour as he lowered her onto the aft deck. She decided to ignore it.

The yacht was a forty-four-foot steel cutter built for ocean cruising. Cherry could tell at once that this sturdy beast was well-equipped for the kind of cruising Victor might have in mind—there was plenty of room to stow a substantial cargo of drugs.

Ciaran was full of blarney as he gave Cherry a tour of his father's boat, all the while subjecting her to a barrage of flashing smiles and gentle arm nudges. He was getting on Cherry's nerves.

'Why is your father letting her go?' she asked.

'He's only loaning her out. Some guy wants to sail her over to the Caribbean and back again.'

That would be Victor.

'I'm trying to persuade the old man to get me on the trip as crew but he's not keen.'

I bet he's not, she thought. It's one thing letting a drug smuggler use your boat to bail you out of a financial mess, quite another to let your son go along for the ride.

'You must know the guy who's setting it all up,' Ciaran said. 'Could you tell him I know this boat like the back of my hand?'

'I don't think he's short of crew.'

He turned the heat up under his grin. 'I'm sure if you smiled sweetly he'd give me a hearing.'

They'd returned to the rear of the boat, where the raised aft deck allowed for a cabin in the stern.

'This is something,' she said, keen to change

195

the subject.

Though not large, it was a spectacular space, with a sea view on three sides, dominated by a four-poster bed.

'It sure is,' said Ciaran, perking up. 'This is the cabin all the girls want.'

'I'm sure.' She kept her voice neutral, keen not to encourage him.

But Ciaran was not the type to be discouraged, especially when he had information of importance to impart.

'My father shot a movie in this cabin last summer. Did I tell you he's a film director?'

'It's a bit small in here to make a movie, isn't it?' she said.

Ciaran's hand was now on the small of her back. Even through the waxed jacket she could feel the pressure. 'Not the kind of movie my old man makes.' The wide-spaced blue eyes were no longer innocent as he directed her gaze to the bed in front of them.

Suddenly a lot of things made sense. Ciaran's father made blue movies. Victor had his hooks into a pornographer. On reflection it was not a surprise.

'We were sailing off Mustique. Always combine business with pleasure, that's what Dad says.'

'You were there?'

'Sweetheart, I was in it.'

Cherry suddenly felt claustrophobic. She had to get off this boat.

He obviously mistook the expression on her face or maybe he wasn't sensitive enough to note the curl of her lip.

'How about you?' he said suggestively. 'Ever wanted to be in the movies? You've got the looks for it.'

Several retorts sprang to mind. Instead she said, 'Maybe I could get you on the Caribbean trip after all. Just give me your contact details.'

He beamed at her and produced a card from somewhere in his skimpy clothing.

'If you change your mind about the movie,' he said as he walked her back to the car, 'you know where to find me.'

She drove fast through the rain, eager to get back to the hotel and Max.

*   *   *

Ralph hadn't exactly answered Alan's question.

'Why do you want to know how to stop horses?'

So Alan told him about Lee's fall at Haydock on Gremlin, his own lacklustre ride on Nightswimmer at Towcester and, of course, the performance of Gremlin at Ascot on the day he'd won with Itsmyparty.

'You said yourself, Dad, that Gremlin had been got at. I didn't want to believe you but, thinking about it, I'm sure you're right. I mean, you'd know, wouldn't you?'

They'd never talked in detail about his father's past sins. 'I made mistakes,' was all his dad would say, 'and I paid for them too.'

Now Ralph put down his empty mug and said, 'This is because of your pal Lee, isn't it?'

'Yes, Dad. If Olympia was nobbled then whoever did it killed him.'

Ralph sighed heavily. 'They wouldn't have done it on purpose.'

'Does that make it any better? I reckon sending

Lee out to jump round Haydock on a doped-up horse makes them responsible for what happened.'

Ralph nodded. He looked weary all of a sudden, no longer the spry lover of an entertainment icon but a has-been jockey and ex-con who was tired of his disreputable past. Eventually he began to speak.

'In my day it was acetylpromazine—ACP. It's a tranquilliser really, a stopping drug. Give it to a horse about an hour and a half before the race and he loses all his fizz.'

'Is that what happened to Olympia and these others, do you think?'

Ralph shook his head. 'I doubt it. Back in the late eighties, early nineties, you could mask it so it wouldn't be picked up. But tests have got better. I don't think you could get away with ACP now though I daresay there's something new.'

Alan thought of his conversation with Clive when he'd suggested the same thing. The Jockey Club man hadn't denied it was possible. It seemed the most likely explanation.

There were other details he wanted from his father now he had him in a forthcoming frame of mind.

'How did you get hold of the drugs, Dad?'

'I was working with this other fellow—it was his idea. He gave me the syringes on the day, ready made up. All I had to do was identify the horse and do the business.'

'How did you get access?'

Ralph grinned. 'I was still doing a bit of training then so I could get in and out of the stables with no problem. Sometimes it was a bit tricky getting the animals on their own. I'd have to come up with some ruse to get a stable lad out of the way but there was always a moment when they weren't watching. It only took a few seconds to put the needle in—I didn't have to find a vein or anything.'

'I see.' It made the absence of Kevin, Tim's travelling head lad, all the more galling. He had to know something about what had happened to Olympia.

'I'm sorry, son.'

Ralph didn't say what he was sorry for—it could have been a number of things.

*   *   *

Cherry came into the room as Max was on the phone to his father, which gave him an excuse to wind up the conversation. She looked wet and weather-blown—even the walk across the car park was an ordeal in this gale—but her wild hair and flushed face gave him a thrill.

'Have you been out all morning?' he asked. She'd dropped him off at the Dougherty farm first thing. 'Where have you been?'

'Just driving around. It's lovely, even in the rain.' She chucked the Barbour onto a chair and kicked off her trainers. 'I had a look around Tralee.' She pulled her sweater over her head and levelled a look at him. 'I missed you.'

He held out his arms and tumbled her onto the bed. He'd missed her too, he realised. Women often said these things to him but it was rare for him to feel the same way. No, not rare—he'd never felt the way he did now. He'd spent the morning at the yard, learning to tune in to the moody terror of a horse he was due to ride at Cheltenham, defying the wild weather as he worked flat out on the

199

gallops, listening to old Tom's words of wisdom and storing them away for future reference. It was the kind of work he loved. And yet, holding Cherry in his arms now, how he wished he'd spent the day with her sightseeing in the rain.

*   *   *

Soon after his father left, Alan had an unexpected visitor: Roisin.

'You're not much of a blackjack player,' was her opening remark.

'I didn't know you were a croupier.'

She pushed past him into the cottage. 'There's plenty you don't know about me.'

'You could at least have said hello.'

'I'm supposed to maintain a professional distance from the players. What would all the other punters think if they knew we were acquainted?'

Acquainted—that was a neat way of putting it.

They were now in the kitchen.

'Tea?' He pointed to the kettle but she shook her head.

She had her hands shoved deep into the pockets of her jacket and her wide sinuous mouth was set in a thin line. She was angry with him, not for the first time. She'd looked exactly the same the last time she'd stood in this kitchen.

She must have been thinking of that occasion as well. 'Noel says you've raised the money for the horse. Congratulations.'

'Thanks.' Now was his opportunity—better take it. 'I'm sorry for what I said about Lewis. It was stupid of me.'

'Yes, it was.'

200

God, she was a hard act. If she hadn't come to mend fences—and for one delightful moment he thought he'd provoked her into doing just that—why on earth was she here?

'Have they fixed the roof yet?'

Of course, she was checking up on the property for her brother. There were some missing slates over the porch.

'A guy came up from the village yesterday and sorted it. Do you want to look?'

She shook her head. 'It's OK.'

'Are you sure you won't have a drink? I've got wine and whisky.'

'I'm driving.'

So what? he wanted to say. Let's kill off a bottle of wine together. Two, even. Don't drive home. Stay the night. Stay with me.

She stepped towards the door. That was it? She was leaving already? Why on earth had she come?

'Look,' she said in the hall, 'if you visit the casino again, please don't sit at my table. If the management found out, they wouldn't be happy. It could be misconstrued.'

'How?'

'The fact that you're staying in my brother's cottage, for a start. They don't like workers mixing with punters. If you ran a casino you'd be paranoid too.'

'I don't think I can afford to play with you anyway.'

She let that pass.

'Also,' she looked embarrassed, 'apart from Noel, my family don't know I work in a casino. Could you keep it a secret?'

'Sure.'

'My mother wouldn't approve and you might bump into my dad when he comes over to Cheltenham, so—'

'It's OK.' He stopped her. 'I've forgotten it already.'

They were standing at the front door, so close together he could feel her breath on his face.

'Are you sure you won't stay?' he said.

She shook her head, setting her black hair dancing about her face.

He watched her cross the road and get into her car. He didn't know why but he felt gloriously happy. She'd driven all the way up here when she could simply have picked up the phone. It was a long way to come to tell someone to stay out of your life.

*   *   *

The rain lashed the windows but Max had never felt cosier, bundled up in bed in a luxury hotel in the west of Ireland next to a sleeping Cherry, with no worries on his mind beyond the prospect of steering the best horse he'd ever ridden round Cheltenham in two days' time. Even the ever-present tumour of anxiety in his gut that expanded and shrank according to his mood—the little lump labelled Tortoise—had almost vanished. Here, outside the jurisdiction of the Metropolitan police, he was free of it. Well, almost.

He knew he wasn't everybody's favourite at Dougherty's yard. He'd been expecting a hard time from the horse—Black Mountain's reputation as a cussed animal had gone before him—but the coolness from other parties had come as a surprise.

In the end, the horse had been easier to deal with than the people. After the first day, when Black Mountain had tried all manner of tricks to unsettle and unseat him—and failed—the animal had been honest to a fault. The same could not be said of the kid, young Connor, who'd greeted his welcome with surliness.

Pauline Dougherty, Tom's wife, hadn't been so obvious with her disapproval but there'd been no warmth in her smile and a curtness in her manner when they'd first met that had taken him aback. At least the Dougherty men, Tom and Noel, had been hearty and welcoming though Max was well aware that he was not their first choice as jockey. But that went with the territory—being the son of the owner had its drawbacks as well as its advantages.

At least now, after his second day at the yard, he felt he'd proved himself in the saddle and got to the bottom of some of the mysteries. Noel had been more forthcoming as he'd given him a ride back to the hotel. The problem with Connor was simple— the boy didn't like anyone else riding Black Mountain.

'He's a mercenary little sod, too,' added Noel. 'He thinks the sun shines out of your father's arse because he keeps slipping him tips.'

That could be easily sorted. A couple of Euro notes would soon get the kid on his side—why hadn't he thought of that?

The mother was a more intriguing case. 'She had the bed in Roisin's old room made up for you,' said Noel. 'Even though we told her you wanted to stay in the hotel, she wasn't having any of it. Then, of course, when you showed up with that young lady of yours she saw the sense in you going elsewhere.'

Max chuckled at the thought of shacking up with Cherry in the old Dougherty farmhouse.

'What's so funny?' murmured a voice into his chest.

He told her.

'So we could be lying in some poky little single bed beneath a candlewick cover with pony pictures on the wall?'

'And Old Ma Dougherty outside tut-tutting to every creak of the bedsprings. Yes, indeed.'

Thank God they were here instead.

He reached for the bottle in the ice bucket on his side of the bed. There was still some champagne left.

'Max?'

'Mm.'

'What do you think of Roisin?'

'I think my old man's a lucky sod.'

She hauled herself up on one elbow so their noses were almost touching. There was no escaping her probing gaze. 'No, seriously. What do you think of her as a person?'

He considered the matter. He'd not given Roisin much thought before, except in the obvious sense and as a stick with which to beat his father over the difference in their ages.

'She's a smart girl. Bit of a dark horse. She works as a croupier at a casino in the West End.'

'Really?' The hazel eyes registered surprise.

'The old man swore me to secrecy before we came over. The Doughertys aren't supposed to know—her mother would reckon she's on the road to damnation.'

Max thought this was a bit of a hoot but Cherry did not appear to share his amusement.

204

'So what's her agenda with your father?'

He shrugged, a token twitch of the shoulders, for much of her weight, warm and delicious as it was, bore down on his chest.

'Dad's smitten but I'm not sure about her. He tells me he daren't crowd her or she'd take off. He'd much rather have her tucked up at home instead of spending her nights in a casino but she won't have it.'

This time Cherry did smile. 'Sounds like she's got his measure then. Do you think they'll get married?'

He blinked. 'You must be joking.'

'No.'

'She'd run a mile if he offered. She doesn't want to tie herself down to some bloke thirty years older than she is.'

'How do you know? Have you talked to her about it? Has her brother said anything?'

What was this—the third degree? 'No,' he said, 'but that's the impression she's given Dad. Anyway, it stands to reason. By the time she's forty, he'll be over seventy and scarcely able to piss straight. Doesn't make sense.'

'And you're happy about all this, are you?'

'Sure. Why wouldn't I be? Good luck to him.'

She nodded slowly and rolled off him, the interrogation over. 'OK,' she said.

It wasn't an OK of agreement, more an OK-if-that's-what-you-think.

'You're not jealous, are you?' he said, a thought occurring. 'Roisin's a looker all right but as far as I'm concerned she's not in your league.'

She laughed. 'Thanks, Max, but what either of us looks like is not the issue.'

'So what *is* the issue?'

'How much is your father worth? He's seriously rich, isn't he?'

'But she's not after him—it's the other way round, if anything.'

She gave him a look that had pity in it. 'It's called reverse psychology. You've just told me she's a dark horse.'

'I've talked to her, Cherry. She's an honest girl straight off the farm.'

'Off the farm and into a casino, which her family don't know about. Ask yourself what other games she might be playing.'

Max poured the remainder of the champagne into her glass in the hope of shutting her up. There were better things to do in this situation than talk about his old man's love life.

But Cherry was not to be deflected—naturally. In Max's experience, which was extensive in bedroom situations, a girl had to be allowed to blow off steam before her energies could be pointed in more entertaining directions.

'Have you ever considered,' she said, having put her glass down untouched, 'that you're a bit like royalty?'

What?

'Prince Max,' she went on. 'The only son of King Lewis, heir to his entire kingdom.'

He grinned happily. 'If you say so, Princess.'

'We're not talking princesses, we're talking new queen. After that come the little princes and princesses.'

'You mean Dad starting a family with Roisin?'

'Bravo, Max. You got there.' She looked smug as she scored her point. Her small pointed chin jutted

206

and a gleam of triumph shone in her eye. Right then he didn't know whether to smack her mouth or kiss it.

He wasn't a complete fool. Ever since his mother's death women had been making a play for his father. Naturally, as an adolescent, he had resented them all, suspicious that at any moment he would have a new mother foisted on him. But Dad had laughed off all contenders and played the field with ruthless regard for his own pleasure—much as Max now did himself.

But Roisin *was* different, that was Cherry's point. She was the only one of his father's companions who, beyond the initial seduction, had played hard to get. And the only one who his dad had wanted more the longer the affair lasted. Maybe Roisin was playing a cunning game and maybe she wasn't, but now he thought about it seriously, he could imagine his father asking her to marry him.

'Jesus,' he said. Then, 'I've nothing against Roisin.'

'Would you like her as a stepmother?'

'That would be a laugh, wouldn't it?'

'And those little half-brothers and sisters?'

'I like kids. I wouldn't mind a few myself one day.'

Cherry sat up cross-legged to face him and reached out to stroke his cheek.

'Sure, but be realistic, Max. Think what a new family would do to your position.'

Max *was* thinking. All his life he'd known that what belonged to his father would one day pass to him. It was preposterous to imagine otherwise!

Or was it?

Cherry's fingers were tracing his jaw, then hooking round his neck. 'Come here,' she breathed, pulling his lips onto hers. He hugged her tight, skin to skin. Thank God for her. She was soft and feminine—and tough. He held her as if he could absorb that core of strength in her. She'd made him face up to the truth and he thanked her for it.

'Maybe I've got it all wrong,' she said when they broke apart.

'Maybe,' he said without conviction.

The bedside phone rang and he extricated himself from her with reluctance.

It was Noel.

'Just wanted to keep you in the picture, Max.'

'Yeah?'

'It's the weather. The forecast's not good. They've been cancelling ferries all day.'

Black Mountain was due to make the crossing to England the next day.

'I just thought,' Noel said, 'that you might want to warn your father.'

Max slammed the phone down with a curse under Cherry's questioning gaze.

'Trouble?'

'You could say that. It looks like Black Mountain might not make Cheltenham.'

She reached for him again but he held her off. He had to phone his father.

Now he had two new suspicious lumps to sit next to the Tortoise tumour gnawing at his guts.

Cherry placed a soothing hand on his arm as he dialled his father's office.

At least he had her.

Chapter Eleven

Tom Dougherty stared through the rain-streaked windows of the horsebox at the rows of cars massing on the dock. He wasn't a fellow given to bad language and he was respectful of those who buttered his bread, but at the present moment he could cheerfully have called down curses on the head of Lewis Ashwood.

Beyond the ferry port, out in the Irish Sea, the white-tipped waves raced towards them beneath a gun-metal grey sky. The prospects of sailing today did not look good. But unless they made the crossing, Black Mountain would not be lining up for the Bula Hurdle at Cheltenham tomorrow.

Truth to tell, Tom himself would not be unduly worried about that. As far as he was concerned the horse came first and Black Mountain was a difficult traveller. The animal had never travelled on water and Tom feared he might react badly to the motion of even the calmest sea—and the boiling grey swell stretching towards the horizon could hardly be described as that. So, from his point of view, if they had to turn for home and skip Black Mountain's Cheltenham trial he wouldn't be too disappointed. There would be other times and other races; keeping Black Mountain safe and sweet-natured, that was what counted. And it would have counted that way for Michael O'Brien too, the horse's last owner.

But Lewis Ashwood was no easy-going horseman from the old days. He saw things differently. The new owner, despite the lip-service he paid to Tom's judgement, was used to making big decisions. That's how he'd made his fortune. And no matter how rich he was these days, he'd come from nothing; he knew the value of money. He'd not flashed out on a potential Champion Hurdler to have the horse languishing in his box on big race days.

So even though the prospects looked hopeless, even though Tom was longing to quit this rain-swept dock and head for home, he couldn't. Lewis's orders were clear: if it were humanly possible, he must get Black Mountain to Cheltenham.

Tom spotted Noel returning to the vehicle in the rain, the wind moulding his overcoat to his body, setting it flapping with every long stride. He hauled himself up into the driver's cab, bringing with him a salt-filled gust of the world outside. They'd been taking it in turns to take a break in the ferry terminal; it was a golden rule never to leave Black Mountain unattended. Even though he travelled everywhere with Connor's pony, Patch, for a companion, he could suddenly get lit up for no reason.

'It might be slacking off,' Noel said in answer to his father's unspoken query. 'The forecast says so at any rate.'

'So when do they think?'

The ferry had been due to sail at nine that morning and they'd arrived at eight only to find that the weather was delaying departure. It was now nine thirty.

'They're not saying. It's likely that livestock won't travel.'

Tom nodded. That made sense. But Lewis Ashwood wouldn't be happy.

'What do you mean, they won't sail with the horse?'
Max held the mobile away from his ear. The wind
might be battering the Lexus as it sat in the car
queue for the ferry but it did nothing to quieten the
enraged tones of his father sitting in his office in
London. 'If it's fit enough to sail with a boatload of
passengers then they'll take the ruddy livestock
too.'

'No, Dad. It doesn't work like that. The horses
have to stay in the horsebox on the vehicle deck. If
it's too rough there's a chance of the box tipping
over.'

'Rubbish.'

'Look, I've just spent five minutes arguing the
toss with some rear admiral. They haven't made
the decision yet but it's very likely they won't take
the horse. I'll call you when I know for sure.'

There was a curse on the other end of the line.
Then the connection was broken.

Cherry looked at him from the passenger seat.
'Rear admiral?' she said.

'Well, some jobsworth in a uniform. Whoever he
was, he made it clear that there was nothing I could
say that would make any difference.'

Cherry didn't care one way or the other whether
Black Mountain made the trip, except insofar as it
helped her provide a shoulder for Max to cry on.
This damp interlude in the Emerald Isle had
proved useful in advancing their little romance and
she was determined to make the most of it.

She put her hand on Max's thigh and gave him a
sympathetic squeeze.

211

'I assume he took it badly.'

Max didn't look at her as he nodded. 'You could say that. Shoot the messenger, it's always been his style.'

'It's not your fault, baby. Anyway, it's out of your hands.'

This time he turned to her. 'He won't see it that way. You wait, he'll be back on the line in a moment. He'll have me hiring some fishing boat to take the horse across.'

'Poor you,' she said. Privately, she was amused that the all-powerful Lewis Ashwood had met his match—even he couldn't alter the weather. She kept the thought to herself and began to massage the tension from the back of Max's neck.

'That's nice,' he said, which was something.

When the phone rang again he pushed her hands away. 'Hi, Dad.' He knew his father's habits all right.

Cherry looked out at the rolling grey sea, pretending disinterest. Max wasn't saying much so it was hard to pick up precisely what was going on, though she could tell from his tone that he didn't like what he was hearing.

'You're joking! How the hell am I going to do that?'

She watched a white plastic bag whirl by the windscreen, to be whisked high over the line of parked cars ahead.

Max was protesting. 'But I've been in the terminal, Dad. They haven't even got a cashpoint, let alone a bank.'

He fell silent again while she continued to stare out of the window. A full minute went by.

Finally, he said, 'Yeah, OK. But I wouldn't hold

212

your breath.' He ended the call.

Before he even told her what Lewis had said, she'd guessed.

*   *   *

'I hear you've got a celebrity on board today, sir.'

'Oh?' Captain Murray Watson wasn't paying much attention to Marie, the shipping office manager, as he sat at a spare desk in the ferry terminal. He'd just got off the phone to his wife and conversations with her tended to use up all of his available energy. What was it about approaching the age of fifty that so obsessed her? Well, he knew the answer to that. It was the excuse to embark on a spending spree, not that she'd ever needed one before.

'I've always wanted to go on the Orient Express,' she'd just told him, not for the first time. 'You can go from Paris to Istanbul and spend five nights in the lap of luxury, waited on hand and foot.'

'It's only a ruddy train, for God's sake.'

'And it's only my fiftieth birthday. You might be satisfied with a drinks party for the neighbours and a chewy sirloin at the Pheasant but I'm not. I can't think what's happened to you, Murray. There's no romance in you these days. Not that there ever was much.'

And that's how the conversation had ended, unhappily, and not for the first time. And what was so wrong with the Pheasant Inn? They'd had a jolly good night when he'd turned fifty. She'd thought he was romantic enough then, though it was something of a distant memory these days.

'How much do you think it would cost to go on

213

the Orient Express to Istanbul?' he asked Marie.

Her face lit up. 'Is this an offer, Captain?'

He should be so lucky. Marie had eyes as blue as a summer sky and a cheeky gap between her gleaming white front teeth. She was also, he was painfully aware every time he admired the swing of her hips in her tight office skirt, only two years older than his daughter.

Her fingers were rattling over the computer keyboard. 'Here we are,' she said after a moment. 'I've got up the web page.'

'Really?' He'd not expected an answer to his question but she was a remarkably helpful young woman. She was one of the many he'd miss when his retirement came round in the New Year.

'Paris to Istanbul,' she was saying. 'Looks like that would set you back around three thousand six hundred pounds.'

He groaned inwardly. It was pretty much what he had expected. Still, it was Barbara's fiftieth and there were big brownie points on offer . . .

'Each,' Marie added.

Each! Jesus wept.

She looked at his gloomy face. 'Does that mean our little holiday's off then, Captain?'

He raised a smile. 'I'm sure you can get one of your younger admirers to take you instead.'

She rolled her eyes. 'Fat chance. I'd stand a better chance putting money on that horse.'

'The horse?'

'Your celebrity passenger, like I was telling you before.'

Had she? Maybe it *was* time he retired, he didn't seem as alert as he used to be.

'He's a famous jump horse. Black Mountain,

214

trained over in Kerry and never been out of Ireland. I've been chatting to one of the lads who's going over with him. He says he's running at Cheltenham tomorrow.'

Watson looked out of the window and noted the white caps still dancing on the waves. Time to get in touch with Belfast for the next forecast and make a decision on the sailing—though the situation was pretty obvious.

He got to his feet. 'Sorry to disappoint you, my dear, but I don't think your famous racehorse will be leaving today.'

*   *   *

Cherry sat impatiently in the car outside the bank. Max had been inside for a good ten minutes. Cherry wondered how much longer she'd have to wait. It could be a while. It all depended how fast people moved when a multimillionaire like Lewis Ashwood snapped his fingers. And, of course, how much cash they had to rustle up.

'Bung the captain—that's typical of my dad,' Max had said when he'd put the phone down on his father. 'He thinks everyone's got a price.'

Just then, Max appeared on the pavement, heading for the car. People moved fast indeed, it seemed. Cherry was impressed.

She studied him as he turned the key in the ignition. There was a bulge in his top jacket pocket, just where the seatbelt pulled tight over his breast.

'OK?' she asked in a neutral tone.

He nodded, his face pale and his jaw clenched. He was wound up tighter than a drum. She'd have

215

to see what she could do about that later.

'Let's go,' he muttered and set off with a loud squeal of tyres.

Daddy's little boy racer, Cherry thought to herself. She'd see about that too.

*   *   *

Only one man decides whether or not to sail. Only one man decides whether to load the livestock: the captain. That's what Tom had told Max and he'd been taking horses and farm animals across the Irish Sea for years.

Max had to talk to the captain.

'I think he's gone on board, sir,' said the first attendant he asked in the terminal, a lad with acne. 'We're loading the cars now.'

Max's heart leaped. Maybe there'd been a change of circumstances. Maybe he wouldn't have to go through with this ridiculous charade of his father's.

'What about horseboxes?'

'I'm sorry, sir. It's too rough to allow the livestock to travel.'

'Look, chum, it's vital my horse gets on this ferry.'

'I'm sorry, sir. It's the captain's decision.'

'Let me speak to the captain then.'

'I'm sorry, sir, but the captain is not available at the moment.'

Max took a deep breath. 'Say "I'm sorry" once more and I'll knock your teeth down your throat.' Right now nothing would give him greater pleasure.

The lad gulped.

'Look,' Max said, taking a pen and a scrap of paper from his pocket, 'my name is Ashwood. My father, Lewis, owns the horse that is waiting on the dock. May I have your name, please?'

The boy hesitated.

'Well? I'm sure my father will want to know the identity of the idiot who prevented his horse from running at Cheltenham.'

The boy's mouth opened and closed, while his eyes scanned the crowded concourse. 'Er, I'm not really the right person . . .' Suddenly his expression changed and relief shone from his eyes. 'Marie!' he called. He must have spotted assistance.

A pretty young woman in a business suit appeared at Max's side. 'Can I help you, sir?' The boy had already slipped away.

Max forced a smile onto his face. He'd handled the lad badly. Tempting though it was, he wouldn't get anywhere by thumping someone.

He identified himself straight away and threw in his father's name, which registered this time. Fortunately she was nowhere near as gormless as her colleague.

'It's such a shame, isn't it? We were very excited to be carrying a star like Black Mountain. Unfortunately the conditions are too dangerous.'

'Really? The weather's improving. The radio forecast said so.'

'These things are difficult to call, sir. We have to rely on the captain's judgement—he's very experienced.'

'May I speak to him?'

'Now is not the best time, as I'm sure you appreciate.'

She was stonewalling him too. Max made an

effort to keep his temper in check.

'Look, miss. My father will go ballistic if his horse can't run tomorrow. I only need a moment— just so I can tell Dad I've taken it to the very top.'

He thought she was going to say no again and he wasn't sure how he'd have handled it. His façade of politeness was fragile. Fortunately he didn't have to put his self-control to the test.

'Well,' she said, 'you're in luck because he's not boarded yet. Let me see if he'll have a word with you. It'll have to be quick.'

'Fine,' he said eagerly. 'A minute or two will do.'

After all, how long could it take to offer someone a bribe?

*   *   *

'We might as well be on our way, Dad. No point in keeping poor old Blackie cooped up longer than we have to.'

Tom Dougherty grunted, his eyes on the mobile phone perched above the dashboard of the cab. Noel knew what was going through his mind. He wouldn't drive off the dock with Black Mountain until every last chance of making the sailing had gone. Those had been the last instructions issued by Lewis over the phone and, much as Tom disagreed with them, he was a stickler for the rules.

'Come on,' urged Noel, his father's stoic demeanour suddenly irritating. 'Max isn't going to change anybody's mind, is he? Let's say bye-bye to Cherry and get going.'

Tom shook his head. 'A few more minutes won't make much difference. We'd best stay till it's official. I don't want any complaints after.'

Noel knew what he meant. For all his geniality, Lewis Ashwood was the kind of man who liked things to go his way. When they didn't, he would doubtless find someone to blame.

'Right you are,' Noel muttered and settled back into his seat, his eyes on the entrance to the ferry terminal. Max couldn't be much longer.

*   *   *

'Sir, do you have a moment?'

Murray Watson did not. Matters had been delayed long enough this morning and he was eager to get back on board his ship and sail without further delay. On the other hand, the question was posed by Marie, to whom he was well disposed. By her side was a fair-haired young man with an aggressive gleam in his eye.

'Mr Ashwood owns Black Mountain,' she was saying. 'The horse we were discussing earlier.'

'Actually, my father, Lewis Ashwood owns him,' said the man. 'I'm just the jockey.'

The captain understood at once. 'Delighted to meet you,' he said, offering his hand. 'I imagine you're disappointed that we can't take your horse.'

'Not half. My father is going to be hopping mad if we don't get him to Cheltenham. You've got to let him on board.' The jockey's voice rose above the general clamour in the terminal hall.

Murray saw Marie gesturing silently towards the office, just a few yards away. He nodded and steered the irate passenger through the door, pulling a piece of paper from his pocket as he did so.

'The thing is, Mr Ashwood,' he said in his most

219

conciliatory tone, 'it's a matter of safety. Here's the latest weather report, just faxed through from the Met Office in Belfast. We've got Gale Force Eight out there and I can't take horses.'

The jockey ignored the fax. 'I thought it was down to the captain. That's you, isn't it?'

Murray was starting to get annoyed but he kept it in check. 'Ultimately, the decision is in my hands and in my judgement—'

'Look, Captain, let's cut the crap. We need to get that horse on board and if you look after us, then we'll look after you.'

For a moment Murray didn't understand. He was tempted to say that Ashwood would look after him best by clearing off and letting him do his job. But the fellow had produced an envelope from inside his coat and was holding it so he could glimpse its contents.

Banknotes.

'There's fifteen thousand Euros there. That's ten thousand pounds, near enough. You could get a nice new pair of spectacles with that—so you can read your weather fax properly.'

Murray knew what he should tell this little shit to do with his money. But the forecast was improving and the decision, as he had said, was ultimately down to his judgement.

For God's sake, nothing was going to happen to the precious animal beyond a spot of seasickness.

He took the envelope without looking Ashwood in the eye, his mind already busy with the commands he must issue to take account of the new sailing conditions.

His overwhelming thought as he pocketed the money, however, was that a jaunt on the Orient

Express was possible after all, thanks to Black Mountain.

*   *   *

Cherry could tell the moment she spotted Max leaving the terminal that he had been successful. The swagger was back in his stride and, as he drew closer, his expression told a story. The tense jut of his jaw had been replaced by a small satisfied smile.

She was perched up in the cab of the horsebox next to Noel and Tom—she'd got fed up with sitting on her own in the Lexus. She could tell the pair of them were itching to turn round and go home. They didn't have a clue.

'Here's your man,' muttered Tom.

'At last,' Noel said with feeling, before adding hastily, 'not that I'm eager to see you go like, but it's a bit of a drive back.'

She patted his arm. 'It's OK, Noel. But I think you're being a bit premature.'

Noel's ruddy face broke into a broad grin. 'You think we're getting on the ferry? Bet you a pint we're not.'

'Mine's a large vodka and tonic when we get on board.'

As his big hand closed over hers to seal the bet, Max pulled open the driver's door.

'Panic over. Black Mountain is sailing.'

'In this?' Tom nodded towards the angry sea.

'I've spoken to the captain. The Met forecast's good.'

Tom stared at Max in disbelief. 'Really?'

'He's just had a fax from Belfast. It's easing off.'

Tom shrugged. 'All right then. If that's what the

221

captain says.'

Noel cast Cherry a wry glance as she slid out of the passenger door to join Max. 'Remind me never to bet with you again.'

She laughed. 'See you in the bar.'

*   *   *

A girl was being sick in the heads as Cherry washed her hands. The room was just like a regular public toilet and hardly deserved the nautical term. But Cherry was a sailor at heart; she enjoyed being at sea, even on a floating pleasure palace like this. The ferry was longer than a football pitch, equipped with all manner of eateries and games rooms and boutiques. A person could pass the morning as if they were at their local shopping mall and never know they were at sea at all. Except, on this particular morning, the shopping mall was lurching from side to side.

Cherry returned to the bar in the stern where Noel and Tom were stoically sitting out the voyage. A cabin was available to them but its claustrophobic interior was the least pleasant spot to pass the time.

The pair of them were looking grey-faced as they nursed soft drinks. She herself was feeling perky, especially after the vodka Noel had bought her.

'Feeling rough?' she asked.

'We should never have sailed,' said Tom.

'Dad's worried about Blackie,' said Noel. 'He's not done this crossing before.'

From what Cherry had heard, that was the point of the trip—a rehearsal for the Cheltenham

Festival in the spring—but she knew enough not to say so. Instead, she nodded sympathetically and asked after Max.

'He's gone up top. Said he needed some fresh air.'

Cherry found him on the deck, leaning against a rail with the full force of the wind blowing spray into his face. He threw an arm round her and kissed her hard. He tasted of salt.

'Isn't this fantastic?' he yelled into her ear.

It was but she wasn't dressed for these conditions. She pulled him into a more sheltered spot and snuggled into his arms.

'Just think of all those rubber-legged fools down there coughing up their breakfasts,' he said.

'You're in a good mood.'

'Why wouldn't I be?' He beamed at her cheerfully.

Now was the moment. 'How much did you pay him?'

'Ten grand in Euros.'

'No!' she said, amazed. 'Your dad must be keen.'

'He is. Ten grand's nothing if he ends up with a Champion Hurdler.'

'Gosh.' She licked the lobe of his ear. 'Clever you. How did you put it to the master?'

He told her.

*　　　*　　　*

Noel made his way unsteadily to the Guest Services desk. He'd never been much of a one for sea travel and couldn't seem to adjust to the rise and fall of the floor beneath his feet. Thank God he was on board a big boat, he couldn't face the thought of something smaller. Dad had much better sea legs than him but he'd refused to let the old man undertake this errand. He'd returned home to take the strain off his father and, like it or not, it was his job to go below and check on Black Mountain.

He made his request at the desk, where an attendant asked if it was really necessary; obviously they were keen to keep passengers off the car decks while the crossing was in progress. Though he would have preferred to lurch back to his seat, Noel insisted.

He was asked to wait for a moment then a rating appeared to lead him down into the bowels of the ship. It seemed a longer way than Noel remembered, down steep and narrow metal stairs. He clung fast to the handrail as he went, not altogether trusting his footing. Ahead, his guide skipped down nimbly, keeping up a stream of amiable chatter.

Eventually they reached a door which opened on to the car deck. The vast area was jammed solid with vehicles, packed so close to each other it seemed the only way across was to clamber over roofs and bonnets. Noel could see the horsebox some three rows in and half a dozen car lengths to his left, on the floor of the deck. Just beyond it, lorries and high-sided vehicles were lashed to the ramp rising towards the great exit doors, ready for a quick departure.

Barely lit, echoing with unidentifiable creaks and clangs, the huge swaying metal hall was an eerie place.

Noel's guide was amused by his discomfort. He pointed to a high-sided lorry nearby which was making strange tinny clonks.

'It's a meat van. That's the sound of frozen carcasses banging against each other as they hang down.'

Nice.

'Why is the floor wet?' Noel asked, looking suspiciously at a puddle of liquid running along the decking.

'It's diesel. All the lorry drivers fill up to the top before they sail because fuel's cheaper than in the UK. Sometimes we get a bit of spillage.'

Which would explain the smell, Noel thought. He stepped gingerly onto the vehicle deck and wedged himself between a camper van and a Range Rover. There was barely room to take a step and he fell against the rear window of the van as the ship moved beneath him.

'Would you like me to come with you, sir?' asked the rating.

Noel refused the offer. 'No, I can manage.'

He took his time working his way to the horsebox. Parking vehicles on a ferry was an art. There was just about enough room to open the door and no more. As he squeezed between lorries he listened carefully for sounds of an animal in distress. If Black Mountain were in trouble he would be unlikely to suffer in silence. But Noel heard nothing. That was a good sign. He reached the horsebox and opened the grooms' door at the back and looked inside.

'Blackie,' he called softly. 'Patch—how are you doing, lads?'

A shuffling came from within, followed by a fluted wicker of recognition from Patch. Noel couldn't see the pony who was beyond the partition, but Black Mountain was looking down at

225

him in contentment, munching at his hay net. Everything was fine.

'I'll see you boys later,' he said. 'Won't be long now before we're back on dry land.' And as far as he was concerned, the moment couldn't come soon enough.

Outside the box, the swaying, creaking ship seemed more hostile than ever. Funny how he'd not even noticed the movement when cocooned with the horses.

Across the deck Noel spotted his guide waiting by the door. He raised his thumb as he squeezed his way towards him.

The movement seemed more exaggerated than before. Had the weather got worse? He couldn't believe it was just him—he ought to be getting used to it by now. He put his foot down blindly and felt liquid slosh over his trainers. Great—diesel in his socks was just what he needed.

As he reached the last row of vehicles, the floor rose alarmingly beneath him and a bang like a gunshot echoed around the cavernous space. What the hell was that? It was followed by metallic cracks and thumps, as if rivets were popping and steel links were being forced apart. Above and behind Noel, vehicles were parked on the ramp and, as he looked, he could swear they were moving. Towards him.

He sprang for the side of the deck, just one car's width away. But as he leaped his wet foot slipped from beneath him and pitched him into the gap between the two vehicles.

I've had it, he thought as a deep and ominous rumbling filled his ears and a bright yellow fourteen-wheeler squashed him flat.

The house was dark when Captain Murray Watson, formerly of the Royal Navy, the now suspended master of the ferry *Dragon Force*, reached home on the outskirts of the Forest of Dean. Barbara, of course, was out playing bridge and Chrissie, his daughter, was still away at university in Nottingham, so he had the place to himself. That was good.

He was tempted to head straight for the drinks cabinet but he couldn't afford to do that. There were other tasks that required a clear head.

The nightmare of the past eight hours had played itself over and over in his mind on the drive home but he had to put that to one side too. Not that it was easy.

The accident on the car deck would have been bad enough if it had been confined to damage to property. A failure of equipment, a deficient weather forecast—these things were reprehensible but, ultimately, understandable. Someone had been bloody inefficient in securing that lorry. Or there'd been a balls-up in the safety checks. It would all come to light in the investigation that was already underway. He could be pensioned off, under a cloud maybe but able to hold his head up in the world. After all, worse things happened at sea than a few bent vehicles.

But the loss of a passenger's life was a hanging offence. Especially when he himself knew where the blame really lay. That the victim should be one of the men minding that damn horse—there was an irony, though not a poetic one.

Poor fellow.

Murray took notepaper from his desk drawer. He wept over the note to Chrissie but she was a big girl now, with a smart boyfriend and a good career ahead of her.

The letter to Barbara took a little longer. He couldn't face retirement and a life of useless indolence, that's the line he took. Today's unhappy events had hastened his decision, that's all. He knew he was a dull old stick these days—she'd be better off without him in the long run. In the envelope, together with the letter, he placed the bundle of Euro notes. He had no doubt she'd be smart enough to squirrel them away before anyone else got wind of them.

There was no confession in the letters though he knew he'd not be able to withstand the questions that lay ahead. This was the only way out which would, please God, preserve his reputation.

Finally Murray turned to the Glenfiddich. He filled a crystal tumbler to the brim and took it with him to the garage. He savoured the rich peaty taste as he found the piece of hose he was looking for and taped it to the exhaust of his car.

If he could have chosen an exit, it would have been at sea, the last man on board ship rounding the Horn or expiring like Nelson in the gunsmoke of battle. But that was hardly possible—or deserved.

He finished the whisky as the engine hummed.

We're not all heroes, he thought.

Part Two

Chapter Twelve

DC Hattie Barber dabbed a wet tissue at the stain on the back of her skirt without conviction. Serve her right for sitting down in the old lady's flat while she took the statement; she could have been parking her backside in anything, from soup to dog mess. The place had been a smelly tip. But then Mrs Greening was eighty-six and half blind, which made the whole visit pretty pointless. There was no chance the old girl could identify the youths who had petrol-bombed the garden flat across the road, even if she'd spotted them in broad daylight at ten yards—which she hadn't.

Hattie sniffed at the grubby tissue. Not dog anyway, that was something. She just wished she hadn't worn the grey skirt. The phone rang as she chucked the tissue in the bin beside her desk.

A Mrs Maclean was downstairs: could DC Barber spare five minutes?

DC Barber didn't know a Mrs Maclean and she never had any minutes to spare, let alone five.

It was in connection with the death of Basil Jacobs.

That put a different complexion on things.

Hattie scrabbled amongst the pile of files on the floor. She now realised who her visitor was. She'd spoken to her in the days following the discovery of Jacobs's body, when the case had been hot and DI Pollock, the senior investigating officer, had got Hattie digging into the dead man's background. She'd spoken to Jessie Maclean once on the phone at her home in Edinburgh. She'd sounded like

231

Maggie Smith in that old film, *The Prime of Miss* ... whoever, all refined and school-marmish. But there'd been nothing refined in what she'd said about her first husband, the late Mr Jacobs: 'I told him often enough,' she'd announced down the phone, 'that he'd die in the gutter.' Mrs Maclean had revealed more than a hint of satisfaction, it seemed to Hattie, in being proved right.

More to the point, the woman had been unable to shed any light on her ex-husband's movements. 'Don't be daft, young lady. I've no' heard from him in twenty-five years.'

Hattie wondered what on earth the woman was doing here now.

Jessie Maclean turned out to be a solidly built matron, expensively dressed in a claret and charcoal jacket and skirt, with not a strawberry-blonde hair out of place. Hattie felt scruffy in comparison, but she was used to that. She ushered her visitor into the cleanest interview room and offered her coffee, which was wisely declined.

Mrs Maclean began with an apology for her unscheduled appearance and thanks for Hattie's willingness to make herself available. She referred, with an air of embarrassment, to their phone conversation and explained that she was down in London for a few days.

Hattie was only concerned to get to the point.

'I'd like to know,' the lady said, 'how you are getting on with the investigation into poor Basil's death.'

Poor Basil? This was a change of tone since their previous conversation. Hattie wondered what had brought it about. She kept her voice neutral however. 'We've done a fair amount of legwork:

door-to-door enquiries, leafleting households in the area, witness appeals in the media. But, to be honest, Mrs Maclean, we're still waiting for a breakthrough. So far nothing of any real use has turned up.'

'Oh dear.' The woman's big pink face folded in distress. 'So Basil's murderer is still out there roaming the streets and you have no idea who it is?'

That was about the size of it. Plus, of course, what trail there might have been had gone stony cold by now and everyone had more pressing problems on their plate than rooting out the killer of a shabby loner like Basil Jacobs. Mickey Pollock's feeling was that he'd got into a punch-up at chucking-out time with a fellow drunk. The other party must have legged it unobserved. They'd discounted a mugging as there was a quantity of cash in his wallet.

'The investigation is still open,' said Hattie optimistically.

'Oh dear, oh dear,' her visitor repeated. 'I thought that these days, what with all the new technology, you'd be sure to find the man responsible.'

Funnily enough, she had put her finger on the only hopeful element in the equation. Hattie seized on it.

'We do have some DNA evidence. We found traces on Mr Jacobs which might belong to his assailant.'

'Traces? What do you mean?'

Vomit, that's what Hattie meant. There'd been watery bile on the alley floor and smeared over Basil's grimy windcheater, as well as blood. The blood was Basil's but not the sick.

Hattie didn't think her squeaky-clean visitor would appreciate these details.

'We found physical evidence of another person at the crime scene.'

'You mean the murderer?'

Mrs Maclean positively relished the word, rolling the rs in her soft Edinburgh brogue. Maybe she did want the grisly details after all. Hattie decided that the Scotswoman wasn't going to get them from her.

'Possibly,' Hattie replied.

'That's fine then,' said the other woman, visibly brightening. 'You can just look him up. You've got a database of criminals, haven't you?'

If only it were that easy. Press a button and, bingo, here's your bad guy. Hattie kept the smile off her face as she said, 'We've not come up with a match so far. If this person has not been arrested then his profile won't be on the national DNA database.'

'I see.' Mrs Maclean didn't look as if she did. Her face had fallen again. 'Oh well, it's a cruel world, isn't it? It's just not nice when something terrible like this happens to your own.'

Excuse me?

Mrs Maclean was climbing to her feet but Hattie was resolved to get to the bottom of her change of heart before she departed.

'When we last spoke, Mrs Maclean, you gave me the impression that Mr Jacobs had ceased being involved with your family since you split up, which was in . . .'

'January nineteen seventy-eight,' Mrs Maclean supplied. 'You probably weren't even alive then, young lady.'

Hattie grinned. 'As a matter of fact, I was three.'

They were both standing, Hattie looking down into the shorter woman's face. She read something there that intrigued her. Maybe the former Mrs Jacobs only needed a little push to reveal the real purpose of her call.

'Forgive my impertinence, but what's made you change your opinion of your first husband?'

Mrs Maclean hesitated and fumbled with the buckle of her rather stylish handbag.

'Well, I know you must have lots of more important matters to deal with . . .' Her voice trailed off.

'This is a murder investigation, Mrs Maclean. There *are* no more important matters. Why don't you sit down again?'

The other woman subsided gratefully back into the chair. 'I'd rather,' she said, 'that you called me Jessie.'

*   *   *

Today, Roisin reminded herself, she could not give way to her feelings. At Leopardstown races, like the rest of the family, she was on parade and must not let anyone down. Black Mountain was running his first race for eight months and the eyes of the Irish racing world, and more, were on them.

Though she knew their motives were of the best, she wished people would think before they opened their mouths.

'Such a terrible tragedy your Noel's not here to see this day' was a sentiment expressed, with variations, by almost everybody she met. There was no reply she could make, not one that wouldn't

235

shatter her brittle composure into a million fragments, and so she just nodded or murmured 'Thank you' and changed the subject to the racing. The idea of discussing Noel's death and the whole ghastly drama of the ferry accident was too terrifying to contemplate.

Fortunately, Lewis was by her side every moment and he'd step in when she was having difficulties or squeeze her arm in a gesture of reassurance when some well-meaning acquaintance began running off at the mouth. She had an understanding with Lewis now, a secret one, and the knowledge that she'd said yes to him was a great comfort. On an occasion like this, she didn't know how she would have managed without him. She had to remind herself that this was a big day for him, his first race as Blackie's owner, and she mustn't spoil it.

She had to be strong for everybody, as she had been strong for the two months since Noel's death. But all she really wanted to do was to curl up in the dark and cry.

*   *   *

'Sorry, Hattie.' DI Pollock plonked the phone back into its cradle; it had interrupted their conversation twice so far and Hattie had only been in the room a couple of minutes. 'Why exactly did the Scottish widow pay you a visit?'

'She's not a widow. She divorced Basil Jacobs back in nineteen eighty and married again. Her second husband is still alive so technically—'

He cut her off with a wave of his hand and she cursed her tendency to be pedantic.

236

'She came because of her guilty conscience,' she said quickly.

This time she had his undivided attention.

'Are you telling me she confessed to his murder?'

'No, guv. She dismissed him as a grubby loser for twenty-five years. She expected him to end up in the gutter, she said so. And now she's feeling guilty because . . .' She hesitated for a beat. This was the good bit. 'Because he's left her over a million pounds.'

The DI's jaw literally dropped. 'I thought old Basil had bugger all,' he protested. 'I was told he lived in a fleapit and had five hundred quid in his current account.'

'That's right. He worked three mornings a week doing the books for a couple of shops and spent the afternoons dumping what he earned at Coral's and William Hill.'

'So what's the real story?'

'It turns out he made loads of money on the Stock Exchange through the eighties and nineties and played it canny when things went flat. That's what his solicitor told Jessie. Apart from some charity donations and money left to his local for a memorial booze-up, it was all bequeathed to her. After inheritance tax and other odds and sods she'll receive one point two mil and she's out there spending it as we speak.'

'Did she know she was in for this little windfall?'

'She swears blind she didn't. Her behaviour is certainly consistent with her story. For years she thought he was a dead loss and when he died she virtually said good riddance. Now she's having a little crisis of conscience.'

He nodded. 'Every silver lining has a cloud, I

237

suppose. Have a word with our friends in Lothian and Borders Police, just to see if the family checks out.'

'Even if she knew about the will, I don't think Jessie's got it in her to sneak down here and whack Basil on the head, guv.'

'Maybe not, but it always makes sense to check out the money trail.'

Pollock was already back on the phone before she had left the room.

*   *   *

At last Max Ashwood sat on Black Mountain in earnest.

About bloody time, he thought as Tom Dougherty legged him up in the parade ring at Leopardstown.

The attempt on the Bula Hurdle at Cheltenham back in December had been cancelled. In the circumstances, Max supposed that was reasonable. The irony was that Black Mountain, supposedly the most neurotic horse in training, had survived the palaver on the ferry without turning a hair. Safe in his horsebox with his pony companion, the horse had arrived fit and eager to race. Max thought they should have run him. It had been a real drag to miss out.

He flashed a smile at the knot of spectators around Black Mountain, just a quick one as he knew that gloom was still the preferred order of business at the Dougherty yard. Personally, he thought it was a bit over the top. Two months had gone by, for God's sake. Weren't the Irish supposed to be a carefree crowd? Seize the day and enjoy the *craic*, for tomorrow we snuff it. Like poor old Noel. Or Saint Noel, as some people would prefer him to be known.

It was understandable that old mother Dougherty would still be cut up about the accident but Roisin had turned into a gloomy stick, giving up her job and spending half her time back here in the Emerald Isle. And his father, of all people, wasn't much better, flying over to Kerry at every excuse to 'support' the Doughertys. Of course Lewis had his motives for holding Roisin's hand, which was another reason why Noel's death had proved so bloody inconvenient, giving Lewis the opportunity to make the big play for Roisin under the guise of Good Samaritan.

Max held his father's eye, reading more than encouragement in the steady gaze and shout of 'Good luck.' Lewis had stuck his neck out for him in opposing the trainer and insisting he was given the ride. Max couldn't afford to let him down. Just to add to the pressure, the international press were out in force to watch Black Mountain's first race in eight months.

The weather was keen and wet but it didn't deter the crowd who had turned out in their thousands and crammed into the bars, betting hall and restaurants. The weather wouldn't deter Black Mountain either, Max knew that much. He'd renewed his acquaintance with the horse over the past couple of days in the filthiest of west coast weather and the horse had been more than game. He seemed to revel in the worst the elements could throw at him.

Despite his lay-off and rumours about his wellbeing, Black Mountain was a very short-priced favourite. Tom Dougherty had him looking hard and ready to do battle. It made Max's spine tingle just to sit on him. Many people had been openly critical of him getting the ride on his father's horse but, sod them, he was as good a rider as any other and he'd bloody well shove it down their throats.

His only regret was that Cherry wasn't in the crowd to watch him do it. She had remained in England to do some job for Victor. Well, too bad. It was down to him and the horse.

'Come on, you black brute,' he muttered to the animal. 'Show me you're as good as you're cracked up to be.'

*   *   *

Cherry was spending the afternoon in about her least favourite place, the cellar of the Sussex farmhouse, with definitely her least favourite people, Chris and Brian Spot.

The subterranean room was furnished with a large oval table. Rucksacks and carrier bags were piled at one end and from the nearest spilled a jumbled pile of banknotes.

Victor's primary business, the importation and distribution of cocaine, generated a lot of money. But it was a strictly cash business and the revenue collected by Chris Spot's network of dealers filtered upwards in the same grubby tenners and twenties that had changed hands out on the street. Every so often the wads of cash had to be counted and, when it came down to it, Victor didn't trust anyone outside his inner circle to do the counting. In practice that meant himself, the Spots and, occasionally, Cherry. It was a job she hated. Being

240

alone with the lecherous Chris and his acid-tongued stick of a brother gave her the creeps.

Brian's eyes, like pale boiled sweets, fastened onto hers. 'I suppose you remember how to count?'

She ignored him and took a seat. Chris took the chair next to her, invading her personal space. Through the musk of his aftershave she could detect an undercurrent of body odour.

He turned to her with a jowly grin.

'So, Cherry baby,' he said, 'what colour knickers are you wearing today?'

It was going to be a long afternoon.

*   *   *

Max had always listened respectfully to Tom Dougherty's advice. He'd be a fool not to take on board the opinion of the trainer who had turned Black Mountain from a no-hoper into a world-beater. But, when it came down to it, a man's opinion was not fact; you couldn't touch it or set your watch by it. Even a man like Tom Dougherty could be wrong.

From Tom's information, and from what he'd observed himself on videos of past races, Black Mountain had just one way of running. It wasn't complicated: he simply went to the front and stayed there, relentlessly grinding the opposition into the dust. It took a special horse to win this way, one strong enough to make all the running and see off all challengers. But Black Mountain was a special horse and he'd not been beaten in the last two years.

Halfway round the two-mile course at Leopardstown, Max knew he had the race won.

241

The pair of them were a dozen lengths in the lead and the animal was eating up the ground beneath them as if he were possessed. To Max, there seemed no point in belting along like a hound of hell when there was no chasing pack to speak of. Ease off the gas, keep something in the tank for another day, that was his inclination.

But Tom had told him to keep the horse going at a good tempo. 'He's stronger than you think,' he'd said. 'You've never ridden a horse like Black Mountain before. When you think you're in top gear, you're still only in third.'

Max had no doubt about that, the horse was obviously a phenomenon. He could be doing handsprings on Black Mountain's back and they'd still win. Fifty yards from each flight of hurdles, Max could sense the horse weighing up his stride. And he was fast, like greased lightning, with so much strength and flair that he never had to get in close. When it came to jumping, it was just a long stride or a very long stride. This was a genuine champion hurdler and a bloody strong galloper to boot.

The one specific instruction Tom had given him beforehand was to kick for home at the last hurdle on the far side. They were approaching it now, still ten lengths ahead of the field. Surely Tom wouldn't think it necessary to gee him up in these circumstances? He kept sitting quietly. He had everything covered—or so he thought.

Turning out of the wide shallow bend into the home straight, Max sensed movement from the chasing group. He snatched a look over his shoulder and saw that a horse in blinkers had thrust out of the pack.

242

No problem. Max gave Black Mountain a smack on the shoulder and asked him to show what he could do.

To his alarm, there was no discernible increase in speed or effort from the horse beneath him. The other horse was pulling alongside now and, as they took the penultimate hurdle at the mouth of the home straight, they were overtaken.

Max was in a panic. This wasn't meant to happen! Where was the response from the so-called wonder horse? Where was his class? He expected a surge of power but that didn't happen. Black Mountain was galloping on as before. At one pace.

Though he'd spent time getting to know the horse at the yard, Max had no knowledge of him when it really mattered. Like right now, lying in second place with one hurdle left to jump in front of a packed stand at Leopardstown with every man jack of the watching throng expecting him to win.

How on earth could he face his father if he lost this race?

But, as Black Mountain cleared the last obstacle still two lengths down, he realised maybe he wasn't going to lose. He'd been looking for some pace from his mount and that hadn't been forthcoming. On the other hand, he was now aware of a gathering momentum in the long stride beneath him. Black Mountain was too big and formidable to react quickly, he needed time to get up to his top speed—time Max should have given him four furlongs from home. He should have kicked him on at the last hurdle as instructed.

But this was a horse who hated to be beaten. From the moment he'd sensed the competition

243

he'd been working hard to get a full head of steam into his huge frame. Thirty yards from the winning post, Max felt him hit top gear and knew he'd win after all.

How lucky was that? Max thought. There was the length of a city bus between the pair of them as he crossed the line but Max knew the truth of it. He'd squeaked home by a whisker.

$$* \qquad * \qquad *$$

Alan was familiar with the walk from the changing room to the parade ring at Newbury racecourse but today felt like the first time he'd ever done it. Everything about this occasion and the race ahead seemed different. For the first time ever he was taking part not just as a jockey but as part-owner and, in many respects, as part-trainer too. Today was Grain of Sand's debut as a jumper and Alan was more nervous ahead of a race than he had ever been before.

He wasn't the only one either. As he approached the disparate group of people huddling together in the sharp winter wind, he could see the tension in their faces. Even Linda Parsons, tricked out in a golden yellow fake-fur coat and gleaming black leather boots, looked suitably concerned. Cyril Ogilvie wore his habitual look of mild amusement but he was fussing anxiously with his gloves and ignoring any comments aimed in his direction. But Geoff Finney, Lee's father, was most visibly affected by the circumstances. He said nothing to Alan, just wrung his hand with the kind of intensity that left him in no doubt that Geoff was thinking of the events that had led them all to this point. Alan

244

had to put on a good show for the living, but more than anything he wanted to do his best for Lee.

Tim legged him up into the saddle and ushered him off without preamble. There wasn't much left to say.

Fortunately Sandy was not affected by human concerns. His ears were pricked and he was eager, Alan could tell. It had been some while since the horse had been to the races but he recognised the set-up and he liked it. He cantered happily down to the start, looking about him with some confidence.

It wasn't a big race, just a dozen runners in a novice hurdle, a couple of whom, like Grain of Sand, were making their debut. Notwithstanding his inexperience, Sandy was installed as the odds-on favourite. Word about how well he jumped must have got out. Tim had been more cynical. 'It's down to our Linda,' he'd said and it was true that La Parsons had featured on back and front pages posing with Sandy. Whatever the reason, it all added to the pressure of the occasion as far as Alan was concerned.

The thing to be aware of in novice events was horses swerving from left to right in front of you. If a horse didn't fancy jumping he would look for a way out. Quite often you could be on a good jumper with a clear view of the hurdles when suddenly a horse could steal your line and you'd have no space left to jump in.

Alan lined up on the inside, aiming tight to the wing. You needed to be brave to do this because, if your horse decided to run out, you'd have little time to react and the consequences were serious. But at least on the inside horses could only run across you from one direction.

Grain of Sand skipped over the first flight without any fuss and Alan kept him handily placed as they raced down the far side of the course. Everything his horse did, even in this soft ground, seemed effortless. As a cluster of half a dozen horses led round the far bend and into the straight he eased over to the stand side rail. There was still half a mile to go and three hurdles to jump.

Alan's plan had been to hold Sandy up for as long as possible but as he looked round he could see there was no point. He let out a reef of rein and in a matter of strides, the race was over. Alan allowed himself one more quick glance behind him after they had winged the last flight. There wasn't another animal within twenty lengths.

My God, this horse was seriously rapid.

They won by a country mile, easing down at the line, and Alan had not even touched him with the whip.

In the winner's enclosure, his fellow syndicate members showered the pair of them with hugs and handshakes and slaps on the back. All the pre-race tension had evaporated as swiftly as dew on a summer's day. Geoff looked as if a boulder had been lifted from his brawny shoulders.

'Lee would have been proud of you, son,' he said to Alan.

'Maybe,' Alan allowed, 'but he'd have been prouder of the horse.'

And that was the truth.

*　　*　　*

The narrow Sussex roads were dark and dangerous and Cherry forced herself to drive slowly, though

what she wanted to do above all was put her foot
down and fly back to London as fast as she could.
Her hands were shaking on the wheel. Really, she
shouldn't be driving at all.

The afternoon had been as nauseous as she had
anticipated. When she'd not responded to any of
Chris's coarse innuendo he'd begun to address his
remarks to his brother as if she weren't there,
referring to her as 'it'.

'It used to be quite tasty when Vic was shagging
it. Now I wouldn't touch it with a bargepole.'

There was much worse than that, of course, but
she didn't want to think about it.

Brian had cackled along to his brother's
crudities, just once turning to Cherry to say, 'You
know, now Victor's kicked you out of bed you
could always go back on the game.'

But the verbal abuse was not what had thrown
her off balance.

When they'd finished and the cash was stashed
away, she'd made for the stairs. Chris had barred
her path. Brian was still at the table, working with
his calculator.

'So what colour are they?' he said with a leer.
'Your knickers.'

'Get out of my way.'

She tried to push past but he grabbed her arm
and backed her up against the table.

'Get off me, you pig!'

But he pushed her down on the table so she was
bent over backwards, his big hands pinning her
arms above her head. Worse than that, a thigh like
a side of pork was thrust between her legs. Then he
had both her wrists in one big fist and he was
reaching down, pulling up her skirt.

She couldn't believe this was happening. She screamed at him and wriggled like a worm on a hook as she was bared to the waist.

Surely he wasn't going to rape her?

He smirked as he stared down at her.

'Baby blue. Very nice. Why didn't you tell us in the first place?'

Then he let her go.

She scrambled for the stairs and ran, their laughter in her ears. In her haste she fell full length on the gravel outside before she reached her car.

Now, as she drove back, her self-esteem wounded worse than her body, she forced herself to get a grip. Think of ways to even the score.

There'd been times during the day when the brothers had discussed business and she'd picked up some valuable titbits. Like Chris's next meeting with his Scouse contacts. And Brian's scheme to launder the cash they were counting through a third party.

What's more, they'd let slip the identity of the freelance money-launderer, a regular at Victor's club called Scott. Cherry didn't know much about him but she could soon rectify that.

But right now she couldn't wait to get home to Max.

Chapter Thirteen

Following Pollock's instructions, Hattie had done some homework on Jessie Maclean. According to the Edinburgh police, the family were upstanding members of the community; her husband was a

248

doctor and elder of the kirk. On the night of Basil's death the pair of them, accompanied by friends and family, had been celebrating their wedding anniversary at a local restaurant.

'I can send you the photos,' Jessie said. 'They're the kind with the date stamped on the back, so that would give us an alibi for the murder, wouldn't it?'

Jessie, Hattie had concluded, was a fan of police dramas on the TV.

This was their second long phone conversation since the woman's return to Scotland and Hattie had little doubt it would prove a waste of time. But there was something about Jessie's situation that intrigued her. She reckoned they'd hit it off well enough for her to try and satisfy her curiosity.

'Basil must really have loved you, mustn't he?'

There was a pause. Would Jessie bite? Eventually she said, 'It was so long ago.'

'And you must have loved him too.'

Jessie tutted softly. 'I suppose. I didn't know many people down in London, it was my first time away from home. Basil seemed a clever lad. I thought he'd go far.'

'Is that why you married him?'

'I married him because I was pregnant. My family are very strong in the kirk, like my husband. I had no choice.'

'So,' Hattie was calculating, 'you had a child with Basil?'

'I lost the baby. Three weeks after the wedding. If I hadn't been such a wee mouse, rushing to do the right thing, I need never have married him at all.'

And today you wouldn't have a million pounds burning a hole in your pocket, Hattie was tempted to say but held her peace. It must have looked as if life had played Jessie a cruel trick a quarter of a century ago, but her luck had turned. Hattie was fascinated.

'Is that when you left Basil?'

'Och no. I stayed with him for eighteen months. Then I realised he loved something else more than me.'

Hattie could guess what that was. 'Gambling?'

'Aye. It was poker two or three nights a week. He was away till midnight playing cards with his friends. It was as bad as if he was seeing some other woman. He promised to give it up but . . . When I realised he'd be out playing poker till the day he died, I left.' Jessie laughed softly. 'You know, my husband's very strict. He hates gambling. He wanted me to refuse Basil's money. Water from a poisoned well is what he called it.'

'But you don't agree?'

Jessie laughed again. 'At least I'll die in luxury, thanks to Basil. It turns out he was a clever lad after all.'

Hattie didn't disagree.

*   *   *

While the coffee brewed, Max flipped to the back pages of the paper. He soon found what he was looking for.

THE MOUNTAIN IS BACK—IRISH
WONDER HORSE
STEAMROLLERS ALL-COMERS
Even an eight-month lay-off, a tragic accident
at sea and a change of jockey could not derail

250

Black Mountain's winning streak at Leopardstown yesterday. In a masterly performance, the Kerry-based hurdler showed why he is still the hot favourite for the Champion Hurdle at Cheltenham in March.

The article continued in a similar vein; it was accompanied by a photo of Max and Black Mountain in the final dash for the line.

The writer had failed to spot that Max's tactics had nearly lost the race. Only Tom Dougherty had been aware of that and Max had made sure to have a quick word of apology before he'd dashed to catch his plane back to London. Tom hadn't said much—when did he ever?—but Lewis had seemed thrilled with the performance and that was what really counted.

But significant as this victory was—the best of his career and his first in Ireland—Max couldn't savour it in the way he would have wanted. The reason was on page nine of the same paper, in the gossip column. Beneath a photograph of Lewis with his arm round Roisin in the Dublin wind he read: 'Braving the elements at Leopardstown races yesterday, property tycoon Lewis Ashwood cheered home the latest acquisition to his equine portfolio, champion Irish hurdler Black Mountain. Helping to keep him warm was lovely Roisin Dougherty, daughter of the horse's legendary trainer, Tom. My information is that a spring wedding is a good bet but get your money on soon, the odds are shortening as we speak!'

Max wanted to dismiss this as pure tabloid tittle-tattle but it wasn't so easy to do. His father's intimacy with Roisin was developing just as the woman lying in his bed next door had predicted.

He wondered if Cherry was still asleep. He poured coffee into two cups and tucked the paper under his arm. If necessary, he'd wake her.

The room was dim but her hair gleamed golden on the pillow and the pale skin of her bare shoulder, turned towards him, seemed to reflect light.

His flight had got in at ten to seven the previous evening and he'd rung her all the way from the airport, bursting to tell her of his ride on Black Mountain. But he'd not been able to contact her. She'd told him she couldn't be sure when she'd be through with her job for Victor but expected she'd be free for dinner.

He hadn't become worried till around nine. By then he'd left messages on her home phone and her mobile. Where was she? Why hadn't she called him?

It was at that point, after half a bottle of wine, when anticipation had begun to curdle and anxiety turned to suspicion.

Precisely what was this mysterious job? She'd avoided giving him details—was that deliberate? The slower time dragged by, the likelier it seemed that the job was an excuse for something else. That was the trouble with going around with a woman who turned heads. You always had to worry that someone else was about to take her off your hands.

Cherry had eventually turned up at ten thirty, looking drawn and unkempt, in a skirt with a ripped hem and a dirt smudge down one cheek. Not that he noticed at first. She was the kind of woman who'd look good in a bin bag. To him she had the kind of tousled glow that came from

252

rushing straight from the bed of another man.

She stared at him for a moment in the doorway, her expression unfathomable, then flung herself into his arms. Guilt was how he interpreted it as she clung to him, shaking like a flu victim.

He dragged her inside and shut the door. 'Where have you been?' he hissed.

'I've been driving—I came straight here. Please, Max, just hold me.'

He gripped her as if he might break her in half. That was how he felt.

He was about to say, 'What's his name?' when she murmured, 'I thought they were going to rape me.'

That halted his suspicions in an instant.

She told him about being sent to an out-of-the-way farm on a job with two of Victor's men who had it in for her. Then he noticed her filthy hands and broken nails, and the gash on her ankle.

'I'll kill them,' he said. He felt like killing someone.

'No, Max, don't get involved. I know how to deal with them.'

He protested but, in the end, privately conceded it wouldn't be wise to take on Victor's guys. It hadn't made him feel any better.

Max had not seriously thought about her work. Personally, he liked Victor but being associated with such a sinister character wasn't good for Cherry any more. Not now she was part of his own life.

He'd gone to run her a bath and when he returned he found her weeping on the bed. By the time he'd finished comforting her, the bath was cold and he had to run her another. It was the first time he'd seen her cry.

Afterwards, when she'd crawled clean and damp into his arms, they'd not been capable of talking about anything. And there was something he had to say to her.

He put the coffee and the paper down on the bedside table and sat on the bed.

He laid a hand on the warm skin of her shoulder and gently shook her.

*   *   *

Cherry had not been asleep when Max came into the room. She'd been replaying the events of the day before, pondering her moves. What should she say to Victor? How should she behave when she next saw Brian and Chris? She had a fair idea how she was going to get even, but what was the best way to conduct herself so that suspicion would not fall on her?

Then there was Max. The intensity of her reaction the night before had taken her by surprise. She'd needed Max's arms around her. She'd looked for strength, sympathy, passion, and she'd found it. That was a surprise too. She felt his hand on her shoulder and allowed herself to be turned towards him, opening her eyes.

'How do you feel?'

She smiled at him lazily. 'Better.'

'I've brought you coffee. And I thought you'd be interested in my write-up in the paper.'

How sweet. She sipped from the cup and flicked her eyes over the race report. 'Fantastic,' she said. She supposed it was expected.

'There's more.' He turned the pages to the

254

photo of Lewis and Roisin. Since their conversation a couple of months ago, in the hotel in Kerry near the Doughertys, Cherry had not gone out of her way to put the poison in. She hadn't needed to.

'It's only newspaper talk,' she said after she'd read it. 'They look good together though, don't they?'

He stabbed at the page angrily. 'This is just the beginning. They'll be selling the ruddy wedding to *Hello!* next.'

She shrugged. 'If that's how it works out. You'll have to learn to live with it, Max. There's nothing you can do.'

'I've been thinking.' He took the paper away from her and gripped her hands in his. 'Suppose you and I get married.'

Her heart thumped. This was a genuine shock.

'I'm serious,' he said, reading the consternation on her face. 'Look, I'm on my knees.'

He was too, he'd slipped off the bed and was kneeling on the floor.

Careful, she told herself. Play this cool. Don't let him think you trapped him in a moment of weakness.

'You want to marry me just to beat your father to the altar?'

'No!' He gripped her fingers tightly and leaned over her, his face inches from hers, his eyes blazing. His intensity thrilled her. 'Look, I don't want you carrying on with Victor, working with those evil bastards. Make an honest man of me instead.'

'What about your father? Are you sure you're not just saying this to steal his thunder?'

'Don't be stupid. He's desperate for me to have

255

a good woman at my side. He'll be thrilled.'

Cherry wasn't so certain of that.

'Come on, darling, put me out of my misery. Yes or no?'

It was yes of course.

'I've got one proviso, Max. If your father doesn't approve, we'd better think again.'

'Of course he'll approve. And if he doesn't, so what? It's our happiness at stake here, not his.'

She liked the sound of that. My happiness as Cherry Ashwood, daughter-in-law to a chunk of number sixty-three on the *Sunday Times* Rich List. She'd sell Victor Bishop down the river to Janice and escape into jet-set land. Houses, yachts and the very best lawyers; she could leave her past behind and become a new person.

She loosened her hands from his grip and placed them round his neck.

'OK then, Max. I accept. I'll marry you.'

His mouth descended on hers. It was a good kiss.

When they broke for air, he murmured, 'I forgot to say. I love you.'

'Me, too,' she breathed.

Maybe she really did.

*   *   *

Alan should have been on top of the world. Yesterday's performance by Grain of Sand had been all that he could have hoped for. The syndicate's pre-race tension had been transformed into post-race ecstasy and the whole group had repaired to Linda's hotel for an early celebration supper that had extended late into the evening. The bill had far exceeded the prize money for winning the race.

What's more, the evening had yielded a small job. Cyril Ogilvie had asked him to cast an eye over a novice chaser while he was riding at Plumpton. It was pleasing that the bookseller valued his opinion enough to pay him for it and it kept the flame of Blades Bloodstock burning.

Alan had been trying as best he could to develop the business he'd started with Lee. On days when he wasn't race-riding he was looking for either horses or buyers. Every horse was assessed for potential and value. As it turned out, in this case there was nothing to report. The horse looked all right but he didn't use himself properly when jumping. If he had to get in close, he was awkward and clumsy and Alan knew that he would be a poor jumper for the rest of his life. Horses either had talent or they didn't. The animal he rode himself wasn't much better and finished way down the field.

All in all, it wasn't a great day.

Alan was about to leave when he spotted Jane leading round a runner for the last.

*   *   *

Cherry looked at the bouquet of red and white roses lying on her desk. Next to it was an open, tissue-lined box containing a cashmere sweater of dusty pink.

Victor stood in the doorway, gauging her reaction.

'I still want a proper apology from those two,' she said.

He nodded thoughtfully. 'I wouldn't set your

257

heart on it, darling. I reckon this is the best you're going to get.'

She savoured the texture of the sweater between finger and thumb; soft, silky smooth and expensive. It wasn't enough.

'They treated me like dirt. They said—' She stopped herself. She'd made a point of never telling tales to Victor; it was poor strategy and, in any case, Vic always found out the truth. 'Anyway, I bet they never even bought this stuff. You did.'

He grinned. 'I know your size, sweetheart.'

'OK.' Time to step back. 'Just don't ever send me off to work with them on my own again. I don't trust them.'

'Sure.'

She held the sweater up against her reflection in the mirror. 'Thanks, Vic. This is lovely.'

After he'd gone, she walked as far as the park and dialled a number on her cheap, pay-as-you-go phone.

'This is Scorpio. I've got some information for you . . .'

*   *   *

Alan waited for Jane to come round again.

'How about a drink after this?' he suggested. It had been a while since they had caught up.

She hesitated. She'd mentioned to him in the past that Donovan, her boyfriend, was jealous of her past relationship with Alan.

'Yeah, go on,' she said finally and named an out-of-the-way pub they'd used before. 'I'll be buying,' she added. 'Wild Willy here's going to hack up in this race.'

Alan stayed on to watch and, after a bright start, Wild Willy faded on the run-in and finished well down the field. It looked like he'd be the one doing the buying tonight.

*   *   *

Chris Spot had only ever served one serious length of time in prison: ten years for armed robbery, reduced to seven on appeal, of which he'd served five. He'd got out at the age of twenty-eight and not done an honest day's work since, which meant he'd spent almost twenty years outside the law and outside prison—quite a result. He put his survival down to a combination of factors—skill, caution and paranoia being among them. 'And the greatest of these,' he'd often said to his brother, 'is luck.' He was well aware of what a lucky bugger he was.

He got the all-clear from the Scouse crew as he was twiddling with the car radio, trying to get Talk Sport. The prat who'd been using this jam jar had tuned all the stations to Radio One. He'd have to have a word.

He gave up on the radio and called Olly for an OK on the handover point, a lay-by on the road towards Billingshurst.

'There's been three cars in the last hour,' said Olly. 'One bloke had a ten-minute kip, the others had a quick leak and scarpered. It's all cool right now.'

Cool? Who did Olly think he was? Come to think of it, he was probably the bloke who'd mucked up the car radio. Anyhow, it was time to get weaving.

The lay-by was on the top of a gentle hill, with

views along the road in both directions. That's why he liked it. Over the years he'd offloaded in many locations but none of them was as good as this. The Scousers knew it too, which made it suitable for this evening's business. He wouldn't have used the same RV twice but he trusted Sefton Billy. He ought to, the hairy Scouse git was married to his niece.

He parked up just inside the entrance to the lay-by, reversing so that he was facing the exit slip. No point in hanging around once the business was done. He could see Olly's vehicle on the far side, just on the edge of the amber pool of light spilling from the toilet block, the only building in the clearing.

He got out, zipping his jacket up tight. He'd give Olly cool—it was bloody freezing.

Down at the bottom of the hill he could make out a pair of headlights approaching from the north. He watched the car climb the hill and make the turn. An old Escort slowed to a crawl and a youthful face peered at him from the passenger side as the car crept past. Chris recognised one of Billy's boys.

The Escort parked out of the light and two men got out. One of them, the passenger, walked briskly over to Chris, pulling a cigarette pack from his pocket. Chris refused the offer, he'd given them up after lung cancer took his dad. He could see the other man, the driver, making a call on his phone. He'd be telling Billy all was cool, no doubt. It wouldn't be long now.

*　　　*　　　*

Alan was wondering what had happened to Jane.

He'd been nursing his half pint in the pub for almost an hour and wondered if he'd been stood up. He picked up his phone and dialled again. He had two numbers for her, a mobile and one for the flat she shared with another girl from Rafter's yard. The mobile, as before, was turned off and no one answered at the flat.

He had the address of Jane's flat; it was probably worth going by, if only to push a note through the door. To his surprise, the door was opened when he knocked. The girl inside was still wearing a coat—she must have just got in. Jane wasn't with her.

'I wasn't expecting her,' said her flatmate. 'She's probably out with Don.'

'When will she be back?'

She gave him a satirical look, the kind you give to someone slow on the uptake. 'I don't think she will be. Not tonight anyway.'

So he *had* been stood up. Obviously this Donovan had snapped his fingers and all thoughts of her arrangement with himself had gone out of her head. He stamped irritably back to his car.

* * *

In the lay-by, three minutes crept past, with the Scouse kid sucking on his gasper and polluting the night air. Chris was tempted to tell him he was signing his own death warrant but saved his breath as a car's lights lanced through the night air. A minute later, a Range Rover pulled into the car park and circled the area, coming to rest beside Chris's car. Sefton Billy, teeth and blond-streaked hair gleaming in the soft light, gripped Chris's

261

hand. Chris could see why young Haley had fallen for him.

But now was not the time for social pleasantries.

'Got the gear?' Billy said. He was holding a briefcase in his other hand.

Chris nodded and opened the boot of his car. The drugs were packed in two cardboard cartons labelled Tate & Lyle. He opened the first and moved aside the top layer of sugar bags.

Billy gave the goods a quick check and nodded. 'Jacko,' he said and the kid loaded the first box into the back of the Range Rover.

Billy put his briefcase into the boot of Chris's car and Chris was about to open it, just to look at the money, when everything went pear-shaped.

Lights blazed around them and, beyond, dark shapes leaped out of the bushes.

Voices were screaming: 'Stay right there! Customs and Excise!'

Chris wasn't having any of that. He slammed the boot shut and ran to get into the car. A hand landed on his shoulder and he ducked and squirmed, jabbing with his elbow even as he yanked the door open.

His assailant clung on, trying to force his arm up behind his back, and Chris had to turn and smack him with his other hand, twice, both good shots out of the old boxing locker. The man dropped away and Chris scrambled for the driver's seat. He was half inside when—*crunch!*—the door was slammed on his leg, then he was yanked from the vehicle and thrown to the ground. A foot thudded into his groin, sending a dizzy wave of agony through his body. Then a weight descended on his chest, cutting off his shout of pain. He found himself being rolled onto his face and, through a mist, dimly heard the metallic click of handcuffs.

As his cheek, wet with blood and tears, was pressed into the gravel, a voice whispered in his ear, 'Give up, mate. You're going nowhere.'

The worst thing was, it belonged to a woman.

Chapter Fourteen

Lewis raised his voice above the hubbub in the Canary Wharf bar, trying hard to minimise his disapproval. 'It's a bit sudden, isn't it? You've only known her a couple of months.'

'So what?' Max thrust his jaw out in the petulant fashion his father knew so well. 'Two months is a long time.'

'For you maybe.' Lewis finished his drink—Roisin had him on slim-line tonic—and longed for something stronger. No, he mustn't.

'You sound like some father in a Victorian play. You'll be asking if she's bringing a dowry next.'

Lewis didn't want to argue. Max had been shaping up well recently and he'd put that down to Cherry. And the events of last December—the death of Roisin's brother, God rest his soul—had sobered everybody up.

'Cherry is a lovely girl. All I'm saying is, what's the rush? Take your time and get to know her better. Make sure she's the right woman for you.'

'Like you're doing with Roisin?'

Lewis had known that would come up. He wondered how much his relationship with Roisin had to do with Max's sudden decision to get married, as if marriage was the preserve of the younger generation. Or was it just the boy's urge to compete?

'Son, I don't know what's going to happen to Roisin and me.'

'But you know what you'd like to happen, don't you?'

Lewis did indeed. He'd lost his heart to the Irish beauty and he hoped his long campaign to wear down her resistance was reaching an end. He was so close. They had a private agreement but she refused to acknowledge it openly, saying it was too near to her brother's death.

Anyway, he had no intention of having the subject of this present conversation sidetracked by Max. His affair with Roisin had no parallel with his son's sudden infatuation.

'Have you even met Cherry's family?' he demanded.

'Her mother's in Australia and she has no contact with her dad. She doesn't know where he is.'

'So she's got no family to speak of.'

'So what? I love her, Dad. You said yourself I should find a good woman and settle down. And you think she's great, don't you? That's what you said.'

Lewis lifted his glass reflexively to his lips. Of course, it was empty. He said the only thing he could in the circumstances.

'Congratulations, son.'

Then he pushed his way to the bar to get them both a proper drink.

* * *

264

'Here you are, one fancy lager and a dry white wine.' Janice set the glasses down on the table and said to Ray, 'If you ask me, she ought to be getting them in for us.'

Cherry knew this was a cue for her to ask why but she disliked giving the woman the satisfaction. She'd find out soon enough.

Janice had insisted they all meet face to face which, in the circumstances, was lunacy. With the arrest of Chris Spot, Victor and his crew were on a war footing and paranoia was running rife. On the other hand, Victor was now spending so much time away from the club, plotting damage limitation with Brian, that he'd never notice her absence. She'd insisted on picking the location: the bar of a restaurant on the top of a west London shopping centre. The risk was minimal.

Janice was smirking at her over her glass. 'I paid Chris Spot out for you. You should be grateful.'

Ray was grinning too. 'You should have seen her. Just about kicked his balls into the middle of next week.'

That didn't surprise Cherry. She could imagine Janice wading in with her feet and fists. Not that Cherry could allow herself to show any kind of gratitude to these two. Given half a chance, Janice would do the same to her.

'So why have you dragged me out here?' she said. 'Vic's in a complete lather about Chris. I've got to be bloody careful.'

'Sorry, but we want you to look at some photos.' Ray's unexpected apology was interesting. For the first time he was conceding her value to their operation.

He slid a plastic envelope across the table towards her. Inside were a series of small photographs; head shots of three men, each in full face and profile. She knew them all. They'd been picked up with Chris as a result of her tip-off.

'What can you tell us about these characters?'

She thought of refusing, stringing it out at least, on the principle that it went against the grain to make it easy for them. On the other hand, the sooner this meeting was over the better.

She identified them all and they homed in on Billy, picking her brains about Chris's deals with him: how often, how big, when and where. He was a vicious little toad and it was a pleasure coughing every little detail she knew about him.

Finally, Ray put his notebook away and stood up, signalling the end of their meeting.

'You're doing the right thing, you know,' he said.

Was she? One thing was sure, there was no going back. With Chris Spot out of the picture and looking at serious time, she had dealt Victor's operation a serious blow. This was the time to land another.

'Sit down,' she said. 'There's someone else you should know about.'

Then she told them about the handsome American, Brian Spot's money-launderer.

*   *   *

Alan had been puzzling over Jane's failure to keep their rendezvous after the meeting at Plumpton. Though it was possible she'd been sidetracked by Donovan, it wasn't like her not to make contact the next day and apologise. He wanted to ask her about the runners from Ian Rafter's yard that had failed to perform, like Nightswimmer at Towcester and Wild Willy the other day. Maybe she could shed some light on what was going on.

After he finished schooling Grain of Sand, he climbed into his car and headed south for Ian Rafter's yard. He'd catch Jane as she finished work. If she didn't want to talk to him she could tell him so to his face.

He reached the yard too late and was told she'd already left for home. Ten minutes later he was outside her flat. As before, the flatmate—Diana, he'd now discovered—came to the door.

'She's not here.'

'Déjà vu all over again then.' He grinned, she didn't.

'Sorry,' she said and began to close the door.

He stepped into the doorway. 'But that's her car outside, isn't it?' He'd noticed it on the way in, an ancient green and white Mini of which Jane was proud.

To her credit, Diana looked uncomfortable. Alan had no doubt she'd been put on the spot. As she hesitated, Jane stepped into view behind her.

'It's OK, Di,' she said. With a shrug, the other girl disappeared back inside.

Jane looked all right physically. But Alan didn't recognise the uncertain smile as she offered her cheek to be kissed.

'Sorry about the other night, Al. I meant to call you.'

She hadn't invited him in. He drew the obvious conclusion—the boyfriend must be inside—but he made his offer anyway. 'How about a quick drink?'

She shook her head firmly.

'Tomorrow then? You choose.'

'I don't think it would be a good idea.'

'For God's sake, Jane, I'm just a mate. Bring Donovan along too, if you like.'

She shot him a look of panic. What kind of weird relationship had she got herself into?

He made a final plea. 'Jane, I have to talk to you about some of Rafter's horses.'

'Sorry, Al,' she said, stepping back.

'Please. It might help. I'm still trying to find out how Lee died.' She knew how important Lee was to him.

She squeezed his arm. 'I can't,' she whispered and closed the door in his face.

As Alan drove home he replayed the exchange in his head. The Jane who'd shut the door on him wasn't the Jane he knew. She'd put a barrier between them. There was only one reason she would do that. Someone had told her to keep her mouth shut about Wild Willy and Nightswimmer. It reminded him of the way Kevin had behaved over Lee's fall from Olympia at Haydock.

*   *   *

'I think that's fantastic news.' Roisin forced as much enthusiasm into her voice as she could muster. 'You must be very pleased.'

'Hardly.'

The reception on Roisin's mobile wasn't so good at the Dougherty farmhouse, but she could picture the grim expression on Lewis's face as he sat at his office desk in Canary Wharf.

'He's only been seeing this girl for five minutes,' he continued. 'He barely knows her.'

Roisin sat in the broken-down armchair by the window and turned her gaze to the hillside and the wedge of slate-grey sea beyond. This was the view from the window of Noel's room, the reason why he'd positioned this chair just so while he listened to his music and scribbled plans for the yard on a notepad. Noel's things were all around her now, his CDs and books piled on the shelves, his papers scattered over the desk, letters and photographs stuffed into the drawers, his clothes hanging in the big old mahogany wardrobe. All her brother's life was here in this room where he'd lived, on and off, since he'd come home from the hospital as a baby.

No wonder her mother couldn't face stepping over the threshold. And so it was left to Roisin to make sense of it. She'd been at it all day and had made little progress. It was hard. It was all she had left of her brother—how could she bear to throw any of it away? Every scrap of paper seemed precious. But it had to be done. Connor was to have this big beautiful room. Noel would have wanted it that way.

So Lewis's phone call was welcome. She mustn't allow herself to become maudlin.

Nevertheless it was a wrench to shift her thoughts to his grumbles about Max and Cherry. She felt good about this news—why shouldn't they get married? On their short acquaintance, she could tell that Cherry hadn't been born with a hatful of advantages like Max. She was smart, she was beautiful and she had a good job, making a living in the real world. She couldn't claim to know Cherry but she had her vote.

She said as much to Lewis.

'I guess you're right,' he conceded. 'I'm

beginning to think you're always right.'

She laughed. His voice was warm and deep. Comforting.

'So when are you coming back?' he asked. 'I need you here, as you can tell.'

Did he? Did he really need her? It constantly amazed her that a man so self-assured—and successful and powerful and all that that brought with it—should need someone as ignorant and insubstantial as herself.

He was waiting for an answer.

'I'm still trying to sort out Noel's room.'

'Ah.'

'It's terrible, Lewis. His whole life is here.'

'A lot of yours, too, I imagine.'

Was that what made it so difficult? The thought that packing away Noel's things was like putting away bits of her own past that she'd never see again.

She found she was crying. She couldn't help it. He was forced to listen to her tears.

Eventually she stopped. 'I'm sorry.'

'That's OK. You need to cry.'

'Yes, but I mustn't, not here. Not in front of Mum or Dad or Con.'

'That's what you've got me for, Roisin. You can always cry on my shoulder.'

She'd done the right thing in agreeing to marry him. She was sure of it.

*   *   *

When he reached home, Alan made straight for the spare room upstairs. This was the place where he stored all the stuff he didn't want to throw out.

270

There were three months' worth of the *Racing Beacon* stacked on the chest of drawers, assorted golf clubs and a fishing rod, plastic bags of clothes he intended to take to a charity shop and a deconstructed table-tennis table—among other things. It took him a couple of minutes to locate what he was after. He took it down to the kitchen to examine in detail.

He'd not given much thought to the box of Kevin's belongings that he'd been given last year. At the time he'd taken it off the hands of the young couple at Kevin's old flat, he'd imagined he might use it to get into the stablehand's good books when he next turned up. At any rate, it gave him a connection to the lanky lad that might make it easier to get him to open up. But Kevin had not reappeared.

Though Alan didn't like to pry into another man's things, he'd had a quick look inside the carton before he put it away. All it contained were a couple of well-thumbed paperbacks, some magazines—Kevin evidently lusted after classic cars—and a jiffy bag full of cards and envelopes.

Now Alan examined the contents more closely. The cards were old birthday and Christmas greetings, the envelopes—blue, square, bearing Kevin's name and address—all written with the same fountain-penned flourish.

He pulled out the first. 'Dear Kevin, It was very nice to speak to you yesterday as it always is. Da says he is very sorry he missed you but he was held up on his last delivery because O'Riordan needed a hand with a ram who'd fallen into a ramshackle well out by the old pigsty.' And so it went on. It was signed 'your loving Ma', as were all the others.

271

Surely Kevin's mother must know where he had gone?

Or maybe Kevin had simply returned home? He examined the envelopes. They were all posted from County Limerick in Ireland. There was no printed address on the blue lined paper, just a handwritten heading, 'Barn House', on each one.

That was frustrating. How many Barn Houses might there be in the whole of Limerick?

As he packed the stuff away, a white envelope fell out of a magazine. Inside was a photograph. Alan hardly recognised Kevin but the beanpole with a smiling face couldn't be anyone else. The reason for the smile was tucked into the crook of his arm, her hair tied back off her face, looking up at him with an expression of adoration. Alan recognised her as Frankie, a stable girl from Tim's yard.

Once or twice, when he'd run into Frankie, he'd raised the subject of Kevin's disappearance. He'd told her he'd got a box of Kevin's things he wanted to give back but she'd not been helpful. Now he understood why.

He put the white envelope to one side.

*   *   *

All day, Victor's electronics guy had been busy about the club. Cherry presumed he was checking for listening devices, one of his regular duties; today he spent twice as long as usual. Later, Victor returned with Brian and they closeted themselves in the back basement room where there was a firewall guaranteed to thwart all bugs.

Throughout the evening people were shown

272

down the back stairs to the small windowless office. Cherry recognised some of them, Chris Spot's wife, for one, and Trevor Smailes, Victor's solicitor, who had been sitting in on the police interviews with Chris.

Victor appeared at about nine and stood on the back patio, chewing on a cigarette. At the sight of his hunched shoulders and bowed head, Cherry felt her stomach clench. Someone—maybe many people—would suffer as a result of Chris's arrest. But she forced a sympathetic expression onto her face and stepped outside. It was a risk worth taking, she reckoned.

He turned at her approach.

'Are you OK, Vic?'

He shrugged and flipped his cigarette butt into the line of shrubs that flanked the paving.

'We can't get him out of this one, sweetheart. Trev's a miracle worker but his hands are tied.'

Cherry imagined they would be, considering Chris had been caught in the act of selling fifteen kilos of cocaine, so Ray had said, out of the boot of his car.

She slipped a hand into his. 'I'm sorry.'

The silence that followed was companionable. Maybe now was the moment.

'This isn't great timing, Vic, but I want you to know before anyone else. Max has asked me to marry him.'

He looked at her, his face unreadable. 'And what did you say?'

'Yes.'

'Well, blow me.' His eyes lit up. He was pleased—what a relief. 'Good for you, girl.'

'You don't mind, do you?'

'Why the flaming hell should I?' He laughed and grabbed her by the shoulders to kiss her lustily on both cheeks. 'After all,' he added, 'I wasn't thinking of asking you myself.'

She risked a wistful lingering stare. 'Once upon a time, eh?'

He returned her look. 'And a bloody good time it was too.'

'Vic.' A voice came from the doorway, bringing the moment to an end. Good timing, she thought.

The tension returned to his face. 'Gotta go, sweetheart. Remember me to your future father-in-law, won't you?'

Cherry watched him go. So he was still interested in Lewis, was he? No wonder he approved of her and Max. But if he was counting on her to further his cause with Lewis he was going to be disappointed. Once she was an Ashwood, all that would be behind her.

*   *   *

Alan looked out for Frankie when he went up to the yard.

'Look,' he said, when he found her chopping carrots. 'I went through that box of Kevin's things.'

She said nothing but her eyes accused.

'Maybe I did the wrong thing but it doesn't look like he's coming back and it might have been junk. Anyway, I found this.' He handed her the white envelope and watched her remove the photograph. 'I thought you should have it.'

She gazed at it for a long moment. 'I didn't think he'd keep it.'

'You look good together. I didn't realise you

were an item.'

'We weren't. Not really.' She turned her gaze on Alan. 'It was a secret between us. A very short-lived secret.'

'I won't tell anyone, I promise you.'

She shrugged. 'Doesn't much matter now, does it?'

'I found a lot of letters from his mother in Ireland. I was wondering, did he ever say exactly where she lived?'

She frowned. 'Why do you want to know?'

'Well . . .' This was awkward, he wasn't sure how he was going to use the information. 'His mother must know where he is, don't you think?'

'But why are you so desperate to find him? So you can give him back a pile of old letters? Or so you can hassle him some more about how that jockey died?'

Yes was the answer to that question. Because 'that jockey' was his best friend who had died because somebody had fixed the horse he was riding. Because Kevin must know more than he'd let on. Because, frankly, he deserved to be 'hassled'.

Alan tried to think of a way of putting it without alienating Frankie completely.

To his surprise, as he stood there searching for the words, she said, 'Concommon. It's in Limerick. His father sells agricultural equipment.'

Barn House, Concommon, Limerick. He ought to be able to track Kevin's mother down from that. Directory enquiries should be able to supply a number.

'If you're going to get in touch with him,' Frankie said, 'you might as well give him this.' She placed the white envelope in his hand. 'I've got a copy.'

She turned back to her carrots. He was dismissed.

* * *

Lewis ignored his in-tray, the draft minutes of the board meeting and the list of callbacks Jackie had compiled, and concentrated on the slim sheaf of papers in the file on his desk. The information had come back quicker than he expected and in greater detail. He'd not often had cause to use private detectives but they'd always proved bloody good. How he wished, in this instance, that it wasn't the case. Though his suspicions had been abundantly justified, it gave him no satisfaction to have proof that his only son was intending to marry a crook.

Cherry Hamilton, it appeared, had been born Tricia Wilkins—at least, that's what it said on her juvenile court records. All her teenage convictions for shoplifting and soliciting had been in that name, so too a report in the *Littlemouth Gazette* of the fifteen-year-old girl who had beaten all-comers in the Easter Laser Regatta. A photocopied cutting showed a stick-thin blonde girl clinging to a trophy of FA Cup-sized proportions: 'Local girl Tricia beats the boys,' read the caption. But by the time the same paper reported the divorce proceedings of south coast supermarket tycoon Derrick Stevens she had become 'nightclub hostess Cherry Hamilton'. In the accompanying photos—there were several—stick-thin Tricia had changed more than her name. The man in Lewis responded to the stockings-and-cleavage display; the father in him

276

deeply disapproved of the 'red-hot heart-breaker' having any say in his son's life.

But what really set his hackles rising were the final pages of the report. A photograph of Cherry at a charity dinner at Grosvenor House, looking much as she did now, on the arm of Victor Bishop was followed by a brief summation: 'According to hitherto reliable sources, CH was the mistress of gambler/playboy Victor Bishop for three years. She currently works at his club in south London in an indeterminate capacity.'

So much for the devious bitch's job in marketing.

He read through the folder twice more. This relationship had to be stopped. No matter how attractive she was, a woman like this—a convicted thief and prostitute, an acknowledged home-wrecker, an associate of the deeply suspicious Victor Bishop, a person who had flagrantly misrepresented herself in every way—could not be allowed into his family.

The question was, how much did Max know of all this?

Lewis reached for the phone. He intended to find out.

*   *   *

Since her engagement—how unbelievable to be 'engaged'—Cherry had headed home at night to Max's flat in Holland Park rather than her Fulham cottage. Already quite a few of her belongings had found a home there, in his wardrobes and closets and in his kitchen drawers. Each time she'd brought some stuff over she'd asked him if he was happy about it and he'd looked at her in surprise,

277

as if it was unnecessary for her to ask. But she was anxious not to act as if she was taking him for granted. She knew well enough that small matters as well as large ones were capable of screwing things up.

Tonight when he opened the door she could see that something was wrong. His kiss was perfunctory and he walked ahead of her into the living room where she could see he was already stuck into the whisky. He sat on the sofa and reached for one of his racing papers. She didn't like the look of it.

Cherry fetched her own glass and took a seat opposite him. He was a sulker, she'd learned that much about him. He liked to brood on things and make you feel guilty while you guessed what you were supposed to have done.

'What's the matter?' she said. She might as well get it out into the open right away.

'Who says anything's the matter,' he looked up from the page, his eyes burning with reproach, '*Tricia*.'

The hated name stung like a slap in the face. How had he discovered that?

'Tricia Wilkins, isn't it?'

Knowing the name wasn't significant, but what else had he found out about her?

She met his gaze and answered as coolly as she could. 'I changed it. It's not a crime, is it?'

'No, but shoplifting is. And selling your body on the street.'

'I see.' She didn't smoke these days but she'd kill for a cigarette right now to steady her nerves. She had to play this just right.

'So you've been investigating my past?' She kept her voice as cool as she was able. 'Did you hire a

278

private eye?'

'I didn't. My father did.'

So that was it. Should she have anticipated this development? Not that there was anything she could have done about it.

'I'm flattered.' She forced a smile.

'Don't make a joke out of it, Cherry. This is serious. He doesn't want us to get married.'

She noted the 'he' and 'us'. So, for the moment anyway, they were still a team. Lewis couldn't have anything really incriminating on her, could he? Not like her friends Janice and Ray.

'What else has this private eye dug up on me? What other crimes am I accused of?'

He took a brown A4 envelope from the side table and threw it in her direction. It landed on the floor at her feet. She noted the words 'By hand' scrawled across the front and the yellow sticker of the courier company. Lewis must have biked it over that day.

She picked it up and leafed through the contents.

It was embarrassing to come face to face with her juvenile indiscretions. And the old photos—it was like looking at a once-close friend who was now a stranger. She could weep for her fifteen-year-old self clutching that silly regatta cup. But that was not what was required right now.

'Where do you want me to start?' she said. 'Or shall I just leave?'

It was a gamble, he could say yes. But she was pretty sure he wouldn't have the nerve to call her bluff. After all, he said he was in love with her.

'Tell me you never worked as a prostitute, Cherry.'

Of course that would be the most important thing to him. No man wants to marry a real whore, even though it's the pretend whore that attracts them in the first place.

She topped up his glass, then hers, rehearsing what she was going to tell him. The truth was what was required, some of it anyway.

'My mum and dad married young and had me straight away. Mum was only nineteen. Really pretty. Dad was her first proper boyfriend. She told me she was stupid to marry the first man who got her into bed. She didn't like having a baby around, it really cramped her style with men.' Cherry realised she might not be helping her cause by painting her mother as a bit of a tart. But she'd decided to tell the truth. 'Anyhow, my parents didn't get on. They always said they stayed together because of me. Until I was twelve, when my father left us. It wasn't just my mother screwing around, he found another woman and buggered off to live with her in Manchester. I loved my dad. He always had time for me. He taught me to sail and we spent our weekends in boats while Mum pleased herself. So I tried to go with him to Manchester but I wasn't wanted there. Barbara had two teenage children already and she didn't want another. And her kids were horrible to me. So I had to live with Mum. I've never forgiven Dad for letting that happen. I thought he loved me, then I realised he didn't love me enough. I've never seen him since.'

She sipped her drink, letting the spirit trickle and burn down her throat. Talking about Dad was difficult and Max wouldn't want to hear a sob story anyway.

'So, living with Mum while she went through a

string of live-in replacements for my father wasn't much fun. I hated them all and I hated Mum even worse. Naturally I did everything I could to get her attention—staying out all night, smoking lots of dope, sleeping around. There were lots of scenes and rows so I ran away. That's when I got in trouble with the police. Do you really want chapter and verse, Max? You can imagine it, can't you?'

'What about this charge of soliciting?'

She was getting to that.

'I had to have money. I knew other girls who did it, so why not? And, of course, there was a man: Mickey, hair down to his arse, rode a five hundred cc motorbike, was ten years older than me—the usual trophy rebellion boyfriend. He got me picking up guys at chucking-out time round the city pubs. That's how it came about. And I didn't enjoy any of it, if that's what you really want to know.'

He looked sheepish and asked softly, 'How did you get out of all that?'

Just how had she? It was remarkable, looking back. It had been no thanks to either of her parents.

'I still liked sailing and I was pretty good. I crewed for all sorts at the yacht club. That's how I met Derrick.'

'The supermarket bloke? I thought you picked him up in a nightclub. Like you did me.'

'I started sailing with him. He had a fantastic boat, a thirty-five-foot cruiser, but he didn't really know how to handle her. Lots of us used to crew with him but he took a shine to me.'

'Father figure,' said Max.

It wasn't a particularly perceptive intervention but she welcomed it. She was carrying him with her,

281

at least.

'Derrick got me to go to college, he let me sleep on his boat until I could sort out a bedsit and he gave me money.'

'In return for what?'

She shrugged. 'We were close, both of us had things to give the other, he made me feel good about myself. But when I wanted to move on, he didn't want to let go. I got a job behind the bar at some dive—it wasn't a proper nightclub—and I started meeting men more my age. Then Derrick's wife started cutting up really rough and made a meal out of their divorce, citing me. I tell you, Max, the only thing I'm really ashamed about in here,' she shook the fan of papers at him, 'is these stupid pictures of me in stockings. They *are* tarty. The rest of it is just life—I did what I had to do at the time.'

He nodded, as if conceding that she was right, as indeed she was.

'Dad's making a big thing about Victor.'

'That's just because Victor rubbed him up the wrong way with some business proposal. You know all about Victor and me. I never made a secret of the fact that we used to be together.'

'But Dad didn't know and now he finds out you're working in his club.'

She felt like laughing out loud. If that was the worst thing Lewis had on her she had got out of jail. So to speak.

She sat beside Max on the sofa.

'Look, pretending to have some big-deal job in business was as much your idea as mine. You didn't want your father to think I was some nightclub pick-up.'

She watched closely as he digested what she'd

282

told him. Then held out her hand.

'Are we still friends?'

He took the hand—as she knew he would. That felt better, to have him in her grip.

She allowed herself to be pulled into his arms. His kiss this time was not perfunctory.

'What are we going to do about Dad?' he said eventually.

'I don't want to come between the two of you, Max. If he's saying it's me or him, well, he *is* your father.' And he's worth a fortune. Only a fool would let that slip.

'And it's my life. I want to marry you, not him.'

Thank God for that, Cherry thought, a bit of backbone at last.

She couldn't be certain of him yet, however. She had one more card to play.

So she played it.

Chapter Fifteen

Hattie Barber couldn't get Jessie Maclean out of her mind. The police investigation into Basil Jacobs's murder was back at square one. Jessie's revelations, diverting though they were, had taken them no further towards the solution of the crime. At least that's how DI Pollock and the rest of the team saw it.

Hattie wasn't so sure. It didn't do to go on gut instinct as a detective. No officer went into the witness box in the Crown Court and said, 'I've got this funny feeling the defendant did it.' However, they all said things like that in the office or the pub.

You just sensed when something was up.

Hattie knew that Jessie had revealed an aspect of the case that was relevant. In all that wash of words about her and Basil there was some little nugget that would lead her to the killer. She had a funny feeling about it.

Not that she let on to her colleagues. They had dismissed Jessie's intervention as a red herring but Hattie had made the mistake of allowing her lingering interest to show. As a result, she was now the butt of too many Jessie-inspired wisecracks for her liking.

'What you drinking, Hat?'

'White wine, please.'

'Och aye the noo, lassie, sure you wouldn't rather have a large Scotch?'

It didn't rise much above that level but the result was that she kept her mouth shut about anything to do with the Macleans. It also meant that she couldn't—wouldn't anyway—ask anyone to help her in her self-imposed task to return to all the households they'd visited in their first door-to-door enquiries after the crime.

One of the problems in solving Basil's murder was working out where he had been in the hours before his death. Their first assumption, and it was still the prevailing view, was that he had been drinking in a local pub. The post-mortem revealed sufficient alcohol in his bloodstream to suggest that he had been sipping spirits steadily for at least a couple of hours before he died; and an analysis of the half-digested food in his stomach had come up with crisps, bread and cheese. Pub food, in other words.

But enquiries at every public house in the

vicinity had yielded nothing of use; the same went for the three private drinking clubs in the area. Nobody remembered seeing him. And Basil, a big barrel-shaped man with a grey beard down to his collar, was a memorable sight. Though it was possible he had sat around boozing unremarked in a public place, Hattie wasn't convinced. She'd been inclined to the theory, along with Pollock, that Basil had been drinking with someone else and that they'd fallen out, resulting in the fight which had killed him. In those circumstances, it wasn't surprising that no one admitted to seeing anything. The clientele of Kilburn pubs weren't known to be the most forthcoming when the police came calling.

But those suppositions had been formed before Hattie spoke to Jessie, when little had been known about the victim himself. From the squalor in which Basil lived, and the alehouse/betting shop nature of the mourners at his funeral, she'd made some glib assumptions about the kind of man he was. A lonely, broke gambling addict. A loser. She'd not been entirely wrong, of course, but she'd missed something.

Basil might have lived in unhygienic circumstances but he could have lived in luxury if he'd wanted to—he had a million quid tucked away.

And though he lived on his own, he was no loner. How many people had there been at his funeral? Seventy-odd, Hattie had counted.

Basil lived just the way he wanted to. A selfish but successful creature of habit.

What had Jessie said about her ex-husband?

'When I realised he'd be out playing poker till the day he died, I left.'

285

That was it.

Hattie's new theory, and it was blindingly obvious now that it had occurred to her, was that Basil had been out playing cards on the night of his death. Playing in a private card school in a house not too far from where his body was found. Maybe he'd had a row with one of the other players and he'd followed him into the street? Maybe one party owed the other money. Or had been cheating. Or—well, there were many possibilities.

At the time Hattie and her colleagues had carried out the house-to-house interviews they'd been looking for witnesses to the fight in the street or people who'd own up to knowing the victim. Now she had another reason to knock on people's doors—to find Basil's card school. Let Pollock take the mickey out of her when it led her to Basil's killer.

*   *   *

'I don't see that this is so bad.' Roisin was sitting cross-legged on the large dishevelled bed in Lewis's St John's Wood home, wearing just his pyjama jacket. Spread across the sheets were the pages of the report he had commissioned on Cherry. 'A lot of kids go off the rails but at least she's managed to get her life together.'

Lewis was sitting next to her, his hand on her thigh, while she read. She had returned from Ireland the night before and it was fantastic to be back in this big warm room basking in Lewis's love. She'd missed him.

But her reaction to the dossier on Cherry was obviously not what he wanted.

286

'She worked as a prostitute!' he exclaimed. 'I don't want a woman like that in my family.'

'It says here there was a pimp. Some man was exploiting her.'

'That's every tart's excuse.' He got up from the bed and pulled on his dressing gown. She could see how angry he was from the way he yanked the belt into a knot.

She didn't want to quarrel but she had to speak up. 'She was sixteen, Lewis. You can't be too judgemental.'

He sighed. 'OK. Leaving that aside, she lied to me. She told me she was a marketing executive for a software firm, that she met Max when she was entertaining clients at the opera.'

'Maybe there's an explanation.'

He shot her a look that bordered on contempt. 'Rubbish. She's the mistress of a professional gambler and she works in a nightclub.'

'I just think you should give her the chance to explain herself. Maybe she was intimidated by the thought of meeting you and made something up.'

'For God's sake, Roisin, the bloody woman's on the make. She's after my money and she's trying to get it by tying down my son.'

His face was red with emotion and he was shouting. Roisin could imagine how intimidating he might be in a business confrontation.

She deliberately kept her tone cool as she said, 'Isn't that the kind of thing people might say about me?'

'What?' He looked confused.

'That I'm some girl who works in a casino trying to tie you down so I can get at your money.'

'Roisin, there's no comparison between the two

287

of you. She's a fraudulent woman with a criminal record and you're . . .' He floundered. 'You're just the opposite. And I love you.'

His face softened and she held her hand out to him. He sat next to her on the bed, his anger banished.

'And Max doesn't love Cherry?' she said slyly after they'd kissed.

'I bet he's changed his mind now he's seen the dossier.'

Roisin wasn't so sure about that. If you loved someone why would a secret past spell the end of it all? But she didn't want to argue. Now she was back in England, all she wanted was Lewis's arms around her. For the moment, Max, Cherry and everyone else for that matter were not important.

*   *   *

Lewis had a midday meeting up at the Elmwood Glade site but he'd been hanging on for Max's call and it came through just as he was about to leave the office. Too bad. The architect could wait.

Max's voice sounded distant on the phone. 'I've read that stuff about Cherry.'

'And?'

'I can't believe you got a detective to check her out.'

'I'm sorry, but in my position you learn to take nothing at face value.'

'Meaning what exactly?'

Was the boy stupid? Was Max going to make him spell it out? Of course he was. Nothing was ever easy with Max.

'Look, son, she's a gold-digger. A fraud with a

288

criminal record who's lied her way into your affections and now she's trying to lie her way into our family.'

'Hang on, Dad, she's never lied to me. We cooked up the story together about her job.'

'What on earth for?'

'Because you'd been having a go at me about not finding a suitable girlfriend. It so happens that Cherry is perfectly suitable but I met her in a club and I knew you'd hold that against her.'

So there *was* an explanation, much as Roisin had predicted. Not that Lewis was inclined to let it persuade him.

'I'm not saying give her up completely. Have fun, enjoy her company, she's a lovely looking girl. But, believe me, she's not the kind you marry.'

'You're not going to put me off her, Dad.'

'Do you really want a convicted prostitute for a wife?'

In the silence that followed, Lewis wished he hadn't had to say that. But there was no shirking the truth.

'She told me about it. It was a long time ago and she was desperate. It's not important to me, Dad. I want to marry her.'

How Lewis wished Max was sitting across the desk from him. Maybe he could shake some sense into him. But Jackie was standing in the office doorway tapping her watch. He waved her away, he couldn't give a damn if he was late.

'Listen closely, Max. If you go against me I shall be looking for a new jockey for Black Mountain at Cheltenham. And everywhere else.'

'This is more important than riding Black Mountain.'

'And if you marry her without my blessing, I shall redraft my will and the pair of you will get nothing. Tell that to your little tart and see if she still wants you.'

Max's voice was cool. 'She'll still want me. I guarantee it.'

'What? Because she says she loves you?'

'Yes. And because she's carrying my baby. She's pregnant, Dad, and I'm going to marry her whether you like it or not.'

*   *   *

Cherry dried her hands carefully under the grumbling hot-air dryer in the ladies toilet off the rear staircase of the club. The machine was infuriatingly slow but today she didn't care, she stood there as if in a dream. She had plenty to think about.

The pregnancy idea had been germinating for some weeks. If all else fails, she'd thought while pondering how to nudge Max into a proposal, I can tell him I'm having his baby. It might be just the last little shove needed to propel him into action.

But the way things had worked out she'd not needed to do it. Then, when Lewis had started to dig up the dirt of her past life, she'd blurted it out, just to make sure Max was securely on her side.

The thing was, at the time there'd been a chance it was true. She'd stopped taking her contraceptive pills when she'd first decided Max was her escape route and, funnily enough, the night Max had sprung the private eye report on her, she was three days overdue. But now, just a few minutes ago, her period had arrived, several days late. In the normal course of events, she'd be relieved. The irony did not amuse her.

She had no intention of telling Max about this latest turn of events. The last thing she should do was give him any room to back out. For the moment she was under no pressure; she could 'lose' the baby at any point over the next three months and he wouldn't be any the wiser. Maybe it was for the best. She had to face the possibility that if it all went wrong with Max she'd be better off not carrying a child.

She peered into the mirror. She didn't use much make-up during the day—she'd never needed to. But there were shadows under her eyes and a deepening of the little furrow, like a punctuation mark, that appeared between her eyebrows when she was worried.

She reached into her handbag for the lipgloss, her fingers brushing across the box of tampons she'd just rushed out to buy. She felt a pang for the baby that never was. To be carrying Lewis Ashwood's grandchild—that would be something. The old tyrant wouldn't be able to kick her out of his son's life if she really was.

She focused on her reflection in the mirror. All things considered, she still looked pretty damn good. She forced a smile onto her lips and Max Ashwood's fiancée, the blooming mother-to-be, smiled right back at her.

*   *   *

At first, Alan didn't recognise the rider coming towards him. He could see it was a woman, lithe and elegant in the saddle, taller and slimmer than

291

any of the girls in Tim's yard.

He knew the horse she was riding, however. It was one of two owned by Lewis Ashwood, who'd moved them from their previous trainer when his son had been caught in bed with the trainer's wife. It was one of the better pieces of gossip of the last few months.

Realisation dawned just as the newcomer came close enough for Alan to make out familiar features under the riding hat. He'd not seen Roisin on horseback for some months. He remembered what an effortless rider she was.

As he turned his horse alongside her, they exchanged awkward greetings. He'd not spoken to her since Noel's funeral and he was conscious that she must be acutely aware of her brother's absence here in Lambourn where they used to spend time together.

'Are you still working at the casino?' he asked.

She shook her head. 'They weren't happy about me being off in Ireland for so long. I'd had enough anyway. I'd made my point.'

What point was that? he wondered but thought better of asking. 'I never told anyone about it,' he said. 'Your secret's still safe.'

She laughed. He'd forgotten what a fabulous mouth she had, full and curving, and those rock-pool sparkling eyes. He looked away, not wanting to be caught staring.

'You can tell who you like now,' she was saying. 'I confessed to my mother and she didn't care. It seems a bit silly but I just wanted to prove my independence.'

He nodded. There was one thing he was dying to ask her but he held back, fearing the answer.

Instead he said, 'So what now? Are you looking for another job?'

'Actually, I'm getting married to Lewis.'

So there it was, the news he didn't want to hear.

'Congratulations.' It almost choked him. 'Is that official?'

'We haven't announced anything yet. I'd rather you didn't mention it.'

He laughed, a hard dry sound. 'Don't tell me, it's another of your secrets.'

She blushed. With her hair up under her riding hat and her cheeks glowing, she looked almost schoolgirlish. Far too young for that old goat.

'I'm glad I found you,' she said as she reached over to pat Sandy's caramel shoulder. 'I wanted to say how thrilled I was about this fellow.'

He assumed she was referring to the struggle he'd had to get the money together. It seemed like ancient history now. 'It turned out OK. I managed to scrape together enough people who wanted a share.'

'I didn't mean that. I meant about your win at Newbury. I hear he's an absolute flying machine.'

This time his laugh was of genuine amusement. 'Did you hear that, Sandy?' He scratched the horse's ear. 'He had a whole career on the Flat and nobody called him that.'

'But you won by twenty lengths and he was scarcely out of breath. Hurdles must really suit him.'

'How do you know?'

'Dad got a tape. He looks at every horse who might end up running against Black Mountain. He was impressed.'

Alan couldn't imagine Sandy, his little novice

hurdler, up against a legend like Black Mountain. But the time of his Newbury win had been exceptional for a novice. Almost four seconds faster than the handicap on the same card.

'Where's he running next?' she asked.

'Wincanton. The Kingwell Pattern Hurdle.'

'And the Champion Hurdle after that?' She shot him a mischievous look. 'So you *are* thinking of taking on Blackie.'

Alan wasn't but he knew that others of the syndicate were. Linda, of course, because Cheltenham was one of the great stages and therefore her natural habitat; and Geoff, because he dreamed his dead son's dreams for him. Even Tim had been heard to murmur that it might not be out of the question.

'To be honest, Roisin, I don't know. It seems unbelievable to me. He could fall on his face at Wincanton.'

But she was grinning at him, those eyes dancing. 'But wouldn't it be fantastic? Your horse and ours in the greatest hurdle race of the year? You've got to go for it, if you get the chance. Promise me.'

He'd been telling himself it didn't really matter if Grain of Sand didn't perform at Wincanton. Suddenly it seemed to matter a lot. Any idea Roisin was keen on sounded pretty good to him too.

'I promise,' he said.

Of course, he thought to himself as he set off for the gallops, what would make it truly fantastic would be to go to Cheltenham and defeat Black Mountain. He might have lost Roisin to Lewis Ashwood, but there was still a chance of beating him on the racetrack.

As Cherry finished dragging a brush through her thick honey-blonde hair, the stillness of the small room was disturbed by the sound of men's voices raised in anger. At once she was pitched back into the here and now. Max, Lewis and her so-called pregnancy had to be pushed to the back of her mind; there were more immediate matters to deal with.

She cracked open the door to get a better idea of what was going on. Victor's private office was situated two flights down and the noise was echoing up the stairwell. It sounded as if the irate conversation was taking place just outside the office door. So much for security.

Brian Spot was defending his brother. 'He'd cut his own throat before he said a word. We both would.'

'I hear you.' Vic's tone was conciliatory. 'I know Chris wouldn't do anything deliberate but maybe he let something slip.'

'No!'

'I mean, it's not a coincidence, is it? Three days after Chris gets busted they lift your guy.'

Cherry's heart beat faster. So they'd acted on her other tip and arrested the money-launderer, Scott. She smiled as she listened to Brian bellow a string of curses.

'Just calm down, Brian. I'm not blaming you or Chris. But we've got a big problem and you've got to sort it.'

There was a pause, then an unidentifiable mumble from Brian followed by the sound of

295

footsteps coming up the stairs.

Cherry backed away from the door and hid in a stall, just as a precaution. She gave it five minutes then flushed the toilet and ran the taps. She stepped out of the door into the hall and walked straight into Victor.

He looked awful, worse than he had the other night.

'You wanna come with me, Cherry?' It wasn't a question.

She followed him down the stairs and into his office, deliberately taking deep breaths to slow her heartbeat. Brian Spot wasn't the only one who needed to stay cool. Suppose Vic knew she'd been eavesdropping and had been waiting for her to come out. Suppose that wasn't all he knew.

She shivered as she took one of the straight-backed chairs ranged in front of the desk. Once, just after they'd opened the building, she'd called this room the 'headmaster's study' and Vic had been amused. He didn't look amused now.

'You cold?' he said, observing her reaction.

'It's OK.' She knew he deliberately kept the temperature low in this windowless cell. He said he didn't want anyone falling asleep during business. Fat chance of that.

He sighed, appearing to weigh his words before he spoke. Had he found out about her? Was this the end? She didn't think her nerves could stand it.

'There's things going down, sweetheart,' he began. 'I ought to put you in the picture.'

Thank God.

'They've charged Chris, haven't they?' she said, a neutral remark just to show she was aware of recent events. Not too recent though.

'Yeah,' he nodded his head.

Chris Spot had been remanded in custody on assorted charges of drug trafficking. The trial was many months off but no one was in any hurry. The chances were that by the time Chris got out of jail he'd be eligible for a bus pass, if such concessions still existed.

Cherry wondered where she'd be in twenty years' time.

Victor was speaking. 'It's a bloody shame, actually it's an effing tragedy, but Chris is out of the picture. He can't do nothing for us right now except keep his trap shut.'

He spoke the last words with emphasis and Cherry seized on them.

'You don't think he'd tell tales, do you?' she said.

Victor's mouth tugged downwards. 'Between you and me, Chris has gone soft. The last time he got out of the nick, *Ghostbusters* was at number one. Now he's got three kids under fifteen and a villa near Estepona. It won't be so cushy in Belmarsh.'

'Come off it, Vic. He may be a complete pain in the arse but he's not a grass.' She put some vehemence into the words.

'That's what I would have said but something else has gone down. I can't help thinking, why now? Could the Old Bill have wheedled something out of Chris without him realising?'

'What's happened?'

'That American friend of Brian's was arrested this morning.'

'Scott Robinson?'

'Yeah.'

'That's terrible. And you think they got to him through Chris?'

Victor nodded. 'Chris got busted by Customs and Excise and the next day the Met's money-laundering squad who did Robinson took a call from a Customs intelligence officer.'

Cherry's stomach lurched. The mention of Customs and Excise was ominous.

'How do you know that?'

'How do you think? I spend a lot of money making myself popular with all kinds of people, even rozzers. Unfortunately, this particular pal of mine doesn't have an inside track on either Chris or Scott, but he does know there's a Customs link. So what do you think's going on, sweetheart?'

She could hardly think at all at the moment. She was in a panic. Fortunately, Vic supplied his own answer.

'I reckon Chris is doing a deal with the Customs geezers, seeing if he can earn himself some wiggle room. Perhaps some of those charges might go away if he plays ball. His bust and the link with the Cussies—it's too big a coincidence. It's got to be Chris.'

'I never liked the filthy sod,' she said. Take a free hit, why not?

'Yeah, I know.' The yellow eyes bored into her. 'One way or another I'll find out who's behind this.'

*　　　*　　　*

Alan stared at the scrap of paper by the phone in the kitchen and tried to think clearly. He'd found it hard to concentrate since running into Roisin earlier in the day. She'd seemed different to the woman he'd sparred with last autumn, different also to the grief-shocked girl who'd stood over her

298

brother's grave. Now she was mellower, sadder but less anxious, more at home in her own skin. Was that what the prospect of marriage did for you? Or was it what Lewis Ashwood had done for her? In which case, if he was a true friend, he should put aside his jealousy and be happy for her.

But he wasn't big enough for that. Seeing her this morning had just reinforced how much he desired her. She'd been polite and pleasant to him and it had knocked him for six. It was mad.

As they parted she'd said, 'You will come to the wedding, won't you?' and he'd agreed without thinking. But, now he thought about it, he realised how insupportable that would be. He'd say no when the invitation arrived. And he'd do his best not to see her again. It wasn't healthy to fall in love with another man's wife.

He forced his attention back to the number he'd written down a few minutes ago and picked up the phone. Directory enquiries had been efficient in coming up with the contact for O'Shea at Barn House, Concommon, in Co. Limerick. This was his link to the elusive Kevin. All he had to do was dial and speak to the man's mother. Tell her he had a box of Kevin's things and ask how he could get hold of him.

Maybe Kevin himself would be there. He could be talking to him within thirty seconds. Simple. Or was it?

Kevin had made it clear he had no wish to discuss Olympia and Lee's death. Quite possibly he'd left the country to avoid discussing it with anyone. He was hardly likely to open up to Alan on the telephone. And maybe his parents were under instructions to keep his whereabouts secret.

Alan put the handset back in its cradle. He needed to think up a better story. At the moment, though, his thoughts kept veering down the one path he didn't want them to take.

Damn Roisin Dougherty—soon to be Roisin Ashwood. No wonder he couldn't think straight.

*　　*　　*

The little house in Fulham smelt stale and neglected; Cherry hadn't been home in days. This evening, though, it was where she needed to be. Just a few hours alone in her sanctuary and she'd feel strong enough to resume the fight.

She ignored her answer-machine and its blinking light, climbed the narrow flight of stairs to the bedroom and dragged the bedclothes over her head. Curled on her side in the comforting dark, just for the moment she felt safe. It was an illusion but she savoured it all the same.

She'd been scared many times before in her life. When Mickey the biker had told her what he'd do to her if she ever withheld money from him again. In Bellwood when her boss-eyed cellmate had threatened to use her face as an ashtray for calling her a fat lesbian. Just the other day, with Chris Spot's hand up her skirt at Cookfield Farm.

But she'd survived those moments and the survival had made her stronger. She had to harness all that strength now while she tiptoed a path through the minefield of her present life. Somehow she had to get to the other side in one piece.

She fell asleep, as if a switch had been pulled and plunged her into a profound and dreamless void. When she woke she had no idea of where she was or how much time had gone by. She lay in the black warmth and savoured the feeling of nothingness. Then her anxieties began creeping back. The conversation with Victor. Her later, almost hysterical, call to Janice.

'He knows!' she cried. 'He knows about you people. He's got a spy!'

Janice had said reassuring things. That no one except her and Ray even knew who Scorpio was. That she was too valuable to be exposed in any way. That she must keep her nerve.

Tell me something I don't know, she'd thought. 'Don't expect to hear from me in a hurry,' she'd said and hung up.

And now, lying in the dark, she heard a creak on the stair.

Someone was in the house. Footsteps were climbing in steady, ominous thuds on the wooden stairs.

I hope they make it quick, she thought. No razors or rape or long drawn-out confessions. One bullet will do.

The door opened. There was the click of a switch but light did not penetrate her dark. She wasn't breathing. *I'm dead already.*

'Cherry?'

It was Max. She'd given him a key but he'd never used it before.

Light flooded into her cocoon and then his face was next to hers. She put her arms round his neck and held on, overcome with relief.

'I called the club and they told me you'd left,' he said. 'You've not returned my messages.'

She didn't bother to reply, just clung to him.

'I spoke to Dad. He says we mustn't get married.

301

He won't let me ride Black Mountain and he'll cut me out of his will.'

A new fear seized her. Was Max about to dump her? If so, she had no weapons left to use. The baby had been her last ploy.

'Did you hear me, Cherry?'

He was lying on the bed next to her. She took her arms from round his neck. If he was going to cut her loose, she had no energy left to fight.

Tell me the worst.

'I said it didn't make any difference, that we'd go ahead anyway.'

She felt numb, unable to take it in.

'Cherry, say something. You will still marry me, won't you?'

Finally she spoke. There was only one thing to say.

She'd make it safely through the minefield yet.

Chapter Sixteen

As he plodded along the expensive residential streets of Primrose Hill, warm winter rain running down his face, Lewis's headache began to fade. Roisin had cajoled him into taking his hangover and his bad temper out for a run. He'd cursed her as he'd laced up his trainers and set out in the gloom of the early February morning, but he had to admit he felt better for it.

He knew he should do more to keep himself fit. The discomforts were minor compared to the benefits. What greater incentive could there be but Roisin herself? He was well aware she was two decades younger than he was and he had to stay healthy for her sake.

As a rule Roisin would have accompanied him but this trudge through the rain was a personal act of penance.

He hadn't meant to drink so much the night before and he certainly hadn't meant to shout at her. But the one had led to the other after she'd opposed him over Max.

'I don't understand you,' she'd said when he'd recounted his phone conversation with his son. 'Aren't you the least bit pleased about the baby?'

He hadn't been last night. He'd just seen the pregnancy as a strategy engineered by Cherry to snare Max. 'She's tricked you,' he'd screamed down the phone. 'Do you even know it's yours?'

Of course Max had said he was sure it was, but how could he be? Cherry was a liar and a convicted tart who worked as a nightclub hostess. 'Face the facts,' he'd said to Max. 'You can't be certain about anything to do with that woman.'

But Roisin had taken Max's side and spoken up for Cherry, arguing against Lewis when he'd talked of stopping Max's allowance and altering his will. It had infuriated him.

'You're being naive,' he'd said. 'This is my son and my money she's after. Just stay out of it, Roisin. You don't know what you're talking about.'

He'd said other things too that had been meant to wound. He couldn't remember everything exactly but he'd woken on the sofa with a blanket round his body and a band of steel gripping his head. Roisin had appeared to find his situation amusing—which was a relief. She'd listened to his apologies and then suggested he take to the rainy streets to straighten himself out.

He took the road to the northern entrance to the park. From there a short uphill stretch led to a commanding viewpoint from the summit of the hill. It was the route he and Roisin usually took. On a good day you could see clean over the whole city.

He laboured up to the top and emerged from beneath the winter-bare trees to the clearing favoured by walkers, dog owners and flab-fighters such as himself. It was permissible to halt here for a moment before taking the downward plunge to Regent's Park. On this grim, dank morning he had the spot to himself.

Roisin had told him not to be such an old grouch. To look for the good things, to give Cherry the benefit of the doubt, to look at the big picture. He'd have a grandchild—wouldn't that be great?

He sat heavily on a bench and stared up at the scudding grey clouds, his chest heaving.

He supposed the situation wouldn't be without its compensations. He'd not seen much of Max as a baby, he'd been too busy empire building. But he'd done a turn of baby-minding whenever he could. In the small hours usually, when Ruth was simply too tired and his brain was still buzzing from the events of the business day. To his surprise, he'd found that holding little Max in his arms gave comfort to them both. Lewis and the gurgling baby had shared special moments together when the rest of the world was asleep. He'd sometimes thought he'd got on best with his son when Max had been just a sweet-smelling bundle of needs that could be simply satisfied.

It struck Lewis that a baby was a clean start. He couldn't blame a grandchild for the crimes and stupidities of its parents. He knew that once the baby was placed in his arms it would be impossible to keep up a fight with Max and Cherry. When the child came into the world, the game would be changed forever.

The rain had stopped and the clouds were thinning. Suddenly a shaft of low winter sunlight played over the buildings and birdcages of the zoo below, then picked out the skyline of the city beyond. Look at the big picture, Roisin had said. As usual she was right.

Lewis made up his mind. He'd swallow his hurt and shelve his suspicion. If he went to war with the mother of his grandchild he could only lose.

*   *   *

As she sat at the kitchen table, looking through the open door into the high-ceilinged living room of Max's flat, Cherry conducted a mental stocktake. It was mercenary of her but she couldn't help it. The apartment was worth a lot, obviously, but was it in Max's name? She had a feeling, from some papers she'd discovered in the chaos of his desk drawers, that he paid some peppercorn rent to a property company which doubtless was part of the Ashwood empire. The car, she now knew, was financed by a bank loan which in turn was paid out of Max's monthly allowance from Lewis. Suppose Lewis heaved him out of the flat and shut down the monthly cash injection?

Well, they wouldn't starve. They could live in her house and she had a few quid stashed away. The money she earned from Victor was generous but, bearing in mind that she was doing her best to put him out of business, it couldn't be relied on.

Cherry wasn't too perturbed. She'd always had to fight for what she got. Though Max had fallen into her lap like a ripe plum it was unreasonable to expect that his father would be so easy to pluck. He'd fall in time, she was sure of it. First she had to make sure of his son. A quick wedding would be best, followed by a miscarriage. And if they had to live off bread and cheese in her tiny house after the honeymoon, then so be it.

As she ruminated she'd heard the phone ring and seen Max sprawl over the sofa to grab the receiver. Now he appeared in the kitchen doorway, a grin plastered across his face.

'Guess what? The old bugger's caved in.'

She didn't know what he was on about.

'That's Roisin on the phone. We're invited to dinner at Dad's on Sunday night.'

She must have looked fearful because he added, 'It's OK. Peace has broken out. Roisin will tell you—she's hanging on to speak to you.'

Cherry's thoughts were in a jumble as she picked up the receiver. She was geared up for a long campaign. It was too much to hope that for once in her life something would turn out to be easy.

She'd only met Roisin once and found her disconcertingly likeable. The Irish girl had pumped her for information about the fateful ferry crossing which, obviously, Cherry had recalled in selective detail. She'd told Roisin how much she'd liked her dead brother—which was no lie. Short though the conversation had been, it had formed a bond between the two of them.

'Hi, Cherry. I just wanted to say I'm thrilled about you and Max. And the baby.'

'Thanks, Roisin.'

'And don't worry about Lewis. He's a bit old-fashioned about some things but you and I can sort him out.'

Cherry had been confident she could manage that on her own but she wasn't averse to receiving a little short-term help. 'That's great to hear, Roisin.'

She reminded herself there was no point in getting too attached to the Irish woman. In the long term there wasn't room for both of them in the Ashwood family.

*   *   *

Hattie hadn't had much luck in resuming the door-to-door enquiries into Basil's murder. For one thing, she realised she'd bitten off more than she could chew. Like all parts of residential London, Kilburn was densely populated. By herself and in her spare time, it would take from now until the end of the decade to revisit all the households covered in the initial investigation. By which time, half the potential witnesses would have died or moved on. Already she'd been drawing blanks because bedsits had changed hands and another old lady was in hospital. 'She's never coming back neither,' confided her neighbour. 'Couldn't manage the stairs even if she did.'

Somehow there had to be a way of narrowing down her search.

Her thoughts turned to Basil's funeral. She'd been surprised by the number of people who'd turned out. Among them, surely, was someone who knew if he attended a regular Tuesday night poker game and where it was held. But she and another detective had attended the ceremony and the wake, so-called, which had followed in a pub in Finchley. They had talked to as many of the mourners as possible and it was from them that they had formed the impression of a man who spent all his free time at the racecourse, the bookmaker's and the casino. There'd not been much talk of playing cards. Perhaps Basil's gambling tastes had changed in the years since he'd been apart from Jessie? No one they'd talked to had seen him on the night of the murder.

Hattie was disappointed. She'd invested a lot in her theory of Basil's gambling night and she was reluctant to give up on it just yet.

She speed-dialled a number on her phone and it was picked up on the first ring, as she knew it would be. Martin was her ex-boyfriend who seemed to live his life in front of the computer. She'd broken off their romance six months earlier but he'd not done the sensible thing and got himself another girlfriend. Frankly, this was a bit of a pain but she couldn't deny that it was useful to have a spare man available when you needed one. Like when you wanted to go to an unfamiliar pub on a weekend and get friendly with the regulars.

He sounded pleased to hear from her and thrilled to learn he was taking her out that evening.

'Unless you've got some other plans,' she added. She couldn't expect to take him for granted.

'Absolutely nothing,' he said.

He was too honest for his own good, but she wasn't complaining.

*   *   *

308

As he added an onion and some bay leaves to the joint of beef sitting in the oven tray, Lewis knew he was earning credit with his wife-to-be. Roisin had been surprised when he'd volunteered to cook the main course for their dinner with Max and Cherry, particularly since he'd given her the impression he didn't rise to more than the odd burned banger on the barbecue. But fast-cooked rib of beef, seared on the outside and bloody within, was his one culinary weapon. He'd produced it from the armoury at moments of crisis in just about all of his serious relationships.

He slammed the meat back into the oven and poured himself a glass of wine. Chef's perks. Good boy treats. He deserved them.

Since he'd decided to like Cherry rather than lump her, he'd been a very good boy indeed. His party piece in the kitchen was just the trimming.

'You're right,' he'd said to Roisin. 'The girl's had a tough upbringing and I won't hold that against her. If Max loves her then I'll back him.'

'And you'll stop all this talk about cutting his allowance and changing your will?'

'If she gives me a grandchild I imagine I might have to make some special provisions.'

Roisin had hugged him and he'd savoured her approval.

All the same, he intended to have a few words with Cherry at a suitable moment during the evening. She'd lied to him about her job—she couldn't blame that on a misspent youth. She had to realise he didn't like being taken for a fool.

He had his opportunity sooner than expected, within ten minutes of their arrival. He left the three of them in the living room to dash to the kitchen and make sure the meat wasn't overcooking. There was nothing worse than overdone beef, in his opinion.

'Are you sure you wouldn't rather stick that fork into me?' said a voice behind him.

Cherry had followed him down the stairs. She wore a tailored red sweater and a black skirt, not in the least tarty but it showed off her figure just the same. Lewis imagined how sensational she could look dressed to kill for a night out. She'd also look pretty good in a T-shirt and shorts on the deck of a yacht. Max had picked a girl for all seasons. Lewis supposed he couldn't complain about that.

'I'm sorry we've got off on the wrong foot,' she said.

He put the fork down, left the meat where it was and reached for his wine glass. 'I thought we'd got off on the right one. But that's when you were some kind of business executive.'

'I didn't think you'd like the real me. And you don't, do you?'

She was very up-front—was she trying to provoke him?

'I don't like being lied to. Though I know now that you have plenty to hide.'

She nodded. 'You see? That's why I did it. Because I really wanted you to approve of me and I knew you wouldn't. I'd have told you everything in the end, but who knew it would work out between Max and me?' She reached for his wine glass and took a gulp. 'Sorry, I'm so nervous talking to you like this but we've got to clear the air, haven't we? I mean,' she put her hand on her stomach, 'for the baby's sake.' She put down the glass. 'I shouldn't be drinking, should I?'

Lewis was well aware there was calculation in her behaviour. She'd slipped into his personal space and shared his drink, moving close to give him the benefit of the sincerity in those pale hazel eyes. And she'd played the baby card.

He'd already decided that there wouldn't be a fight—why else was Cherry here, about to eat the food he'd cooked in her honour? She wasn't taking much of a risk in confronting him like this. They both knew how it would end up. Though not just yet.

'You can ask anything you like about my murky past,' she said.

When it came down to it, her scandalous youth didn't matter that much. There was really only one thing that needed clearing up.

'You work for Victor Bishop.'

'Yes.' She smiled, as if she wasn't bothered by this line of enquiry at all. 'Do you know him?'

'We've met once or twice. How would you describe your relationship?'

'Come on, Lewis. It was in that report you gave Max. I used to be his girlfriend.'

'And now you work for him?'

'He's got a club near Streatham, the Poison Ivy. It's better than it sounds. The restaurant's good. Why don't you come along one evening?'

He ignored the offer. 'What exactly do you do there?'

'I'm like a manager. I try to ensure the place runs smoothly so Victor can get on with his other stuff.'

'And that would be?'

She shrugged. 'He's got all sorts of business interests. He owns properties all over the world.

311

And he goes racing a lot, of course.'

Lewis pondered this response. It was hardly informative but she couldn't be expected to suddenly spill the beans on her long-time mentor. He couldn't criticise her for being loyal.

'How long do you intend to carry on working for him?'

She grinned and glanced downwards. The baby card again. 'I suppose it can't be much longer.'

'Why don't you finish now? I can cover your salary, if that's a problem.'

She looked surprised. Had he done her a disservice in judging her to be simply mercenary?

'Thank you but I thought I'd stay on till the wedding.'

Not simply mercenary then, her ambitions were grander. Well, he'd concluded that already.

'And have you thought when that would be?'

'We'd like to keep it simple. So, in the circumstances, the sooner the better. Subject to your approval, of course.'

Was this the shape of things to come? Lewis wondered, with the pair of them negotiating behind Max's back. He supposed it could be worse. When it came down to it, he realised he could do deals with this woman.

'And then you'll stop working for Victor Bishop?'

'Yes.'

He put the meat back in the oven. Another ten minutes should do it.

Something else occurred to him.

'I don't want Bishop to come to the wedding.' He'd not meant to blurt it out like that, so it sounded like an order.

Cherry didn't turn a hair. 'Neither do I,' she said.

So they ended up in agreement. As he ushered her out of the kitchen on the way to fetch the others, he reflected again how much she reminded him of his first wife.

*   *   *

The landlord at the Wheatsheaf remembered Hattie, she didn't even have to flash her ID.

'So you've not caught the bastard who killed him?' he said as he poured their drinks.

'Not yet. That's why I'm here. Have you got a moment to answer a couple more questions?'

'Does it look like it?' He gestured to the bar, where customers were bellying up two deep and a lone pink-cheeked barmaid was gingerly dispensing pints of Guinness. 'Come back Monday morning and you'll have my undivided attention.'

'Just tell me,' she said quickly, 'are any of Mr Jacobs's friends in tonight?'

'Try in the back,' he said, jerking his thumb towards the rear.

Hattie headed purposefully through the crush, Martin trailing behind her, clutching their glasses. She turned and gave him an encouraging smile.

'I hope you know what you're doing,' he muttered as they stumbled into a room blue with smoke.

This back area of the pub was used for games. Hattie and Martin found a space against the wall with a ledge to place their drinks. Their arrival had been greeted with a few stares and, in her case, several frank appraisals of her scoop-necked sweater and leather trousers.

313

'I bet that bloke wouldn't be ogling you if he knew you were a copper,' muttered Martin.

Hattie didn't bother to reply; it was one of Martin's regular lines. Instead she ran her eye over the clientele in her turn, looking for any familiar faces from the funeral and wake. No candidates sprang immediately to mind. She paid particular attention to the group clustered around the fruit machine. She could imagine Basil spending hours feeding his small change into its greedy metal mouth. And from what she now knew, she could also picture Basil coaxing a regular jackpot from its innards.

'See who you're looking for?' Martin was pretty clued up on the case. Though they were no longer a couple she'd never got out of hitting his speed-dial number; he'd always been a good listener.

Hattie was about to answer his question in the negative when a big man waddled out of the gents. He looked familiar. Hattie watched him make his slow progress to the dartboard where he reached for a pint glass and swallowed half of it. He picked up the darts lying by the glass and took his turn at the board. She studied his profile as he threw. That big beak of a nose was unmistakable. Had he been at the funeral?

She'd find out.

*   *   *

Cherry didn't think the meal had gone too badly. It had been a bit awkward in the kitchen with Lewis but that was to be expected. Basically, she'd put one over on a top tycoon, one of the country's richest men, and that gave her the kind of buzz that

314

banished the nerves now constantly fluttering inside her. The prize she sought—marriage to Max and sanctuary within the golden cage of the Ashwood family—had been sanctioned by Lewis himself. All that remained was to get Max to the Register Office. How long would that take? Three weeks? Four? Long before her failure to show signs of pregnancy could become a talking point, at any rate.

The talk at dinner had been of weddings but not, principally, hers. Maybe Lewis wished to reassert his authority but no sooner had he raised his glass to toast herself and Max, than he held it aloft again.

'There's another cause for celebration,' he announced.

Cherry noted the glance Roisin gave him, an embarrassed 'not now' look that he ignored.

'I've finally worn down my Irish rose. Roisin and I are getting married too.'

To his credit, Max bellowed a string of *fantastics* and *congratulations*. Cherry gave Roisin a meaningful hug and bestowed a kiss full on Lewis's lips which he returned with enthusiasm. Cherry had no doubt that once she got into the dutiful daughter-in-law role she'd be able to play him like a fish.

Roisin, sweet though she was, would be more of a problem.

Naturally, she and Max pressed the pair of them for details. It was obvious Roisin felt a degree of reluctance which, Cherry gathered, was due to Noel's death; the ferry accident still cast a long shadow over the Dougherty family. Roisin swore them to secrecy for the moment. 'It's not official

315

and I'd rather it didn't get out.'

Lewis laughed. 'Don't worry, we'll turn it into the biggest knees-up of the summer.'

Roisin didn't look happy. 'I'm not sure that's such a good idea, Lewis.'

'Well, I do, my darling. To every thing there is a season and all that. A time to mourn and a time to bloody well let your hair down.'

He'd been hitting the bottle a bit, that was obvious.

There was no talk, Cherry noted, of making it a double wedding. All things considered, that was just as well. If it was anything to do with her, there would only be one marriage anyway. It had just dawned on her how to bring this about.

*   *   *

The man with the big nose introduced himself as Lenny.

'Weren't you at Basil Jacobs's funeral?' Hattie said.

He shot her a surprised look. 'Was you there too? I didn't see you.'

'We all looked a bit different then, didn't we?' She certainly had, in her charcoal suit with her hair up, not loose and flowing like tonight.

'Yeah, I could only make the service,' Lenny said. 'I was on the afternoon shift.' He'd already told her he worked on the Underground. 'How d'you know Basil then?'

So she came clean. Now she'd broken the ice there didn't seem much point in not doing so.

He was flabbergasted. 'You're Old Bill? I don't flaming believe it.'

She showed him her warrant card.

When the amazement had faded he seemed amused. 'Blimey. A cracking little bird like you. I'd never have thought it. And what about him?' He looked towards Martin.

'He's my boyfriend.' Why had she said that? It seemed to satisfy Lenny, however. 'Look,' she said, 'can I ask you a couple of questions?'

He nodded and sipped his beer.

'Was Basil a card player?'

Lenny almost choked, beer frothing from his mouth. Alarmed, Hattie thumped him on his back and then realised he was laughing. He mopped his face with a grubby paper tissue as he recovered.

'Oh dear,' he said at last. 'Is the Pope a Catholic? Yes, old Bas was a card player all right. Poker, pontoon, brag—anything if you could win money at it.'

'How about a regular card school?'

'Oh yeah. You'd never see him in here on a Tuesday or a Friday. They were his card nights. He'd do casinos and other stuff in the evenings, like the dogs, but they weren't regular like Tuesdays and Fridays.'

'Where did he play?'

'Ally Pally.'

Alexandra Palace? That was miles from where Basil's body had been found. And it wasn't on any easy tube or rail link Hattie could think of.

'That was on Fridays,' Lenny added.

'What about Tuesdays?'

Basil had died on a Tuesday. *Please say Kilburn.*

Lenny pondered the question. Finally he said, 'I dunno.'

'Was that Ally Pally too?'

317

Lenny shook his head vigorously, the thought was ridiculous. 'No. Tuesdays he played with Paul.'

'Paul who?'

'Just Paul. Basil didn't have a big mouth, you know? Not like a lot of blokes. It took a while to get to know him but when you did, he was a diamond. All he ever said to me about Paul was that he was a bit dodgy.'

'Meaning what?'

Lenny shrugged. 'You know. A bit of a ducker and diver.'

'So he did talk about him?'

'Not really. Just to say he was round Paul's so he didn't see the match, that sort of thing.'

Martin appeared at her elbow, making a how's-it-going? face; she despatched him to get in another round of drinks. Lenny proudly revealed her real identity to his pals and she fielded their questions about the progress of the murder enquiry. They were congenial company and eager to help. Unfortunately, they couldn't.

'So,' said Martin as they returned to his car an hour later, 'did you get what you want?'

'I dunno,' she said, attempting to imitate Lenny. She'd allowed herself to be bought a couple of real drinks and suddenly she was feeling light-headed. 'All I've got to do is find some ducker and diver called Paul who lives in Kilburn.'

Martin watched as she fumbled with the seatbelt. 'He'll stick out a mile then, won't he?'

That sobered her up fast. Paul. That's all she had to go on. But it was more than she'd had before.

*   *   *

318

Roisin felt dog tired. The evening with Max and Cherry had been an effort and now she just wanted them to go so she could cuddle up in the safety of Lewis's arms and sleep. She took refuge in the large bathroom on the first floor and splashed water on her face. She supposed one day she'd get used to houses like this, with unnecessary chandeliers in the halls and gold taps on the bath.

Only, she chided herself, that was the wrong way to think. Once she was Mrs Lewis Ashwood she could rip all this vulgar stuff out and start again, stamp her own taste on this house—and the others. She'd visited Lewis's Eastside apartment in New York but not the villa in Umbria. Lewis had staff to run these places but she knew he was suspicious of some of the arrangements that had been put in place. She'd formed the impression that, once she was his wife, household administration would be part of her job description. Why did that feel like a burden rather than a challenge? Many women her age would love to boss people around while wielding a large chequebook.

She met Cherry in the hall outside. It occurred to Roisin that Cherry would be just the type to make a success of organising Lewis's domestic affairs. Perhaps she'd be able to rope her in to help.

Roisin held the bathroom door open but Cherry didn't go in.

'I was looking for you,' she said. 'I just wanted to say thanks.'

'I didn't do much. Lewis did all the cooking.'

'That wasn't what I meant.' Cherry's hand found Roisin's. 'If it wasn't for you, I wouldn't be allowed through the door. Lewis was all set to

319

excommunicate Max until you stepped in. God knows what he was going to do to me—burning at the stake would be too good.'

Roisin laughed. 'Don't be daft. It was never that bad.'

'Yes, it was. You know he put a private detective on me. You've probably seen the report.'

Roisin nodded. She felt the pressure of Cherry's fingers and saw the intensity in her eyes.

'I don't know how you did it but you turned him round and I can't thank you enough.'

Roisin was embarrassed. She'd never been good at receiving compliments and Cherry's sincerity was unnerving.

'It's OK,' she said. 'He'd have come round anyway.'

'All the same,' Cherry was squeezing her hand as she spoke, 'it was noble of you in the circumstances.'

'Oh? What circumstances?' Roisin looked puzzled.

'I mean,' the blonde woman continued, her eyes big in her pale face, 'I understand how you can forgive Lewis, but to forgive me and Max too just shows what a wonderful person you are.'

'What do you mean?'

'You know. About the ferry accident. You must love Lewis very much.'

Roisin stood like a stone as Cherry leaned forward and kissed her on the cheek. The touch of her soft lips was like ice.

The ferry accident? This was something to do with Noel's death?

With a final squeeze Cherry released her hand and turned to walk away.

'What about the accident?' Roisin didn't

recognise the voice as her own. 'Tell me everything you know.'

'You mean Lewis hasn't said anything?'

It wasn't sincerity in those big eyes now, it was amusement.

'Tell me!' she hissed.

It was obvious Cherry had every intention of saying her piece, she was just playing with Roisin.

It was surprising how quickly you could change your opinion of someone.

But Roisin was no longer interested in Cherry, just in the story she began to tell. It tallied with all that her father had told her. The dreadful weather that delayed the ferry sailing, the expectation that the horsebox would not be allowed on board, the last-minute reversal of that decision.

But what she'd not heard had been the reason for the captain's change of mind.

'Max was on the phone to his dad on and off all the time we were waiting on the dock. I couldn't hear what Lewis was saying, of course, but it was obvious he wasn't happy about them not taking Black Mountain. Max had already had a row with someone in the terminal about it but Lewis just wouldn't accept the decision. After the last of these calls Max told me Lewis wanted him to bribe the ferry master. I stayed in the car while he drove to the bank and collected some money that Lewis wired over. We parked back at the ferry port and Max went into the terminal. He looked like he was off to the dentist. I could tell he didn't want to do any of this but, you know how it is, what Daddy says is what goes.'

Roisin concentrated on Cherry's face. Was she making any of this up? She no longer trusted her.

321

'Anyhow, when Max came back he looked like he'd just got out of jail. Relieved and excited all at the same time. I knew before he told us that the horse would be sailing. Later, on the boat, I got it out of him how much he paid—ten thousand pounds in Euros.'

'I don't believe you.' To Roisin the words sounded hollow, but she couldn't just accept this horrible story. Its implications were too dreadful.

Cherry nodded. 'I don't blame you. Denial is the best way to deal with something like this. If Lewis wanted you to know about it I'm sure he would have told you.'

'I stood up for you, Cherry. I thought you were being treated unfairly and you tell me lies like this.'

Cherry reached to take her hand again but Roisin pulled back.

'Go away. Get out of this house.'

'Please yourself.' Cherry smoothed her skirt and tugged at her sweater as if her appearance was the most important thing on her mind. 'Shoot the messenger—that's how Max said his father reacted when he told him the horse couldn't sail. If you really don't want to believe me, Roisin, don't ask your father whether Max drove off for fifteen minutes when we were waiting on the dock. Don't ask him how the ferry company changed their minds at the last minute after Max had been in the terminal. And don't start wondering why the master killed himself when he got home that night.'

Roisin said nothing further as Cherry turned and descended the stairs. But her words were lodged inside Roisin's head. Much as she wished it, there was no way Roisin could make them disappear.

322

Chapter Seventeen

When she was sure Lewis had left for the office, Roisin took a plastic folder from the table on her side of the bed. She'd only recently begun to think of any of Lewis's territory as 'hers'. That was ironic.

Downstairs she could hear a clatter of dishes as Lewis's housekeeper set about clearing up from the night before. There was plenty there to keep her busy. Roisin had intended to sort out the remains of the dinner party but, after her conversation with Cherry, she had not even gone downstairs to say goodbye. She'd locked herself in the bathroom and pleaded illness.

'I've got a migraine,' she'd said to Lewis through the door. 'I'll sleep in the spare room.'

He'd protested. 'I didn't even know you had migraines. You've never had one before.'

She'd not replied, just remained in the bathroom until he started shouting that he was going to call a doctor. When she emerged, she must have looked suitably convincing for he insisted on taking the spare room himself. And when he'd crept in that morning she'd just played dead.

Now she removed the newspaper cuttings from the folder and spread them on the table by the window that overlooked the garden. Even in winter it looked pretty; there were buds on the magnolia and the early-flowering cherry. In the summer it would be ravishing but the summer was a world away.

She'd kept the reports of the ferry accident, not as a ghoulish memento but as a chronicle of a significant event in her life. She'd scarcely been able to read them at the time but knew that, some day in the future, she must try and make sense of what had happened. It seemed that day had come sooner than she had thought.

The first coverage of the accident had focused on Noel's Black Mountain connection, with pictures of Noel next to the horse on almost every front page. Then, after the suicide of the ferry captain, Murray Watson, the emphasis shifted. There were photographs of Watson in his Royal Navy days, looking every inch the distinguished military commander—handsome, dependable, the kind of man you could trust with your life. Accompanying this shot was one of his wife, making a statement to reporters at her front gate, looking solemn and baggy-eyed but nevertheless with neat lacquered hair and fresh lipstick. Behind her was a thin girl in a shapeless sweater and a look of blank misery on her face—the dead man's daughter Christine, according to the caption.

Captain Watson, it seemed, was a man of impeccable record who had made an error of judgement in allowing Black Mountain to board in the heavy sea conditions. The Marine Accident Investigation Branch had been called in. It was expected that the inquest on Captain Watson's death would be adjourned until such time as the MAIB report would be available. In the meantime, the Watson family asked for their privacy to be respected while they grieved for a loving husband and father.

At the time, Roisin had reacted with fury— where were the words of regret and remorse for Noel's death? It was all very well this Watson doing the noble thing but what use was that? Creating another family tragedy seemed pointless.

'They're going on like the man's some bloody war hero,' she'd screamed at Lewis. 'He's a coward, that's all. He couldn't face taking the blame for Noel's death.'

'Don't get worked up about him,' Lewis had said. 'Try not to think of him at all.'

Now she wondered exactly why he had said that.

She shuffled though the little pile of cuttings and found a yellow Post-It note with a phone number scribbled on it. She'd copied it from a letter she'd received in the days following Noel's death. The letter had been to the point:

Dear Ms Dougherty,
You will probably not want to receive this but when I saw your picture in the paper I had to write to you.

I am the daughter of Murray Watson, the master of the ferry on the day your brother died. As you must know my father subsequently took his own life.

I'm finding it very hard to come to terms with what has happened, though I know I must somehow. Part of that is to say to you and your family how terribly sorry I am for what happened to your brother. I'm sure you will not want my condolences but believe me they come from my heart.

There is no need for you to reply to me. I'm sure you wouldn't anyhow but I wanted you to know that your family is in my prayers.
Christine Watson

On the top of the page, a mobile phone number had been written next to a printed West Country address. Though Christine had said she didn't expect Roisin to contact her, obviously she had hoped she might do so. And, once her emotions had settled, Roisin had considered it.

Here were two families linked by mutual grief. And the daughter, ghost-pale and shell-shocked in her photo, looked just as Roisin had felt. Maybe a healing connection could be forged between them.

But time had gone by and Lewis had grown in Roisin's life; he stood like an oak next to her, offering shelter, strength, comfort.

Some oak—it appeared he was rotten to the core.

No, she mustn't rush to judgement.

She dialled. As the phone rang, Roisin prepared a message to leave on the voicemail. Suddenly it was answered.

'Hi! Who is it? I'm dashing out.' The voice was loud and energetic, not what Roisin was expecting.

'Is that Christine Watson?'

'Yeah, yeah. Hurry up or I'll miss my bus.'

'Roisin Dougherty.'

'Who? Oh.'

Silence fell like a curtain.

'Christine? Are you still there?'

'Yes.'

'I got your letter. Can we talk? Not now, you're in a rush, I know—'

'It's OK. I don't care about the bus now.'

'Thank you.' Roisin hesitated. She wasn't sure where to start. 'Look, can we meet?' This would be better face to face. 'I'll come to you.'

'Really? But I'm in Nottingham, at the uni.'

'That's fine. I'll drive up from London.'

'Well . . .' Roisin could hear that she was taken aback by the urgency in her voice. Too bad.

'How about today?' Roisin said. 'I can be with you this afternoon.'

'This is very sudden, isn't it?'

'Does that matter?'

'No, not at all. I'll be out till four.' And she gave Roisin her address.

*   *   *

Victor Bishop didn't play much golf. It was one of those games that took up too much time. He'd rather be at the races. But this morning he was combining business with so-called pleasure, playing a few holes at Trevor Smailes's local club in Surrey. The empty course on a wintry Monday morning was an ideal place to review the nasty surprises of the last few days. So far, however, he'd listened in silence to the solicitor make small talk with the third member of the group, Brian Spot.

He addressed the ball, focusing his aggression— and he had plenty of that—in his special way. His driver made a satisfactory swish through the air as he smacked the ball with his full force, sending it sailing high up into the air and, for once, straight down the fairway.

'Great shot,' said Brian.

Victor could feel the sweetness of the hit tingling throughout his body. He pointed his club at Brian. 'It's in the mind,' he said. 'I just picture your brother's head on the tee.'

Brian's face fell. 'Not that again. Chris is the one who's been grassed up. Tell him, Trev.'

327

The solicitor, dapper in his golfing clothes, was busy practising his swing; plainly he did not want to be involved. With reluctance he turned to Victor. 'I attended all of the interviews. I can assure you Chris said nothing incriminating whatsoever.'

'But he's not going to say it in front of you, is he? You're not with him twenty-four hours a day.'

Trevor tugged nervously at his two-tone golfing gloves, as pristine as the rest of his equipment. He wasn't comfortable being in the firing line.

'You've got to get this nutty idea out of your head,' said Brian. 'The fact is, Chris was grassed up. He must have been. Customs was waiting for them at the handover.'

Victor wouldn't accept it. 'Look, we know the Cussies were sniffing around Chris's boys last year. They're not stupid. He got slack and they did him. But how did Customs get on to your Yank, eh? Just three days later. There's a link and I bet it's your flaming brother.'

In the silence that followed there came the *snick* of Trevor slicing his drive into the trees that flanked the right side of the fairway; he had all the latest gear but the solicitor couldn't hit the ball straight to save his life.

'We've been over this,' muttered Brian as he placed his ball on the tee. 'You've got no proof.'

Victor shrugged and waited till Brian was at the top of his wonky backswing before his next comment. 'Has Robinson coughed up my money yet?'

Brian's driver wobbled in its descent, but then it always did that; he wasn't the most orthodox player. Nevertheless his ball scudded and bumped its way down the middle of the fairway, landing some fifty yards behind Victor's but in Position A to cope with the dog-leg turn to the left.

Brian bagged his club. 'He's banged up, Vic. He can't sort it where he is.'

'He'd better. If I don't get my nine hundred grand I really am going to start playing golf with someone's head.'

* * *

Roisin caught herself touching 100mph on the motorway. She stamped on the brake and drove deliberately in the slow lane for the next few miles. She enjoyed driving fast but not when her thoughts were elsewhere. Right now they were flying all over the place, reinterpreting the past couple of months in the light of what Cherry had said. And in every interpretation, her saviour Lewis—her lover and future husband—emerged as a complete bastard.

But suppose Cherry had been lying? Roisin had to be sure before she acted.

All the same, she had packed her bags, clearing all her belongings from Lewis's house. She'd left the clothes he'd bought her hanging in the wardrobe and the jewellery on the dressing table.

Her first impulse had been to confront him directly, the moment Cherry and Max left the house the night before. It wasn't cowardice that stopped her, just the thought that she had no real evidence to challenge him with. Only what Cherry had told her. He could have denied it in that cold-eyed boardroom-bully way of his which was impossible to penetrate and then she'd never know the truth.

So she'd decided to get away, taking what she

needed with her in case she never went back.

What should she do about Lewis for now? She'd turned off her phone but doubtless there would be messages piling up for her. He thought she'd been ill so he'd be doubly solicitous.

She wasn't going to pretend all was well. But, on the other hand, she couldn't confront him until she was more certain.

In the end she did the obvious thing. 'I'm going back to Ireland for a few days,' she said. 'I don't like to leave Mum alone right now.'

That was unanswerable; he could hardly complain about her devotion to her grieving mother.

'It's a bit sudden, isn't it?' he complained. 'And you're not well.'

'I'll be better in Ireland. Sorry, Lewis, my battery's about to go.' And she'd cut him off. Not original maybe, but effective.

The address Christine had given her was in Lenton, an area Roisin instantly recognised as a student quarter. The large Victorian terraces were fronted by scrappy front gardens filled with overflowing wheelie bins; curtains in a variety of unpleasant 1970s patterns hung uncertainly in the front windows. The door she knocked on had been painted a perky fuschia pink some time in the last century. It didn't look so perky now.

It was opened by a tall skinny lad with an earring and cheekbones sharp enough to cut paper. He seemed to know who she was and pointed her through a door off the hall to her left. 'I'll get her for you,' he said, disappearing up the stairs.

The room was obviously a communal sitting room with two old sofas leaking stuffing grouped around a hearth and an old-fashioned black plastic-cased TV. The walls were booklined and the table in the window was littered with papers and a scattering of CD cases. But the vase on the mantelpiece held a display of brilliant yellow chrysanthemums and there was a cosy feel to the place. The contrast to the formal perfection of Lewis's opulent London home was stark.

'Hi, Roisin.'

She hadn't heard Christine come down the stairs but she was in the doorway, a small, slim girl lost in a loose check shirt worn over a high-necked black sweater and jeans. Her dark hair was held off her forehead by an Alice band and her eyes were huge grey pools in her ghost-white face. Behind her hovered the boy with the cheekbones, looking on proprietorially. Was that his shirt? Roisin wondered.

She was clutching a bottle of wine and she held it out, feeling foolish. This wasn't exactly a dinner party.

Christine thanked her for it and gave the bottle to the boy who disappeared into the house. Roisin sat on a sofa, which seemed to suck her in, as welcoming as a big soft bed. Christine perched in the corner of the other one, at right angles. Late afternoon sunshine filled the room and a clock ticked somewhere, the noise loud and clear in the nervous silence. Roisin didn't know where to start.

'Are you angry with me?' said Christine.

'No.' What was the girl thinking?

'Only, after you rang I got thinking, why is she coming all this way? And why now? But I spoke to Stefan and he thought maybe, with my father being involved in your brother's death, that you'd have this anger you'd need to resolve.'

Stefan, Roisin gathered, was the lad who'd let her in. The girl's boyfriend, watching out for her.

Roisin couldn't help smiling. 'Is Stefan studying psychology?'

'English, actually.' Christine raised a smile herself. 'It's just that, putting myself in your shoes, I'm not sure how I'd feel about meeting me.'

Roisin didn't know herself, she was still trying to work it all out. 'I haven't come here to make a scene, Christine.' The girl looked relieved. 'There's just some questions I'd like to ask about your father.'

'Call me Chrissie. Only my mother calls me Christine. But, sure, go ahead.'

Roisin searched for the right words.

The door opened and Stefan entered carrying a tray. 'I've made you some tea,' he said, his eyes darting inquisitively.

Chrissie sent him away after he'd put the tray down. Roisin imagined him standing guard outside the door. She ignored the tea and pile of crumbling biscuits. There was only one way to do this: plunge right in.

'Why do you think your father killed himself?'

As Roisin had feared, the girl's big grey eyes filled with tears and she felt her own prick in sympathy. It was going to be a long evening.

*   *   *

Ralph Morrell's old BMW was a comfortable machine to travel in. And though, like most jockeys, Alan didn't much enjoy being driven, he made an exception for his father. It took him back to when he was a kid. Funnily enough, sitting in the back seat with his father at the wheel was very much like being a kid again, only the woman in the passenger seat was not his mother but Linda Parsons, the nation's favourite middle-aged sweetheart. 'Pensioner's totty' was how she described herself, so maybe driving with the pair of them wasn't much like being a kid after all.

They were on their way back from a day at Exeter races, where Alan had been dumped by his third ride of the day before they had even completed the first circuit of the three-mile chase. His first thought, as he had painfully levered himself out of the mud, was that he had damaged his wrist. That would be a blow. He had to be fit to ride Grain of Sand at Wincanton in a few days. But on the long trudge back across the course the pain had eased and now, sitting in the comfortable leather embrace of the BMW with an ice pack on his wrist, he was confident he would be OK.

'Hey, genius.' Linda turned to face Alan. 'Next time I ignore your advice, shoot me before I put the money down, will you?' Having punted shrewdly and drunk liberally, she was in a jovial mood. Her only bad bet of the afternoon was one Alan had warned her against.

'What made you so sure,' she continued, 'that Nautical wasn't going to win?'

Nautical had the form to win in the mares-only novice chase and had caught Linda's eye in the parade ring. Alan's attention had been taken not so much by the horse as the fact that Ian Rafter trained it.

'Just a hunch,' he said. 'There's been some disappointing runners from the Rafter stable

333

recently.'

'But he trained the winner of the first,' Linda protested. 'That's why I wanted to back her. And she looked so good in the ring.'

This was true. Nautical had also looked good for the first half of the two-mile three-furlong race then she had run out of steam and tailed off embarrassingly. Alan hadn't been surprised. He'd noticed Nautical slipping in the betting and been aware that there was only one other serious contender. If he'd been allowed to bet—which, as a jockey, he wasn't—he'd have stuck his shirt on Susannah Superstar, who had duly obliged at 7 to 2.

He didn't know what to say to Linda. That he suspected there was something illegal going on at Ian Rafter's yard? That his friend who worked there was too scared to talk to him about it? That there were certain races where the honest punter, such as herself, might just as well set fire to her money as stake it on a horse to win.

Ralph saved him the bother.

'Al reckons that race was fixed, don't you, son?'

'Really?' Linda sounded excited rather than outraged. She turned to Ralph. 'I suppose you two would know all about that.'

So Linda was aware of his father's disreputable past.

'Leave Al out of it, Linda,' Ralph said. 'He's never done anything dodgy on a racecourse in his life.'

'How did you know then?' Linda demanded.

Alan found himself telling her the story of Olympia and Nightswimmer and Jane who now wouldn't speak to him, explaining, too, the mechanics of laying odds on the internet betting exchanges. Linda loved it all—it appealed to her sense of drama.

Ralph, who'd kept silent, suddenly spoke up.

'I remember,' he said, 'when I was an apprentice at a yard near Oxford, one of the other lads was from a local farm. His big brother used to keep a greyhound and they knew all sorts of tricks to make money out of him. One of them was to take the dog down to the river on the way to the races. They'd stick him in a harness, lower him into the river and let him swim for fifteen minutes against the current.'

'What was the point of that?' said Linda. 'The poor animal would be tired out.'

'Exactly. They'd do this a few times to make sure the dog didn't win. Then, when everyone thought he didn't have a chance and the odds were good, they'd lump a load of money on him. No swim before the race this time. Do you see?'

Alan didn't know whether Linda had worked it out, but he had. If you exhausted an animal before a race he'd be too tired to win—but he'd pass any drugs test going.

Why hadn't he thought of that?

*   *   *

The tea had been replaced by Roisin's wine and, when the other housemates began to return, Chrissie led her upstairs to her room where they wouldn't be disturbed. The pair of them sprawled across the large double bed which dominated the small space; it was the only place to sit.

A large photograph of Chrissie with her father

stood on the dressing table—taken, Roisin guessed, in Chrissie's last year at school. The pair of them were standing on the summit of a hill, smiles of triumph on their faces, his arm round her waist, her head on his shoulder.

By now Roisin knew how close father and daughter had been; that her real mother had died of a brain tumour when Chrissie was eleven; and that she dismissed her stepmother, Barbara, as shallow and mercenary. 'She'll be married again in a couple of years,' Chrissie had said. 'She's on the lookout for a man already.'

In all the daughter's talk of her father, she'd not come up with an answer to Roisin's first question. She didn't know why her dad had killed himself. Not really. The question gnawed at her.

'When he was at home, my dad was as soft as toffee. I could get him to do anything and so could Barbara. She had him dancing to her tune all the time. But at work he was different. I know that because the men he served with in the Navy told me and because I've been with him when he was working for the ferry company. Anything to do with his ship and his command and he was the boss. If he made a decision he'd stick to it—and he'd defend it to the hilt. Even if he'd made a mistake in sailing with the horse on board, he'd have made it for the right reasons. And he wouldn't have been afraid to say so afterwards. Do you see what I mean?'

Roisin did indeed. It had seemed strange to her that a ship's captain, no matter how filled with remorse, would not stand up for himself. There could be many reasons for the unfortunate accident on board—vehicles not secured properly, a failure of safety equipment, deficient procedures in allowing Noel onto the vehicle deck—which the forthcoming MAIB report would doubtless raise. For the captain to pre-empt the whole business by killing himself suggested that there were other reasons for his state of mind.

Thanks to Cherry, Roisin had an idea what those reasons might be but she still hadn't summoned the nerve to bring the matter of bribery into the open.

Chrissie had shown Roisin the note her father had left her on his death. It was short and uninformative. Murray Watson loved his daughter more than anything or anybody in the world. He was proud of her and knew she had a fine life ahead. He hoped he'd been a good father to her and that she would forgive him this moment of indulgence. He had no choice.

If Roisin had not cried herself out already she'd have started up again. 'What do you think he meant by "I have no choice"?' she said.

Chrissie carefully folded the sheet of paper and put it away. 'I wish I knew.'

'The papers said there was a note for your mother.'

'He said he couldn't face retirement and she'd be better off without him.'

'And do you believe him?'

She raised a wan smile. 'Maybe it was the thought of her nagging him all day to spend money he hadn't got.'

'So they didn't get on?'

'Everything was fine as long as Barbara had something to amuse her. You know, a party to plan, a holiday to look forward to. She couldn't just be happy, that's what Dad used to say. He was supposed to provide entertainment for her all the time.'

Was that enough reason for a man to kill himself? Roisin wondered.

Chrissie reached for the wine bottle and refilled her glass; Roisin's was still full.

'You know,' Chrissie said, 'I've imagined the wildest things. Like Barbara having a lover and getting him to kill Dad and make it look like suicide.'

'And forge the letters he left behind?'

'I know, it's stupid, isn't it? But she was up to something, I'm sure.'

'You really think she had a lover?'

'Maybe. Suppose she was about to leave Dad and he found out. And when the accident happened it just pushed him too far. That could be why he went on about her being better off without him in the note he left her.'

Roisin studied Chrissie—was it the wine talking?

'Have you got any evidence she was being unfaithful?' she asked.

Chrissie giggled. 'You mean, like love letters or hotel receipts or those funny phone calls where the other person hangs up? No.' She gulped her wine. 'Anyway, I wasn't there during term. All I know is that's the kind of thing she'd do. And she had a load of cash just after Dad died—that's suspicious, isn't it?'

Roisin's heart stopped. She slowly lifted her glass to her lips and sipped. She spoke slowly. 'Really? Where do you think it came from?'

'When I got home after she found Dad's body she was in a terrible state. I was too. It was like sleepwalking through days that never ended. Well, you know, don't you?'

Roisin said nothing.

'Barbara put on a good front for all the reporters who turned up but she was like a jelly inside. I'd make her take the sedatives the doctor gave us and put her to bed. I didn't take them myself. I stayed up and went through all of the important things. I made sure the will was in place and sorted the household admin, like bills that had to be paid. Anyway, I found a load of banknotes in her jewellery box, which was a stupid place to put them. It's the first place a burglar's going to look, isn't it?'

'How much?'

'Enough to keep you going for a bit. Enough to run away with someone. It was in Euros, so maybe that's what she was planning to do.'

Euros. That's what Cherry had said. It proved it, surely. To be certain, Roisin said, 'Like a couple of thousand?'

'Much more than that. Fifteen, twenty thousand—I didn't count it all. Where would she have got that kind of money?'

Roisin knew but she wasn't sure it would be wise to tell Chrissie.

'Did you ask her about it?'

'I didn't want her to know I'd been snooping among her things And when I next looked, the money wasn't there.' She looked at Roisin sharply. 'You must think I'm mad.'

'No. But I think you're looking for someone to blame for your dad's death and Barbara is a pretty handy scapegoat.'

'Who's the psychologist now then?'

'Sorry.'

They both grinned.

Roisin looked at her watch. It was eight in the evening and she could hear music and loud conversation floating up the stairs. She didn't know what she was going to do with the rest of her life but she knew one thing: she wasn't going back to Lewis.

'Are you hungry?' she said. 'I can order a takeaway.'

Chrissie's pale face glowed in the dim light. She was smiling.

'There's always hungry people here,' she said.

Suddenly they were hugging with a fierce intensity.

Thanks to Chrissie, Roisin now knew the truth but she couldn't bear to tell the girl the real reason her father had killed herself. The notion that her beloved father had betrayed his principles and taken a bribe would be terrible for her to cope with. For Chrissie's sake, Roisin hoped she would never find out.

*   *   *

Max surprised Cherry. When she got back late from the club he told her he had been to the Register Office and booked a date for the wedding. She flung her arms round his neck in elation.

He'd booked it for the week after Cheltenham. She did a quick calculation. The date was not ideal for her purposes but she guessed she could live with it. By the wedding she'd be ten weeks pregnant, in theory anyway. It would be sad to lose the baby on her honeymoon but that couldn't be helped.

'I love you,' she said and hugged him tight.

340

The sound of the phone disturbed their embrace. Max disentangled himself with reluctance and she went to the kitchen to fetch a drink. She allowed herself to savour the glow of satisfaction his words had lit within her. A wedding date, that was something. She wasn't out of the woods yet but this was a significant milestone on her path.

Max was calling from the front room.

'It's Dad,' he said, holding out the receiver. 'Roisin's gone missing and he wants to talk to you.'

'Why me?' she said innocently but took the phone.

'Hello, Lewis.' She injected warmth into her voice. 'I hope Max has thanked you properly for last night. We had a marvellous time.'

But he wasn't in the mood for niceties. Well, she could imagine that he wouldn't be.

'Have you heard from Roisin?'

'No. What's wrong?'

'I don't know where she is. She said she was going back to Ireland but she's not arrived and I can't get her on the phone.'

'Oh dear,' she offered.

'Did she say anything to you last night?'

'Not about going to Ireland.'

'Was she OK? She complained of a migraine after you'd left and I couldn't get any sense out of her.'

That was interesting, Cherry thought. She might as well go along with it. 'Roisin didn't say anything about not feeling well but I thought she was looking a little pale.' That bit was true at any rate.

'You were up there long enough. What were you talking about?'

He sounded suspicious. Time to mollify him.

341

'To be honest, Lewis, I was thanking her for her support. I wanted to let her know that you and I had cleared the air. And that I knew it wouldn't have been possible without her help. Of course, I also told her how happy I was that you two are getting married.'

'Right. I see.' The gruffness in his tone had eased.

'Look, Lewis, I'm sure she's fine. I mean, she's a pretty independent woman, isn't she? It might not occur to her to check in with you tonight. If I were you, I'd go to bed.'

There was a short pause before he spoke again. 'I suppose you're right, Cherry.'

Max was looking at her curiously as she ended the call.

'What was that all about?'

'Like you said, he hasn't heard from Roisin.'

'What's that got to do with you?'

She shrugged. She had no intention of telling him the truth—let him work it out if he was able. 'I think your dad just needed a bit of reassurance.'

'From you?'

'Good, isn't it?' She snuggled up next to him on the sofa. 'We're going to take care of him, you and me.'

He stroked her belly softly. 'And the little one.'

Who?

It was an effort sometimes to remember she was pregnant.

Chapter Eighteen

Roisin reached the Dougherty farm at breakfast time. By rights she should have been tired but for the moment she was keeping exhaustion at bay. She'd thought she might sleep on the ferry in the small hours but, on reflection, that would never have been possible. If there had been any other means of travel open to her she would have taken it, but she couldn't put her car on a plane.

Her mother had not been surprised to see her step through the door.

'Your Lewis has been on the phone ten times,' was her greeting. 'You won't be able to skitter around like this when you're a married woman, you know.'

'I'm not married yet,' she said. She kissed her mother and studied her with concern. The older woman had had enough trouble to contend with recently and here she was bringing more. But there was no way to avoid it.

'You'd better call that man of yours,' said Pauline, 'and put him out of his misery.'

'Not before I speak to Dad.'

She walked through the yard in search of her father. He was the only person she could talk to about what she had discovered about Noel's death. And what she had to tell him would have a profound effect.

She followed the path up the slope from where she could look down onto the long paddock. As expected, dimly visible through the early morning mist, her father was overseeing the horses. She was in no hurry to join them. This was a labour of love for him, he might as well enjoy it while he could.

At length he turned for the path back to the yard. Con and Black Mountain led the string. Con was on a tight schedule as he had to change and cycle to school. Roisin waited till he'd passed through the gate into the yard before she hailed her father.

Tom allowed himself to be kissed, looking keenly into her eyes. He knew something serious was up.

'Come and help me do the horse up,' he said. 'And tell me what's on your mind.'

Tom rubbed Black Mountain down as she talked. He interrupted her from time to time with softly spoken instructions and she fetched a hoof pick and changed the horse's water. He didn't fill the gaps in her tale with unnecessary queries or expressions of emotion. He nodded when she described Cherry's version of events while waiting for the ferry to depart.

'Max did drive off, right enough. He couldn't have been away more than twenty minutes. Not that even.'

She told him about her flight from Lewis's flat and her trip to Nottingham to see the captain's daughter. And Chrissie's discovery of the banknotes.

When she had finished, Tom stood in silence for what seemed an age. Then he said, 'It's all my fault. I let Lewis buy me with this fellow here.' And he laid his hand fondly on Black Mountain's muzzle.

'No, Dad.' She wasn't having that. 'He bought the horse and asked you to carry on training him. That's fair enough.'

'Roisin, I know what those sort of men are like. They think they can buy everything in life. I knew he was trying to buy you and I should have said no. If he'd taken Blackie to another yard none of this would have happened.'

'And if I'd seen through him earlier then it wouldn't have happened either. We can't blame ourselves, Dad. He's the villain here, not you or me.'

In the silence that followed, Black Mountain began to investigate her father's pockets for food. Tom allowed him to extract a carrot.

'What are you going to do?' he said.

'I thought I'd come back here. I've had enough of London.'

He smiled for the first time that morning but the smile vanished as he said, 'I meant about Lewis.'

'I never want to see him again.'

'There's people investigating the accident. You could tell them what you know.'

She shook her head. 'The captain is dead. He's paid his price already.'

'But the findings will be made public. It's a good thing for men like Lewis Ashwood to get a bloody nose from time to time.'

'I can't do that to Chrissie Watson, Dad. She's lost someone too and none of this is her fault.'

He nodded. He accepted what she said.

'Do you want me to deal with Lewis for you?'

Should she let him? Surely it was her job to tell Lewis to get out of her life.

'No, Dad. I've got to tell him myself.'

He put a big, bear-like arm round her shoulder. 'When you've done it, let me know. And I'll get him to remove his horse.'

'Dad, I'm so sorry.' She buried her face in his chest and he held her tight.

Black Mountain began to hunt for another carrot.

When they got up to the house, Pauline told them that Lewis had been on the phone again. He was flying over that morning.

*   *   *

Roisin drove to Shannon airport and mounted guard by the arrivals gate. She knew Lewis's travel habits well enough to predict he'd be stepping off an Aer Lingus flight from Heathrow shortly before one o'clock. It was the only direct flight in the middle of the day and Lewis was not a man to waste time being shunted via Dublin or Manchester.

Her father had queried her decision to go and meet him.

'I don't want him coming to the yard, Dad. He'll get round Mum somehow and make a scene in our home. I'm going to get rid of him on neutral territory.' And she'd turned down Tom's offer to accompany her. This was her dirty work.

The airport announcements seemed distant, as if she had cotton wool in her ears, but that was the only sign of her fatigue. When this was over and done with she'd sleep but, until she'd cut Lewis Ashwood out of her life, rest would be impossible. Cotton wool or not, she'd hear every word that came from his guilty lips.

He was among the first to emerge through the gate, cashmere overcoat slung across his shoulders, his leather overnight bag in his fist. He didn't see

346

her at first as he headed for the Hertz desk. She stepped into his path.

'Roisin!' He dropped his bag and flung his arms wide.

She refused his embrace.

'What's the matter, darling? Are you still not well? You shouldn't have come to meet me, I've arranged a car.'

'Don't bother, Lewis. We can talk here. Then I want you to go back.'

He stared at her as if she had spoken Chinese. 'Are you sure you're feeling all right?'

She ignored him and turned for the stairs to the first floor. He followed as she led him into the self-service restaurant and found a table that was reasonably isolated. It would have to do.

He put his bag and coat on a chair and looked at her without speaking, assessing the situation. He wasn't a fool.

'I'll have a coffee,' she said.

'And then you'll tell me what this is all about?'

She nodded and took a seat. She watched as he queued at the counter. Already he looked diminished in her eyes, greyer and slower than he'd always seemed. A man more her father's age than her own. She looked away.

'Well?' he said, taking the seat opposite her. 'What's up?'

She forced herself to look directly into his eyes. 'I don't want to see you any more, Lewis.'

He shook his head, as if denying her words. His mouth stretched into a small smile. 'This is a joke, isn't it?'

'No. Our relationship was a mistake and I'm sorry I encouraged you. It stops right here.'

He leaned back in his chair. 'I understand if you're having cold feet about the wedding. I've been pushing, I know. I'll back off and you can take all the time you like to think about it.'

He looked unconcerned, his tone reasonable and his gaze benevolent. As if she'd been wasting her breath. It infuriated her.

'You're not listening to me, Lewis. This is not some negotiating position. I want you to piss off out of my life and never come near me or my family again.'

The vehemence in her voice had an effect this time. She could see confusion in his eyes.

'Why, Roisin?'

At last.

'You know why. Because you killed my brother.'

He stared at her helplessly—she'd got through all right. Then his face hardened.

'Have you gone crazy? That's a ridiculous thing to say.'

'Don't deny it, Lewis. I know.'

'For God's sake,' he reached across the table and grabbed her hand, 'how on earth could his death have had anything to do with me? I was five hundred miles away.'

She jerked her fingers free, sending coffee splashing. 'You might not have been there but Max was. You were on the phone to him all the time. You wired him money and got him to bribe the ferry captain to take Black Mountain.'

He looked stunned and sat there motionless, his sleeve in a pool of coffee.

'That's a complete lie,' he managed finally.

'Don't bother, Lewis. Like I just said, I know.'

'Who's been spreading this slander? I'll sue.'

She shrugged. 'Do what you like, it won't change a thing. I have proof.'

'What proof?'

'Proof enough for me to know that I should never have got involved with you in the first place.'

'Tell me. I want to know.'

'Why? So you can try and lie your way out? Whatever you say, it's over, Lewis.'

His face seemed to sag. 'I didn't bribe anyone.'

'No, you got your son to do it. It's the same thing. You're a bigshot bully, Lewis. You bribe and buy your way through life and you don't care about the consequences.'

His cheeks flushed. 'Of course I care. I care about you. I love you more than I've ever loved anybody. I'd never do anything to hurt you.'

She didn't doubt the sincerity of what he said but that wasn't the issue. 'Noel is dead,' she said. 'That changes everything.'

He didn't move.

'I understand that you want to blame someone, Roisin, but it was a terrible accident. Please believe me.'

She said nothing.

He reached for her hand again across the table and she pulled back. 'I love you,' he said. 'Everything I have is yours. I can't bring him back but I can make it up to you. Just ask.'

What had she ever seen in him?

'Don't grovel, Lewis. Just go away.'

He sat as if anaesthetised.

She was feeling very tired now but it was almost over. The hissing in her ears was like static on a badly tuned radio.

Finally he got to his feet, picked up his bag.

349

'Dad's going to call you about removing Black Mountain,' she said. 'You might want to make arrangements and save him the call.'

He didn't acknowledge her words, just stared at her as if committing her to memory.

'I'm sorry,' he said finally and turned away. A trail of coffee spots marked his way.

When he'd disappeared from sight, Roisin closed her eyes. She wished she could sleep forever.

*   *   *

'You're in luck,' said the girl on the desk when Lewis asked for the first available flight back to Heathrow. 'There's been a delay on Aer Lingus. If you run you can just make it.'

As Lewis stowed his damp jacket in the overhead locker of the same plane that had brought him to Ireland, he did not feel lucky. A stewardess he recognised from before was doubtless about to remark on his reappearance when he shut her up with a scowl. He'd guessed he'd have to deal with a crisis when he'd chased after Roisin that morning, but nothing like this.

He'd almost forgotten about his part in the ferry accident. After all, what real connection was there between providing an incentive for the captain to allow Black Mountain to sail and the stupidity of the horse's handler? If Noel hadn't gone onto the vehicle deck then he wouldn't have got hurt. But this wasn't an opinion that would cut any ice with Roisin. The fact that her brother had been a fool wouldn't make any difference.

He'd had one conversation with Max about the

affair, just after it had happened.

'Who knows about you talking to the captain?' he'd asked.

'One or two people in the terminal. But when I slipped him the envelope we were on our own in an office. No one saw me.'

That had been a relief.

'So no one knows about the money but you and me?'

'Correct. Don't worry, Dad, I've forgotten it already.'

So how had Roisin found out? Maybe she'd been talking to Tom and put two and two together. Max wasn't the most discreet of operators. It was possible his behaviour on the dock had been suspicious.

Whatever the reason, Roisin had found out and now he'd lost her. There would be no going back from this.

The picture she'd painted of him had hurt, that he was just a bully with deep pockets, that he only knew one way to deal with a problem—to pull out a chequebook. That wasn't true. He wasn't just a money bags. He knew the value of people and relationships. It was just that, as a businessman, sometimes you had to stick your neck out to get things done. If Roisin had stayed with him she would have come to appreciate the simple truths of living in the real world. Maybe she was too young for him after all. He should be setting his cap at a more mature woman, one who wasn't still weighed down by the crap of youthful idealism.

But he loved Roisin, his pure Irish beauty. And now she loathed him—he had seen it in the way she'd shrunk from his touch.

He tried to push the pain and humiliation to one side. She knew things that must remain secret— how was he going to ensure that they did? It didn't matter that whatever 'proof' she had uncovered was unlikely to stand up in a court of law. If the story of his sweetener to the ferry captain became public, then it could be damaging in all sorts of ways. These days a prominent businessman had to guard his image with care.

He thought it unlikely that Roisin would start broadcasting her discovery. Those principles that had driven her to cutting him out of her life would prevent her spreading poison about him, surely. But could he rely on her natural discretion?

As he sat there, lulled by the drone of the plane's engines, he considered his options. Roisin was lost, he accepted that, but there was one thing he could do that might make her think of him more kindly—and ensure that she kept her secrets to herself.

*   *   *

For all her fatigue, Roisin didn't sleep as much as she would have liked. Breaking the news of her split with Lewis to the other members of the family had not made for restful circumstances.

It had taken a while for her mother to grasp what she was saying.

'I know girls these days don't like to be rushed to the altar. I wouldn't make him wait too long though, he's not got time on his side like you.'

'Ma, you don't understand. I'm not going to marry Lewis.'

'Sure, you say that now. You might think

352

differently in a week or two when you're pining for your London life. And I wouldn't blame you.'

The difficulty was that Roisin and Tom had decided not to tell anyone of the real reason for the rupture.

'Mum won't be able to keep it to herself, Dad. Everyone will want to know why I've broken it off and she's bound to confide in someone. Might as well broadcast it on Radio Kerry.'

Tom had agreed. 'She's going to need a reason though.'

'I'll think of something,' she said.

But she hadn't, at least nothing that satisfied her mother. When the penny had finally dropped that her daughter's relationship was over, Pauline had kept coming up with questions.

'Why should the age gap matter to you now? You've spent months telling me it makes no difference and suddenly it does.'

'It's just part of it, Ma. He's not the man I thought he was.'

'Oh really? He's an upstanding God-fearing fellow, as far as I can tell. And he's more successful than any of the fancy jackeens you could hope to meet over here. You do realise the kind of living you're throwing away, don't you?'

Roisin felt no pangs for the lifestyle of the rich but she knew the same could not be said of her mother—a woman who had scrubbed and toiled all her days. She must have been looking forward to some of the material benefits of becoming Lewis Ashwood's mother-in-law. Roisin felt bad about it but it couldn't be helped. If her mother knew the truth she'd spit in Lewis's face no matter how much money he held in his fist.

353

Finally, Roisin said, 'Lewis is by no means as God-fearing as he makes out. He only told you he was a believer because he knew you wanted to hear it. That's how a hypocrite like him operates.'

That had shut her mother up but she'd gone about the house as if there had been another death in the family.

It was Con, however, who'd taken it worst of all, once it had been explained that Black Mountain would be moving from the yard. He'd said nothing, he couldn't. The pain had gripped him from the inside, twisting his face into a grotesque mask of grief, and then the tears had begun to flow.

Roisin had found it hard to sleep with the sound of Con's sobs echoing through the thin walls.

During the night she heard footsteps on the stairs and toing and froing in the yard. She got up to find her father, his shabby old coat pulled over his pyjamas, standing in the hall, holding a torch.

'It's the boy,' he said. 'He's gone to sleep in the stall with the horse and I haven't the heart to shift him.' He sighed heavily. 'It could be Blackie's last night, I suppose.'

There'd been a call in the afternoon from Jackie in Lewis's office to say that instructions about Black Mountain would arrive the next day.

'I'm so sorry, Dad,' she said.

'Con'll get over it,' he said, putting his arms round her. 'You had no choice.'

Her father's embrace was a comfort but she lay awake all night all the same.

The morning brought a letter, couriered from London. She read it with disbelief.

Dear Roisin,

Let's keep this businesslike. I'm sure you wouldn't expect me to proceed any other way.

Following our meeting yesterday I accede to your request to sever our connection. For my part, I do so with deep regret. You know the depth of my feelings. I promise I will make no attempt to contact you or involve myself in your affairs in the future. I would like to place on record the regard I have for your entire family and how much I regret the events of last December which ended in unforeseeable tragedy.

Concerning Black Mountain. You are correct in assuming that I acquired the horse to ensure he continued to be trained by the man best suited to the task: your father. I think it would be a pity if the change in our relationship should affect the relationship between the horse and his trainer.

Consequently, I propose to turn the ownership of Black Mountain over to you. In return I ask for no payment, only the discretion that is owed by any intimate friend to a former partner.

I shall forward the necessary paperwork in connection with the transfer of ownership in the next few days.

Roisin, please accept this offer in the spirit of our past friendship.

Lewis

She didn't want anything of Lewis's. Not the clothes he'd bought her, the jewels, his houses—or

355

his horses. He was responsible for the death of her brother. There was no way round that.

But it wasn't just her sense of propriety that was at issue.

She showed the letter to her father. She could see the light that suddenly shone in his face as he read it. But it faded as he returned the letter and said, 'You do what you think is right, Roisin.'

'It's no better than blood money,' she said.

He didn't reply, just looked in the direction of the stables where Con was saying his last goodbye to Black Mountain. The boy had refused to go to school that day and nobody had opposed him.

Roisin followed his gaze. Was she being selfish? After all, blood money was a kind of justice.

'I don't want anything of Lewis's,' she said. 'But that doesn't mean somebody shouldn't benefit.'

She went back to the house and got Jackie on the phone.

'Tell Lewis I accept his proposal provided he puts the horse in Con's name.'

Two minutes later she returned to the yard and walked out into the paddock, calling to Con. She was about to turn his darkness into light. If only someone could do that for her.

*   *   *

'What?' Max stared at his father, scandalised. 'You've given the horse away?'

'Keep your voice down.' It was mid-morning, too early for the lunchtime crowd in the Canary Wharf bar, but all the same Lewis noted one or two office types lounging around. 'Your big mouth's caused enough trouble.'

Lewis wasn't feeling overly sympathetic to his son. Max seemed to care more about his chances of riding Black Mountain than his father's broken romance.

'Honestly, Dad, I swear to you I told no one.'

'How else did it get out then?'

Max shrugged. 'Maybe Captain Whatsit spilled the beans before he topped himself.'

Lewis hadn't considered that. On the face of it, it didn't seem likely. But Watson's daughter had been in touch with Roisin; he remembered her telling him she'd had a letter from the girl.

'I haven't heard from Tom Dougherty,' said Max. 'Do you think I might still get the ride?'

Lewis shot him a pitying look. 'Roisin knows you set up the captain. You've got more chance of being the next king of England than ever getting back on Black Mountain.'

Max glared at him. Lewis knew what he was thinking, that somehow his father should fix the situation. 'My train set's broken, Daddy. Please buy me another one.' If only it were that simple.

'Oh well.' The little boy look slid from Max's face. 'I don't reckon Black Mountain's going to win the Champion Hurdle anyway.'

'Why on earth not?'

'Because, apart from the fact he's a crotchety devil who's never raced out of his own backyard, he's one-paced.'

Lewis laughed. 'Rocket-paced, you mean.'

'Sure, but it takes a while to get him firing. He'll always be vulnerable to a horse with a turn of foot. And there's another reason.'

'Yes?' Lewis was listening. Max was telling him things he didn't know and, for once, he was impressed.

'I reckon I know the horse who's got the beating of Black Mountain. Grain of Sand. I've watched him work up at Tim Davy's yard.'

The name rang a bell. The late lamented Noel Dougherty had had some connection with the owner, who'd had trouble raising money to keep the horse. Lewis had expected to be tapped up himself at one time but the approach had never come.

'He's kept his Flat speed, Dad, and taken to hurdles as if he was born for it. I've talked to the lad who rides work on him. He says Sandy goes up through the gears like a Formula One racing car.'

'Why don't I know about him?'

'Because he's only had one outing over hurdles—a nothing novice race at Newbury. He walked it. But he's in the Kingwell at Wincanton this afternoon.'

'Sounds like I should get some money on him.'

'I wouldn't know about that. I don't bet.' And Max winked.

Lewis raised a grin and his son's hand landed on his. 'I'm sorry about Roisin, Dad.' Better late than never, he supposed.

*   *   *

Alan had never been more nervous before a race. The Kingwell Hurdle at Wincanton was a true test of Grain of Sand's ability, as it was each year for Cheltenham hopefuls. Sandy had been entered for both the Novice Hurdle and the Champion Hurdle at the Festival. How he performed today would decide which race he would run.

358

But if the contest was a trial for the horse, it was also one for the jockey. In fact, Alan thought as they hacked down to the start, it was worse for him because he knew exactly what was at stake. As far as Sandy was concerned, this was just another day at the races and, so far in his career, he'd always enjoyed those.

The race in prospect was bound to be a tougher encounter than the novice hurdle at Newbury where Sandy had crucified the opposition.

'You won't have it all your own way today,' Alan murmured as he lined up amongst the seven other runners.

It was a classy field, with some of the contenders familiar to race-goers from past heroics, together with a couple of newcomers already tipped to feature at Cheltenham. That category, of course, also contained Grain of Sand. Alan reminded himself he had no cause to feel overawed in this company—not yet anyway.

In Sandy's previous race at Newbury, Alan had held him up on the inside towards the rear of the field, fearful of running his race too soon. Today was different. Though it was mid-February the course was dry and quick, and there'd been talk beforehand about a fast time. In particular, commentators were relishing the prospect of a duel between the current Champion Hurdler, Tiger Tim, and Narcotic, who'd finished third to him at the Festival; if the two of them went head to head, it might even produce a record.

However, when the starter let them go, it was another novice, Big Beau, who led the way. He had bags of early speed and took the runners along at proper Champion Hurdle pace for the first mile and a quarter before he began to tire. At that point Narcotic took over and Alan let Grain of Sand track him through. For a few strides before leaving the back straight, the jockey on Narcotic took a pull; trying to get some air into his mount's lungs ready for the downhill run for home. The rest of the field bunched up behind him.

Alan had Sandy glued to the leader's tail, ready for him to make his move. They were travelling easily as Alan steered Sandy into Narcotic's slipstream and then, approaching the penultimate hurdle, moved alongside to challenge. Both horses were now flat to the boards and Alan was pushing for all he was worth.

The last hurdle was coming up fast; it was just a short run-in from there to the winning post. As Alan realised they were close to another win, he registered a blur of movement on his outside. Tiger Tim was making his move.

The two horses took the hurdle in line and battled stride for stride towards the post. Alan couldn't believe Sandy had anything left to give but he hit him once with the whip. Incredibly, the horse switched up to overdrive for the last few yards. As he crossed the line they were three lengths clear and going away from their rivals. And they were one second inside the course record. More important from Alan's point of view, there was now no doubt that Sandy would run in the Champion Hurdle.

He thought of Roisin Dougherty. It was what she had predicted. She'd be in the parade ring at Cheltenham on the arm of Lewis Ashwood. There was something to look forward to.

It didn't really take the gloss off his victory.

*   *   *

'That's a nice horse, all right.' Tom Dougherty was watching the replay of the finish at Wincanton.

'Nice?' Roisin was on her feet, still fizzing from the way Grain of Sand had burned off the opposition. 'He's a serious contender.'

'Blackie'll handle him all right. He's got more firepower than any of those others.'

Roisin, still mesmerised by Grain of Sand's performance, wasn't so sure. But she had no desire to dampen the mood of optimism that had swept through the Dougherty house with the knowledge that Black Mountain was to remain part of their lives. Better than that, Blackie was officially one of the family and not a word could be said against him.

The papers for the transfer of ownership had arrived that morning. They'd seemed straightforward until Roisin had read the final clause: 'In consideration of this Gift, Roisin Dougherty and her family agree not to divulge to a third party any knowledge or information concerning Lewis Ashwood, his family or associates without the written approval of the Donor.'

'He's done it again,' she hissed as she showed the words to her father. 'He's buying my silence with the horse.'

He nodded. He wasn't surprised, obviously.

'It's OK,' she added. 'I'm not going to insist we send Blackie away.' She couldn't do that now, not to Con or her father. She didn't want the bribery to come out anyway, for Chrissie's sake. But this was typical Lewis, the noble gesture that masked self-

361

interest.

Next time, if there was ever to be a next time, she'd find a man with principles.

*   *   *

The man without principles watched the Kingwell Hurdle on a portable television he kept in his office for just this sort of occasion. Given what Max had told him about Grain of Sand, Lewis was not surprised by his victory. He was elated nonetheless. Everything about the horse looked right and, in seeing off Tiger Tim and Narcotic, he had already beaten two of the fancied Champion Hurdle contenders. If any horse had a chance of beating Black Mountain, it was Grain of Sand. And suddenly Lewis very much wanted to beat Black Mountain.

His elation stemmed from the seed of an idea that had popped into his head when he remembered the financial problems of Grain of Sand's owner. Why not buy the horse himself? That way he'd still have a runner in the Champion Hurdle and Max would have his ride—Daddy would have fixed it, as he always did. And, now he'd seen the horse in action, he'd have a serious chance of putting one over on the Doughertys.

Lewis was not a man who wilted in the face of life's disappointments. The loss of Roisin had cut him to the quick. He'd grown to expect the touch of her fingers on the back of his neck and her legs tangling with his in the middle of the night; his clothes shoved to one side in the wardrobe to make way for hers and the fridge stuffed with yoghurt and salad and half-eaten bars of chocolate. His

362

house was empty without her and, if he'd given way to it, he could have mooned around like a depressed adolescent, obsessing over what might have been.

Bugger all that. The week after Ruth's funeral he'd bought a Ferrari and driven a blonde to the races, just to prove to himself he was alive and kicking.

Today he fancied buying a racehorse. Some people might think he was mad to give one away and then buy another. But he wasn't some people.

He had Tim Davy's mobile number. There was no time like the present.

Chapter Nineteen

Max came home in one of his moods. He'd had a drink or two, Cherry guessed, and he looked as if he wanted to punch someone in the mouth. Could be that someone was her.

'You told Roisin, didn't you?' he said, slamming the living-room door behind him.

'About what?' she replied innocently.

'About getting that bloody horse on the ferry. I saw Dad this morning. Somehow Roisin's found out. He thought I'd told her but it was you, wasn't it?'

He wasn't the brightest button in the box sometimes. The pair of them had been celebrating Roisin's retreat to Ireland for days and it seemed he'd never bothered to ask himself why.

'I did it for your benefit, Max. Roisin was a threat. Lewis couldn't be allowed to marry her.'

He grabbed her by the hair and yanked her head back viciously.

'My father, in his almighty wisdom, has given Black Mountain to Roisin. You know what that means, don't you?'

She stared at him uncomprehendingly, needles stabbing into her skull. 'Let me go.'

Max ignored her, yanked hard again so her head jerked back. His face, rigid with anger, was inches from hers. She tried to push him away but he was immovable.

'That means, you stupid tart, that you've just lost me my ride in the Champion Hurdle.'

Good God, was that all he was worried about? Some effing silly horse race. She was tempted to laugh in his face. Dare him to smack her about as he was dying to do. If she showed up at Victor's with bruises on her face there'd be hell to pay. Victor would fix it so Max couldn't even ride a seaside donkey.

These thoughts flashed like sparks through her head, together with the knowledge that she could lose everything she'd schemed for right here.

Ignoring the pain in her scalp and his whisky breath in her face, she said, 'I'm so sorry, Max.'

His grip relaxed and his snarl softened.

The hand that had futilely attempted to push him away crept up his chest to stroke his cheek.

'I never meant that to happen,' she murmured. 'Please forgive me.'

He let go of her hair and held her close, burying his face in her neck. After a moment he began to sob and she patted his back as if she were comforting a child.

She hoped that these were tears of remorse for

so nearly beating up his pregnant partner, though she feared they were for himself and his lost dreams of Cheltenham glory.

Later, as she swallowed painkillers in the bathroom and repaired the mess he'd made of her hair, she reflected on the hard road she'd chosen. But it was too late to turn back now.

*   *   *

The dinner to celebrate Grain of Sand's victory was held at Linda's large and chaotic west London house. She'd planned the occasion well before the event, encouraging all the members of the owning syndicate to attend, along with partners and friends. It was quite a party.

'What would you have done if Sandy had trailed in last?' Alan asked the hostess as he opened bottles of wine in the kitchen.

'We'd have had a wake, darling,' she said. 'I'm in showbiz, remember? The party must go on.'

It was far from a wake. A dozen of them sat down to eat at a vast Victorian six-legged table extended to its fullest. A couple of cheerful young girls, Linda's nieces, chased in and out with plates of food. Ralph topped up glasses as if it were a crime to see one half full. Alan was flushed with success.

Tim Davy asked for quiet, which was ignored. He resorted to a request in the voice he used on the gallops which silenced the room in an instant; even Linda looked impressed.

Tim grinned and apologised for the interruption. 'Before we all get too sloshed to think clearly, I've got some news. I had a phone call just after the race. We've got a prospective buyer for Sandy.'

A couple of months ago these words would have been the answer to Alan's prayers. Now, a knot of anxiety lodged in his gut. Suddenly, he didn't feel hungry any more.

'We're not selling,' shouted Linda, voicing Alan's sentiments.

'You mean someone's actually placed a bid?' said Cyril.

Tim nodded. He consulted a scrap of paper in his hand, though it was surely unnecessary. 'For four hundred and fifty thousand pounds.'

There was a communal intake of breath. The sum was more than four times what Alan had paid for the horse at Tattersalls.

'We're not selling,' said Linda, though less resolutely than before. Alan knew that her sharp mind would already have calculated a £70,000 profit on her original stake.

'Can't we hold on to the horse and sell him after Cheltenham?' said Geoff. 'It would be grand to have the winner of the Champion Hurdle.'

Everyone agreed with that.

'This buyer won't wait for Cheltenham, if that's what you mean. He wants to run the horse in the Champion Hurdle himself. So it's yes or no to this offer now.'

'Suppose we say no and then Sandy wins at Cheltenham,' said Geoff. 'What's he worth then?'

'Millions, surely,' cried Linda.

'No.' Tim was quick to pour a bit of cold water. 'This isn't Flat racing. There's no stud value in Grain of Sand. It's more likely to be in the region of six hundred thousand.'

'Oh.' Linda was deflated. 'All things considered,

that's not a great deal more than what he's offering now.'

Geoff spoke again. 'Suppose he doesn't do much in the Champion Hurdle, what's he worth then?'

Tim shrugged. 'Who can say? A lot more than we paid for him certainly but probably less than this. It's a generous offer.'

'A bird in the hand,' murmured Cyril. He turned to Alan. 'What does our syndicate manager think? You're being awfully quiet, Alan.'

Alan was reluctant to say what he really thought. He wanted to keep Sandy whatever mad money was on the table. He wanted to ride him in the Champion Hurdle and other top races for years to come. The rides at Newbury and Wincanton had given him a thrill like no other he'd experienced as a jockey and he knew that maybe he'd never be on such a top-class animal again. Besides, a Champion Hurdle win might rekindle his career. But that was an entirely selfish point of view.

'After Lee died,' he said, 'when Sandy was injured and I had no idea how I was going to pay for him, I'd have been amazed if you'd told me this was going to happen. I'd have taken the money like a shot. But now, knowing he's a real champion in the making, I just want to keep him.'

'Fair enough,' said Geoff. Other heads nodded in agreement.

'Hang on,' said Alan. 'That's just my personal feeling. We've got to look at it from a business point of view. If we accept the offer, we walk away with ninety grand each—that's a four hundred and fifty per cent return. As Tim says, even if Sandy wins the Champion Hurdle we're unlikely to make much more than what's on offer here. And,' he added reluctantly, 'things can go wrong. He's only had two races.'

'Think of the fun we'll miss out on,' said Linda. 'I want lots more dinners like this.'

'There's always an excuse for a celebration. We could reinvest some money in more horses.' Alan wondered why he was playing devil's advocate so scrupulously. Was it the lure of the money?

'Suppose,' said Tim, 'I go back to our buyer and ask for half a million.'

'Good idea,' said Cyril.

The others agreed and looked at Alan. 'Don't settle for anything less,' he said. It was a crazy sum of money.

A thought struck him. 'Hang on, Tim. Who is this bidder? He's not some time-waster, is he?'

Tim laughed. 'Oh no. I thought I'd told you. It's Lewis Ashwood.'

Alan's thoughts raced. How typical of Ashwood. He already owned the big favourite for the Champion Hurdle but here he was buying up another hot contender. Just as he'd bought Roisin. He supposed it was one way to win but it made Alan sick.

*   *   *

Cherry planned her approach to Victor carefully. They'd hardly spoken since the night he'd told her about the Customs and Excise link to Scott Robinson's arrest. He'd been like a bear with a sore head and she'd been aware that lots of people had been getting it in the neck—Brian Spot, for one. Not that she was going to lose any sleep over him.

But she couldn't allow a distance to develop

368

between herself and Victor. They'd always been close. She had to know whether she still enjoyed his confidence.

The club gym closed at eight in the evening and that was the time Victor chose for his workouts. Cherry gave him a good forty minutes to work off his aggression before she put her head round the door.

He was on the treadmill, red-faced and panting hard. There was no one else in the room.

'Don't overdo it, will you?' she said, closing the door behind her.

Vic stumbled off the machine, his vest wet through. His breath came in short urgent gulps. She handed him a towel.

'I've been smoking too many fags,' he said, scrubbing his face and neck with the towel, as if he were removing more than sweat.

'Are you OK, Vic? I've been worried about you.'

He slumped on a bench. 'Why should you care? You're about to swan off with Maxsie boy.'

She sat next to him. 'But I do care. You've been looking a bit stressed out.'

He laughed. 'You'd be stressed out, sweetheart, if someone owed you nine hundred grand and you couldn't get hold of that someone because they were banged up.'

'Scott Robinson, you mean?'

'He was in the middle of doing a deal with us when he got nicked and his end hasn't come through.'

That was interesting.

'You mean that cash I was counting with Brian and Chris?'

He nodded.

369

'What, all of it? He takes the money, gets arrested and we're left empty-handed?'

'Not quite that bad. He transfers a slice into one of Brian's offshore accounts. We hand over all the moolah we want washed, he reckons it up, then the balance gets paid in. Only the Yank's got himself pinched before the second transfer's gone through. The word is that he didn't get a chance to spin our cash before he got lifted.'

'Can't we get it back?'

'We could if we knew where he'd stashed it. Brian says he's got some lock-up in Essex but Essex is a big place. I'll get to him in the end but right now it's difficult.'

Cherry took in the implications of this remark. She didn't doubt Victor could get to Robinson in prison but he'd need inside help.

'You'll work it out,' she said. 'You always do.'

'You're right, darling. So I do.' He stopped mopping his face; his breath was coming easily now. To her surprise he started to hum a tune.

She stared at him, perplexed. 'What's that?'

'Simon and Garfunkel. You're too young.'

But when he sang the words, her confusion vanished. Cecilia—the name of Ciaran Fitzmaurice's boat.

'So the trip's on, is it?'

His grin was wide. 'You don't want to know, sweetheart.'

But he was wrong about that.

*   *   *

Alan spoke to Roisin the morning after Linda's party. It wasn't that simple a process.

370

He'd scarcely slept, mulling over the likelihood of losing Sandy to that smug plutocrat, Lewis Ashwood. He'd never met the man and yet he loathed him. Lewis had annexed the one woman Alan had ever had real feelings for—ill-founded and irrational though they might be—and now he was out to steal Alan's horse. If he'd known Ashwood was behind the bid for Grain of Sand then he would have spoken emphatically against accepting. He'd been a fool to be so scrupulous. His one hope now was that the businessman would not be fool enough to pay such an inflated asking price.

Sometime in the small hours it had occurred to Alan that he had a way of finding out what was behind Lewis's bid. He could ask Roisin. The thought had taken root. Even if Roisin wouldn't tell him what was going on he'd have the pleasure of talking to her. It was a small thing but it weighed heavily in the balance, heavier by far than the thought of Lewis's money. Ashwood could turn Alan's finances on their head with the small change in his pocket. It was an insult.

When he'd last seen Roisin, riding out at Tim Davy's, she'd given him her mobile phone number. He'd deliberately thrown it away once he'd decided that seeing her wasn't good for him. He regretted that now.

Consequently he called the Dougherty yard in Ireland; he'd be able to get a message to her that way at least. Pauline Dougherty was delighted to hear from him.

'That was such a kind letter you wrote to us about Noel,' she said. 'And it's great you're doing so well with that horse of yours.'

Then she surprised Alan by saying, 'I'll just get Roisin for you.'

Roisin had told him she'd been spending time in Ireland; he'd obviously caught her on a visit.

'Alan.' Her soft lilt down the phone conjured an instant picture of her in his mind. 'This is funny, I was going to call you today.'

'You were?'

'Dad and I watched you on Grain of Sand. Congratulations. You were just great.'

'It didn't have much to do with me. I only sat on the horse.'

'Oh please.' He couldn't see her smile but he heard it in her voice. 'And there was I thinking you were such a bighead.'

Is that what she'd thought? He didn't care. It just made him feel good to talk to her.

'Roisin, can I ask you a question?'

'Sure. Ask away.'

'Why is Lewis trying to buy Grain of Sand?'

The line fell silent.

'It's a bit of a cheek me asking, I know. You don't have to answer.'

Her voice sounded different when she spoke next. 'Alan, you should know that I'm no longer involved with Lewis.'

'No longer involved'—what did that mean?

'I've moved back to Ireland. Lewis and I are going our separate ways and I know nothing about him buying your horse.'

'You mean you're not going to marry him?'

The split second before she answered seemed to stretch into an age.

'Alan, I wouldn't marry Lewis Ashwood if he was the last man alive.'

372

How sweet that sounded. It was all Alan could do to swallow the whoop of joy that bubbled up in his throat.

But this wasn't his business—not directly anyway—and he could tell that he had stumbled onto private territory.

'Are you OK, Roisin?' It was a silly question. Whatever had happened in her life had obviously been swift and dramatic.

'I will be. There's one thing though,' she continued. 'Black Mountain now belongs to my brother Con. I imagine Lewis is trying to buy your horse so he'll still have a chance at the Champion Hurdle.'

Alan was confused by this sudden turn of events but, by the time he put the phone down, two things were clear in his mind. Roisin was a free agent and fair game for any prospective suitor; and Lewis would pay through the nose to buy Grain of Sand, now he no longer owned Black Mountain.

He speed-dialled Tim Davy's number. Maybe there was still time to scotch the deal. Or put a million-pound price tag on the horse's neck—there was just a chance Ashwood would be fool enough to pay it.

Tim sounded upbeat—as he would in the circumstances.

'I've just got off the phone to Lewis,' he said. 'Guess what? He's agreed to half a million.'

Alan was too late.

'Just one bit of bad news,' Tim added, 'from your point of view, that is. I couldn't persuade him to keep you on board as jockey. His son Max is going to ride.'

There was a surprise.

Alan tried to put Sandy out of his mind. If the horse and his Cheltenham preparation was no longer his concern then he had time on his hands. He had no decent rides booked for the coming week. Suddenly a trip to Ireland in search of Kevin, the missing stable groom, seemed like a good idea. The fact that it would take him to within a few miles of the Dougherty farm and Roisin was entirely coincidental.

*   *   *

'What do you mean, you're packing it in?' In a corner of the pub, Janice glared at Cherry. They'd given up coffee bars.

'I'm getting married, giving up the day job to be a housewife and mother.' Might as well keep up the baby front. Stay in character as much as possible.

It didn't cut much ice with the Customs agent. 'You?' she snorted with contempt.

'You don't think I'm capable of settling down?'

Janice ignored the question. She was no more interested in answering it than Cherry was in hearing her response. 'I don't know that we can allow that. The operation is in a very crucial stage. We've got Sinbad under pressure.'

'And who's helped you put him there?' She'd just passed on the information about Scott Robinson's Essex lock-up. Quite possibly the police would be able to squeeze its location out of him before Victor could track it down. Janice had looked interested. 'I've done my bit,' Cherry continued. 'Soon I won't be able to help you any more.'

'I see.' Janice sipped thoughtfully. She drank bitter from a pint glass—what was she trying to

374

prove?

'Look,' Cherry said. 'There's got to be an end to it sometime. I've stuck my neck right out for you.'

Janice gave her a weary look; they'd had this conversation before.

Cherry considered a new tack. She wanted a clean break from this crew as much as she wanted away from the criminal world. She lived in dread of being dragged out of her wonderful new life spending the Ashwood millions to appear in court testifying against Victor. Might as well slit her wrists now.

Obviously the lock-up titbit wasn't strong enough to get her off the hook for good.

'How about,' she said, 'I give up one last job.'

'What job?'

'An ocean run. A yacht coming in from the Caribbean. A couple of hundred kilos on board at least.'

'Of what?'

'Coke.'

Janice was interested, Cherry could tell by the tightening of her thin lips.

'What yacht? When?'

'I don't know.' She sipped her drink. 'Yet.'

'We need loading port, destination, route and time. Anything and everything you can find out.'

'Of course. It's all up in the air at the moment but it'll happen.'

'OK.'

'And then I'm out? Off the hook for good with no comebacks?'

'I'm not sure I can guarantee that, Cherry.'

'You'd better or it won't happen.' She finished her drink. 'And it's Scorpio, remember?'

Alan was about to ask for the cheapest vehicle available from the car-hire desk at Shannon airport when he remembered that he no longer had to count the pennies. Instead of a Ford Fiesta he plumped for a Mercedes E200 and, as he dumped his luggage in the spacious and squeaky-clean boot, he reminded himself that there were lots of ways he could loosen the financial straitjacket he lived in. Maybe he should use some of Lewis Ashwood's money as a deposit on a home of his own. He could certainly trade in his knackered old car. Maybe he'd buy a horse.

He'd rather still have a share of Sandy and a ride in the Champion Hurdle.

He slammed the boot shut and plotted his route to Concommon. It didn't look too far on the map, about twenty miles south of Limerick City. And only about fifty from the Dougherty yard near the mouth of the Shannon.

It would be permissible, surely, once his visit to Concommon was over, to call Roisin. As he drove south he rehearsed what he might say. 'I'm in the area, looking at horses—can I drop in and bend your father's ear?' It was feeble but he'd do it anyway. If she really gave him the frost he'd just pay his respects to her parents and go. What did he have to lose?

It was a damp afternoon and the rain fell harder as he approached his destination. The land around was flat pasture, boggy brown and dull green under a mushroom grey sky. As houses began to appear along the narrow straight road and he passed a

376

church and a pub, all built of stone as grey as the heavens, he realised he had arrived in Concommon. He drove on, looking for the centre of the village, only to find he had passed it. Concommon was a one-street town and he had driven the length of it in less than a minute. How hard would it be to find a man in this insignificant place? He was about to find out.

Alan turned the car around, taking care not to bury the Merc's panels in the hedgerows. Maybe it hadn't been such a great idea to hire a fancy car. He drove back slowly and parked in front of a building with a glass front and a green hoarding with 'Culotty's QuickPick Foodstore' written in fresh gold paint. Next to it was a pub with a similarly spruced-up air about it. This seemed a reasonable place to start.

The shop was much like any small-town self-service store in England and the woman at the till disclaimed any knowledge of an O'Shea family in the village. 'But I'm not local,' she added. 'I'm from Cork.'

He asked her for Barn House and, naturally, she didn't know where that was either, though an old lady trailing a basket with one tin of cat food gave him directions to a turning north of the main street. She didn't know any O'Sheas, or so she said.

It took Alan twenty minutes to find the turning, an overgrown lane that appeared invisible from whichever direction you approached. After another ten minutes of twisting and turning along the puddled ruts of an unmade road he came to a gated driveway and buildings beyond. He left the car in the lane and tramped up the drive, past evidence of building work and other refurbishment.

A cement mixer stood where there should have been a lawn and the roof of a long low building next to the main house had been stripped to its beams.

Alan hailed a man in wellington boots and a Barbour who was scanning what looked like a set of architectural drawings. He turned out not to be local either.

This was, however, Barn House and the booted man was its new owner. An Englishman from Kent. He had no idea if the previous occupants had been called O'Shea or not, he'd only dealt with the agent.

Though he was affable enough, the man was obviously busy and, as he said pointedly, there wasn't much daylight left.

As Alan trudged back to the car, he wondered if he'd done enough. Had honour been satisfied?

Hardly. The reason he was here was to find out what had happened to Lee, his dead friend who, ultimately, was the reason why he was some £100,000 richer. He'd been slow in acquitting his debt to Lee but at least he was here now—it was not right to give up just yet.

He drove back to the centre of the throbbing metropolis that was Concommon and booked a room for the night at the pub. Unsurprisingly, the landlord was not a local; he was from Dublin.

*　　　*　　　*

Cherry used the phone she kept to call Janice to get in touch with Ciaran Fitzmaurice. As promised, she'd used her influence to include the boy-band hunk on the cruise of the *Cecilia*—the drug run

378

from the Caribbean. The lucky fellow. It was about time she got some thanks.

He'd given her a card that wet and windy day he'd shown her round his father's boat. She fished it out—'Ciaran Fitzmaurice: Creative Contacts'— and called the number he'd scrawled on it, emphasising as he'd done so, 'This is my *personal* contact number.'

He answered the phone with a sulky 'Yeah?' which changed immediately the moment she announced herself. She used the name he knew her by.

'Of course I remember you, Lindsay. I wanted to call and say thanks for getting me on the trip but I didn't have your number. Don't tell me you want to try out for the movies after all?'

It was as easy as that. She declined the movie offer, but not in such a way he'd think the door was firmly shut. And they chit-chatted about his trip— which was when? Had he heard?

'You just caught me. I'm flying out to Trinidad tomorrow. Uh-oh, hang on a sec.'

Then there was the sound of a voice in the background, a female one naturally, and a scuffling, as of a hand being placed over the phone.

A few moments later he was back, his voice low. 'Sorry, Lindsay, gotta go. You know how it is.'

She could imagine.

'Thanks for calling and maybe we could, er, get together some time after I get back.'

'Maybe. Can I call you while you're away? You know, just to make sure it's going OK. I feel a little responsible.'

'Oh baby, that's so sweet. This number'll be good. Next time, I promise, we'll have time for a real talk.'

Putty in her hands. It was that simple.

* * *

Alan wasn't much of a boozer—weight-watching was a reflex for a jockey his size. But the snug of the Concommon Inn, he realised, was no place for a Diet Coke drinker if he wanted to get in with the locals. The first problem was finding some. People were friendly enough, he found as he stood at the bar with a pint of Guinness at his elbow, but no one seemed well-acquainted with the village.

Eventually, he fell into conversation with a mechanic from a garage ten miles away. 'Who did you say you were looking for?'

'A fellow called Kevin O'Shea. His family used to live at the Barn House up the road.'

The mechanic repeated the request to a bald man in a check shirt who sucked ruminatively on an unlit pipe and passed him on to a fellow with jug ears. And so it went on. Occasionally Alan was met with a nod of the head and a question or two he couldn't answer. He knew practically nothing about the O'Sheas. He certainly didn't know if Kevin had a sister who'd tried out for *Pop Idol* or whether his father played the squeezebox. And each conversation became a lengthy affair, with rounds being bought and sport, for the most part, being discussed. The Cheltenham Festival was on many minds and he found himself chatting away merrily. However, he kept his own involvement—not that he now had any—under wraps. When Grain of Sand was mentioned as a worthy rival for Black Mountain he kept his mouth firmly shut.

380

Eventually he found himself in the corner, next to an old man with a ginger beard and grey hair. The Guinness he'd drunk had dulled his sense of purpose but when the barman referred to his companion as 'Mr O'Riordan' something stirred his memory.

'Did you used to keep pigs?' he asked him.

O'Riordan squinted at him. 'My father used to but I got rid of 'em. Couldn't stand the smell.'

'But you've still got a pigsty, haven't you? And an old well nearby.' He remembered that letter from Kevin's mother in reasonable detail, considering.

The farmer pulled on his pint, his eyes on Alan the whole time. 'How do you know that?' he said.

'Kevin O'Shea told me. Your farm's next to Barn House, isn't it?'

'It sounds like you're telling me.'

'And once, a few years back, a ram fell down the well and Kevin's dad helped you pull it out.'

'Is that so?' O'Riordan's eyebrows, which were ginger too, shot up his forehead. 'Remind me who you are again?'

'I'm Alan Morrell. I'm a pal of Kevin's from when he was working over in England. I need to get in touch with him to return some things.'

The other man finished off his drink. His eyes were sky blue, untarnished by the years that had taken their toll on the rest of him. They bored into Alan's as he said, 'You're out of luck, son. There's never been any O'Sheas living round here.' He plonked his empty glass back on the bar. 'Not one.' And he turned his back.

Alan had had enough of the Concommon Inn for the moment. As the Guinness flowed, so the volume of conversation grew, supplemented by the football commentary from the television. He couldn't hear himself think. Outside, the rain had turned to an insubstantial drizzle. It helped to clear his head.

How much had he drunk? he wondered as he stood by the wall that fronted the pub's small car park. He felt more boozed up than he'd been since, well, since the other night at Linda's.

And just what had he got out of this? Nothing relevant to his Kevin quest, that was certain. It was as if the O'Sheas had never existed in this place. The closest he'd come to Kevin's family was meeting a farmer with a ginger beard who didn't like the smell of pigs. He chuckled tipsily to himself. He was no loss to the detective profession, that was for sure.

Headlights lit the road and a dark van pulled up across the entrance to the parking area. The passenger door slid back and a thin youth with long hair jumped out and dashed for the pub door. A moment later he reappeared and headed straight for Alan.

'Are you the feller who's looking for Kevin O'Shea?'

Up close he was older than he looked, with a ratty beard and dark sunken eyes. Crooked teeth gleamed in his smile.

'That's me,' Alan replied. Hope bloomed within him. 'Do you know him?'

'Might do,' said the man and butted Alan in the face.

Alan felt his nose crunch and blood fly as he staggered. The pain was as bad as being kicked in the head by a horse, though horses didn't follow up with a blow to the stomach. He fell to the ground and rolled, a jockey's reflex, but it did him no good as boots thudded into his back and legs. There had to be more than just the small man. He could hear laughter.

'That'll do,' said a voice. 'Hurry it up now.'

Then he was picked up and thrown onto a metal floor. Doors slammed and an engine growled. The van was on the move.

Chapter Twenty

'OK, you sack of shite, tell us who you really are.'

Alan was in a room without windows. A cellar, he thought. Or maybe a garage. There was no lighting but some natural light spilled from above, penetrating the gloom. He'd been put on a chair drawn up to a table and facing him were two shadowy figures, one bigger than the other. The smaller one must be the man who had headbutted him outside the pub. He'd caught a glimpse of teeth.

Alan put his hand to his face, carefully. He hurt in a way he recognised from past injuries.

'You've broken my nose,' he said in a voice he barely recognised as his own. He was in shock.

'Yeah. And that's only the beginning, bucko, unless you start speaking straight.'

'What do you want to know? My name's Alan Morrell and I'm looking for Kevin O'Shea so I can give him back some stuff he left in England.'

'You're just an old pal of his?'

'Yes.'

'He doesn't remember any old pal called Alan.'

'I used to work with him, for God's sake. At Tim Davy's yard. I'm a jockey.'

'Oh yeah?'

The small man who'd headbutted Alan moved forward holding a hammer in his right hand. He raised it above his head and brought it down hard, crunching it into the wood next to Alan's elbow.

He pushed his face into Alan's. 'I don't think you're a jockey. And you won't be by the time I'm through with you.'

It dawned on Alan that this greasy psychotic was going to smash his arm to a pulp.

'No! Wait, you're making a mistake,' he cried, his voice feeble and desperate.

The man raised the hammer again.

From outside came the sound of a car engine and the man froze. Footsteps sounded then a shaft of artificial light speared into the room. A tall figure was silhouetted in the doorway.

'Good timing,' said the man with the hammer. 'You want to watch me do his arm?'

'No,' said the tall man. 'Let him go. He's all right.'

If Kevin O'Shea wasn't Alan's friend beforehand, he was now.

They took him away in a different vehicle, a battered Volvo estate, with Alan sitting in the back and Kevin driving. Only the small man remained now and he sat up front, jabbering to Kevin, all the while shooting anxious glances over his shoulder. Alan gathered that he was Kevin's half-brother, Declan, and that he was sorry—very sorry.

'But, with all due respect, you turn up in some fancy car, asking right and left about Kev, your great mucker who says he's never heard of you.'

Kevin nodded. 'Sorry, Alan, it wasn't till I saw you that I remembered.'

True enough, he and the tall lad hadn't been particular friends. 'That doesn't give you the right to assault and kidnap me,' he said.

Declan shrugged. 'I thought you were one of those English bastards who fixed our Kev.'

'What do you mean?'

'Show him,' said Declan.

The car was turning into a drive. Kevin parked in front of a large, grey, stone house.

'Go on,' Declan urged him.

Kevin switched on the internal light. Then he held up his right hand. Alan leaned closer, trying to focus through the sapping pain in his head. Kevin's little finger and ring finger had been crudely severed at the second joint. The scar looked raw and angry.

'Jesus Christ,' Alan murmured, aware at once of the implications. For a man who liked to ride horses, the loss of those digits was a blow; you'd have to learn a new way of gripping the reins.

'My dad calls me Russ Conway,' said Kevin with a grin.

'But how did it happen?' Suddenly a broken nose didn't seem so bad.

'I'll tell you tomorrow. Declan's going to fetch Doctor Murphy then Ma's going to find you a bed. Is that all right?

Alan didn't have the strength to argue.

*   *   *

At the sound of footsteps outside, Victor looked up

385

from the newspaper spread over his desk. Brian walked in, his face as long as a wet weekend—which was pretty much how Victor felt himself.

'You've seen it already?' Brian pointed to the paper.

Yes, Victor had seen it. The gleeful report that a crack money-laundering squad from Scotland Yard had recovered £5 million in drugs money stashed in a secret hideaway in Essex.

'You reckon Robinson did a deal?' Brian said.

'Of course. Coughed the money for a lighter sentence. Got no balls, some of these kids.'

Brian sank into a chair. 'Five mil—it's a bloody joke. I reckon they make it up.'

Privately, Victor agreed. Drug values and drug money were always exaggerated. But that wasn't the point.

'Nine hundred grand of that's ours,' he growled. 'Best part of a million we won't ever see again.'

'Yeah.'

Silence fell.

Finally, Brian said, 'Sorry, boss. I wish I'd never suggested we outsource.'

An apology was something but it didn't put food on the table.

*   *   *

Alan sat at a big well-scrubbed kitchen table holding a tea towel full of crushed ice to his face. The doctor had said he didn't think the nose was actually broken, though if Alan couldn't breathe through it in a few days he ought to seek further help. For the moment, however, ice packs and painkillers were all that were required.

He wasn't sure what hurt the most, the swollen nose, his bruised body or the headache—which very likely came from too much of the black stuff the night before. By his elbow was the remains of a vast fried breakfast, which had been difficult to eat for a variety of reasons. Opposite was Kevin, sipping a cup of tea. Kevin's mother, who had busied herself around the two men for the past half hour, had finally left the room.

Kevin spoke first. 'Are you going to tell me what you're doing chasing after me? And don't tell me it's so you can give me back a box of letters and magazines.'

'How do you know about them?'

'We've had a look in the back of your car. Nice motor.'

'I hope you haven't damaged it.'

Kevin shook his head. 'We borrowed the key. You were sleeping like a baby.'

The doctor had given him a pill. It had knocked him out for twelve hours. That and the Guinness.

'I only want to talk to you about Olympia. The day he ran at Haydock and Lee got killed.'

Kevin groaned. 'I knew it. I should have left you to Declan last night.'

'Olympia was fixed somehow, wasn't he? You travelled with him. You ought to know. Or was it just your job to turn a blind eye and let someone else nobble him?'

The thin man said nothing for a moment, then held out his mutilated hand. 'You know, at night I imagine I've still got my fingers. He broke the little one before he cut it off and it still hurts. Doesn't seem fair, does it?'

'At least you're still alive.'

387

'It was never the idea that someone would get hurt. They just wanted to make sure Olympia didn't win.'

'What did you do?'

'They've got a special horsebox with an equine pool inside and it fills up from a water tank beside it. You put the horse in, it's like putting it into a starting stall but when the door's closed it's watertight up to five feet. I told the lad who looked after Olympia to stay in bed and I would take him out to stretch his legs. We had the lorry parked outside the track by the car park. It was easy. We swam him for twenty minutes, dried him off and brought him back.'

'I assume they were paying you.'

'Of course. My salary was peanuts in the yard and I was working all hours. I thought I'd got a girl pregnant and I needed the money. Once I'd started I just carried on. It paid well and then you could make on the side too, if you knew something wasn't going to win.'

'On the betting exchanges?'

'That's right. That's why we were doing it, so they could lay the horse. And if you picked the right race you could probably find the winner too. It wasn't only our yard.'

Alan knew that well enough.

'So why did you stop?'

Kevin glared at him, affronted. 'Why do you bloody think? Lee wasn't just your mate, you know. I was only in it for a few bob and when he died I felt terrible. I knew I couldn't hack it any more. They didn't like it when I told them.'

Alan nodded at Kevin's hand. 'So they did that to you?'

'I told them I was stopping and they said I couldn't. I said I'd rather go to the police and tell them all I knew—I was in that much of a state. They came for me one night and told me I had to get back to fixing the horses. I said eff off and they chopped off my fingers. Said if I breathed a word, next time it would be my head. I believed them so I came back here.'

'And now you're telling.'

Kevin grinned. 'I don't care now. No cocky English bastard is going to find me here. Do you reckon?'

Alan nodded. Kevin was pretty safe, provided he never went back to England.

'So you might as well tell me who these people are.'

'What are you going to do with the information?'

'Hand it over to the Jockey Club. They're looking into all this.'

Kevin laughed. 'Good luck. They're not going to frighten Victor Bishop.'

Alan had never heard of him.

'He's a gambler and nightclub owner—I don't know the half of it. He's the man who cut off my fingers.'

'Nice.'

'There's others who pay off lads at yards who've got access to the horses overnight.'

Alan had a thought. 'Do you know of a fellow called Donovan?'

'Sure. He used to do the business at Ian Rafter's.'

Alan wasn't surprised to hear it. No wonder Jane had been so reluctant to talk to him.

'Look, Kevin, there's a guy at the Jockey Club

called Clive Jones. You've got to talk to him. If you don't blow the whistle, someone else will and you'll come off worse.'

'Worse than being killed by Victor?'

Alan was silent for a moment. 'You may be safe here but other people aren't. What happened to Lee could happen to someone else. You can't just turn your back on it.'

Kevin didn't respond at first. 'I'll think about it.'

Alan stared into his eyes through the fog of pain in his head. This was probably the best he was going to get right now. He wrote down his numbers and passed them across the table. 'Call me.'

Kevin inclined his head—it could hardly be called a nod—and put the paper into his pocket.

Alan was curious about one more thing. 'The girl who got pregnant?'

'She lost it.'

'Was that Frankie, at Tim's yard?

Kevin narrowed his eyes. 'You know about her?'

Alan nodded. 'She keeps your photo, you know. She'd like to hear from you too.'

*   *   *

The call Cherry had been dreading finally came: the summons to meet Lewis for lunch. The invitation was only for her—Max was up at Tim Davy's yard, working with the new horse.

She'd managed to avoid speaking to Lewis since the day after Roisin had fled, when he'd got Cherry on the phone and asked her what she'd said to Roisin the night before. After that, when the break-up became official, she'd written to Lewis offering her sympathies—a letter was so much

390

more personal sometimes. Since then she'd always managed to be out of the way when he called. But there was no escaping this encounter.

He looked grim, baggy-eyed and stressed out, without that sleek, bronzed, well-fed look that came so naturally to the super rich.

'Oh, Lewis, you don't look well. Poor you!' She fussed and fluttered around him but she could tell it didn't cut much ice. 'This business with Roisin has hit you hard, hasn't it?' Might as well go straight to the heart of the matter. If he was going to quiz her again about her conversation with Roisin, it would be less suspicious if she brought it up first.

He sipped his Scotch and stared at her. 'It's been rough.'

'Tell me to mind my own business, but what happened? She seemed absolutely fine when I spoke to her that night. Did she say why she went off like that?'

Of course, what she really had to find out was whether Roisin had shopped her. All was not lost if she had, however; she would simply have to play a harder game.

Lewis said, 'She decided she didn't like me any more.'

'So there's no hope of patching it up?'

This was an important question. She couldn't imagine there was any way Roisin would be coming back to play Mrs Lewis Ashwood but it was as well to be certain.

'No.'

Cherry didn't allow the awkward silence to develop. She orchestrated a symphony of chatter, about the fantastic Grain of Sand, about the

391

wedding (just think, if Sandy wins it could be a double celebration!) and, of course, about the baby.

Lewis watched her balefully throughout, drinking more than eating, assessing her every move.

At the end of the meal, strictly a one-course-and-coffee affair, he said, 'Where are you going to have this baby?'

A good question. 'There's a choice of hospitals locally. The GP says I don't have to decide just yet.'

His mouth turned down. 'Cherry, you're not having any grandchild of mine on the NHS.' He pulled a slip of paper from his pocket. 'Theo Goodhill's the top gynaecologist in this country. We go racing together. He's expecting your call.'

'Oh Lewis, that's so kind of you!' She clutched his hand—what the hell did she say now? 'But I couldn't possibly.'

'Of course you could. I'm paying.'

'No, I mean I have every confidence in my GP. She's a bit of an earth mother herself, got four kids of her own. I really don't want to move from her care.'

'You've got nothing to lose. Go and see Theo. If you don't like him it's no skin off your nose.'

'That's true.' She picked up the paper. She'd spin it out and play for time.

He seemed mollified.

Was that it? Could she go now?

While they waited for the bill to arrive, he said, 'When you spoke to Roisin that night, did she mention her brother's death?'

'Only in passing.' She'd thought this through. 'Just to say how great you'd been in helping her come to terms with it. I think she only mentioned it because I was on the ferry too. I'd been in the bar with Noel just before he . . .' She dropped her voice. 'Before the accident.' She didn't think she'd overdone it.

The waiter returned at that moment with Lewis's credit card slip.

'Thanks so much for lunch, Lewis. You will take care of yourself, won't you?'

He allowed himself to be kissed on both cheeks on the pavement outside.

'Call Theo,' was his parting remark as she climbed into a cab.

Cherry waved as the taxi pulled into the traffic, then took the paper with the gynaecologist's phone number from her handbag and crumpled it into the ashtray.

Finally she leaned back and allowed the tension to drain away. Not for the first time she reckoned she'd got away with it.

*   *   *

Alan found driving hard, his head and body hurt like hell but he'd laid off the doctor's painkillers so he could concentrate on the unfamiliar road. There was one advantage to being a jockey—he was used to dealing with pain.

In any case, the discomfort was worth it. Kevin had come clean like a man confessing his sins. Alan now knew who was responsible for Lee's death. He also had an insight into the scams being carried out in racing and who was behind them. That had to be worth something.

He'd got Roisin on the phone directly this time.

Had she sounded pleased to hear from him? It was hard to tell. All his carefully rehearsed approaches of the day before had deserted him.

'I'm here in Ireland—can I come and see you?'

'Sure you can.' If she was surprised she didn't sound it and calmly gave him directions.

'I'll be a couple of hours.'

He sang to himself as he drove north to the Shannon estuary. The sound reverberated within his skull, merging with the purr of the engine. He couldn't sing for toffee but he didn't care. Life was great.

*   *   *

Lewis didn't go back to the office after lunch with Cherry. His usual escape in times of emotional turmoil—throwing himself into his work—was failing him these days. If he went back to Canary Wharf, the hurly-burly of the business day would wipe the memory of his lunch with Cherry from his mind. He didn't want that. He needed to brood on the nuances of what she'd said and the way she'd said it. Just because she looked angelic didn't mean she wasn't lying through her teeth. He'd had proof of that already.

He drove to Lambourn, taking it carefully because he'd drunk too much, but the trip had only occurred to him after he'd said goodbye to the little witch outside the restaurant. If work was no longer his solace, he'd find comfort elsewhere. His new horse, Grain of Sand, was balm these days to his troubled spirit. And he'd have the chance to catch Max. He had an important question to put to his son, who had gone to stay in Lambourn for a couple of days. There wasn't long to go now to the Champion Hurdle and Lewis had suggested Max spend as much time as he could getting to know Grain of Sand.

After visiting the horse at Tim Davy's, Lewis found Max in the local hotel. Max only wanted to talk about Sandy, which was OK by Lewis. He liked to see his boy appreciative of the chances that had been put his way. He knew he'd spoiled Max as a child but how else could he have behaved? Most of his life as a father had been snatched between punishing sessions at the office, building the kind of wealth that meant he could buy his son anything he wanted. He was still doing it.

'I saw Cherry for lunch today. She seems very keen on this GP of hers.'

Max looked vague. 'I don't know much about it.'

'I don't want to interfere but I do want the best for this baby. If it's all right with you, I'm prepared to pay for the best pre-natal care we can get.'

'Great.'

'Have a word with Cherry, will you? I've given her the name of a gynaecologist—make sure she sees him as soon as possible.'

'Sure.' Max grinned. 'Thanks, Dad.'

Now was the moment. Lewis gripped his son's arm.

'Did you tell Cherry about paying off the ferry captain?'

The words wiped the smile from Max's face. He blinked but the twitch of the lids could not obscure the hesitation in his eyes.

'No, of course not.'

'She was there though. Did she know what you were up to?'

The certainty was back in Max's gaze. 'Absolutely not. I guarantee it.'

'Are you sure?'

'Relax, Dad. I swear she didn't notice a thing.'

Lewis let it go although he wasn't convinced. Max had been issuing denials all his life—why should this one be the truth? He hoped to God it was.

Back at the office he had a new dossier from his private detective. Discreet enquiries had been made about the ferry captain's daughter, Christine Watson. How much did she know about her father's part in Noel Dougherty's death? The dossier didn't contain the answer. But it did reveal that Roisin had spent the afternoon before her departure to Ireland with Christine in Nottingham.

Lewis would get to the bottom of this somehow. He had to, it was eating him up.

*   *   *

For all her coolness on the phone and the casual way she had informed her parents—'Would you lay another place for supper, Ma?'—Roisin was thrown by the thought of Alan's sudden arrival. When they'd spoken the other day he'd given no hint that he was likely to be in Ireland. Surely he'd not just turned up because he knew she was single again?

According to Noel, Alan had carried a torch for her. When she'd asked her brother why Alan was so aggressive about Lewis, he'd replied, 'He's just jealous.' And Roisin had known there was truth in it. The way Alan looked at her these days, with a stare that demanded more than she could give, was a sign.

But Alan had been right about Lewis, hadn't he? Along with the desire in his gaze she'd seen the disapproval when she'd told him she was marrying Lewis. He didn't have to say he thought it was wrong that she was giving herself to a rich man old enough to be her father, it was plain from looking at him.

That made Alan unique amongst those whose opinion she valued. Noel had encouraged her romance with Lewis, and so had her father, though he regretted it now. They'd all been wrong except Alan, even if his motives were blinded by his own desires.

For all that, she wasn't sure she wanted Alan around right now. She was still trying to sort out her feelings about Lewis. Though her opinion of Lewis had changed overnight, it wasn't possible to uproot such an attachment without leaving a big hole. She had learned to depend on Lewis in so many ways. He'd become her confidant as well as her lover, helping to ease the grief of Noel's loss. But how could he have done that—comfort her for the death of her brother—and not confess his part in it? And then when she'd confronted him with what she knew, he'd looked her in the eye and lied through his teeth about the bribe. It was a betrayal worse than if he'd seduced another woman.

And maybe she'd got it wrong about Alan too. It was quite possible he was no longer interested in her, that it was simply contempt for her choice of partner that she'd read in his expression. In which case, why was he coming? Whatever his motives, she told herself, Alan's sudden appearance was a piece of opportunism that should be treated with suspicion.

Her mistrust dissolved the moment she set eyes on him.

She watched from the house as he stepped out of the kind of car she'd never associated with him—it was far too smart—and slowly made his way up the path, dragging his foot. There was a smile on his face as she opened the door but it made him look even more grotesque. His nose had swollen to twice its normal size and seemed to be packed with bloody gauze, he had two black eyes and a ribbon of Elastoplast down his cheek.

'Hi, Roisin,' he mumbled. 'It's good to see you,' and he steadied himself against the door frame.

'Ma!' she yelled. 'Come and give me a hand.'

Within five minutes they had him lying on the bed in Con's old room and Pauline had his shirt off revealing the mass of bruises beneath. Roisin extracted a promise from Dr O'Leary that he'd pop in on the way back from surgery and she'd unearthed some painkillers from Alan's bag which she'd brought up from the car.

'It's OK,' he kept saying. 'It looks worse than it is. I just fell off a horse.'

'A horse wearing size twelve boots,' muttered Pauline as she peered at the bruises on his back.

The doctor came and changed the dressings on Alan's nose, and Con appeared, demanding to know what jackeen owned the Merc parked in the yard. When he discovered that Alan was the jockey who'd been riding Grain of Sand, he set up shop beside the bed and bombarded him with questions until Roisin demanded he leave Alan in peace.

'You can't half pick 'em,' Con muttered as they went downstairs for supper. 'Your fellers are either too old or half dead.'

'He's not my feller,' she snapped.

'If you say so.'

Roisin felt mean. She'd distrusted Alan's motives but his phone call had turned out to be just a cry for help. All the same, she'd been aware of his eyes on her as she moved about the room. So she'd not been wrong about everything. Maybe he did fancy her.

Was that really so bad?

*   *   *

Alan stared for a moment at the round yellow object with a familiar cartoon face. After a few seconds it arranged itself into something recognisable: a Bart Simpson alarm clock. He was in Connor Dougherty's old bedroom in the Dougherty farmhouse in Ireland. And—he peered closer at the clockface—he'd just slept for almost sixteen hours.

It hadn't been unbroken sleep. He'd been aware of the wind during the night, of the creaks and groans of the unfamiliar building, of voices and footsteps as the household came to life. There'd been someone in the room too; the click of the door handle, the shuffle of footsteps and the touch of a soft palm on his forehead. But he'd not been able to stir. It had all been part of his dreams in which a river of blue-black hair flowed over his pillow and a woman's voice whispered, an Irish lilt like a song in his ear.

He sat up and a jolt of pain in his ribs reminded him what had brought him to this little room. He gingerly moved his head from side to side. The battleaxe throb had gone, replaced by a distant ache. An ache was OK. And he could breathe through his nose once again. Even better.

He pushed the covers back and swung his legs out of bed. He was wearing a pair of green and white striped pyjamas, several sizes too large. Sexy.

As he lurched to the window, the door opened and Roisin came in.

'So you're alive,' she said. 'How are you feeling?'

He grinned stupidly.

'Absolutely fantastic.'

*   *   *

Away from his home environment, and the female presence lurking in the background, Ciaran Fitzmaurice sounded much more forthcoming—which was excellent news for Cherry.

'Hiya, honey,' he cried, as if they were already lovers or, at the very least, best friends. 'I've been hoping you were gonna call. I've been lying in my lonely bunk just longing for the sound of your voice.'

What a bullshitter.

'A lonely bunk doesn't sound like you,' she said, playing him along. 'You mean you're not in the four-poster?'

'You remember that, do you? The place where all the hot action takes place. Not on this trip though. That's Captain Helmut's cabin. He's a pain in the ass.'

That would be Helmut Muller, a skipper who'd made several drug runs for Victor. He was entitled to be a pain in the ass since he was responsible for making sure the whole expedition didn't go belly

400

up and land them all in jail for the next ten years.

Cherry had no idea how much Ciaran knew. She'd only been able to get him included on the return trip because one of the regular crew had signed on for a Pacific crossing, preferring to go round the world than make a nice chunk of change. Well, good for him. If Cherry had anything to do with it, he'd made the right decision.

'So you're in Chaguaramas?' she said.

'Yeah, you know it?'

She knew it all right. It was a bit crowded for her taste.

'We're off to one of the islands tomorrow. Apparently we've got to take some stuff on board, then we're heading back to Europe.'

'How long do they say it's going to take?'

'Can't wait till I'm back in your part of the world, eh, babe?'

How true that was. Within reach of HM Customs and Excise would do.

'Helmut reckons ten days, maybe less. Personally, I like to take my time when cruising. You know, savour the experience. In fact there's only one experience I prefer to savour.'

Yeah, yeah.

'You sound like just my kind of guy.' Might as well lay it on thick.

'So you just hang on for a week, Lindsay, and then, I promise, we'll make sweet music together.'

She couldn't wait.

*   *   *

Alan found his way outside in the afternoon. He wanted to say a proper hello to Tom Dougherty who'd briefly looked in on him the evening before. Alan had scarcely managed a word.

Tom was feeding some bullocks in a barn beside the stables.

'How do you manage to do it all?' Alan asked after he'd thanked Tom for his hospitality. He remembered from conversations with Noel that, apart from the horses in his yard, there was a farm to run.

Tom smiled. 'I get up early,' he said. 'And I have a bit of help here and there.'

Alan supposed that added up. These Irish horse folk were tough.

'I'll be feeding Black Mountain in a minute,' said Tom. 'Our Con's dead keen for you to see him.'

Alan was keen himself. He'd heard many stories about the big horse but he'd never had a look at him in the flesh.

Roisin appeared at her father's side and scowled at Alan. 'Don't you think you ought to take it easy?' she said.

'I feel fine. I prefer being out of the house.'

'If that's the case,' said Tom, 'you could take the harrow to the gallop. I've got a stretch of all-weather out there and it needs shaking down.'

'No, Dad,' said Roisin. 'See the state of him! You can't ask him to drive a tractor. He looks like he's been run over by one.'

Both men laughed, then Alan turned to Tom.

'I wouldn't mind,' he said. 'I like tractors.'

*   *   *

Roisin woke in the dark to the ringing of her mobile phone. She grabbed it by reflex. 'Hello,' she

402

said, weighed down by sleep.

'Don't hang up,' said a familiar voice.

Lewis.

She was instantly alert.

'I promise I will never call you again, if you answer one thing.'

It was two in the morning. She could hear the desperation and the whisky in his voice. She should hang up.

'What is it?'

'Was it the daughter who told you about taking a pay-off?'

The daughter—he meant Christine Watson.

'What do you know about Chrissie Watson?'

'I know she's a student in Nottingham and you went straight to see her when you left my house. Did she tell you something?'

Oh Lord, this was a nightmare. The last thing Roisin wanted was Lewis sticking his dirty hands into Chrissie Watson's life. The poor kid had enough to deal with already.

'Listen to me, Lewis. Chrissie knows nothing about her father accepting a bribe.'

'She didn't tell you?'

'No!'

'Then it must have been Cherry. Was it?'

Roisin wanted no part of this conversation. Of Lewis or Cherry or any of them. And what did she owe Cherry, after all?

'Was it?' repeated Lewis.

'Yes,' she said and ended the call.

Chapter Twenty-One

'He's a lovely man is Alan.' Pauline Dougherty was stirring minced beef and onions into a gloopy mixture in a bowl; meat loaf was on the menu.

Roisin peeled potatoes. She did not respond to her mother.

'Our Con's loving it with him here.'

Roisin knew where this was heading. Her mother had been playing versions of the same recording for the past five days, ever since Alan had staggered from his sickbed and thrown himself into the work of the yard.

Next her mother would be reminding her how much her younger brother missed Noel and how having Alan about the place was just what Con needed.

She might then go on to say that, after Lewis, Roisin could do worse than a man like Alan. He might not be so rich but he was younger, he mucked in and he was more like one of them, even if he was English.

Her mother hadn't said these things but it was plain to her daughter what was going through her head.

Pauline added garlic, tomato puree and what looked like half a bottle of Worcestershire sauce to her mixture.

'I think it's lovely,' she said, 'that Alan's going to be riding Blackie at Cheltenham. I'm sure he'll be lucky for us.' She began to pour her gloop into two well-used baking tins. 'God alone knows we could do with a bit of luck.'

That was true enough. The latest misfortune had befallen Con three days ago when they'd got a call to say he'd sprained his wrist in a playground fight. Alan had taken over riding Black Mountain at that point and one thing had led to another.

'I think Al ought to ride Blackie in the Champion Hurdle,' Connor had announced over supper, when Alan was out of the room. 'What do you think, Dad?'

Tom had continued to chew for a moment. 'We've promised the ride to Billy Flynn,' he said, referring to the Limerick jockey who'd ridden the horse in the past.

'But I want Al to ride him,' Connor protested. The boy had watched the video of Alan winning on Grain of Sand at Wincanton many times. 'I'm the owner, aren't I? It's down to me.'

Tom pointed his fork at him. 'So you'll tell Billy, will you?'

Con had stared back defiantly. 'I will and all.'

Roisin knew that he would. Connor saw things in black and white and if Alan was the best rider, that settled it. He'd not been keen on Billy after the jockey had given Black Mountain more cracks of the whip than was necessary to win at Naas the previous year.

In the end, Tom had nodded. 'As a matter of fact, I agree with you, son.' He'd looked at Roisin. 'Shall I ask him then?'

Of course she'd said yes.

*   *   *

What a way to find out you had just lost £53 million—twiddling a dial on a radio as Victor had

405

just done. According to the radio, that was the street value of the cocaine found on the yacht *Cecilia*; it had been seized in the Atlantic a hundred miles east of Barbados by *HMS Leicester*. This was a triumph for the Royal Navy, working in conjunction with the US Coast Guard. 'We are proud of the part we have played in this combined operation,' said the commanding officer. 'Counter-drug initiatives are among the Royal Navy's prime objectives in these waters.'

Victor had only turned on to catch the racing bulletin, part of the build-up to Cheltenham which was, in turn, part of the few days' relaxation he'd promised himself. The bedroom door opened and a girl came in, wearing just a frilly apron and a lipglossed smile; she carried a breakfast tray. She was part of the relaxation too.

Well, so much for that.

'Hop it,' he growled. He was already hauling on his trousers.

She made a little moue of disappointment and exited. Two minutes later she was back in her street clothes to say goodbye.

'Is it me?' she said, her concern genuine. 'Please don't tell them at the agency.'

He handed her some cab fare. 'Don't worry about it.'

He stared at his reflection as he shaved, as if seeing himself for the first time in ages. Too much grey in the hair, too many furrows on the brow. He was getting older. He ought to be taking it easy.

No chance of that now.

* * *

Alan was aware things weren't going as he'd have liked with Roisin. She seemed angry with him and resentful of the way he fitted so neatly into the Dougherty family, like a missing piece of jigsaw.

Was it the way he'd turned up? Collapsing on the doorstep like a casualty of war, almost demanding to be taken in? He'd stuck to his story about falling off a horse and embellished it a bit, saying the animal had belonged to a farmer whose son used to work over in England. Roisin had not pressed him about it. Was this out of sensitivity, or simply that she wasn't interested?

Roisin had not revealed anything about her own situation either: the sudden break-up with Lewis and the transfer of Black Mountain into Connor's hands. The lad didn't understand the cause of his good fortune, that was plain. He'd told Alan it was because Roisin was a moody one and she'd gone off Lewis, which hardly explained why he now owned a champion racehorse. He'd said he wanted to write to Lewis and thank him but Roisin had forbidden it and Tom had backed her up.

It was a puzzle and Alan was intrigued but Roisin showed no signs of wanting to confide in him. He'd have asked her straight out but for his suspicion that she didn't want him around. His confidence was low anyway because he looked like a refugee from a horror movie. The bruising on his face and body had developed a spectacular mosaic of colour, from yellow to purple and every tone in between. He didn't hurt any longer but he looked worse than ever.

All the same, he had to tackle Roisin. The morning was sunny and he went looking for her.

'Fancy a spin? I've got the car just sitting there.

And you can show me the choice of local hotels.'

'What for?' She sounded surprised.

'I can't take up space in your house any longer. I'm like the man who came to dinner.'

'Have you mentioned this to Mum or Dad?' She looked at him with suspicion. 'Connor won't be happy if you go.'

And how do *you* feel about it, Roisin? he wanted to say, but didn't.

'Have we done something to upset you?'

'No! You've been fantastic to me.'

'Or is it that you've got what you wanted and it's time to back off?'

'I'm sorry, Roisin, I don't understand.'

'I mean, now you're on Black Mountain for the Champion Hurdle. That's what you came here for, wasn't it?'

He was dumbfounded.

'You think I could do that? Get beaten up so you'd all be nice to me and I'd sneak a ride.' He laughed—it was a joke. 'I've heard of some funny ways of getting a job.'

'What do you mean you got beaten up?'

He ignored the question, regretting his slip of the tongue. 'Do you really think I came here to talk myself onto Black Mountain?'

'Why did you come here, Alan?'

'To see you, of course.'

Her face softened.

He rushed on before he lost his nerve. 'We've never been close but I've always thought we could be. I mean, I'd like to be.'

He suspected he was being terribly uncool. It was difficult to be cool with a face all the colours of the rainbow. She'd seen him in those ridiculous pyjamas too. Maybe that's why she was grinning.

'OK. Take me for a ride in your fancy car then,' she said. 'But you can forget about hotels. With that face, you'd frighten the other guests.'

* * *

Cherry could feel Max's eyes on her as she made coffee.

'You're not feeling sick or anything, are you?' he asked.

'No.'

'Constipated? Sore tits?'

'What on earth are you on about, Max?'

'I've been looking up the symptoms of early pregnancy. What about dizziness?'

'I'm feeling just fine, thanks. I must be one of the lucky ones.'

'What does this Goodhill bloke say?'

'Who?' She knew at once from Max's face that she'd mucked up. Then it came to her—Lewis's sodding gynaecologist. 'Oh, Theo Goodhill—sorry, memory lapses I do have.'

'Is that a pregnancy symptom? Anyway, what does he say?'

'I haven't seen him yet.'

'You ought to get on with it.'

'So what? I've got my own doctor. It's my body and my business and I don't like to be told what to do.' And she slammed her cup down, cracking the saucer.

He grinned at her in an infuriating way.

'What's so bloody funny?'

'You.' He held out his arms. 'Irritability, that's another symptom. So you have got some of them.'

409

She let him put his arms around her. Time to make up. 'I'm sorry, Max. I am a bit up and down at the moment.'

'You see? Mood swings.' He held her carefully, as if she might break. 'So you'll ring Dad's doctor?'

'I think I've lost his number.'

'I'll get it for you.' He looked into her face. 'Then you'll make an appointment?'

'I promise.'

For after the honeymoon—when it would be too late.

*   *   *

For once in his life Lewis didn't know what to do. Cherry was the last woman in the world he wanted as a daughter-in-law. She'd cynically chased Roisin out of his life and thrown a hoop of steel round his son. Soon that hoop would be legally binding and she'd have insinuated herself into the heart of his family.

Lewis was convinced the reason Cherry had scotched his chance of marriage—and maybe children—with Roisin was to enhance her own future. Girls like that, with a history of deceit and immorality, never liked to share. Cherry would have had her eyes on his wealth right from the start. And he had no doubt she would target any future woman he set his heart on, especially if she were young enough to give him a family.

Lewis had considered offering Cherry money to go away. It was obvious she could be bought. But the time had passed when he could have got her agreement for a few thousand. Now things had progressed to the point where it would be

410

expensive, especially since he'd have to buy her silence over the ferry captain. She'd make him pay through the nose for that, he had no doubt.

But money wasn't the issue—which was ironic. Roisin would never know that, when it came to the crunch, it wasn't the cash that concerned him.

Cherry, the evil siren who had bewitched his son, was carrying his grandchild. There was no way around that fact. In these circumstances, he couldn't pay her to go away because he and Max would lose the child. It was unthinkable. As was the prospect of having that devious little bitch take a centre seat in his life.

He didn't know what to do.

*   *   *

Janice regretted asking for a meringue. It splintered under her fork and left gobbets of cream on her chin. It might taste effing gorgeous but it only reinforced the sinfulness of eating it in the first place. Her skirt was too tight and she resented spending spare cash on clothes for work.

The scumbag opposite her didn't have any of these problems. Cherry bleeding Hamilton, a jumped-up little drug-runner who'd sell her own mother down the river, was about to escape scot-free into a life of riches. Ray had agreed, they'd all agreed right from the top, that if she delivered on the boat they'd let her go. And she'd come through, like she always did. Cherry was the best grass Janice had ever worked with and she hated the blonde cow's guts.

They were in some posh café—it said *salon de thé* on the door—not a million miles from the Ritz.

411

Cherry had insisted on a celebratory touch to their last meeting. 'Don't worry,' she'd said to Janice. 'You won't have to pay. My treat.'

Just who did she think she was?

Janice didn't like being patronised. She'd have preferred a pint in some spit and sawdust boozer, not that they'd ever find one in this part of the world. As it was, she was painfully aware of her pitiful appearance in comparison to the well-heeled women all around, not to mention the blonde sitting opposite. Cherry's new leather coat was draped casually over a vacant chair and she wore a cream dress in a delicious wool and silk mixture; the shoes, she'd told Janice as she sat down, had come from Jimmy Choo in New Bond Street. The whole outfit must have cost a bundle; a month's money for Janice, probably. There was something wrong with the world.

'I'm impressed you could call in the Navy,' Cherry said. 'And that they found the boat. It's a big ocean out there.'

Of course—she was a sailor.

'There was some kind of freak storm and boats got into difficulties. When the *Leicester* went to assist, they found your yacht caught up in it.'

'So it was just luck?'

'We'd have got them at this end anyway.'

Cherry popped a piece of éclair into her mouth. How come she didn't make a mess? Janice fantasised about taking that chocolate log and smearing it down the cream dress.

Instead she said, 'How's Sinbad taking it?'

Cherry pulled a face. 'Not a happy bunny.'

'We'll tie *Cecilia* to Sinbad, you know. He's on borrowed time.'

412

'As long as you don't involve me.' Cherry looked at her. 'I'm out now. That's official.'

'Nothing's official.' Janice paused, she wished she didn't have to admit this. 'But we won't be taking further action on the Jimmy Morton testimony. I suggest you keep your nose clean in the future.'

'Oh I will.' Cherry was removing banknotes from her purse. 'I'm about to enjoy a life of luxury.'

She dropped a fifty on the table—far too much. Janice knew she was only doing it to rub it in.

It wasn't right.

*   *   *

They'd driven west to the mouth of the Shannon, then through Tralee to the Dingle Peninsula. Alan felt like a tourist but he was happy to be one with Roisin as his guide. They stopped and climbed a hill to find a good vantage point overlooking Dingle Bay. High clouds were scudding in on the westerly breeze but occasionally the son shone through, lighting up the waves and the mountains.

Alan was thrilled to be standing on the western edge of Europe. 'And out there,' he pointed to the seaward horizon, 'is America?'

'Newfoundland, I think,' she said. 'About two thousand miles away.'

He liked the sound of that. This was a remote and lovely place.

'So have you come back here for good?'

It was a moment before she answered.

'I don't know. It just feels right to be here at the moment.'

Was she going to come clean about Lewis now?

413

He waited but she said nothing. He couldn't let it pass.

'You're not going to tell me about Lewis, are you?'

This time she turned to face him. 'I made a mistake.'

So that was it? A big case of cold feet?

She added, 'I'm in shock. I've only just discovered what he's really like.'

Alan wasn't much wiser.

'And what about you?' she said. 'Are you going to tell me who thumped you?'

Touché.

'It was a misunderstanding. I was looking for a friend from England and asked too many questions. My fault really.'

He could see she didn't believe him but if she was going to hold back then so was he.

So they were on an equal footing, at least. It was an improvement on the days when he'd played the peasant to her Lady Muck.

She put her hand on the sleeve of his coat, a heavy waterproof he'd found hanging in the hall. 'I think we're going to get a sunset.'

Out at sea, the clouds had thinned, and the sun was sinking like an orange ball towards the horizon. They watched in silence, her hand still on him and Alan imagined he could feel the warmth of her fingers on his arm.

It was dark when they got back to the house.

'Noel's coat suits you,' she said as they walked up the path. 'I think you should keep it.'

* * *

414

Victor was on his own, with nobody watching his back, so he hoped this wasn't a set-up. But there were some circumstances where there was no alternative to sticking his neck out. He doubted if he was in any danger in the car park of the Old George near Biggin Hill, but he kept his eyes open all the same.

After ten minutes a car parked on the far side of the pub and a bulky figure in a jacket with a sheepskin collar got out. He headed as if to the side entrance then stepped into the shadows and, two seconds later, slipped into the passenger seat next to Victor. This was Graham, one of Victor's contacts inside the Met, the one who'd told him about the Customs interest in Scott Robinson's arrest. He'd rung Victor late that afternoon to arrange this meeting. Some information could only be exchanged face to face.

Victor had nearly put him off. He'd spent the day in a panic over the loss of the *Cecilia*. Tracks had to be covered, arrangements unravelled and troops given a volley. But here he was. There was no point in paying top dollar to an inside man if you didn't listen to what he had to say.

Graham didn't bother with any preamble.

'The drug bust on that yacht came after a Customs tip. You've got someone in your set-up who's talking to them.'

'I've been thinking it's Chris Spot.'

'No.'

'Chris has gone soft. He might be doing a deal.'

'He'd know about this, would he? He's been banged up for weeks.'

That was the problem. Chris knew there was a boat in Ireland that was due to make the Caribbean

415

run. But he wouldn't have known the timing, it was too recent.

'Who then?' he said.

'I don't know.'

'What are we sitting here for then?'

'Because I can find out for you. It'll cost.'

Victor sighed. 'I reckon I pay you enough already.'

'You're not paying me, you're paying my Customs contact.'

'You mean there's a Cussie offering to sell me information?'

'That's correct.'

Bloody hell. What was the world coming to?

'How did this Cussie know about you and me?'

Graham paused, considering his answer. 'I'm known to have good contacts. It's my job.'

Victor let it pass. He was thinking about rats. Someone squealing from inside his team would account for the arrests of Chris, Scott, and now the *Cecilia* bust. Whoever this was had to be dealt with, no matter the cost.

'How much?'

'A hundred grand.'

'Jesus. What's your cut?' he asked. He knew Graham of old. The policeman thought himself above dealing with the likes of Victor but he couldn't resist the cash in hand. He wouldn't move a muscle without being paid.

Graham ignored the question. 'For the money you will get a name. Also a log of meetings, phone calls and supporting evidence to confirm the identity of your informant.'

'Who is it, Graham?'

In the dim light Victor could make out the look

of contempt on the policeman's face. 'I don't know. That's valuable information which the officer has not shared with me. We'll meet tomorrow and I'll give you the necessary documentation.'

'OK.'

'And you'll bring the money, of course.'

'Sure.'

When you get rats in your house, you send for the rat-catcher. And you pay the price.

*   *   *

Hattie was disappointed with herself. Her mother always used to tell her off for not seeing things through. Going to Guides, learning the flute, doing karate—these were all activities she'd begun with enthusiasm and dumped when things got tough. And now, as an adult, Hattie could see the truth in her mum's criticism. She was always giving up when books got boring and diets got too tough. And relationships. She'd started seeing Martin again and, when she'd confided in him about this, he'd said, 'But you never stop beating up on yourself, do you?' He had a point.

Her disappointment now was her failure to find this possible witness in Kilburn. She'd been all fired up after her visit to the pub in Finchley and when she'd got to work the following week she'd checked the door-to-door names and statements on the computer. Officers had come across three Pauls in their enquiries: one was a thirteen-year-old who'd been in bed at the time of the murder; the second, a pensioner, had been at his ballroom dance class and was alibied until breakfast the next morning by a lady friend of a similar age; the third was thirty-

417

five and lived on his own.

Hattie had visited this last Paul with high expectation, which had been dashed once he proved to her that he'd been in Manchester on that night for a pharmaceutical sales conference. And after that her enthusiasm had nosedived as the hurly-burly of her everyday work had swamped her. It seemed like every six months there was a new initiative to stamp out gun crime.

But she wasn't giving up on her theory. Today she had time to check out a block of purpose-built flats across the way from the alley where the body had been found. Putting herself in Basil's position, she could imagine taking a short cut that way to head down the high street to the tube station.

There were twelve flats in the building and, once inside, she remembered it. The deaf granny with six cats next door to the Indian family on the first floor, and on the top the man who looked like a nightclub bouncer who was actually a Pilates teacher. Half the doors did not open to her ring; it was still too early for some office workers. But Mr Pilates was at home.

He confirmed all the earlier details he'd given. This time she asked if he was aware of regular social gatherings in the building.

'You mean people having parties? Not in this block.'

'I was thinking more like, suppose you had people coming round one evening a week to do a class.'

'But I don't do any classes at home. I work at a studio.'

'Sorry, that was just a for instance. Suppose you did.' She was fishing—she didn't want to put any

418

ideas in his head.

'No. There's nothing like that. Not unless you count the bloke next door. His mates are always round to play cards.'

Oh really?

'When do they come?'

'Tuesday nights, every week.'

Bingo. Thank you, Lord.

He misinterpreted the sudden lift to her features.

'None of that lot would be seen dead in a Pilates class, believe me.'

'Next door's number eleven, isn't it?' She consulted her notes. And then she saw it. 'Mr Gideon McCartney.'

'No one calls him Gideon. They call him Paul.'

Well, they would, wouldn't they?

*   *   *

Graham had set up a different rendezvous for the handover: an Indian restaurant in the back streets of Croydon. It was a slight risk for the two of them to be seen together in a public place but Victor reckoned the danger was greater for the policeman. He understood that Graham wanted the opportunity to count the money and a restaurant toilet was preferable to sitting in the car somewhere.

Graham was already at the table when Victor arrived. He politely declined the offer from the waiter to take his briefcase and took a seat.

'I've ordered something for both of us,' said the policeman. 'It'll save time.'

Victor nodded and indicated the case. 'You want

to go and count it now?'

Graham certainly did. He grabbed it and made for the Gents.

Victor was impatient for the information he'd been promised. But he sipped his lager and waited. He had no worries Graham would slip out the back or otherwise cheat him. He knew where Graham lived. And what would be the point? The name he was paying so handsomely for was only of value to himself.

Food was carried to the table, which Victor ignored. He wasn't narrow-minded or anything but he hated all Asian cuisine.

Eventually Graham returned and placed the briefcase on the red velveteen banquette next to him. Victor could tell that he was satisfied. It was his turn now, though satisfaction was not what he was paying for.

'Well?' he said.

Graham reached into his jacket pocket and produced an A4 envelope which he passed across the table. Then he began to spoon pilau rice onto his plate.

There were several sheets of paper inside the envelope. It was headed 'Scorpio'.

It began with a summary paragraph.

Scorpio came to the attention of Customs & Excise Investigation Division last autumn as a result of information received from US Customs. The information incriminated this individual in 'coopering' drug consignments off the south coast of England in 1999/2000. Considering Scorpio's position in the criminal empire of a top ID target, Victor Bishop, a direct approach was made. As a result, Scorpio was persuaded to offer information concerning the Bishop organisation and their ongoing criminal activities. This information proved to be of considerable value and has resulted in several recent successes in the fight against drug-trafficking in general and in curtailing the activities of Bishop in particular. These successes include: the seizure of cocaine worth just under £1million at Billingshurst, West Sussex, and the arrest of four individuals, including high-ranking gang member Chris Spot; the closure of a multimillion-pound money-laundering enterprise run by Scott Robinson, a US citizen with connections to organised crime in America, who is currently awaiting trial; and the well-publicised seizure of cocaine worth in excess of £50 million on the yacht *Cecilia* at the beginning of an importation run to the south coast. In consideration of this assistance, the ID has agreed not to proceed with charges against Scorpio who, it is understood, is intending to withdraw from all future criminal activity.

Two pages accompanied the top sheet. They listed phone calls and meetings with Scorpio, including dates, times and locations—a complete log of contacts with the informant over the past five months.

Victor scanned the list, quickly computing past events—absorbing a page of data was something he was good at. Some dates meant nothing to him, other days and their events were clear in his memory.

He knew where the finger was pointing now and suddenly it was blindingly obvious. He'd check this log out carefully, he wouldn't rush to judgement, but the weight of certainty was already bowing him down.

The final page was a photograph, generated off a computer in poor colour. Scrawled underneath in biro was Scorpio's real name.

He'd never gone much on astrology but one thing he did remember was Cherry's birth sign. Born 9 November. Scorpio.

*   *   *

Mr Gideon Paul McCartney, naturally, was not in. Hattie found a Costa Coffee round the corner and killed some time. When she returned there was still no sign of McCartney and there was a limit to how much time she could waste.

Martin was taking her out later. He'd not told her where they were going—it was one of his surprise dates. So far they'd been bowling, ice skating and to a piece of radical theatre at the Tricycle. It was like having a new boyfriend instead of the old one back. Maybe that's because she'd said he was predictable last time she'd dumped him. Whatever the reason, she appreciated the effort he was making and she didn't want to be late.

She promised herself she'd return soon to talk to this Paul. She couldn't remember much about him from the first visit, which was poor. She was meant to be a trained observer. She concentrated hard and conjured the image of a small pasty-faced man of about forty. The flat had been neat but not very

422

homely, with framed James Bond movie posters on the wall and a glass coffee table. Anything else? Another table, full size, with a green cloth on it and the smell of stale cigarette smoke.

She'd be back. Next Tuesday evening seemed like a good time.

*   *   *

Victor did not go to bed. He spent the night reviewing the past few months, what he'd told Cherry, what she knew, where she'd been—testing everything against the log of events that the Customs agent had supplied. He tried hard but he couldn't find anything on the log that disproved the charge against her. There was not one date or time when he could say for sure she couldn't have done that.

According to this log she'd passed on information about his gambling and behind-the-scenes racing contacts, and key locations like the farm in Sussex. But one thing stood out as damning: the *Cecilia*. Cherry was the first to know about the yacht, because he'd sent her to check it out. And she'd got pally with the kid who showed her round and, later, got him on the run as crew. So she could have found out the timing of *Cecilia*'s return run from him. Certainly, no one else on his UK team could have supplied this information.

It was at this point, at two in the morning, that Victor broke out the whisky. He was known as a hard man but he had his sentimental side. He found some old photos: Cherry as he'd first known her, trying to look sophisticated in an evening gown, sailing a dinghy through a big sea, sunbathing naked by the pool at his villa in Spain. In his way he'd loved her. She'd been his girl and he was proud of her. *Was* proud of her.

How could she betray him? Well, he could understand it. It was not unknown but he'd never have thought it of her. Why hadn't she come to him after the Cussies' first approach? He'd have worked some way out for her, even if it wasn't as glamorous as the one she appeared to have organised for herself: marriage to Lewis Ashwood's son.

He pondered his next step. He had to make a business decision. To face up to the challenge of Cherry's behaviour and see it as an opportunity. Was there a way to turn Cherry's betrayal to his advantage?

By the time he reached the bottom of the bottle, he reckoned that there was.

Chapter Twenty-Two

Lewis took Victor's phone call at home. It was a moment or two before he placed the voice.

'How did you get this number?'

'Easily.'

What a cocky bastard he was.

'I've got a question to ask you,' Bishop said. 'Are you happy your son is about to marry a convicted prostitute?'

The short answer to that, of course, was no.

'I know all about Cherry's dubious past,' he said.

'You wanna bet?' Bishop chuckled. 'You haven't answered my question. Are you happy about the marriage?'

Lewis said nothing, unsure whether to tell Bishop to get lost or to hang up.

'Because if you're not,' Bishop continued, 'then I might be able to help you.'

'What are you after?' Lewis demanded. He wanted no connection to this man, it was potentially ruinous. All his instincts told him he'd be well advised to keep Victor at arm's length.

'Meet me and find out. But if you're happy for the wedding to go ahead then I won't waste any more of your time.'

Lewis was thinking hard. He'd not managed to come up with a scheme to thwart Cherry but Bishop knew her better than he did. Bishop, repulsive though he was, might be the only person who could stop the marriage. Obviously there would be a price, but it might be worth paying.

'It won't hurt you to listen,' the other man said.

Lewis supposed that it wouldn't.

*   *   *

At first, if he were honest, Alan had not been impressed by Black Mountain. In comparison to Grain of Sand, it was like getting into a vintage car after a modern high-performance vehicle. One was big and classically cumbersome, the other versatile and instantly sensitive to the commands of the driver. A flick of the switch on Sandy and the horse was up or down the gears—nimble, fleet of foot, effortless. Black Mountain was none of these things. You had to ram the pedal to the floor to get any response and, even then, it took a while to register in the animal's lumbering frame.

425

But Alan soon realised there was more to the horse than could be discovered on a couple of outings. His normal work morning involved going three times up Tom's all-weather gallop. It was only five furlongs long but set into the side of a steep hill and Black Mountain always appeared stronger on the final section than on the previous two. There seemed no end to his stamina. Brute strength was not necessarily required to pilot him successfully, or else Con would have had no chance of controlling him. Alan settled for allowing the animal to get used to him.

Two days after Alan and Roisin had enjoyed the sunset over the Bay of Dingle, the weather changed. The sea boiled and the sky grew darker than the bruises on his ribs as the wind swept the rain in from the west. Hailstones bounced off the roof of the stalls and congealed in icy puddles in the yard.

'You don't want me to take Blackie out in this, do you?' Alan said to Tom.

The trainer cocked his head on one side. 'It won't bother him, but if you don't fancy it . . .' He shrugged, leaving Alan little choice. He was on trial here so he couldn't bottle out.

He'd encountered worse conditions, he supposed. At Aintree once when the north-westerlies had dumped an ocean of water on the course an hour before the first race. By the time it had got to Alan's only race, the last of the day, it was like trying to ride through a swamp. Half of the runners were pulled up before the finish, but Alan had stuck it out and he won, so maybe it was a good omen.

Here, at least, the all-weather gallop was firm

underfoot. They only had to contend with riding head first into a gale that threatened to blow the hillside flat. Black Mountain put his head down and hurled himself forward, his big frame knifing into the wind as if inspired by the challenge. Alan just sat against him, enjoying the sensation of power. At the end of two miles round Cheltenham, would it be enough to hold off Grain of Sand? If the ground came up soft then it just might.

It was an incredible feeling to be hurtling into this deadly wind, like riding a cannonball. He'd never travelled so fast on any horse—or was it just the illusion of speed as the wind rushed past in the other direction? Whatever the truth, he knew he'd just had a glimpse of what Black Mountain was all about. The animal was an elemental force.

He turned Blackie and rode him back, with the gale behind them. It was a phenomenal sensation, like riding the wind itself. He couldn't wait to do it again.

When he got back to the yard Tom was waiting. 'You see?' he said. 'The tougher it is, the better he likes it.'

Alan was speechless.

*   *   *

Victor was relieved Lewis had taken the bait, not that it would have altered his course of conduct but it was satisfying—and surely profitable—to be proved right. Lewis Ashwood did not want the likes of Cherry marrying his son. Victor had been prepared to open Lewis's eye to the kind of woman she was, but it sounded as if the businessman had a fair idea already. That should make things easier.

427

Their meeting had been arranged for an upstairs room in a trendy drinking club in Soho. Lewis looked bloody awful in Victor's opinion. Aside from the bloodshot eyes and sunken cheeks, there was a general couldn't-care scruffiness far removed from his spruce public image. Victor had noted some of the gossip-column speculation about the failure of Lewis's relationship with that pretty Irish girl. He could understand how that might knock a man for six.

Lewis had obviously decided to come clean about Cherry.

'I hired a private detective,' he said. 'He dug up a whole lot of stuff about her going off the rails as a kid. Theft and prostitution. Time in some institution or other. Working in nightclubs. Cited in a divorce case. Not what I would ever have wanted for my son.'

Victor nodded sympathetically. He could see how Cherry didn't have the most attractive CV from Lewis's point of view.

'But Max and one or two others talked me round. Cherry assured me that all this was in the past—though she'd lied to me recently. Anyway,' Lewis gulped his drink, 'she then did something which I'm not prepared to talk about. It was unforgivable. So you're right in thinking that I am not happy about this marriage.' He sighed heavily. 'I'll come round in time, I daresay.'

Victor nodded. 'You might do. Provided Customs and Excise don't decide to press charges against her. That would be a bit embarrassing for you, wouldn't it?'

The blood drained from Lewis's cheeks. 'What charges?'

'Drug-running. You know she's a handy sailor? If you're bringing stuff in by sea you need people like Cherry. So I'm told.'

'She was arrested for that?'

'Not at the time. It's four or five years ago but the Cussies have only just found out about it. We're talking sizeable amounts of gear, worth millions. Be a big trial if it ever gets to court. And the papers will love Cherry, especially if she's your daughter-in-law.'

Victor wondered if he'd overdone it. Lewis looked as if he were having a seizure. His knuckles whitened as he gripped the glass in his hand but, remarkably, it did not break. Eventually Lewis said, 'I've got to put a stop to it.'

'Look,' said Victor quietly. 'I know Cherry better than you. We go way back. I'm sure I can persuade her to leave Max alone.'

'How would you do that?'

'A bit of carrot and stick. I'll offer her some money to join her mother in Australia.'

'You think she'd go?'

'I've only told you the carrot part. I don't think it's in your interests to know about the stick.'

Lewis thought about that. He seemed to accept it. Then he said, 'She's going to have a baby.'

Oh. That was a wrinkle Victor had not anticipated, though it did explain a few things. Like how come Lewis hadn't fobbed her off with a fat cheque.

'You sure it's Max's?' he said.

'To be frank, I'm not a hundred per cent sure she's really pregnant. She won't go near the gynaecologist I've lined up for her. It wouldn't matter but the wedding is too damn close.'

429

'Even if she is pregnant, it's not a problem. She can have an abortion.'

The bloodshot eyes bored into Victor. 'That's my grandchild.'

'Possibly your grandchild. Cherry has always been popular with the guys at the club. And even if it is, so what? Max will find another girl and have a family. Stick with Cherry and you could be bringing up the kid while she does ten years.'

Lewis nodded, an indecisive punch-drunk reflex, as if he'd taken too much punishment. 'You fix it then,' he said.

That was better. 'OK.'

'What's it going to cost?'

'You remember we once discussed your Elmwood Glade development? I'm still interested.'

Lewis stared at him dumbly, as if this was a shock too many.

*   *   *

Alan had been absent from home longer than he intended. It was hard to tear himself away from Roisin and the warm-hearted care of the Dougherty farm. But the phone call he'd been hoping for from Kevin finally came through and reminded him of his other responsibilities.

'All right,' said the Irishman. 'I'll talk to your Jockey Club fellow but he'll have to meet me here. I'm not going back to England. Tell him to leave a message at the pub.'

'Thanks, Kevin. I'm glad I talked you round.'

'It wasn't you, mate. I gave Frankie a call and she persuaded me. She said she'd come over if I sorted this out.'

Alan was delighted to hear it. He wished Kevin well and called his father to say he was flying back.

Ralph was surprised. 'I thought you were going to work with that new horse of yours till Cheltenham.'

'I'll discuss it with Tom, but I reckon I've done enough. And there's something I've been putting off.'

Then he told Ralph about Jane.

*   *   *

Roisin had said all along she wasn't going to Cheltenham with the rest of them. Connor had jumped through hoops so he could go to Tuesday's race, poring over his school books when he'd normally be in the yard with Blackie or watching TV. Even Mr Doyle, his headmaster, had said that considering Con was the owner of the Irish favourite for the Champion Hurdle it was his patriotic duty to attend. So Pauline was making the trip as well. Roisin would be the only Dougherty not rooting for Blackie in person.

'We need someone to keep an eye on the farm,' she'd said when Pauline had tried to persuade her.

'Fitzgerald and his lad from up the road will do it,' Pauline had protested. 'They owe us from last summer.'

Roisin pulled a face; she resented being made to spell it out. 'Lewis will be there.'

'And so what? You can avoid one man in fifty thousand, surely? Besides, I know someone else who will be there and he'll need all the support he can get on our Blackie.'

'You'll just have to shout twice as loud then,

won't you, Ma,' she'd said huffily and was instantly ashamed of herself.

But that conversation had taken place days ago, before she'd spent the afternoon with Alan. Before she'd seen him develop an understanding with Black Mountain and grow into Noel's coat as if it had been his all along.

She'd urged him to take it with him when he left and he'd declined, adding, 'Maybe I could borrow it next time. I mean, if I'm ever back here again.'

'Sure you will be,' she heard herself say and she watched the Merc, now covered in mud and farm muck, as it disappeared up the lane.

All the same, she still wasn't going to Cheltenham.

*   *   *

'There's a few tricks in here even I didn't know about,' said Ralph. He'd just been reading a summary of Kevin's evidence that Alan had put together.

'Surely not?' said a dry voice from the sofa on the far side of the room.

Alan grinned. They were in Linda's house and their hostess was supposed to be minding her own business but it wasn't possible to keep her out of matters as scandalous as race-fixing. Her antennae were working overtime.

Ralph ignored her. 'Mind you, not a lot of people realise if you deprive a horse of water for a couple of days it will cut its performance by forty per cent. Most people only think about giving them a bucket of water before a race to stop them. The trouble with that is that you can't always make

432

them drink.'

'That's bloody obvious.' Linda couldn't resist butting in once more. 'If I deprived you of water for two days you wouldn't run well either.'

'It might seem obvious but it never occurred to me. I've never seen a horse without a water bucket. It's just a reflex to make sure it's filled up. Anyway, it's down here as one of their methods. Plus anything you can think of to tire an animal before the race. Swimming them, putting them on walkers, loading them with weights during the night.'

'And no doping,' added Alan.

'That's the point, isn't it? Tire a horse out and he's not going to give of his best but nothing will show up in a test.' He looked at Alan. 'What are you going to do with this information?'

'Go to the Jockey Club.'

'Those old farts have still got it in for me.'

'All the more reason to help them out now.'

Ralph didn't disagree. 'And what about your friend Jane? She's likely to end up in trouble, isn't she?'

'I'm sure she's not involved, Dad. I think she's been frightened into covering for Donovan.'

'She'll still end up in hot water if she doesn't come clean. Before the Jockey Club get involved would be best.'

Alan was well aware of it. 'I wish I could get Jane on her own,' he said. 'I'd drive there right now but she won't talk to me.'

'Maybe I could have a word with her,' suggested Ralph. 'Suppose I pitch up at this flat of hers and pretend to be her uncle.'

An explosion of laughter erupted from the sofa. 'You'll get yourself arrested for being a dirty old man.'

'Come off it, Linda.' Ralph was affronted.

'I'm serious. Middle-aged man with wolfish grin accosts young girl and claims to be a long-lost relative. No chance. You leave it to me.'

Alan and Ralph stared at her.

'Don't worry, I'll think of something that won't scare the pants off her.'

'But Linda,' Alan suppressed a grin, 'she'll know you already. Everybody knows you.'

She got to her feet and stalked towards him. 'Listen you, what do you think I do for a living? I'm a sodding actress. I pretend to be someone else.'

Alan supposed she had a point.

*   *   *

Alan and Ralph watched from the security of Ralph's BMW as Linda walked away from them towards the building where Jane lived. A few minutes earlier all three of them had watched as Jane's Mini drew up outside. Linda had adjusted her dark wig for the nth time and set off.

'This is a farce,' Alan said. 'Maybe I should have gone.'

'Linda's very good in farce,' murmured Ralph.

Alan held his tongue. A long ten minutes went by. Then the phone in Ralph's pocket rang.

He listened for a minute, then started the engine.

'What?' demanded Alan.

'They're going to meet us round the corner. We'll find somewhere quiet to have a chat.'

Alan stared at him in amazement.

'Linda came clean the moment she got in there.

Told Jane you were really worried about her and knew she was in trouble. Apparently the poor kid burst into tears.'

They waited round the corner until two figures appeared, Linda's arm tucked protectively through Jane's.

'Linda's pretty good at straight parts too,' added Ralph as the two women reached the car.

They found the empty back room of a country pub. In the car Jane had been remorseful.

'I'm sorry, Al. I was horrible to you, wasn't I? But Don was so jealous of you. He said if I talked to you we'd be washed up.'

'Are you in love with him then?' Alan asked. He'd not realised their relationship was so strong.

She stared straight ahead, her mouth turned down. 'I used to be. Before I found out what he's really like.'

'And what is he like?'

She turned to him and he could read the fear in her eyes. 'He's the meanest man I've ever met.' And she began to cry.

Now she nursed a drink and looked again at Linda. 'I thought I knew you. That's why I let you in.'

'I've just got that kind of face, dear.' She patted Jane's arm. 'Tell Alan what he needs to know.'

'I can't.'

That's what she'd said to Alan before. She probably didn't realise how much he knew already.

'Look, Jane,' he said. 'We know there's a conspiracy to slow down good horses and lay them on the betting exchanges. Why don't you tell us what you know.'

'You don't understand. It's not me. Don knows

435

where my family live. He knows where my sister goes to school. He told me what he'd do to them if I ever said anything.'

Alan could understand her reluctance but she didn't know the whole picture. 'There's a stable lad in Ireland who's going to talk to the Jockey Club. The whole thing's about to blow wide open and Donovan's going to be in the frame anyway. Off the record, just tell us what you know.'

She shook her head. 'I want to, but . . .'

Her former boyfriend obviously had her petrified.

'The other thing is that, if there's arrests and prosecutions, you don't want to get mixed up with the other side. If you don't come clean now, there's a danger you'll be seen as protecting Donovan.'

She gave him a long shrewd look. Then at last she began to talk.

'The first I knew of it was Wild Willy at Plumpton. Remember? There'd been a bit of a party the night before, someone's birthday, and it didn't finish till four in the morning. I didn't think there was much point in going home for two hours so I went straight to the yard. I thought I might get some sleep before everyone turned up. Only, when I got there I found I wasn't the first.

'There were working lights on in the yard and I could hear the horse walker going. So I went to see what was up and found Donovan walking Wild Willy. He wasn't pleased to see me but he pretended it was perfectly normal to be walking a horse at that time. He said he was doing research on animal sleep patterns for his brother who was doing a postgrad degree in veterinary science.'

'What?'

436

'Yes, I know. It was complete rubbish but he sounded very plausible and I was half asleep. He said he'd only walked Willy for five minutes. Anyway, he said he'd get into trouble with Ian if it got out and swore me to secrecy. It was only later, after the race, that the penny really dropped. Willy was deliberately walked before the race to tire him out. Then I remembered how Nightswimmer had lost in the same way and I was angry. I would have told you all about it, Alan, if I hadn't run into Don and told him what I thought of him. He said it was just coincidence and forbade me to talk to you. He knew we'd been out together and accused me of carrying on with you.

'Later on, I realised he was just suspicious of you, Alan, because you'd been on Nightswimmer and he'd seen you talking to me at Plumpton. We had a row and he turned nasty, told me if I breathed a word he'd say I was in on it and had helped him. Then I knew he didn't care for me at all. He was just using me because I had a senior position in the yard. He'd started as a casual but everyone trusted him because he was with me.' She finished her drink in one swallow. 'Even though he's left the yard I still keep looking over my shoulder. He really did threaten my family and I believe him.'

She looked as if she might cry again. Linda gave her a hug and Ralph presented her with a fresh glass of wine.

'Jane,' Alan leaned forward, 'do you know where Donovan is now?'

She gulped her drink. 'He's got a job as a security guard at Cheltenham. I'm dreading the thought that I might run into him tomorrow.'

Alan looked at Ralph and read the concern in his eyes. The thought of Donovan guarding Cheltenham racehorses set alarm bells ringing.

He had to phone Clive at the Jockey Club right away.

*   *   *

Sitting in the lounge of the late-night ferry, Roisin told herself she was a fool. If she was going to the races she should have gone with everybody else thirty-six hours earlier. Now she was faced with a lonely drive through the night to Cheltenham once the ferry docked. At least she wouldn't be alone on the road—half the passengers were Cheltenham bound judging by the shouts and laughter echoing from the bar.

It was an adventure though. Even travelling on the ferry took some courage. She didn't know if it was the same ship Noel had died on and she didn't want to know. His spirit was with her, all the same, on her pilgrimage to watch Black Mountain's assault on the Champion Hurdle. If there was any justice, Blackie would win for him.

Why had it taken so long for her to realise she had to be there to see it?

It always took her a while to see things clearly. She ought to trust her instincts more.

Her instincts had warned her off Lewis at the beginning but she'd ignored them.

Her instincts were giving her a message now, about Alan.

She wasn't going to ignore them this time.

*   *   *

Ralph had to pinch himself. The idea that he was part of a Jockey Club security operation was hard to come to terms with. For years he had been the number one bad guy in their book and yet now he had been welcomed into the fold. As Clive Jones had said when they first met a couple of hours ago, 'Poacher turned gamekeeper, eh?' Ralph had agreed but privately he'd thought it was his chance for redemption.

He'd been mending his ways ever since Linda had come into his life, though that stunt at the casino when he'd won the money for Alan had been a bit of a lapse. He'd not used that hooky mobile phone since then—it had a sensor inside which, once the roulette wheel was spinning, could predict where the ball would end up to within six places. Of course, the casino authorities would be on to gadgets like that now but that wasn't the only reason he hadn't used it again. These days, with Linda on his arm and back on good terms with his son, it was more important to go straight. And tonight's little operation set the seal on it.

He and Clive were concealed in an empty stall in the overnight stables at Cheltenham racecourse. They had been there for a couple of hours, just before the changeover of security personnel. The new shift included Donovan—Clive had checked his status with the Cheltenham management—and their mission was to observe the guard's behaviour throughout the night shift.

Ralph wasn't quite sure how Alan had wangled him onto Clive's team. As an experienced horse-fixer he'd be alive to any funny business but then so would Clive—it was his job, after all. It was also true that Ralph would be able to identify Donovan, having regularly seen him at racecourses. All the same, Ralph had the feeling that Clive had included him as a favour to Alan. 'I owe him one,' Clive had said and Ralph was happy to leave it at that.

He was conscious that they were surrounded by millions of pounds of horse flesh. In this section of the stable, approximately thirty of the best National Hunt horses in the country were getting a night's rest before one of the biggest days of their lives. Not that they would know it.

'That's him.' Ralph indicated a stocky man in overalls walking the line of boxes. His long black hair gleamed in the working lights and Ralph could make out tattoos on his forearms below his rolled-up sleeves.

They observed closely as he entered a stall diagonally across from their hiding place. He remained out of sight for some minutes.

Ralph had a fair idea of the animals around, he'd tried to memorise the layout. By his calculations Donovan was in the stall occupied by War Head, a much-fancied contender for the Arkle Chase, the race preceding the Champion Hurdle. He kept quiet, however; Clive would be just as aware as he was.

Eventually Donovan reappeared and continued his walk along the boxes. Then he returned to look in on War Head once more. This time he stayed outside the stall, observing the horse within.

Ralph had no doubt that something was up.

After five minutes Donovan disappeared into the guards' hut.

Clive turned to Ralph. 'I'm going to look in that

440

stall. If he's done something to the horse we've got to nip it in the bud.'

Ralph nodded. There was no point in allowing Donovan to fix the horse and confronting him after the damage was done.

Clive was whispering into a mobile, alerting the two other Jockey Club men who were concealed in the yard.

'You stay right here,' he said to Ralph as he opened the door and stepped into the yard.

Ralph watched, heart in mouth, as Clive swiftly made the distance to War Head's stall. He opened the door and ducked inside.

At the same moment Donovan emerged and made straight for the stall—he'd probably been observing on CCTV, Ralph thought.

The big man moved silently.

Where were the other guys? Ralph wondered. Shouldn't they be springing to Clive's defence?

Donovan was opening the stall. Ralph heard Clive's voice. The words 'Jockey Club' sounded clearly but the rest was lost as Donovan lunged inside and was lost from view.

Ralph didn't think, he just ran across the yard.

The light was dim inside the small space but there was the horse, standing oddly, it seemed, though there was no time to discover why. Donovan had his hands round Clive's throat and was squeezing.

Ralph hit the big man in the kidneys as hard as he could. Donovan threw Clive to the floor and turned.

There were shouts out in the yard behind and sounds of footsteps.

Ralph threw another blow but he didn't know if

it landed because a fist like a hammer landed on the side of his head and finished his night.

* * *

'Jesus, Dad!' Alan was surveying his father's swollen head as he sat in the hospital bed.

'You can talk, son,' muttered Ralph through clenched teeth.

Roisin—a tired but exhilarated Roisin, getting by on adrenalin after her night-time dash and now consumed by this new drama—gazed at them both. 'You make a right pair,' she said. 'Do facial injuries run in the family?'

Jokes were in order because Alan had spoken to the doctor about Ralph and the old man hadn't suffered any permanent damage; neither, thankfully, had Clive who had already been discharged.

'What exactly had he done to the horse?' Alan asked. They'd been through the fight several times but this was the remaining unanswered question.

'He'd tied his front foreleg behind his off. It was bent up behind the knee so the horse was standing on three legs.'

'You mean War Head would have been left like that all night?' Roisin was appalled.

'Yes. And Donovan had thrown away his water.'

'So he wouldn't have been in great shape to run the Arkle,' said Alan.

All three of them contemplated the situation for a moment.

'Well done, Dad,' said Alan. 'Pity you won't get to the racecourse to see him run.'

Ralph shrugged and pointed to the television.

442

'I'll be watching, son. Good luck.'

As they left the room, Ralph called Alan back. 'This Roisin, have I seen her somewhere before?'

'She used to be a croupier at the Golden Thread.'

Ralph's eyes opened wide. 'I always fancied those girls but I never had any luck,' he said. 'Congratulations, son.'

'What's funny?' demanded Roisin as they made for the exit.

'Nothing,' he said. He couldn't explain it to her but it was good to know he'd beaten the old man at one thing.

*   *   *

Connor Dougherty couldn't explain all the feelings that were racing through him, though he knew he had never been so scared. Leading Blackie round the parade ring ahead of the Champion Hurdle he was aware the eyes of the racing world were upon him and his horse. Already reporters had waylaid him as he'd gone about his business of the day and Tom and Roisin had done their best to shoo them away. He was a story in himself—the fourteen-year-old owner of the race favourite—but all he could do was blush in the spotlight of their questions.

What he wanted to say to them was that only Black Mountain was worth writing about and that his brother, Noel, should have been standing here in his place and please, please leave me alone. But he'd not managed even that. Now he just concentrated on Blackie, as his dad had told him. His wrist was still sore but he wasn't going to let on

443

about that. He took courage from the horse; the way Blackie held his head high and strode the ring in his awkward bullish way, as if he didn't care, as if they were alone together back on the gallops in Kerry and all these people didn't exist.

Then he caught sight of a face in the crowd, grinning and sticking his thumbs up; next to him was another smiling maniac, calling out to him as if they were related yet he had never seen them in his life. The Irish fans were out in force and he smiled back, thinking of the lads back home watching him on television. Even Mr Doyle would be watching in his study—he'd told him so.

On the inside, amongst the knots of trainers and connections, he spotted his sister, who'd been snotty about coming over but had changed her tune and appeared out of the blue. Right it was too. It wouldn't have been the same without her even if she was a moody one. For a second their eyes met and she looked on him with pride.

That was it. That's what he felt above all—pride in the magnificent animal beside him.

'You show 'em, Blackie,' he muttered as he led him round. 'Go out and show 'em what you can do.'

*　　　*　　　*

Roisin caught sight of Lewis in the crowd on the other side of the ring, a blonde head by his side. So he and Cherry were here together. In the light of Lewis's late-night call she found that surprising. She turned her back on them smartly. She didn't want to think about either of them. Pray God it wasn't their day.

Alan was in deep conversation with her father.

He was wearing green and white silks, Connor's choice, and the fading bruises on his face lent him a battle-scarred look. Now that his nose had returned to its usual size she was able to appreciate what a handsome man he was. It wasn't something she'd thought about before.

She put her hand on his arm.

'Good luck.' It wasn't really adequate. She wanted to say more. She put her face close to his and hissed, 'Beat those cheating Ashwoods for me.'

His eyebrows rose fractionally, surprised at her intensity. She realised she was pinching his flesh through his shirt. She didn't care. She wanted him to know how she felt.

'Just do it.'

The amusement vanished from his face and he said, 'Yes.'

* * *

Max hadn't been exaggerating when he'd told Lewis he thought Grain of Sand was a better horse than Black Mountain. And nothing he'd discovered about him first-hand had changed his mind. The smart money, he noticed, was on Sandy. Black Mountain was still favourite for the race but his price was easing, Sandy's was shortening by the minute.

In the battle between the two, Max reckoned he had the edge. Grain of Sand was a simple horse to ride, you pushed the buttons and the horse obeyed. Black Mountain was a different proposition, as Max knew from his ride at Leopardstown. He'd nearly been beaten that day. Defeat was only a matter of time and today, Black Mountain's first race outside Ireland with a new jockey on board, could be the day.

In any case, his race plan was simple. Follow Black Mountain and put Sandy in position to show what he could do when it came down to the wire.

*   *   *

Roisin's words were still ringing in Alan's head as they set off. She'd been so fierce! He felt inspired, like a warrior heading into battle with a woman's favour on his sleeve.

Then all other thoughts were gone as Black Mountain led the charge over the first hurdle of the Old Course. Alan had ridden this tricky terrain many times before but he'd never had a winner at the Festival. If he did no more than make up the numbers, this would probably be one of the highlights of his career.

But the horse beneath him was not accustomed to making up numbers. Black Mountain was leading the field of thirteen out into the country and up the hill. Tom had told him that would be the case. 'He only knows one way to run a race and don't try to stop him. There's never been a horse like him. He's like Linford Christie only he runs the fifteen hundred metres, d'ye see?'

There'd been talk not just in the Dougherty parlour but in all the media about the head-to-head between Black Mountain and Grain of Sand. Alan had tried to keep a sense of perspective. There were eleven other runners in the race, among them more Irish horses and raiders from France and the USA. These were top contenders, the cream of National Hunt hurdlers, and he felt that any of

446

them could make a nonsense of the prediction of a two-horse race. Cheltenham races so often defied the pundits.

But at the top of the hill Black Mountain was six lengths clear and the rest of the field was strung out behind him like smoke from a chimney.

The nearest horse was Grain of Sand.

*   *   *

So far, Max reckoned, everything had gone as planned. Black Mountain had shot off like a bullet from a gun and Sandy had followed, tracking the big horse up the hill, making light of the soft conditions like the class act he was. Provided they could stay in touch until the last flight, Max was confident his fellow could take the other. Sandy was itching to up the gears, Max could tell, but he wouldn't go until Max gave the word. What a fantastic horse he was.

His father had looked ill as he stood in the ring before the race. Cherry had gripped his arm, almost as if to hold him up. It had occurred to Max at the time that Lewis had probably caught a glimpse of Roisin.

It was the first time in his life he'd felt sorry for his dad. If he could put the Champion Hurdle Trophy in his hands, that would cheer him up. Lewis would be truly proud of him at last. *Here's my chance to put everything right.*

They were heading downhill now, on the run back to the finish, towards a baying crowd spilling over from the vast stands, his father and Cherry among them, watching every stride of this duel for supremacy.

At the second last flight, Max gave Sandy a slap down the shoulder to keep him up to his work. The horse instantly changed gear and took off. In a matter of strides he was upsides Black Mountain and past him.

Max looked up and saw the last flight of hurdles and the winning post in front of him.

I'm going to win, he thought.

*   *   *

Alan was dismayed. He couldn't believe the speed at which Sandy was travelling. But Sandy was an incredible horse.

As they raced round the final bend, Grain of Sand pulled four lengths clear and Alan was convinced his chance had gone.

Now they were charging to the last hurdle. Alan urged Black Mountain on with all his strength. At the last flight, just when he wanted to see a stride more than at any other time in his life, he couldn't. But Black Mountain came to his rescue. Alan had no idea where the horse's strength came from, to find such a leap at the last. Blackie picked up from outside the wings of the hurdle and landed running just as far on the other side.

Alan struggled to stay with him as they began the final uphill run to the line. With less than a hundred yards to go Alan could see the gradient was finally taking its toll on Grain of Sand. His stride had shortened visibly and he began to wander from side to side. Sandy's tank was empty. But Black Mountain just kept powering forward the way he'd torn into the gale by the Shannon.

They passed Sandy ten yards before the post.

Black Mountain won by two lengths and the crowd's cheers nearly blew the roof off the stand.

*   *   *

Lewis watched the bedlam around him as if he were elsewhere. In business and in life, he'd never seen much merit in coming second.

The ache in the centre of his chest intensified and for a moment he thought he might fall, as if it were possible to fall with the crush of people all around. Then it passed and he was left with just the pain of disappointment.

He'd had his hand on the trophy and it had been ripped from his grasp by a horse he'd given away. How stupid could a man be.

The woman by his side was shouting in his ear. 'Never mind, Lewis. It was a great race.'

What did she care, the jumped-up blonde slut who had his son by the balls and him by the throat. He couldn't even bring himself to think of her by her name—Cherry. Sweet and soft on the outside, with a stone for a heart. How he hated her.

When was Victor Bishop going to keep his promise? The blonde witch had to be on a plane to Australia within the next week or it would be too late.

He'd call Bishop when he got back to London. And he'd make a doctor's appointment. He felt like shit.

*   *   *

It was all Connor could do to lift the great trophy, he was shaking so much with excitement and

449

emotion. Roisin was by his side but she made him go up onto the stand first and hold up the golden cup for the crowd. Then she came and held it too. And Ma and Da came up to great roars and Alan held his silver plate up high and everyone kissed and hugged and Connor cried. He couldn't help it even though he knew they'd be watching on television back home.

He'd thought winning the trophy would make it better about Noel. It didn't do that, but it helped.

Chapter Twenty-Three

This was the first time Victor had missed the opening day of Cheltenham since he was a kid. Even if he wasn't based in England at the time, he'd always made a point of coming home for Cheltenham week. Today he wouldn't even catch it on television.

The meeting was at an Amsterdam hotel he'd used once in the past, for a head-to-head with a Jamaican bigshot who wanted to talk business. The bigshot had insisted on Amsterdam so he could tour the red-light district. Victor had brought Cherry with him so he wasn't interested in any of that stuff. It was as well Mr Big had enjoyed himself. He'd been gunned down in Kingston three weeks later, so their business had come to nothing.

By some irony, Victor was given the same suite he'd shared with Cherry—or did they all look the same? Wood panelling, orange curtains and canal prints on the wall.

His Dutch visitor was dead on time, as Victor

450

had known he would be. Precision was important in his line of work. Victor had never used him before but he was meant to be the best. This wasn't a job he could do in-house. When it came to dealing with Cherry, there mustn't be any link back to him.

Victor supplied the Dutchman with a dossier of material: photographs, addresses, car details and résumé of her habits, insofar as he'd been able to compile them. The Dutchman said not to bother too much as he would familiarise himself with the subject before the event. Then they talked money. Their business took a mere ten minutes.

*　　*　　*

Hattie was fed up. She'd been promised a card school on Tuesday night at Gideon McCartney's and yet no one was at home—despite McCartney's dilapidated Sierra taking up a parking place: she'd checked it on the Police National Computer. She got no answer to her regular ringing on the bell and sat in her car outside for close on four hours before giving up. Next time she saw Mr Pilates she'd let him have a piece of her mind, though given his track record, he probably wouldn't understand her. Obviously tonight had been yet another misunderstanding.

Martin did not agree. She'd been so frustrated she'd called him when she finally got home and he'd turned up with pizza.

'So these people are gamblers,' he said.

'Yes.'

'Just cards?'

'I don't know. Anything that moves, I expect. Basil bet on most things.'

451

'Like horses?'

'What are you getting at?'

He flipped open the paper to the TV page and pointed to a late-night listing, *Today at the Cheltenham Festival*.

'What's that?' she asked.

He rolled his eyes. 'The great detective is investigating the death of a gambler and she doesn't know about Cheltenham.'

'You're really enjoying this, aren't you?'

He grinned. 'Not half. The Cheltenham Festival is only the best jump racing of the season. Today was the opening day. If I were a gambler, I'd bet that your Mr McCartney is in Cheltenham tonight.'

'So when is he likely to return?'

'When it's all over. Friday.'

She guessed she could wait that long—she'd waited long enough already.

*   *   *

Victor was surprised to be called at the club by Lewis.

'Hard lines about Grain of Sand,' Victor said. 'Max went too soon but I reckon the Irish horse would have got him anyway.'

But Lewis did not want to talk about the race.

'What are you doing about the matter we discussed?'

'Don't worry, Lewis. It's in hand.'

'I do worry. The wedding is a week off and she's still here!'

'She won't be for much longer. Guaranteed.'

'Huh.' It didn't sound as if Lewis set much store by Victor's guarantee.

'You should relax, mate. You sound a bit stressed. Take my word for it, she won't make the wedding.'

Lewis grunted and hung up.

*　　　*　　　*

It all came back to Hattie the moment the door opened. Pasty-faced Mr McCartney with his current-bun eyes and sly smile. He was grinning now.

'DC Barber, isn't it?' he said as he ushered her in.

She was surprised. 'You remember my name?'

'Most coppers I've met don't look as memorable as you.'

What a creep.

She avoided the sofa and took a seat at the table, a square oak-finished article with six matching straight-backed chairs. She noticed the green cloth that had covered it on her last visit, folded on top of the sideboard.

She refused refreshment and went through a few preliminaries. This was just a follow-up to her last visit; she wondered if anything had occurred to him in the intervening time.

'No,' he said emphatically. His eyes were on her calves.

She referred to the table. 'Do you entertain often, Mr McCartney?'

'Paul. It's not my real name but that's what everyone calls me.'

She knew that by now. She repeated her question.

'No. I can't cook.'

453

'Do you ever have friends round to play cards?'

That stopped him ogling her legs.

'Er . . . sometimes.'

'How often?'

'Once in a while.'

'I had a word with your neighbour. He said you had friends over for cards about once a week.'

Paul looked as if he'd like to murder Mr Pilates.

'It's none of his bleeding business. We don't make no noise. I kick 'em out before midnight. You wouldn't believe the tenancy restrictions in this place.'

Hattie produced a sympathetic smile.

'Do you have a regular night when you play?'

'I suppose he told you that as well.'

'He did mention Tuesdays.'

'Why are you asking me then? You already know. Tuesday nights I often have some mates round to play a few hands. It's perfectly legal, innit?'

'Of course. Don't worry, Paul, I'm just pursuing a train of thought.'

He didn't look happy. Good.

'So,' she continued, 'would you have been playing cards with these friends on the night of Tuesday the twenty-fifth of November last year?'

'I can't remember. It's a while ago.'

'Really? You seem to have such a good memory for some things—like my name.'

The sly smile returned to his face.

'Though not,' she continued, 'for renewing your road tax. That is your Sierra downstairs, isn't it?'

The smile vanished. 'Come off it, officer, you're not gonna do me for that, are you? I've been away. I'm going down the post office first thing.'

'If you could just concentrate on November the twenty-fifth?'

He took his time. She could almost see the cogs whirring in his brain as he calculated the odds. She waited, implacable.

'You'd be a good poker player, you would.'

She didn't reply, just stared at him.

'OK. I can see you're gonna find out anyway. Tortoise was here that night.'

'Who?'

'Basil. We used to call him Tortoise because he was so bloody slow at poker. Good player though.'

She wanted to smack that smug look off his face, to scream and shout. The little idiot had only wasted three months of her investigation. She tried to keep the anger out of her voice as she said, 'Why didn't you tell me this when I first interviewed you?'

He shrugged. 'I dunno really. I didn't want to get involved.'

Jesus Christ.

'I mean,' he went on, 'old Basil getting bonked on the head wasn't nothing to do with any of us.'

She'd see about that, just as she'd see if there was a chance they could do this creep for obstructing the course of justice.

*   *   *

DI Pollock's expression had run the gamut from amusement to world-weary despair to rank cynicism. Now, as Hattie reached the conclusion of her saga, 'stunned mullet' might best describe the face he presented.

'So you've been charging around on your nights

off, interviewing witnesses by yourself, based on some remark of the blethering Scottish widow.'

'Yes, guv.'

'And you've found a guy who says Jacobs was playing cards at his house on the night he died.'

'Yes, guv.'

'And he's given you the names of four other members who were present?'

'Yes, guv.'

'Crikey.' Pollock was speechless for a moment. 'Why on earth didn't you tell me what you were up to? We're meant to be a team. You're not supposed to go running around like Sherlock Holmes. Even he didn't go off on his own—he had that clot Watson with him.'

'I didn't think you wanted to hear any more about Jessie Maclean. And, with respect, because you were all taking the piss out of me.'

Pollock nodded. 'Take DC Mooney and get cracking with these new witnesses. And Hattie?'

'Yes, guv?'

'You're a bonnie wee lassie.' He shot her a sly wink.

*   *   *

Max's phone rang ten minutes after Cherry had left. Typical—it was probably some other instruction about wedding preparations she'd forgotten to tell him.

'Hello, stranger.' The voice was familiar but for the moment Max couldn't place it. 'Haven't seen you over the green baize in yonks.'

It was Double Top, one of the old card school at Paul's. What did he want?

Max soon found out.

'Have you had a visit from the rozzers yet?'

'What? No.'

'Thought not. I'm the only one who's got your address.'

Max forced himself to keep the panic out of his voice.

'What's going on?'

It was quite a rigmarole. Basically some female detective had showed up at Paul's out of the blue and persuaded him to admit that Basil had been playing cards on the night he was mugged. It was unclear whether Paul had spilled the beans because he fancied her or because she'd threatened him. Max wasn't interested in that aspect of events, he was more concerned by the consequences. Paul had supplied the names and, insofar as he was able, the addresses of the other players and they'd been interviewed in turn.

'I wanted to warn you, Maxie, that you're about to get a visit.'

Because you've just given them my address. Thanks very much.

'What do they want to know?'

'What time we all left. Who went with who. Whether anyone had the hump with old Tortoise and how much money had changed hands. It's like they've got some idea we'd cut each other's throats for a fiver.'

'Right.' Max didn't like the sound of this. But provided he said he went home along with everyone else, he'd be OK, surely? It was just a question of keeping his nerve.

'Oh yeah, one other thing. They want a little swab from inside your mouth.'

457

'Why's that?'
'Why do you think? DNA sample, of course.'
Oh shit.

*　　　*　　　*

Max was shaking. He could hardly tie the laces of his trainers he was twitching so badly. For God's sake, get a grip. He was a man who rode half a tonne of horse over fences for a living, he wasn't supposed to panic.

But what he was facing now required a different kind of courage. The courage to face up to what he had done in a moment of temper and weakness.

So was he going to confess? What alternative did he have? A DNA test would trap him for sure. He'd been sick on Tortoise, hadn't he?

If he confessed now, said it was a terrible accident and he hadn't meant it to happen and it was self-defence anyway—that would be best. He'd get a lighter sentence that way. Manslaughter not murder.

What was a lighter sentence? Ten years not life?

He was about to be a father. He wouldn't know his own child. Cherry would find another man—another father for his kid. Oh Jesus Christ.

There had to be a way out.

He called Lewis. He didn't know what he was going to say but Dad would get him a lawyer, the best. Maybe he could refuse to give a DNA sample. There must be some grounds, surely?

He reached Jackie.

'I'm sorry, Max. He's having some tests in Harley Street and I can't get hold of him at the moment.'

'You must!'

'I'll keep trying but he was incommunicado five minutes ago. I'll get him to call you back as soon as possible. Where are you?'

It dawned on Max he couldn't stay at home. The police could be ringing on his bell at any minute.

'I'll be on my mobile. Or at Cherry's.' He hung up and raced for the door.

He'd go to Cherry's right now and wait for Dad's call. The police wouldn't find him there.

Dead man walking. He'd seen the movie—that's how he felt right now.

*   *   *

Cherry didn't go straight home. She parked the car in the underground park in Hammersmith and headed for the chemist's. There was the honeymoon to think of which, when it came down to it, was like any holiday. For a week's sailing in Cyprus she needed a ton of stuff, starting with suntan lotion. It was going to be bliss, apart from the miscarriage part, but she'd been reading up on that and reckoned she could fake it with the minimum of drama.

She enjoyed filling her shopping basket in Boots, it took her mind off her anxiety about the wedding. After all, her entire life plan depended on it. The moment the ceremony was over she would be safe, with a stake in the Ashwood fortune that no one could deny her.

But suppose something prevented the wedding? Max was flaky enough to get cold feet. And he was suspicious about the pregnancy, nagging her to see the gynaecologist even now. Lewis, of course, was the one pushing him. Suppose they demanded she prove she was pregnant before the wedding went ahead?

Or, and this was another possibility, suppose Lewis had a real heart attack and not just the funny flutter he'd got at Cheltenham? The way he was looking, it wouldn't be a surprise. Thank God the wedding was only two days off. The old monster could keel over and die at the reception for all she cared, provided it didn't disrupt her plans. In fact, that would be just about an ideal scenario.

She took her bags back to the car and headed for Fulham, paying no attention to the motorcycle messenger some fifty yards to her rear. If her mind had been less occupied she might have observed that the same bike had been behind her as she left Max's flat some ninety minutes earlier.

* * *

Max paced Cherry's small cottage. Why hadn't Dad called back? How long did it take to have an ECG or whatever it was?

And where the hell was Cherry? He'd left a message on her mobile but she must have had it turned off.

He didn't know what he was going to tell her. He'd nearly confessed to her. 'I almost killed a man,' he'd said, as a bit of bravado really when they were talking about her misspent youth. It had seemed a good idea to suggest he'd had some experience of life on the street himself.

He could expand on that now, come clean about his situation. Maybe they could flee the country together and lose themselves in the yachtie fraternity she'd told him about. Dad could send

460

him money and the three of them—himself, Cherry and their baby—could live the vagabond life on the waves that they'd fantasised about.

He was upstairs in her bedroom which gave a better view of the street. There, at last, was her car and he watched as she parked on the opposite side of the road and took bags of shopping from the boot.

He made for the stairs. He'd tell her the truth— a version of it anyway. It had been self-defence— who could say any different?

It was going to be OK.

*   *   *

Cherry pushed the garden gate open with her hip and took the four short strides to the front door. She held her bags in one hand while she pushed the key into the lock. She was thinking about packing. She'd need plenty of warm clothes as it was bound to get cold on board a boat. Despite the suntan lotion she didn't think it would be that hot in Cyprus in mid-March.

She heard the swish of clothing and turned to see a motorcycle messenger at her gate. He had a brown padded envelope in one hand and he was smiling.

*   *   *

The Dutchman had done his homework. He'd watched the blonde visit the little terraced house before and had planned for just this moment, with her standing at her front door, completely at his mercy and no one else in sight.

461

She turned at the last minute and looked at him without suspicion even as he removed the gun from the padded envelope.

Such a pretty girl. What a waste.

'Can I help you?' she said.

He fired into the centre of her chest.

She looked surprised and slid to the ground, as if she were sitting on the step, leaning against the door.

He bent over her just to make sure, even though every instinct screamed in him to get away. It took only a few seconds to check and they might be the most important of all.

Her coat gaped wide over her chest and the pastel blue sweater beneath was turning purple with blood. Good job.

He tucked the barrel of the silencer beneath her chin. One more.

Then she moved. Her torso toppled backwards as the door behind her opened and the Dutchman looked up into the face of a man with floppy hair and piercing blue eyes. He didn't appear to see the gun.

'What's happening?' he said. 'Cherry, are you OK?'

The Dutchman killed him too. He had no choice.

As he turned away from the bodies, a telephone sounded from inside the house.

Epilogue

DI Pollock was wearing his most forbidding expression as Hattie entered his office. Was she about to receive a bollocking?

He pointed to the seat opposite his desk. No bollocking then—he delivered those when you were standing up.

The message light on the phone was flashing as usual but he ignored it, turning a biro round in his fingers as he studied her face. It occurred to her that he was groping for the right words. If so, it was a unique situation.

Finally he spoke. 'I've always thought a lot of you, Hattie.' He coughed uncertainly. 'I'd go so far as to say I'm one of your biggest admirers.'

She tried to make a joke of it. 'I wish you'd told me before, guv. I just agreed to marry Martin.'

'Really?' The old Mickey Pollock reasserted himself. 'That's excellent. Congratulations.'

She could see he was genuinely pleased. Then the smile vanished.

'Your Basil Jacobs investigation.'

'Not all mine. It's a team effort.'

'Crap. You listened to the words of the Scottish widow and followed a trail that the rest of us thought was pure fantasy. And off-duty too and on your own which was just bloody stupid.'

'Yes, guv.' So it was a bollocking after all. Sort of.

'I know you've been waiting for the DNA result on your remaining suspect.'

'For two months,' she said. She couldn't resist. It

was bad enough the tests on those card players at Paul's coming back negative but to be stalled by all the hoo-hah surrounding the double shooting in Fulham was bloody frustrating. She'd narrowed her suspicions down to one man, Max Ashwood, and at the very moment she and Mooney had pitched up at his flat to question him, her possible murderer had been getting shot less than two miles away. Her subsequent request for a DNA read-out on the corpse had simply disappeared into the ether, despite her frequent protests.

'I've only just found out myself,' said Pollock. 'The test matches up. Max Ashwood was the guy who was sick over Jacobs.'

'So he must have killed him!'

'Let's just say he had a hand in his death. Maybe it was self-defence. We won't ever know for sure.'

'I know,' she said boldly. 'He killed Jacobs if only because he never called for an ambulance. Pity we won't ever see him in court.'

'Indeed.' Pollock looked embarrassed. 'Officially, Hattie, this DNA match-up does not exist. I don't know what kind of political pull Lewis Ashwood has but it's good enough to bin your result. The case dies with Max. There's to be no discussion outside this office. No leaks to the papers. It stops here.'

'But . . .' Hattie was appalled. 'What about the shootings? Maybe they're linked.'

Pollock shook his head. 'Believe me, they've looked at it all ways up. Max was just a bystander. The girl was the target, she was a Customs and Excise informant who'd been shopping a drugs ring. It's a coincidence.'

'It still doesn't seem right,' she said. 'What about

Basil's family—Mrs Maclean?'

'Do you think she really cares who killed him?'

Hattie supposed not. Anyway, she'd had her satisfaction—the money was in the bank.

'I tell you who this does make a difference to,' Pollock continued. 'That's you. You're not going to get the credit you deserve and that upsets me.' The uncertain expression had returned. Now she realised what was up: Pollock just wasn't used to handing out compliments.

'Bloody good work, DC Barber. Now bugger off and keep your trap shut.'

Hattie blushed. 'Yes, guv,' she said.

*   *   *

The magnolia was in bloom in Lewis's garden. He spent a lot of time there these days, trying to get his strength back, trying to take an interest in the shrubs and birds that he'd never noticed before. And trying not to think about the past.

It wasn't surprising he'd had a heart attack. He'd been lucky, the doctors said. He'd already checked into the Marlborough for a battery of coronary tests when the news of Max's death came through. If you're going to have a heart attack you might as well have one in hospital. That's if you want to carry on living, of course.

There were hedgehogs in his garden, he'd discovered, just emerging from their winter hibernation. A long, long sleep appealed to Lewis right now, though sleep was hard to come by without sedatives. Sometimes he'd come out into the garden at night and watch for the hedgehogs. They were noisy little beasts, snuffling around the

465

undergrowth looking for worms and slugs or engaging in noisy sex. He wondered what Roisin would have made of them if she were still here. She'd loved his garden. They could have hunted hedgehogs together.

But he mustn't think about her. The hard-hearted Irish bitch. She was as dead to him as his son and the hated blonde woman.

The police had been gentle with him, considering his condition and his grief. He'd had to pretend he was sorry about Cherry. He didn't really know why—obviously self-preservation was an instinct that operated beyond the reach of rational thought.

He could hear the sound of voices from the house but he didn't bother to turn his head. It would be Gaynor, the day-time nurse. She often had long loud conversations with her boyfriend on the phone. Lewis didn't mind, as he would have done once. Young Australian women were allowed to be cheerful and raucous.

But she didn't sound cheerful now. 'I'm sorry, Mr Ashwood, I told him he couldn't come through but he wouldn't listen.'

There was a man by her side: a familiar stocky figure in neatly pressed slacks and a blazer. The one man Lewis least wanted to see in the entire world.

Victor Bishop shrugged apologetically. 'I'm sure you don't mind a chat with an old friend, do you, Lewis?'

Lewis considered the nurse. She was an athletic looking young lady but hardly capable of physically ejecting Victor. And neither was he.

'It's OK, Gaynor,' he said.

She shot Victor a poisonous glance. 'You can't stay long then. He's under strict doctor's orders.' And she stalked off up the path.

The pair of them watched her go.

'I was sorry to hear you'd been poorly,' said Victor and took a seat on the garden bench next to Lewis's chair. 'It's been a bit stressful for all of us recently, hasn't it?'

Lewis did not reply. It was important he didn't get worked up about things, that's what his specialist said. Victor being here was a test.

'The police,' Victor went on, 'have given me a bit of a hard time over the Cherry business. Endless interviews, harassment really but that's their style. Water off a duck's back as far as I'm concerned.'

Lewis looked into the other man's smooth, well-polished face. There were no sharp edges at all to his features, just doughy mounds, nothing you could snap off or break. It was a completely undistinguished countenance, remarkable only for the eyes—bottomless yellow pools of evil. Lewis could read nothing there, no sorrow or remorse or pain. None of the things he felt.

Lewis spoke for the first time. 'Max.'

Victor pulled a face, the kind of apologetic look you give when you've accidentally trodden on someone's foot. 'That wasn't meant to happen, believe me. I mean, the girl had just said goodbye to him and then he turned up at her place. He saw the shooter so . . . you know. It was just bad timing.'

Lewis had a cane by his side, to help him get about. He could picture himself hitting Victor with it. Smacking it into his smug smooth face.

He dismissed the thought as futile. Victor would take the cane from him before he could raise it

467

from the ground. Pointless.

'You hired a hitman?'

'Yeah. Like we agreed.'

What? 'We agreed nothing of the kind.'

Victor grinned. 'Maybe not in so many words. But if you recall our meeting when we discussed Cherry, I told you I'd use the carrot and the stick. On reflection, I thought the stick was the best way to go.'

Lewis sat in silence.

'Anyway,' Victor continued. 'I wouldn't worry about it. If I'm OK, you're OK. For the moment I reckon we're both in the clear.'

And now comes the pay-off, Lewis thought. Victor hadn't turned up just to enquire after his health.

'How are you getting on with your Elmwood Glade development?' Victor said. Right on cue. 'I'm planning to move my interests out of the UK. The business climate's a bit difficult at the moment. But I'll be back. It'll give you time to develop that site properly. Build me a nice casino.'

'And if I don't?'

Victor smiled. 'Then I might think of retiring. It's all hard graft here—they've even taken the fun out of racing. I've got those tossers at the Jockey Club on my back. I'd go somewhere out of the reach of Her Majesty's forces of law and order. But wherever, there'll be telephones and a postal service. I'd probably deal with a newspaper first. They'd go mad to get the inside story on the shooting of your son and his girlfriend.'

They would indeed and the police investigation would swiftly follow. Lewis would be charged with conspiracy to murder, with or without Victor by his

468

side in the dock. What remained of his life would be utterly destroyed.

'Suppose I don't care?' he said.

'Then you'll die a lonely old bastard in a nick somewhere. Better to pop off in comfort, don't you think?'

Lewis didn't think at all, he was past all that. He'd made mistakes, terrible mistakes, and now he was paying for them.

'You'll have your casino,' he said. 'Now get out of my garden.'

Victor went without another word.

*　　　*　　　*

Alan hadn't been back to Ireland since before Cheltenham. Though he'd promised the Doughertys he'd be over to join in the celebrations of Black Mountain's triumph—which had been protracted—he'd never made it. Everyday life had overtaken him. Winning the Champion Hurdle had kick-started his career. Suddenly every trainer in the land wanted to book him and every owner wanted him on his horses. It had been his moment and he'd seized it.

Simultaneously, Blades Bloodstock began to take off. He found himself regularly scouting for Cyril and a couple of his pals; and he came across another good prospect at a yard in Yorkshire, a Flat horse who had a natural aptitude for jumping—like Sandy. Learning from past experience, Alan had got his father to bid for him at the sales and the members of the old syndicate had all chipped in. Though they'd never replace Sandy in their affections, once more they had a

469

good young hurdler at Tim's yard, learning his trade for the next season.

So the promised trip to Ireland had slipped back on Alan's agenda.

There was another reason he hadn't returned—Roisin. Their friendship was solid, he knew that from the regular phone calls at eleven at night when the rest of the family had gone to bed. She'd call and they'd talk, sometimes into the small hours, and she'd be apologetic, knowing how early he had to get up and ride out. It was as if she needed those conversations more than he did.

The murders of Max and Cherry had knocked her for six. She'd known them, though not well, but for an intense period whose mysteries she gradually revealed. She said she felt sickened, astonished and—Alan found this bizarre—guilty. As if her bolting from Lewis had precipitated the whole thing.

'Why *did* you leave him?' he asked her finally.

The story didn't exactly change his opinion of Lewis Ashwood. He'd disliked him anyway, on principle. Now he had reason for his animosity.

'Do you think I should write to Lewis?' she'd said. 'He'll be heartbroken.'

'If you feel it's the right thing to do,' he'd replied. He wasn't going to fall into the trap of bad-mouthing a previous boyfriend.

But was he the present boyfriend? They'd not kissed or held hands even. He'd not seen her for two months. There was just the baring of souls around midnight. That could just be laying the foundations of a close friendship. Maybe, after her painful experience with Lewis, that was all she wanted.

It wasn't all Alan wanted but he wasn't going to make a fool of himself by turning up on her doorstep like some puppy begging for affection.

And another thing, she'd not asked him to come. Never in all those conversations had she said, 'I wish you were here, Alan. Come and see me.' And that meant something surely. Such as, I like you at arm's length, on the other end of the phone, but don't come any closer. He was damned if he was going to push himself in where he wasn't wanted.

So why was he now driving the last mile to the Dougherty farmhouse? His heart hammering in his chest at the thought of seeing that river-fall of black hair and enigmatic smile.

It was thanks to Connor. The phone had rung the night before, earlier than usual and it wasn't Roisin. It was the first phone call he'd ever had from the owner of Black Mountain. His voice sounded deeper than before.

Connor didn't beat about the bush.

'What the hell are you playing at with my sister?' He sounded much like Noel all of a sudden. He plunged on without giving Alan a chance to respond.

'Me and Ma and Da have been talking and they won't call you but I don't care. Roisin's been moping around here like a wet weekend ever since she came back from England. We can't get a civil word out of her, yet she's on the phone to you every night. She's always been a moody one but if you're mental enough to take her on, would you please put us all out of our misery?'

Alan had been gobsmacked. 'How old are you, Con?'

'It was my fifteenth birthday last week.'

471

'Are you sure no one put you up to this?'

'You don't think I'm capable of making a phone call? Come on, Al, do you like her or not?'

'Since you ask, Con, I think she's the most fantastic woman I've ever met.'

'Jaysus, do you really?'

'Yes.'

'Well, get your arse over here and tell her. Or you won't be riding for me any more.'

So here he was turning into the rutted drive of the Dougherty farm.

A slim figure in a too-large overcoat that he instantly recognised stepped out onto the track ahead, her dark hair whipping round her face in the wind. He stopped the car and squelched through the puddles towards her.

Roisin opened her mouth to say something but his mind was made up. There had been too many words. He just kissed her, feeling her slender frame tremble beneath the folds of Noel's old coat.

And she kissed him back.